FELICE PICANO
THE LURE

"FELICE PICANO HAS TAKEN THE PSYCHO-LOGICAL THRILLER AS FAR AS IT CAN GO."
—Andrew Holleran,
author of *Dancer from the Dance*

"A HIGH-VOLTAGE THRILLER . . . A PAGE-TURNER WITH A BREATHLESS TENSION AS PALPABLE AS A SKIPPED HEARTBEAT ON EVERY PAGE. . . . ONE OF THE BEST BOOKS OF ANY KIND I'VE EVER READ."
—James Spada, *The Advocate*

"EXCITING, SUSPENSEFUL . . . A STRONG PLOT AND PLENTY OF ACTION . . . BUILDS TO A SOLID SURPRISE ENDING."
—*Publishers Weekly*

"DAZZLING . . . MESMERIZING . . . VIBRANT AND REAL."
—*Out Magazine*

"ELECTRIC . . . WELL-CRAFTED . . . THE KIND OF 'I-MUST-FIND-OUT-WHAT-HAPPENS' NOVEL THAT WILL KEEP YOU UP LATE."
—*The Villager*

THE LURE

FELICE PICANO

A DELL BOOK

Published by
Dell Publishing Co., Inc.
1 Dag Hammarskjold Plaza
New York, New York 10017

For my mother and father

"For the Eye altering alters all. . . ."
—*William Blake*

ONE

FIXING THE BAIT

1

March, 1976

The serene icy morning was shattered by a scream.

Noel Cummings swerved his ten-speed bicycle to a stop at the railing and listened. One sneakered foot remained tight in the metal clamp of the bike's pedal, the other dangled gingerly on the thin concrete abutment.

Nothing.

Despite the frigid wind flapping off the Hudson River, he pulled down the hood of his sweat shirt to hear better.

Still nothing.

The wind whistling through those loose metal flaps of the crumbling warehouses on his right? Perhaps. Or perhaps an early morning driver screeching his tires as he sped around a corner below, on West Street.

He peered over the railing of the elevated West Side Highway, closed to traffic south of Thirty-fourth Street since a nearby section had collapsed almost a year before. Closed to car and truck traffic, that is. Still open to pedestrians; or, more common, to bicyclists like Noel, alone this early March morning at a quarter after six. Below him he could make out the back of a crawling Sanitation Department truck.

It must have been a hallucination, he decided, and put up his hood again.

Looking east, through lines of building walls sheer as cliffs, the night's blackness had begun to give way to a pale cobalt at the horizon. Dawn soon.

Then the scream repeated. Even with his hood up,

he knew it was no hallucination. It was so clear, so close, Noel could make out its direction—to the right, in front of him—and even a few terrified words— "No . . . didn't mean it."

A light flickered on in the second-story warehouse window, level with where he stood. With it the scream ended.

Noel shot across the road to the right-hand railing. Light flickered in the third window; like matchlight, or a cigarette lighter guttering in the wind.

Then he heard the man's voice again, lower, pleading, punctuated by what seemed to be gasps.

Noel leaned far over the metal railing to look in. Debris all over the floor, loose beams hanging half torn from the walls and ceiling. All he could make out were shadowy figures—one shrinking back, two others looming on either side of him. One's arm was extended; something sharply pointed in his hand jabbed forward again and again, each thrust followed by a gasp, a cry, another "No."

"Hey! What's going on in there?" Noel shouted. "Stop that."

The light flickered off.

Out of the sudden blackness someone shouted, "Help me! Please! They're killing me!"

"Finish him off," someone muttered.

"Help me!" the man shouted again. "Please!"

Then Noel heard what sounded like stumbling over broken glass. Was the man escaping in the dark?

Noel calculated the distance from the railing to the open window: a good ten feet. Too far to jump. Debris and broken glass to land on if he did. Glass that twinkled and cracked in the reflected streetlight as the shadows moved over it. He had to help him. But how?

"I'm coming in," Noel shouted. He detached the heavy flashlight he carried clamped to his handlebars, flung it into the corner he thought the attackers were in. It smashed against something, thudded to the floor.

". . . getting out of here," he heard one voice say.

"Are you finished?" another asked.

Broken glass crunched under several pairs of feet. Then the man's cries, his gasps again.

How could Noel get in there? "Leave him alone!" he yelled.

It was a quarter mile to the nearest exit. He'd have to chance it. They were scared by now. They'd leave.

He shouted once more that he was coming in, then spun around on the Atala Grand Prix and shot off north toward Eighteenth Street, adjusting his gears for the highest speed. In seconds he was moving so fast he almost missed the turnoff. He swerved right, swept over the broken concrete exitway like a ski jumper going off a lift, then down the ramp so suddenly the breath was whipped out of him. Lines of white and gray at the bottom of the ramp caught his eye—wooden police horses, obstacles. He had only an instant to avoid them. He jerked left, felt his right trouser leg brush one, leaned over almost horizontal to the road, regained his balance, then turned sharply and was skimming along West Street, over cobblestones, in and out of the steel pylons that supported the highway. One row of warehouses flashed by. Then the open space opposite Westbeth, telephone labs turned into artists' housing. The second line of warehouses began, glimmering ominously in the yellow light of the mercury streetlamps.

He swung the Atala to a soundless stop. Now what?

He'd expected to see fleeing figures, a car taking off.

Instead the street was empty, the cobblestones gleaming with ice. Jesus! and he'd gone over this road at forty miles an hour. What now? There was a man hurt somewhere upstairs. More than likely the men who attacked him, too. What am I doing here?

He had to go in, find the man, help him. But first

park the bike where they would not see it when they came out. The other side of the building.

He spotted one doorway at street level, the door knocked in, hanging on a hinge, so black inside it might be completely enclosed. This can't lead upstairs, he thought. Too much of a trap anyway. Farther along?

He jumped onto the concrete loading platform. Graffiti scrawled on the outside wall in large wavering letters: Keep Away. Pickpockets Inside.

There were more than pickpockets inside.

One wide garage door was opened just high enough to crawl under. Noel edged over and peered in.

It was lighter inside. Huge. These warehouses had been used for loading and receiving from ships; the piers they were built on extended hundreds of feet out into the river. The far end of this one was sagging, as though crushed by a giant hand. The dark western sky looked lighter against the building's darker jagged-metal bulwarks. At least he'd be able to make out someone coming at him.

He slipped in and crouched, accustoming his eyes to the gloom. No one. A jumble of fallen beams. The frosty glitter of glass—or was it ice?—everywhere. Good thing he was wearing his Adidas. He'd hear them before they heard him.

A dozen or so feet inside, he saw that the place was even more immense than it seemed at first: two football fields long, he guessed, from the street to the river end. Concrete floors. Safe for walking, except for the glass. This must have been a driveway. An inner loading platform to his right. Beyond it, darkness. To his left what seemed to be another, smaller building within the larger one: a half-dozen windows, half that many doors, all the glass smashed out of them of course, all the doors off their hinges. What was that darker double-sized doorway? A stairway. The way up to the hurt man. And to the other men, waiting for him.

This is insane, Noel told himself, then started up. The stairs were remarkably clear of litter and glass, as though much used. At the first landing, he stopped. Anyone might get at him from around the corner. He waited, poised to leap aside or back down the stairs. Not a sound. Could this little corridor be the way to the man?

It wasn't. The corridor nearly circled the inside building, going three-quarters around, ending in a pile of stacked beams and one ghostly white urinal stinking to high heaven, graffiti chalked on the walls around it, indecipherable in the darkness. But from here, he could look down on the open warehouse floor below. He saw no one.

He made his way back to the stairway, ascended warily, a step at a time, hugging the railing, until his eyes reached floor level. A huge room. Empty. To his left a bare wall some fifty feet away. Much closer on his right a series of doorways: some closed, some open. These must have been warehouse offices.

He sidled to the nearest doorway. He could see the elevated highway out the window, about chest high. It was the right floor. Now where was the man?

It was lighter in the room now: he could see a robin's-egg blue at the horizon. Couldn't he wait here a few minutes until dawn?

No. Go on. Go in.

A tiny room opened off this doorway. Some newspapers bunched up in a corner he took at first for a crouching man. On one wall were the stenciled words: Dressing Room.

Why was it so quiet? Where was the man? And the others, where were they? Waiting for him behind any doorway. Their shadows thrusting, deadly. The man's cries and gasps. Noel had to find him, not let him die. Insane or not, he had to help him.

He crept forward, edging into first one doorway, then another. At each he waited, slid quietly inside, waited again, poised to jump aside, alert for a movement, an attack. He peered into each darkness, made certain no one was in the shadows, checked the outer room again, slipped out, moved to the next.

At the fifth one he saw the flashlight. The dull burnished shine of its cylinder made him shudder. This was the room.

He paused, looked for a long time at the flashlight's dented side, then slipped into the room and stood still. No one. Just a sign, Smoking Lounge, on the wall opposite the windows. Several discarded doors were thrown into the far corner. The flashlight sat on a pile of debris.

Here I am. Now where the hell are you! . .

Expecting at any moment to be pounced upon, he retrieved the flashlight, grabbing it as if it were a hot potato, though it felt cold through the lightweight racing gloves he wore. Heavy, substantial: real. What about the rest of it—the man stabbing, the victim's scream, his pleading? Was that real? There was nothing to prove it. Nothing but the flashlight.

He wondered if the flashlight still worked, and switched it on. Its glare was blinding, and he swung it down.

The circle of light rested on the doors stacked in the corner. The top one was pale green, speckled darker from top to bottom as though someone had begun to paint it and stopped halfway. The dark layer gleamed wet, looked freshly painted.

Cautiously, he touched the door. It was wet, sticky. Christ, it must be blood! He wiped it off on a pants leg and swung the flashlight in a slow, low arc, half dreading to see what it would show him. At the bottom of the pile, he made out some material, and coming closer, one trousered leg that extended out from behind the doors. It, too, gleamed from the knee to the socks, which—once white—were now dyed dark. A wetly brown loafer was twisted half off a foot.

Noel stood back, holding the flashlight on the leg, unable to move.

Then he went to the door and began to move it. As he did, the leg pulled slowly in. What was that sound? Like a small dog whimpering. Noel heard a dry wheezing. The man was still alive! He'd come in time.

"Don't be afraid," Noel said quietly. "It's me. The guy from the highway. They're gone now. I threw the flashlight to scare them off. I'll get you out."

The wheezing continued, louder now. Noel wedged the flashlight between some loose boards on the right wall, aiming it at the corner to see better. Then, using both hands, he lifted off first one, then another, setting them quietly flat down on the floor.

When the last door was aside, he saw the man.

He lay like refuse thrown in a corner. Both legs were extended, both arms dangled on the floor. His head was fallen forward so that Noel could see only the top of his lank, light hair. He sat in a dark puddle. His sleeves and trouser legs were dappled with dark spreading stains. He'd been stabbed everywhere, over and over.

The man raised his head slightly and Noel heard the sharp intake of breath, the fluttery wheezing, and, barely audible, the muttered words, "Didn't mean it. Didn't."

With that, the man's head fell back all the way against one corner wall. Was it only a trick of the dim light that Noel could not make out a single feature of his face? No, the flashlight shone fully on him. And Noel saw that where the man's nose and eyes and mouth ought to have been was just a dark wetness that seethed and bubbled and welled up. And he realized why he could not see the man's face: they had cut it to ribbons.

"*Oh, my God!*" Noel whispered it under his breath, feeling his stomach knot and constrict, feeling his throat begin to contract. "Christ, help me."

The words helped, and he clenched his eyes shut, feeling the flashlight's dented side, found the button and flicked it off.

Better in the dark. Better not seeing what ought not be seen. He felt a little better already.

He bent down and talked quietly, fast.

"Listen. You're hurt very badly. I've got to get a doctor. You're bleeding. I've got to get help."

Noel felt wetness seep under one knee as he talked. He jerked it up and hunkered.

"They're gone. They won't be back. Just stay still. I've got a bike. I'll ride and get help. I'll only be a few minutes, I promise. Stay still, very still."

"Ssszzz," Noel heard among the wheezing, then he felt a hand brush against his ankle. It made him shudder.

Then, the hissing sound again: "Ssszzz."

"I can't understand you."

The man held Noel's ankle in a loose grip. He reached down and took the hand, holding it in his own. It, too, was wet, bleeding.

"Listen," the man managed to say in a sharply asthmatic voice, very low. "Go . . . cross . . . street."

"I'll get help. Don't worry."

"Cross . . . street . . ." the man repeated slowly, with great effort. "Cross . . . street."

"Across the street?"

The fingers tightened in his hand.

"Across West Street?"

Yes, the fingers replied, tightening again.

"Directly across?"

"Yes," the man said now.

"Why? What's there? Not the police station? That's on Tenth Street, isn't it?"

"Cross . . . street." The man's fingers tightened once more in Noel's. He was wheezing badly again, unable to talk.

Noel looked at him. Then, remembering, and afraid he might see his eyes or what remained of them, he looked away, toward the dull gleam of the flashlight he'd hung on the wall.

"All right. I'll go across the street. Don't worry. Just stay still. Don't move. All right?"

The man's fingers relaxed, and Noel thought he must have lost consciousness, but the wheezing continued. He laid the man's hand gently on the soaked trouser leg, and stood up.

He was shaking so badly, he had to hold on to the doorjamb.

"I'll be right back," he promised, not sure whether the man heard him or not. The room was getting lighter: the sun was about to rise.

Noel half staggered out the doorway, and ran heedlessly down the stairs. Only at the first landing did he come to his senses and remember to be wary. There was no proof the other men had left the building. So he edged along the lower offices, then crawled under the barely open garage door onto West Street.

It was still night below the elevated highway, the cobblestone road lighted yellow.

Across West Street, the man had said. Noel strode across, looking back as he did, to make certain no light went on again in the upper-story window. The man's whimpering rang in his head. His wheezing breath. No face. He had no face left. Stop it! Noel told himself. Concentrate on getting help.

Opposite the warehouse, on the other side of the highway, were two buildings, neither very likely to contain help. On Noel's left was a whitewashed warehouse, seven stories high, the windows painted closed black. One black garage door, locked. One doorway, up four steps, locked, too. Deserted.

The other building was red brick aged with layers of soot. Cages covered the high, deeply set, opaque glass windows from the ground floor all the way up to the fifth level, which appeared to be a huge wire mesh tent, like a gymnasium atop a public school. There was one deeply set doorway with a heavy-looking metal door labeled, Danger: Moving Door.

Even the bulky, greenish air-conditioning unit was enclosed in a meshwork cage.

Then Noel remembered: this was the Federal House of Detention where men awaiting federal trials in New York City were held. Hadn't it been closed a while ago? Sure: he'd read about it in the *Times* four or five months before.

Directly across the street, the man had said. Had he thought he was somewhere else? What was supposed to be here? What would he look like if he lived: his face a mask of scars, or what? Jesus, how the blood had bubbled up.

The door gave a hollow booming response to his knock. Noel held himself ready for it to shoot open. It didn't. He pounded on it again. And again.

Could the man have been so crazed by pain he'd made a mistake? But no, didn't shock set in, and with it, drastic reduction of pain? Noel hoped so, for the man's sake.

Maybe another door. But there was nothing on this side but the caged windows. Around the corner? Nothing here either. Then he saw another sign, this one painted on the wall: Federal Parking. Employees Only. Well, that confirmed what the place was. Or had been. Another doorway, set deep like the one on West Street. Barred over, so he couldn't even reach in to knock. More brick wall. A corrugated garage door. He knocked there, too, but got no answer. I'm wasting time here. I'd better get the bike and ride to the police station, he thought. Now he had reached the end of the building. One more doorway: the delivery entrance.

A sooty glass slot at eye level revealed a small inside foyer, then another glass door too distant and too dirty to see into. To Noel's surprise, this outer door opened at his touch, swinging in easily, well counterbalanced despite its weight.

It was a foyer, all right, dark beyond the glass door.

Locked, of course. Pure fluke the outer one was open. A dull institutional corridor stretched beyond the glass door. Empty.

He set up a tattoo, knocking with his ringed knuckle. No answer. No running feet. No anxious faces. I'd better go to the police station, now, he told himself and turned to open the outer door.

He was jerked back so fast he stumbled backward, as hands pulled at him. Before he could get to his feet, he was behind the glass door, in the corridor he'd been looking at, and hauled around a corner, into pitch darkness.

They'll mangle my face, too, he thought, and his hands went up to protect his eyes.

He could feel two or three of them, holding him securely against the wall, breathing.

"What are you doing here?" The voice was sharp, cold, toneless.

Noel stiffened. "The man . . ." he began.

"What man?" another voice asked, close to his left ear.

"Across the street," Noel managed to get out. "He said to come here for help. He's hurt."

"What man?"

"I don't know who he is."

"What's going on here?" yet another voice asked.

"He sent you here?" the first, the cold-voiced man asked Noel.

"Yes. He's hurt very badly."

"Who's hurt?" the newer voice asked.

"I don't know. Who's out tonight?" The cold voice again.

"No one. Wait, wasn't Kansas out?"

"He was linking tonight," the man on Noel's left said.

"There?"

"Where is he?" the cold-voiced man asked Noel, pushing him roughly against the wall.

"Across the street. In the abandoned warehouse. Second story up. Fifth doorway on the right when you get up the stairs. I was riding by and . . ."

"We'd better take a look," the cold-voiced man said, interrupting Noel's explanation. Then, with another push against the wall, he asked Noel to repeat his directions.

As Noel answered, he heard more men arriving in the dark corridor. There were many voices mumbling around him now, talking hurriedly in low tones.

"I was riding by on the elevated highway," Noel tried to explain again. He was interrupted by another hand slamming him against the wall.

"Shut up!" the man on his right said.

"Who's got a bracelet?" someone else asked.

Noel was seized by the shoulders, spun half around, while someone else grabbed his hands together. He felt something cold, then heard a click. He was handcuffed.

"Wait a minute," he said. "You don't understand. I didn't do anything. I was just riding by and saw it."

"Dry this one off till we get back," the cold-voiced man said. "Where's medical?"

"Outside already," someone answered. "Everyone's out."

"Get the Fisherman," the cold-voiced man said. "And dry this one off."

"Come on," someone else urged. "Let's go!"

"But I didn't do anything," Noel protested. The glass door slammed and he was dragged back by the hands, then pushed in another direction so hard he almost fell. As he was getting to his feet, a heavy door slammed shut inches away. In front of him, he could see a tiny barred window.

"But I didn't do anything. I was just riding by and saw it happen and went to help him."

"Sure, buddy," a flat, older voice replied from the other side of the barred window. "Haven't you heard? They closed the highway."

"I was on a bike. I was riding a bike. It's at the warehouse right now!" he shouted, but he could hear the man's footsteps receding and a minute later, another sound: a door closing. He was alone.

He inched about in the murky darkness. This must be a cell. Not very large. Damp. Cold. Jesus! Here's a case study on the inadvisability of helping people in trouble. No wonder no one else did.

He was shivering, and had to use the wall to nudge up his sweat shirt hood. That was marginally better. But his breath still frosted. His eyes were acclimated to the light now, but there wasn't much to see, just a bare cell with two metal shelves long enough and barely wide enough to hold a man.

This is crazy, he told himself. Crazier than seeing someone being stabbed. But they'd find the man and come back and release him. Realize he was trying to help, then let him go.

After what seemed an interminably long time, he heard noises in the corridor. They were returning. Good. Now they'd let him go. Good thing. He was freezing here.

The cell door opened with a clang, and several men entered.

"Will he be all right?" Noel asked.

"As all right as ground round," the cold-voiced man said, and Noel felt himself lifted off his feet and slammed against the wall.

He was held there, shaken, pummeled. Questions came fast and he could hardly get his breath to answer them.

"Who was with you?" the cold voice asked.

"No one. I was alone."

He was punched in the stomach. "Who was with you?"

"I was riding by on my bike. I was alone."

"Let me do the asking," someone said, shoving in front of the other man. "I was in 'Nam. We had methods." With one hand he held Noel's head back, against the wall, his eyes glittering very close to Noel's. "Now, I'm going to ask you some questions, and for every wrong answer, you're going to have your head bounced off this wall. You hear?"

"No, please. I was alone. I was trying to help him," Noel begged. "I was riding by and saw them attack him . . ."

"How did you know who he was?"

"I didn't. I don't."

"Hey," someone else said, "let me ask. I'll get it out of him."

Noel felt another punch, hard in his ribs.

"Let me," a new voice said. He was punched again, lower.

They were crowding him, all of them pushing and trying to hit him, shifting positions to get at him. They were going to kill him. Kill him here in this freezing cell.

"No! Let *me* ask him!" The voice came from behind them. Instantly all of them stopped.

"It's the Fisherman," someone muttered. They all moved away from Noel.

"That's right." the new voice said. It was authoritative, slightly accented. "Now suppose you tell me what all this ruckus in the dark is about?"

"They got Kansas," someone said.

"What happened?" the man they called the Fisherman asked.

"Looks like a dozen meth freaks with a case of broken glass got at him."

"Bad?"

"Dead."

"Two," Noel offered. "There were two of them. I saw."

"And you were one of them," one man said, punching Noel in the side.

"Who's he?" the Fisherman asked.

"He came snooping around here. Said Kansas sent him."

"Leave him alone. Get some lights on. What is this, a medieval torture chamber? Go on. Back to your posts. All of you. Out."

Noel felt himself being lifted up against the wall.

"Don't hit me," he pleaded. "I didn't do anything."

A light came on in the room, blinding Noel for an instant.

"Out, I said," the Fisherman repeated. "All of you. Mack, stay at the door. I want to talk to him."

Noel was shivering now, sore all over from the assault. The one man remaining in the cell took him gently by the shoulders and sat him down on the metal shelf.

"I didn't do anything," Noel said. "I was just trying to help him. Why were they hurting me?"

"Because they're angry one of their friends is dead. You're all they had to vent their feelings on."

"But I was trying to help him."

"Just rest awhile," the man said. Then: "You cold?"

"Yes."

"Mack, get a blanket."

A blanket was brought in. The Fisherman arranged it around Noel's shoulders, then sat down on the opposite metal shelf.

"Now relax a bit, young man, then I want you to tell me how you came here."

"He told me to get help across the street," Noel said.

"I see," he said, sounding unconvinced. "Go on. I'm waiting."

"I thought this building was closed," Noel said.

"It is. Tell me everything that happened."

"I was riding my bike on the elevated highway," Noel began, gaining confidence now that he wasn't shivering anymore.

As he talked, he looked over the man they had called the Fisherman. He was fifty-five or sixty years old. Middle-sized, he seemed solid looking, although with the dark gabardine overcoat and heavy woolen

pants tucked into rubber galoshes, it was difficult to
ascertain how heavy, how solid he was. He was bare-
headed, and his hair was thinning but ungrayed
brown, slightly creased all around as though he had
been wearing a hat and had taken if off. A square,
clean-shaven face, with thickish lips, heavy jowls,
slightly reddish skin, as though from drinking, with a
large, fleshy aquiline nose. The brow was strong,
squarish, the eyebrows thick and bushy. Only his eyes
were a soft, doelike brown, betraying the easier treatment Noel had just received at his hands. Altogether
an authoritative man: the boss. Noel trusted him, as
much as he could trust anyone in this absurd situation. He would not hurt Noel, nor let him be hurt.

"That's all he said, to come here?" the Fisherman
asked when Noel was done.

"He was having trouble breathing," Noel said. "His
voice was very hoarse. I guess it was too hard for him
to talk anymore so he squeezed my hand, and I asked
if he meant directly across West Street, and he
squeezed it to say yes. That's the only reason I came
here, because I promised him. I was going to the police station."

"That makes sense. Nothing else? He said nothing
else? No names?"

"No. No names. But when he was being stabbed he
pleaded with them to stop, naturally. When I found
him, he must have thought I was one of them returning, that's when he said he didn't mean it."

"He didn't mean it?" the Fisherman asked.

"That's what he said." Noel could hear the broken
wheezing again, see the man's bloody facelessness.
This man, the "Fisherman," inspired confidence, and
Noel suddenly blurted out, "Perhaps it's better he
died."

"Why?" There was a threat in the word, the first
time Noel had felt hostility from his questioner.

"I just mean he was cut up so badly. His face was

. . . I don't think I'll ever forget it. What would he look like if he lived?"

The Fisherman stared gloomily at the floor.

"Do you think he'd been stabbed in the lungs?" Noel wondered. "Could that be why he wheezed so badly?"

"More than likely. Was his throat cut?"

"I don't know. It was just blood from his forehead on down. They'd stabbed everywhere. Everywhere. They wouldn't stop," Noel said, seeing again those deadly pointed shadows on the wall.

Someone tapped on the cell door and the Fisherman signaled him to come in. It was a tall, youngish man with a heavy beard, in denims and a forest-green ski parka.

"We found this in the room with Kansas," he said, in that same cold voice of the man who had so cruelly interrogated Noel. In the dark, he had seemed much older.

He handed Noel's flashlight to the Fisherman.

"That's mine."

"It was wedged into a wall," the man reported, ignoring Noel. "Just above eye level."

"I put it there to see," Noel explained. "He was behind some doors. I needed both hands to move them."

"You see any doors?" the Fisherman asked.

"Three of them. On the floor. The light was out when we got there. Not burned out either."

"I shut it off," Noel said. "I couldn't bear to look at him while I talked to him. I got nauseous."

"Yeah," the younger man said, "either that, or you turned it off after you were sure he was wasted."

"He was alive when I left that room!"

"That's enough," the Fisherman said. "Get back over there and go over that place. All of it. I want answers." The young man turned, glared at Noel, then walked out. "But the way," the Fisherman stopped him, "is there a bicycle there?"

"A ten-speed," Noel said. "Atala Grand Prix."

"It's there."

"Bring it here," the Fisherman said. "Go on. Go. Comb that place."

When the man had gone, the Fisherman turned to Noel. "What were you doing up on the highway?"

"I ride it every morning. For exercise."

"Why so early?"

"I have early classes. Sometimes nine, today at eight."

"Where?"

"New York University. The Washington Square campus. I teach sociology. Social change in action, inner-city problems. A basic penology course."

"So you were riding by as usual and heard a scream?"

"And saw the light."

"I thought you said the flashlight was yours?"

"It is. I saw flickering light. One of them must have been holding a cigarette lighter or something. I threw the flashlight in to scare them off. I told them I was coming in, too. But I couldn't jump it."

The Fisherman listened, then stood up and went to the cell door.

Noel panicked, thinking he would be left there, or the other men called in again. "You believe me, don't you?"

"Why shouldn't I believe you," the man said, not hiding his disgust. "It's the same old story."

He talked in a low voice to someone outside the cell, then came back with a pad and ball-point pen. "Give me your name, address, and phone number. Also where you work."

"I can't. My hands . . ." Noel turned to show them manacled.

The handcuff key was found, and Noel wrote down the required information.

"Here's your flashlight, Mr. . . . Cummings, is it?" he asked, reading the paper.

"I just wish I had hit one of them when I threw it. That might have been one or two minutes less for them to stab. He might have lived then, mightn't he?"

"Why bother thinking about what might have been?" The Fisherman led Noel out of the cell, through the corridor, and into the little foyer outside the glass door. No one else appeared. "I have to apologize for the others. Sometimes they're like animals," he said, taking Noel's hand and shaking it.

Noel took the hand, shook it, looked into the man's sad brown eyes, and said he understood. He was halfway out the metal door when he had a thought. "Shouldn't the police be notified?"

"We are the police," the Fisherman said, closing the glass door with a click.

2

The note from the department chairman arrived faster than Noel expected. It was prominent in the cubbyhole that served as his mailbox in the Sociology Department general office when Noel stopped there between classes the following afternoon.

"Are you sure this is for me?" he asked Alison, Boyle's secretary. She lifted her glasses Eve Arden style, and peered at the envelope the note had come in.

"Put it there myself."

"Is he free now?" Noel asked.

"Will be shortly. Seat?"

"No. I'd rather flirt with you."

"You mean you'd rather try to extort information from me," she said. A tall, slender, vaguely washed out blonde, not unattractively approaching her fifties, Alison had a dizzy and capricious surface that hid a shrewd mind. She knew everything that went on in the department, possibly in the entire school. Noel settled on the edge of the desk and watched her go back to typing.

"You have to admit this invitation is a little sudden," he said. "You know as well as I that Boyle and I talk to each other once a term. The conversation is always the same."

"This one won't be," she declared, then lowered her voice. "Are you in trouble?"

"What kind of trouble?"

She looked around the office, then, certain that no one was listening, she said, "What were the police holding you for? They called here, you know. Spoke to me. They insisted on speaking to *him*. I tried to stop them. . . ." She shrugged.

"Is that all?" he said, with exaggerated relief.

A day and a half had passed and he was still hearing that anguished wheeze, feeling the hands pounding at him, seeing that dread featureless face. But instead of being depressed he was exhilarated. He'd missed his first class yesterday, but had been electric for the others, pulling ideas out of thin air, making associations and connections that had surprised him and awed the class. Half of them had gathered around his desk long after the period bells had rung, asking questions, offering ideas.

This morning had gone well, too, although he was calming down. Frightening as it had been, it had happened to *him*. That made it remarkable. That kept him in high spirits. High enough to tease Alison.

"Promise you won't breathe a word?" he said, taking on her conspiratorial tone.

"I'm not sure I want to hear this."

"I deal drugs. Mostly cocaine. But a little heroin,

too. The cops raided my place." He waited for the appropriate confused/horrified response to register on her face. "Luckily the place was clean. Not lucky, really, I was tipped off. There's this former junkie who runs for me. Actually, he's still addicted, which is how I get him to work for me, and . . ."

Boyle's office door opened. Noel stopped in midsentence and got off Alison's desk. She turned back to her typing. They heard the voices beyond the door, the department chairman, oily smooth as usual, the excited voice of the young man who exited first, shaking Wilbur Boyle's hand. Noel had seen his type before—tousled, dirty hair, granny glasses, denims a size too small, a corduroy jacket with worn houndstooth elbow patches—the costume of the career graduate student.

Boyle spotted Noel. "Did you get my note, Mr. Cummings? Do you have a moment now?"

Not waiting for an answer, he went back into his office.

"Here goes," Noel whispered to Alison and headed after him.

"You must be Noel Cummings," the graduate student said. "You wrote that article *contra* Wilson."

"I admit it."

"Everyone's talking about it in Chicago. No kidding. We think it's a terrific critique!"

"Thanks," Noel said, and would have stayed to find out what else they were saying at the University of Chicago, but Boyle was signaling to him.

"Nice boy," Wilbur Boyle said when they were alone. "Very up on things. Might join our staff next year."

He motioned Noel to sit down, but remained standing himself, looking up at the high windows under the prominent eaves of the old building.

"When I first took this office, I thought how wonderful it would be, right here in the heart of Manhattan overlooking the park. A roof with eaves to keep off sun and snow. Birds singing. All I notice now is pigeon shit."

Noel sat down and automatically inspected the bookshelf. A glance told him not a volume had been moved since his last visit at the beginning of the term. He'd heard such prologues before. They always led into a long, convoluted soliloquy of disappointments, hardships, and department problems. To listen to one was to hear all of them. But to break in was a breach of etiquette.

Noel used the time to prepare answers to Boyle.

The chairman got to the point rather suddenly, breaking off in the middle of a platitude to ask, "By the way, what is all this about, yesterday morning?"

"I witnessed a murder."

The handsome, well-cared for, middle-aged face stopped for a second as though a plaster mask had received a light hammer tap.

"No? Really?"

"Really. I think the victim was a police decoy. I never found out more. He was still alive. He sent me for help. It arrived too late for him. They said they would call to check my story. They even began to beat me up. Their chief stopped them."

"Not a nice bunch," Boyle said, all sympathy and interest. "What happened?"

"Some men knifed him. In one of the abandoned piers on the Hudson River."

Boyle winced, but seemed fascinated. "And they let you go?"

"Here I am."

"If only you'd told me," Boyle said, "you needn't have come to class. I would have found someone else. Or canceled it."

"I didn't mind, Noel said. He was enjoying himself now. "I thought work would keep my mind off it. It was grisly."

"It must have been." Those words said, Wilbur Boyle was once more the unworried, slick university administrator, his hair stylishly long, neatly combed, his clothing meticulous, his tone that of an aging politician. Boyle had made his name with one idea in one book twenty years ago. Since then, nothing had panned out, except this job. He'd done his best to glamorize it and himself.

"What were you doing there? In that area, I mean?"

"I bicycle every morning, before class."

"Sounds invigorating." Boyle shuddered. "And that's all?"

"What else would I be doing in an abandoned pier at that hour?"

"Then you aren't the one," Boyle said, sighing with obvious disappointment.

"What one?"

"No one tells me anything in the department. But I had heard an intriguing rumor that one of the staff was seen at curious hours recently in that area. Getting material. You know, of course, that area is a center of homosexual bars, clubs, haunts of different sorts? I was certain I'd soon be reading a proposal for a ground-breaking study on that milieu seen from within. It's needed. It sounded good. Very good. I'd hoped that person was you, Noel."

"Me?" Noel had been following Boyle with interest. He hadn't heard such a rumor nor did he know of the area's reputation. Boyle's last words startled him.

"Vain hope, I see," Boyle said, curling his upper lip. "Correct me if I'm wrong, but you *do* owe the department a thesis, don't you?"

"I suppose."

"So it wasn't entirely foolish of me to harbor the thought that this would be the long-awaited work?"

"But we've always discussed my ideas beforehand."

"I know. I know. To what end? What was the most recent one? Ah, yes, something about the impact of a drug rehabilitation center suddenly placed in a middle-class neighborhood. What happened to it?"

"The crime rate rose five hundred percent in four

months. A month later it was closed down, reopened in Harlem. It was nothing."

"It might have been something. If you had chosen to do it."

"As a book?"

"The Current Ideas imprint needs such books. That's why I began it. Or have you forgotten?"

How could anyone forget Boyle's pet project? Noel was reminded of it in some way every week. Boyle was using it to show up the other branches of the University Press: it was becoming an obsession.

"Would you really print something like that?" Noel asked, hoping to deflect Boyle onto his favorite topic.

"Like what? The rehab center? Or the murder?"

"No. I wasn't thinking about that."

"Maybe you ought to, Noel. No, don't interrupt. You realize that the social sciences are based on being right on the spot, living it, reporting it. All the great ideas in our field have come from being *within* a society. Look at Mirella Trent. She worked three months as a guard in a women's prison for her book. And it turned out to be the best one we've done in the series. We need more of that. Not more critiques of someone else's ideas in another grad school journal."

When was the last time Boyle had done fieldwork? Noel wondered resentfully. Unless that was what he called all those uptown cocktail parties. He was even more irritated by the department chairman pointing out Mirella's book as a guide. Everyone knew what a sensational muckraking feminist tract that had been: a best-seller that had pulled the Current Ideas imprint out of a financial hole. Not to mention the decisive blow it had dealt to Noel and Mirella's on-again, off-again two-year relationship. Boyle couldn't be ignorant of that, either.

"May I remind you," Boyle was saying now, "that when I first took you on here, I had high hopes. I know you're good in class. Students fight to get into your lectures. But I can no longer guarantee that will be enough to keep you in line for tenure."

There it was—the threat. Noel had been waiting for it.

"You saw that young man who came out of my office before. He's already coauthored one book. He's bright, eager. Why shouldn't he work here?"

"You've made your point," Noel said, standing.

"You have to realize my position, Noel. I have to answer to a dean, a board of directors. I'm attacked on all sides."

"I know." Which he did, from hearing it from Boyle so often. But he didn't care. All he wanted was to get out of that office.

"And you know I hate to exert pressure. It's not my style."

Of course not, Noel thought. It doesn't match your mirror-shine shoes or four-thousand-dollar face-lift.

"Don't let me go into the board meeting this term-ending with empty hands, Noel. Give me something to show for keeping you."

"I will," Noel lied: anything to get out.

Boyle seemed surprised, pleased. "Good. You must know how I detest these administrative duties," he said, suddenly unruffled and friendly again. "Why don't you show me something substantial soon? We'll meet over lunch. Wouldn't that be pleasant?"

"I won't let you down," Noel said at the door. He had to force himself to shake the plump, slick hand.

"Shit!" he said as Boyle's door closed. "Shit!"

What was happening to him?

He was in a black mood by the time he left the uptown IRT and walked to the apartment he had taken on Madison Avenue after Monica died and the five rooms on Riverside Drive had seemed so vast and empty. This place satisfied him. It was a good-sized studio with a tiny kitchen and bath off to one side, a sleeping loft built over a small study area. The ceilings were twelve feet high. He had a working fireplace, long walls for built-in closets and bookshelves. There was traffic, loading and unloading outside from seven in the morning until noon, but by afternoon the neighborhood was quiet and most nights it was country silent.

He had let himself into the apartment and dumped his books when the phone rang.

"Noel? Is that you? This connection is bad. Should I call back?"

"Mrs. Sherman? My side is fine."

"Well, I guess this will do then," she said, her nasal voice unmistakable. "I just wanted to check if you were coming up this weekend."

The minute she said it—half pleading, half reminding—Noel remembered: today was March third. In two days, Monica would have been twenty-eight. They had always visited her parents for her birthday, and after she died, the Shermans had insisted Noel continue the tradition. How they had loved her! How good they had been to him after it happened, never leveling a hint of reproach for letting their only, their wonderful daughter drown. Of course they had known Noel most of his life, were almost family to him. And usually Noel looked forward to seeing them.

"I know it's a long trip, now that we're so much farther away," Mrs. Sherman apologized.

"No problem." Brewster was only an hour and a half by train, a pretty ride along the Hudson River. Noel enjoyed being out in open country in cold weather. He hated the city in winter.

She was armed with train schedules, and they agreed to meet by eleven on Saturday morning.

"Peter is so much looking forward to seeing you," she said. "He made sure to ask if you were coming. We hardly see you."

"I'll be there," Noel said. But the minute he put down the receiver he knew he would do it this year only out of duty. Something was wrong. He couldn't put his finger on it, but it was there, gnawing away at him, not the usual flood of memories, but something else, something different.

He put on a record, one of Monica's favorites—the last Beatles album—and tried to remember her. Nothing happened.

He went to the closet, pulled out a box of photo albums they had collected for years and opened it randomly. The snapshots he peered at had been taken some eight years ago. They were still in college then, living together in a small basement off campus. She'd tried to be a lighter blonde that year and had dyed her hair platinum, and cut it quite short. As usual, she had pulled it off. She had looked like a golden retriever, glossy, smooth, tanned, long-legged.

From that album it was easy to get into the others. Noel sat in the curved-back rocking chair he and Monica had bought on the spot one morning after an all-night party, and went through album after album of photographs: a dozen of them, beginning when they were children living next door to each other in Mamaroneck. Many photos through junior high, she

always a few inches taller, always a bit more mature—
as in that snapshot of them at the Shermans' lakeside
house in Connecticut, Monica staring right out at you,
Noel squinting—a slim, curly-haired boy of thirteen.
The next album covered high school, when he finally
passed her in height and weight, and Monica had
grown radiant in her fair beauty, indomitably high-
spirited, so securely the most popular girl in school
that one could almost overlook the serious, gawky
young man who inevitably appeared next to her—
Noel, the obligatory chaperon. Monica was always the
main attraction, looking seductive at seventeen in her
first bikini (Noel to one side, holding a surfboard); or
ravishing in a cocktail sheath, strand of pearls and
pearl earrings, which he (in white jacket and black tie
with tartan cumberbund) had given her for her twentieth birthday; or fresh and cheerful in her short white
cheerleader's skirt with the tight-fitting bodice, her
hair long and sun-streaked (Noel half in shadow,
wearing basketball shorts and a shirt with the major
letter he had gotten that year); Monica smiling, in every conceivable pose and outfit, and always next to
her, Noel.

That was how it ought to appear, if photography
conveyed truth. It was always Monica for Noel. If not
from the day she stepped into his driveway where he
was patching a flat tire on his Schwinn and introduced herself as the new neighbor, then from only a
month or two after that. She was always first, through
high school and college, work and marriage, right up
to that afternoon on the lake.

He didn't have to look at those last snapshots taken
the day she died. He recalled that day well enough,
even after three years: how much of the margaritas
he'd drunk from the Thermos. How she'd awakened
him after he declared himself drunk and sleepy. How
they'd made love in the little skiff, sloshing around in
a half inch of water, their limbs slithery with it. The
soft undulation, the sun shimmering on the lake. Her

splash afterward as she dove into the water. Her taunts for him to join her. How she had left him alone to nap. Then the vague cries, his slow awakening, and the sudden clear sight of her arm and hand straight out of the water, gripping at air. His frozen terror the instant before he snapped fully awake and dove in. How he had grabbed her crumpled form, slowly sinking downward. How he had dragged her up and into the boat, thrown her over on her stomach, pumped her lungs. How he thought he had succeeded, and got the engine going, shooting back to the dock, praying, cold-faced, with her inert body. How he had listened to the doctor later, watched the old locals shrug, heard that of course cramps were common after intercourse, it happened all the time. And how that night he'd sat in the tiny, freezing cabin with Monica's corpse and slowly realized that after eighteen years of knowing her, being with her, living for her, everything had changed.

As the years passed, that day alone stood out clearly for Noel—the others became vague, even with the photo albums—the day he had failed to save her life. This recalled, he always felt a catharsis. The ritual finished, the records and the photo albums would be replaced in a back corner of the closet, the ghost relaid.

As it was this early evening. Relieved, he threw himself into two dozen impromptu sit-ups, his stockinged toes wedged under the crossbar of the kitchen table. He followed that with more exercises, showered, had dinner, studied, watched a few hours of TV, and went to sleep early.

Lying in bed, he felt exhausted. Somehow Monica seemed further away than ever before. Now school, his career, Boyle's ultimatum, clouded her image. Just before he fell asleep, Noel briefly saw that bloody man with no face.

"Someone's waiting for you," the old man Gerdes, the doorman, said.

Noel lifted the Atala over the threshold and rolled it into the storage closet next to the mailroom.

"Well," he asked, when he had locked the bike away, "where is he?"

"I let him in."

"Into my apartment?"

"He said he was your uncle."

"My uncle? What uncle?" Noel demanded, jabbing the elevator button.

"Don't know. He said he was tired. Not all old men are like me, you know, on my feet all day."

The floor arrow above the elevator pointed to five.

"Why couldn't he sit down here?"

"He said he was your uncle."

It was coming down slowly. At three, now, stopped. Probably Mrs. Davies, holding the door open to get her menagerie in.

"When did you ever meet any uncle of mine? Imagine letting a stranger into my apartment! If anything's missing—"

He withheld the remainder of the threat, as the elevator landed with a thump and sure enough, Mrs. Davies and a half-dozen dogs of various sizes and colors exited in a rushing barrage of fur and barking, their elderly owner spinning about, trying to hold on to their leashes.

Whatever could have been in Gerdes's mind to do

such a thing? Noel wondered as he ascended. Had his Uncle Al come to visit him? Why hadn't Aunt Antonia called beforehand? Was there trouble in the family?

His apartment door was slightly ajar. Music from the radio seeped out into the hallway: Mozart. Noel stood still, took a breath, and slowly opened the door all the way.

Only when it was fully open did he see the man sitting in the rocking chair, bathed in morning sunlight from the tall windows. At first, Noel didn't recognize him. When, a second later, he did, it was with a sudden rush of fear. It was he, the chief of those men in the abandoned Federal House of Detention, the man they had called the Fisherman.

"Come in! Come in!" he said cheerily. At Noel's baffled, apprehensive look the Fisherman got up from the rocker and came to meet him. "I didn't know when you'd be back, so I asked the doorman . . ."

"I know." What did he want?

"You don't seem too pleased to see me."

"I hoped I'd never see you again. I've tried to forget that morning." Noel closed the door, wondering whether anyone else was in the apartment. The bathroom door was open, no one could hide in the kitchen. In the closets?

"I can understand that. Do you have a pet?"

"A pet?"

"You keep looking around as though . . ." The Fisherman interrupted himself with a laugh. "I'm alone. Don't worry. By the way, have you had breakfast yet?"

Noel had been out riding this Sunday morning, enjoying the crisp, almost-spring, late March weather. He'd completed his route—on the East Side since that dawn—then had circled through Central Park, taking advantage of the winding roads closed to vehicular traffic every weekend. All the way home he'd been thinking about his growling stomach.

"Because if you haven't," the Fisherman went on, "I brought a few things. You like delicatessen?"

He opened a white paper bag he'd left on the table. Inside were fresh bagels, pungent lox, some smaller wrapped parcels.

"There is also fresh squeezed orange juice. And coffee. I have a special roast at Zabar's."

Noel was drawn by the food and by curiosity.

"Why did you tell the doorman you were my uncle?"

"What was I supposed to tell him? That I was a police officer?"

Noel didn't answer.

"Is this the kitchen?" the Fisherman said, going into the tiny room and spreading the packages of food on the counter. "Where are your dishes?"

"I'll get them," Noel said, taking off his jacket.

"I got the Sunday *Times*, too. It's over there." He pointed to its thick bulk on the lamp table next to the rocker. "You'll need a sharp knife to cut these bagels. They're fresh. They tear otherwise. Heat some water. I got cream cheese with chives. Do you like it?" He unwrapped the packages.

The small table seated two comfortably. Noel's initial panic had passed quickly, but not his curiosity. The man probably wanted to ask more questions. Or the same ones over again: a small enough price for breakfast and the *Times*.

"I'm here for a reason," the Fisherman said once they were seated.

"I didn't think you'd come to apologize again for my mistreatment."

"You're an intelligent man, Mr. Cummings. University professor and all."

"Not so smart. I still haven't figured out your name."

"Excuse me. Loomis," he said, putting out a hand for Noel to shake across the table. "Anton Loomis."

"Anton Loomis, New York City Department of Police. A detective, right? Some high rank? In which division? Homicide?"

"I used to be captain. I don't hold any rank now."

"Not because you were demoted. You're working for some special group, correct?"

"Close enough."

"That's all the questions I have," Noel said, and got up to cut another bagel. "You, too?"

"I'm overweight already. Mr. Cummings, I came to tell you something about what you stumbled into that morning."

Noel didn't completely believe him.

"I don't blame you for wanting to forget it. It was very unpleasant. But not the first unpleasant matter we've dealt with. And, not the worst. There has been a series of such murders. All of them related. Do you know who that man was you tried to help?"

"One of your men called him Kansas."

"Kansas. A code name. Operative number five. A police detective. Twenty-six years old. Just promoted. A wife. A child. A promising career in the department."

"I'm sorry to hear it. But isn't death an occupational hazard in your work?" Exactly what was he driving at?

"It is. It is. Not like that, though—blinded, bleeding, butchered in a rotting warehouse."

"I agree," Noel said. "I was there. Remember?"

"I remember. But as I was saying, Mr. Cummings, he was not the first of my operatives to be murdered. About a month ago another was found facedown in a snowbank, not four blocks away. His hands were bound, his throat cut, his body mutilated. And it isn't only policemen who are being killed."

"Are you trying to tell me there's a crime wave in the city? I do read the papers, Mr. Loomis."

"This isn't any general outbreak of crime. This is one group or one man. We don't know who. We aren't even sure why. But we can guess."

"Maybe they're ritual slayings," Noel suggested, re-calling what Boyle had told him. "Don't homosexuals consort in that area?"

"Exactly. See, I said you were an intelliegent man. From below Christopher Street all the way up to the twenties, there are dozens of bars and clubs."

"Well, that's who's doing it. Some homosexual-hating psychopath who took your men for what they were decoyed to be."

"So it would appear," Loomis said. Then, with a penetrating glance: "Or maybe that's what we're sup-posed to believe."

"You don't?"

"Do you recall, Mr. Cummings, about a year and a half ago when a man named Robby Landau was found murdered in his apartment? He owned a large and popular discotheque. He'd been stabbed many times, a hundred, more. His underwear was slashed off, the apartment ransacked—things broken, paint-ings ripped. It appeared to be the work of the type of man you just described."

Loomis went on: "What the newspapers didn't say was that Landau was to testify before a grand jury the next day about the South American drug trade. He was a large purchaser of cocaine. If he hadn't agreed to talk, he would have been indicted.

"While you're absorbing that," Loomis said, "try to recall a similar incident a few months later involving Albert Wills, a socially prominent, wealthy, playboy type. Except Wills played with boys, not girls. He was found badly beaten, strangled, stabbed: the works. The assumption was he had picked up a rough hustler, and they had disagreed about money. Except that in Landau's preliminary brief, he had mentioned Wills as another large purchaser of cocaine. Wills was sub-poenaed, too.

"Two other men were found dead in their apart-ment. One knew Wills. Both were pals of Landau. Neither was mentioned in his brief or known to the grand jury. No drugs were found. But the method of death was the same. Only this time the killer was looking for something and, failing to find it, had set fire to the place. A sharp-nosed neighbor smelled the smoke. Only a few files were found charred next to the bodies. Some of the papers pertained to Landau's club. Soon after his death, Landau's parents sold the discotheque to a corporation from Connecticut.

"Others at Landau's club got threatening phone calls. Other clubs catering to homosexuals were harassed by unknown men. Several bars in the West Street area came in for the same treatment—the owners threatened, beaten up. Sometimes, they just disappeared."

"The Mafia?" Noel asked.

"Maybe. Probably not. The techniques are classic syndicate methods. But, the Mafia has more or less abandoned penny ante business like bars and clubs. Nowadays they play the stock market, sit on the boards of directors of multinational corporations. More money there. The one bar in the area which we know to have mob connections was subjected to the same treatment. I can't see them hurting their own people, can you?

"No," Loomis went on, "whoever is behind this wants us to think it's the Mafia or that it's unorganized, merely random. But I think it's quite shrewdly organized. By one man—the man we call Mr. X. The mystery man. The operative who was cut up that morning was supposed to be linking up with Mr. X. Evidently he was discovered to be a decoy."

Noel ate his second bagel, drank his third cup of coffee, and listened fascinated. Loomis was like a TV police series come to life, sitting in his kitchen.

"Mr. X wants everything the Mafia has given up. And more, too. Maybe pornography, more than likely a boy prostitution ring up on Forty-second Street. But those are only sidelines compared to really profitable operations—large-scale drug smuggling, wholesale larceny from the ships that dock on the closed piers on the West Side. We don't know what else. But he seems to be building a little empire right under our noses. And he's not very nice to anyone he feels is in his way.

"We still haven't gotten a shadow of him. Whenever we think we're coming close, there's another club-owner beaten or killed, another operative slain, another takeover completed. Like magic. The man must have a sixth sense about us. It would need a sixth sense, because only those directly involved, and now you, Mr. Cummings, even know that Whisper exists."

"Whisper?"

"That's what our unit's been nicknamed. Because it's so hush-hush. We're not even directly funded. We're staffed by members of the U.S. Drug agency, state and city police. Our salaries are all laundered through an innocuous city agency I cannot name."

"Is that why you were in the abandoned federal jail?" Noel asked, trying to piece it all together.

"Were. We've moved again. I'm not free to say where. I've been in the intelligence business for thirty-five years, starting with the OSS in the Mediterranean, during World War Two. I've never run across anyone so elusive. We're never left with a clue. His men must be professionals, his organization small enough to deal with information leaks and betrayals, but large enough to operate against three of our men at any one time. Our informers report in every day. That morning they had nothing to report. They never have anything to report. It's exasperating.

"Meanwhile," he said, lowering his voice, "after chasing his shadow for so long, I've gotten to know a bit about Mr. X."

Loomis's last words recalled the shadows, the stabbing of Kansas in the debris-filled room. Had Mr. X been holding the cigarette lighter?

"He's smart," Loomis said; "no half-assed petty crook. He has this intuition about policemen: more than caution. More like true paranoia. And I admit this is a long shot, but I'm willing to defend it—he's a homosexual himself."

Noel had followed Loomis's reasoning right to the end. "But haven't all his victims been homosexuals?"

"Or decoys. Exactly. Mr. X's businesses are exploitative. But in order to exploit a certain group you have to know *how* they can be exploited. Mr. X has the magic touch: he knows which bars and clubs are most popular, which are only fly-by-night, or financially shaky. And when he moves in, it's done legally, tight as a drum. My theory is that one day Mr. X just woke up, looked around, saw how much was to be gotten on his own turf and then determined to get it."

"Which is why he's been so careful to throw you off the track," Noel said, "by making it seem as though a psychopath or the mob were behind it. But can't you locate him through the ownership papers of the bars?"

"He's a silent partner. The up front owner is usually some nobody. In half the cases the legal ownership hasn't changed. But we're certain Mr. X has taken over anyway. Everything even vaguely connected with this case has been checked out dozens of times."

"Even me?"

Loomis seemed to be expecting that question. "What do you want to know? You were born October twentieth, 1947, in Alameda, California. Your family moved to Mamaroneck, New York, in 1952. You went to Swarthmore College in 1965, majored in English literature for two years, then switched to social sciences. You studied two years after that, from 1970 to 1972 at Columbia Uinversity, worked part-time in a children's afterschool center on Rivington Street. In 1969 you married Monica Sherman, also of Mamaroneck. You paid two thousand, three hundred and forty-five dollars in income taxes to the federal government last year. You have a savings account and a special checking account at Manufacturers Hanover Trust, its Murray Hill branch. Your health insurance expired three years ago and was picked up by New York University one month later. Your status changed from family plan to individual in a group at that time. Your Social Security number is one four seven, three three, nine eight—"

"All right," Noel said, "I believe you. That's pretty impressive. But I thought you believed I had nothing to do with it?"

"I believed you, Mr. Cummings, but I had to check out your story. You were followed for seventeen days. When you went out bicycling in the morning, one car followed you halfway, another the rest of the way. The day after the murder, you changed routes—which didn't surprise us. You kept to the new route consistently. On Wednesday, two weeks ago, you went to two Fellini movies."

"Are you still following me?"

"You were dropped four days ago. Even if you were deliberately keeping a low profile, you couldn't possibly have looked so clean to us."

"Why shouldn't I? I'm not a homosexual."

"That wouldn't prove a thing."

Noel had an anxious thought. "Did you tap my phone?"

"We're not authorized to do that. But—as I said—you were our prime suspect, until you checked out to be exactly what you seemed to be."

Noel was intrigued—and secretly pleased—that he'd been a suspect. What would Alison say when she heard that? Noel could already see her mouth form an O of surprise. He was surprised, himself.

"Why tell me all this?" he asked.

"To be perfectly frank with you, Mr. Cummings, we're back to square one. So we try something different. Since Mr. X can smell policemen, we get people to work for us who aren't policemen. People like you."

He said it so matter-of-factly, it took a minute for Noel to register astonishment. "Me? You're kidding?"

"Why not?"

"It's not my kind of thing," Noel tried to explain.

"Look around you, what does this place look like to you?"

"Like the somewhat sparsely furnished apartment of a New York University sociology professor. That's why we need you."

"I'm not trained for it. I've never even handled a gun."

"You won't have a gun. You won't need one. It won't be that kind of job. Look at yourself, Mr. Cummings, you're in better shape than most rookies fresh out of the Police Academy. You do two, three hours of exercise a day?"

"Something like that. But . . ."

"How would you like to come down to the academy? I'll lay two-to-one odds you outrun, outjump, outreact, and outthink any man there. We've watched you, you know."

"That may be so," Noel said, trying not to feel too flattered. "But they're trained to think in certain ways. To be defensive. To be cautious. To know how to handle people."

"And you aren't? You're a sociology professor. Isn't that the study of people?"

"In groups, yes, but . . ."

"You'll be *in* a group. I just want you to find me the one in the group that stands out—the rotten apple. My men are fumbling around in the dark. They don't know who or what they're looking for. You could probably spot him on a dime. You've had psychology, too, I know. I read it in your records."

Noel admitted that.

"So, you know what to look for. For you, this straw in the haystack will be bent a certain, unmistakable way, won't it?"

"I suppose. Look, I really feel flattered. But I've got my teaching and all—"

"It won't interfere with your teaching. I'm simply asking you to show up at a certain place for several hours a night. A bar off Christopher Street we're certain Mr. X owns and frequents. All I want is for you to bartend a few nights."

"But there must be dozens of homosexual bars in the city. Why that one?"

"Because this bar attracts the kind of homosexuals we believe he associates with. And because it's the most popular one at the moment."

"That's still pretty hit or miss, no?"

"Maybe. But without knowing who Mr. X is, we still know a lot about him. We're certain some of his victims were once his sexual partners. Others he's set up in the bars as owners or managers fall into the same pattern. Let me show you."

Loomis produced a manila envelope he'd been carrying in a side pocket of his coat, and pulled out a dozen eight-by-ten-inch photos.

The first seemed to be a typical male beefcake pose. A curly-haired, handsome young man, with a small dark mustache, large, light-colored eyes, and a muscular though nor grotesquely over-developed body. He wore only a small bikini. His skin looked oiled.

"Bill Ames." Loomis said. "One of the two men found in the burning apartment."

The next photo was of a dancer in midleap, his body in profile, his head turned full face to the camera. His arms were akimbo and his handsomely boyish face was broken in a wide grin. Dark curly hair and light eyes. Not as heavily mustached as the first man, but of distinctly athletic build, highlighted by the close-fitting tights.

"Rudy Brill," Loomis said. "A friend of Landau's. DOA. It looked like a drug overdose."

The third man was a bit older. Also in superb physical shape, tanned, mustached, blue eyes, wavy jet hair, handsome. He was leaning against the railing of a beach house, the ocean in the background. "This is Landau," Loomis said. "Now do you see?"

Noel sorted through the other, similar photos.

"Well, they certainly seem to fit a particular mold."

"How tall are you," Loomis said, "six feet?"

"Exactly."

"Ames was six one. Landau a half inch taller. The others about the same. Care to look in the mirror and see the other similarities?"

"No, I get the idea."

"You see, Mr. Cummings, you won't really have to look for Mr. X. He's going to find you!"

That gave Noel a chill. Trying to dissuade Loomis, he said, "What if he's changed his type?"

"Unlikely."

"It's sort of hard thinking of myself as, well you know, fitting a certain physical description. As so much meat."

"That's exactly what you will be. A nice juicy piece of bait for Mr. X. As my grandma used to say, it takes honey, not vinegar to catch a bear. Come on, Noel, say you'll do it. It won't take much of your time. You'll be well paid. You'll be doing a service to the community. All you have to do is tend bar a few nights a week and wait until Mr. X comes along. Then we pounce on him. You're perfect. The other operatives were too busy playing Kojak just to wait. You'll never be suspected. Say you'll do it."

That Noel even considered the offer shocked him. He wasn't a doer, he was a thinker. Despite all his exericse, he thought himself an intellectual. Others he'd grown up with had sailed on merchant steamers, worked their way across the Pacific and Indian oceans. Some hitchhiked across country, lived on ashrams in India, communes in the Oregon woods. Not he. He wasn't adventurous. Yet the last few minutes had made Noel feel this was the way to find adventure, to break out of the routines he'd fallen into since Monica's death. He was swept off his feet, riding a higher altitude than he had since . . . since when? Of course, since the morning of the slaying three weeks before.

And then he remembered Kansas, bleeding, faceless, dying in all the garbage and fallen timbers. No. It was too dangerous. He couldn't accept.

"I don't know if you can understand my point of view, Mr. Loomis . . ." he began.

"Wait a minute," Loomis interrupted. "Please. Let me show you how this could be an experience of the most crucial importance to you. Maybe I'm stepping out-of-bounds by saying it, but I happen to know that your current position is not the most secure, so I . . ."

"How do you know that?"

"I just know. Let me be blunt with you. If you come to work for Whisper you'll be able to save your career."

Noel was surprised, amused. "Really? How?"

"Let's say you were doing work on one of the tribes of the Amazon jungle, what would you do to find out how they really live, how they really think? You'd go into the jungle, wouldn't you? You'd find that tribe, live with them, eat their food, even learn their language, follow their customs—"

"Wilbur Boyle," Noel said suddenly.

Loomis looked as though he'd never heard the name before.

"The chairman of my department at school," Noel explained. "You've been talking to him."

"What makes you think that?"

"Because he wants a study on homosexuals as seen from the inside. For his Current Ideas book line. Right?"

"And you need a study to keep your job," Loomis said, without flinching. "So here is it." He waited for Noel to protest. When he didn't, Loomis went on: "We figure there may be more than a half million homosexuals in the city. A huge subculture. Not much studied. I'll place you literally at the crossroads. I'll prepare you better than any anthropologist setting off into the jungle. Whisper has operatives all over the Lower West Side. You'll be trained how to behave, what to expect. On the job, too."

"Sounds terrific." Noel meant it to be sarcastic.

"It is terrific. When's the last time someone handed you a gift like this—all wrapped up with fancy paper, placed on a silver platter?"

Noel didn't answer. Instead he asked, "Did Boyle approach you? Or you he?"

"What's the difference?"

"I just want to know."

"Are you afraid of homosexuals, Mr. Cummings?"

"I'm afraid of *you*, Mr. Loomis."

"Don't be like that. Give it a try. You don't have to commit yourself. I'll provide a guide, you go take a look. Then go talk to this Boyle."

"What if I decide not to do it?"

"Then I'm out of business again until I can find someone who looks like you and knows what you know." Loomis sighed heavily. "I don't like looking for second best, when I can have the best," he said. "It will take time. Meanwhile Mr. X is getting fancier everyday. More and more people are going to be put through his slicing machine."

Noel didn't care to be made to feel guilt over something that really didn't involve him. Coolly, he said, "I'll think about it."

"Take a look first. Then think about it. I'll have someone call on you."

He stood up, and Noel walked him to the apartment door.

"I suppose you read the financial section," Loomis said, looking wistfully at the *Times*.

"Take it, if you want."

When Loomis had his coat on and his papers under one arm, he began to shake Noel's hand vigorously.

"You won't regret this, Noel."

"I haven't committed myself to anything," Noel reminded him.

"I know, I know." Loomis withdrew his hand. Noel held the door open as he left, watching the other man standing in the hall pushing the elevator button. "By the way," Loomis said as though realizing something, "Vega's his name. Buddy Vega."

"The guy who'll call me?"

"Ssshh," Loomis cautioned, looking around. There were two other apartments on the floor, both doors closed.

The elevator arrived, Loomis stepped in. Noel was turning back into his apartment when he heard his name whispered.

"Yes?"

"Thank your neighbor for the *Times*. It was laying beside 4-D," Loomis said, letting the door close on his smile.

5

─────────────────────

"*Is this Noel Cummings?*"

"Speaking."

"Vega here."

"Who?" Noel placed the pencil he'd been chewing on to mark the place in the Levi-Strauss book he was reading, then put it down on the desk, and took a deep breath.

"Buddy Vega. The Fisherman told me you'd know who I was."

"I know who you are," Noel answered, his voice suddenly small and tight. He remembered Loomis's visit all right. He'd been replaying it in his mind all week.

"Good," Vega said. His voice remained flat, expressionless. "What are you doing in half an hour?"

Noel wanted to say he was going out, that he'd changed his mind about the whole business, that Vega ought to forget it.

"Nothing," he answered. "Preparing for tomorrow's class."

Noel heard a child's voice in the background, and joining its shrill piping, a woman talking rapidly in Spanish.

"You got the time to go over to the Grip?"

He didn't. He couldn't. Not end up like Kansas, blood pouring out of his eye sockets.

"That's the name of the bar?"

"Yeah. Get ready. I'll be at your place in half an hour."

Before Noel could tell him not to, the line was dead. He cursed himself for not getting Vega's phone number, and tried to concentrate again on Levi-Strauss and primitive consciousness. It was useless. Exercising was no better. When he looked at himself in the mirror all he could think of was how much he resembled the men in the photos Loomis had shown him. Mr. X's victims.

He finally gave up. He'd just finished dressing when the buzzer rang, and Gerdes announced Vega, garbling the name so it was scarcely recognizable.

Perhaps because of the name, Noel had expected someone different from the man who swaggered into his apartment, looked around disdainfully, made a point of avoiding Noel's hand extended for a shake, and dropped onto the couch.

Not small, wire, ethnic-looking, as Noel had pictured him, Buddy Vega was large, broad-shouldered, with light hair that probably bleached blonder in the summer, a scraggly beard and mustache, wearing a getup from an old Hell's Angels' movie—soiled, antique black leather jacket, fat buckled garrison belt, faded skintight denims, and a ragged work shirt open to his navel, exposing a hairy chest and an abdomen rapidly going to flab.

"I thought you'd be ready," Vega said, annoyed.

"I am."

"You're not going to the Grip looking like that?"

"Why not?"

Noel looked himself over. He wore a turtleneck with light-colored chinos, brown oxfords, and a poplin Windbreaker.

"Because I won't be seen with you dressed like that. That's why. I've got to work there four nights a week, you know. Come on now. If you're serious about this . . ."

"I am serious. What's wrong with how I'm dressed?"

"It's postcollegiate fag. It's East Side. Worse, it's East Side five years ago. No good. No good at all." Vega pulled himself out of the couch, and Noel wondered if Buddy were on drugs, he seemed to move so lethargically. "Let's see your duds."

Vega pawed through the dozens of slacks in the closet, shaking his head. "For Chrissakes, don't you have any jeans?"

Noel grabbed a hanger with a pair of denims.

"Put them on."

Noel undressed quickly and was pulling on one leg of the pants when Vega stopped him with a pained expression.

"Oh, man. Nobody wears fucking underwear anymore. Chuck 'em."

More self-consciously, Noel did as he was told. Vega held up the discarded drawers.

"Jesus! I haven't seen a pair like this since the Marines. That turtleneck job's gotta go, too. And the jacket." He began to rummage through the neatly stacked shirts in Noel's bureau, then turned around. "Those jeans shit!"

"What?"

"They're too baggy. Look!" He dropped onto one

knee and began pulling at the pants in various places. "They're too loose. They should hang low on your hips, be tight in the ass and the legs and especially full at your basket. They shit! Take 'em off. What else do you have? Old things."

Without waiting for Noel, Vega continued his rummaging, throwing clothing onto the carpet, stopping now and then to examine something, then tossing it with the others, muttering all the while.

"I thought the Fisherman had you outfitted. I don't know why the hell I'm supposed to do it. I'm no nursemaid. You'll have to get a full drag tomorrow. And listen, this is your story. You're hard up for work. Unemployment benefits ended a month ago in San Francisco. That's where you're from. Ever been there?"

"Not recently."

"Too bad. You used to work in a bar called South of the Slot. Remember that. And also the Barracks. That's a bathhouse. You're new in town, right? You got here by driving a car someone wanted transported from the Coast. All it cost you was gas and oil. Got all that?"

"I think so."

"Aside from that, keep quiet. You're bound to fuck up. Don't you have any guinea T-shirts?"

"An old one," Noel said, pulling out a shirt he'd gotten back from the laundry a month ago with a large bleach hole. He'd been saving it to use as a dust rag. "It's no good. Look!"

"It's perfect. Put it on. And what about these?" He pulled out a pair of jeans Noel didn't recognize at first. "Here. Put these on."

"Those were my wife's."

"They look like men's pants. Put them on. We don't have all night, you know."

"They're too small for me."

"I'll decide that. Don't you have any sneakers?"

Noel pointed to his Adidas. Vega said, "Finally, the man has a wearable item of clothing. Hallelujah! Put those on, too."

Monica's jeans had been secondhand when she bought them. The pockets and cuffs were frayed. She'd worn them on hiking trips, and that last time at the lake. They felt tight, too tight to wear.

"It's no good," Noel said. "I won't be able to close all the buttons." The metal fly buttons, he meant.

"Leave the bottom one open. They look fine. Now, do you have a file or sandpaper?"

When Noel came out of the bathroom with a fingernail file, Vega was in the kitchen helping himself to a beer.

"Put one hand in your pocket. All the way down so you can hold your dick. Do you hang left or right? Right, I think, hold it there, now file it."

"Is that how you got that rubbed look on your crotch?"

"You're kidding! The way I got mine would take too long. Go on. File away!"

"How's this?"Noel asked.

"It'll have to do. Your hair is all wrong, too. That style is too straight." Then: "Hell, you *are* supposed to be from out of town. Don't go to your regular barber next time. We'll have Vinnie style it. You know, the Windbreaker might do after all. I don't suppose you have any leather? Let's take a look."

He turned Noel to face him, and looked him over as critically as though he were a model about to go out on a runway with a new line of fashions. Noel was able to check his own image in the mirror. The T-shirt was close fitting; the hole stretched tightly from his armpit to expose one nipple, the edge of the shirt was only barely contained by the low-slung jeans. Monica's jeans. He couldn't get it out of his mind: these were the last clothes Monica had worn.

Vega chugalugged the rest of the beer. "Let's go."

"You're not serious?"

"Why not?" Vega was sincerely surprised.

"Look at me."

"I'm looking. Man, you look so fucking hot those
queens are going to trip all over themselves. Get something straight, Professor, I don't know what kind of
crap the Fisherman laid on you, but your job with
Whisper is to look as pretty as you can. That's all.
Don't act smart. Don't talk to anyone more than you
have to. Don't try to be a hero. Just keep quiet, even
mysterious. Hide everything you can about yourself.
Stand behind that bar and look pretty. That's all we
need you for: the wrapping. You're the bait for the big
motherfucking fish to bite on. You got that?" he
asked, patting Noel on one cheek with a dirty fingertip.

"That's what Loomis said, but—"

"But nothing. You fuck up on this, you talk too
much, and you are D-E-A-D, man. Let's go. I don't want
to be late for work."

They hailed a cab and Vega directed the driver to
West Street. Noel had felt funny entering the lobby
dressed so uncharacteristically, but no one else
seemed to notice: not the doorman, not the teenaged
girls who lived on the next floor, not even the cabby.

"We're late, so I won't have the chance to run you
up and down the way I wanted to, showing you off,"
Vega said in the cab, lighting a hand-rolled cigarette.

"Is that grass?" Noel asked.

"Sure. You want some?"

"No. But . . . the driver and all."

Vega tapped the window that separated them from
the cabby. The driver's face looked back at them.
"What you want?"

"You mind if we smoke some reefer, man?"

"Hell, no, bro." The driver smiled. "I got ripped myself."

"Good deal," Vega said, inhaling deeply. "Maybe
you ought to have a few tokes, too, man. You're a little
nervous. You afraid of dying young?"

Noel declined the grass. "You were saying? Showind me off?"

"Going to have to do that tomorrow. I want people to really take a look at you. They will at the bar. But some folks don't go into bars. I want everyone to see you. Everyone. So, tomorrow or the day after, we're going to take us a little stroll. You wear those same pants, hear? We'll go from Sixth Avenue and Eighth Street to Christopher Street, check in a few places there, then down to the pier. Everyone cruises Christopher."

"Looking for sex?"

"Whatever," Vega said, then seemed to come alert. "That's a word you didn't know, right?"

"I wasn't sure."

"Any other words you hear you're not sure of, you ask me. But not in company, you hear?"

They were stopped at a light. Noel was annoyed with Vega. "You don't like me, do you?" he asked.

Vega puffed on the joint, face averted to look out the cab window so that his words came out low, almost muffled.

"I don't like or dislike you, man."

"Why are you treating me like an idiot then?"

"You want to stay alive? Then you listen to me. Hear?"

"Or is it that I'm not a cop?" Noel asked, dropping his voice with the last word so it was barely audible. "Is that it?"

"Something like that," Vega admitted.

"Well, don't worry about that. I'm a professional, Mr. Vega. Maybe not in your line, but in my own. I can take care of myself. Evidently the Fisherman knows what he's doing. No?"

"Maybe," Vega said, not sounding convinced. "Right here," he said in a louder voice, tapping the guard window between them and the driver.

Noel let Vega pay for the ride and hassle with the

cabby about a receipt—no doubt later reimbursed by the Police Department. Meanwhile, he stared at the bar and its environs.

The Grip was located at one end of a block that faced the elevated West Side Highway and the scores of huge moving vans parked under the closed road, a single-story building with stucco up to a series of painted over or tinted windows. The bar had two entrances, a large double door in the middle of the block and a single door at the corner. Both were painted black, with tiny windows set at eye height. Over the larger door was a plaque, the letters burnt in, ranch style, below a crudely drawn black-gloved fist holding a white cylindrical object that extended to the top and bottom edges of the sign. At first Noel thought it was a diploma. A moment later he realized it was probably meant to represent a penis. Better get used to it, he told himself.

There was another, smaller bar on the block and a closed-off four-story building, which might have been a warehouse. Right next to the Grip was another store with no identifying sign. A glance explained why none was needed. Two display windows on either side of the front door were filled with leather gear—full sets of men's leather clothing, from boots to head-over masks, gloves, underwear, pants with front and back panels cut out. More, the windows contained sex tools of every size and description—fake phalluses in all sizes and colors, ribbed or smooth, different kinds of condoms, leather thongs, handcuffs, handkerchiefs, T-shirts printed with obscene illustrations. Floating over the wares on wires, like inane guardian angels, were two inflatable rubber dolls—one male, one female, both of them pinkly naked.

"Let's go," Vega snorted, pushing Noel out of the cab. Once on the street, he added, "Stupid shine, can't write his name." Then following Noel's gaze to the sex emporium, he said, "You ought to go in, you won't believe some of the shit in there. Buy yourself some cock rings and other gear, you know."

He strode into the Grip, Noel behind him.

It was dark inside, with the musty smell of most saloons he'd been in, pulsing with the beat of rock music from speakers not immediately visible, relentless, monotonous.

Vega walked up to the bar, a huge, turn-of-the-century oaken affair which curved around from one room of the Grip into another in a shallow horseshoe. Noel joined him, envying his easy stride in the tight jeans, and wondering if it was off-hours. Loomis had said the Grip was busy all the time, but only a half-dozen men were in the bar. One of these was a curly-haired, Hispanic-looking man who eyed them from the entrance.

"Hey, Miguel!" Vega teased loudly, going up to him, "what's on your mind, eh, baby!"

Miguel stared at Noel with solid, almost dead eyes, then began talking low to Vega. Noel was spooked by the look. Could this be one of Mr. X's hired assassins? Or was he merely interested in Noel? Either way, Noel didn't like Miguel, and stayed at a distance from him.

A bartender appeared suddenly from the other room and came up to Noel. His look was a lot more obvious than Miguel's; he pointed the tip of his tongue to one corner of his mouth, gazed slowly over the bar, up and down Noel's body. "What can I get you?" he said with a slight indeterminate drawl.

Vega broke off his conversation long enough to turn around and say, "This is the guy I was telling you about. Noel Cummings. This here's Rick Chaffee."

Noel put a hand out; Chaffee hesitated, then took it in the open-handed, high-in-the-air peace shake of the sixties.

"I wondered why old Buddy talked you up so much," he said, holding on to Noel's hand. "Now I see."

"Rick's the manager," Vega said offhandedly, then went into a small room off the side.

"Something to drink?" Chaffee offered, fixing a slow lizard stare upon Noel. Unlike Miguel's stare, however, Chaffee's was unmistakable. How many times had Noel seen it when men met women; the evaluation look, he called it—how good will she be in bed? What will she do? What can I do to make her hit the ceiling? Slowly, Noel withdrew his own hand, and glanced over the bottles on the back shelf of the bar.

"Beer'll do."

Chaffee got a can of Budweiser out of a barrel, punched it open on a screwed-down opener. "California, huh?"

"Frisco," Noel said, trying to meet the look Chaffee had given him. Rick was about thirty years old, with long, lank dark hair, thin face, fine features, deep-set dark eyes. Scars in various places on his cheeks and forehead. A rough beard and mustache.

"Must be something in the water out there," Chaffee said.

He punched open a Bud for himself and leaned over the bar.

"Need work, huh?" Without waiting for an answer, he asked, "You ever come in here before?"

"Just got in town."

"I guess you don't have to hang around bars much. You been pushing it much?"

For a second, Noel was confused, then he realized he was being asked if he were a prostitute. He fought down his sudden anger.

"No. Never did it."

"You could," Chaffee said. He tapped his long fingers on the bar, leaned closer, and said, "Tell me, would you rather work here or ball me? You can't do both, you know. I've got ethics."

He'd been waiting for his own reaction to the first proposition. This one was so good, Noel had to laugh. "Could I take a look around?"

"Sure. Look around. You're too pretty for me, anyway. I'd rather have you pulling in business than have a few good fucks and lose you."

"Then I can have the job?" Noel acted sincerely.

"You're on a month's probation. I'll need you three nights a week. Eight o'clock to four in the morning. That's when we close here. Not at three like California."

"Two, out there," Noel corrected, suddenly remembering the fact.

"Whatever," Chaffee said, all business now. "You set up when you come in. We keep two reserves: open and closed. You have to get a key from me for that. Or ask. Count your register when you come in. Note it. Tips are split among everyone on the shift, usually two of us. Free drinks at your discretion. I assume you can mix anything?"

"Pretty much," Noel lied. He'd have to get a bartenders' manual and learn it by heart.

"We have three qualities of booze: house, brand, and top brand. Three prices. Always mix with the house unless someone asks for the others and is watching. No sex, no drugs at the bar. If you want to smoke or ball, go downstairs. Bud will show you the office downstairs. You get a half hour for dinner break. What you're wearing looks fine. Don't you have boots?"

"Yeah. But if I'm going to be on my feet all night . . ."

"Start tomorrow. Eight o'clock. You know the pay?"

"Buddy said . . ."

"It's not much. That's why you'll have to hustle for tips. You shouldn't have any trouble. I'll work two nights' shift with you for a while. Buddy'll probably work with you on the other day. That's Max at the door."

Noel turned around in time to see a large, heavyset man with a nasty, distinctly Teutonic face, dressed in black leather from his boots to his visored motorcycle cap. He'd just come into the bar, looked around, smiled a broken-toothed grimace, and settled himself on a tall stool next to the entrance.

"You have any trouble at all, call Max. He'll cream the guy. Eh, Max?" Chaffee lowered his voice. "He's really a pussycat when you get to know him. But he likes to play rough, too."

Max grunted loudly and, overhanging the stool on all sides, appeared to fall into an immediate sleep.

"Remember," Chaffee warned, "you'll be watched here. So no shit. Okay? Oh, and do us a favor? Don't bring your personal life into the bar."

Noel assured him he wouldn't.

Business over for the minute, Chaffee smiled, and leaning over the bar ran a finger down the front of Noel's chest, stopping only where the jeans began. Noel was so surprised he couldn't help but flinch. "You're going to regret not balling with me. Believe me, you'd bring out the best in me. I'd do things to you you'd never get over."

"I thought you had ethics," Noel said, sipping his beer and gingerly placing Chaffee's hand back on the bartop.

"Tomorrow night at eight," Chaffee repeated without anger, then turned to face a customer who'd just come into the bar.

Buddy came out of a doorway leading to two bathrooms, and to a stairway which, Noel supposed, led down to the office. He waited, but instead of coming over to Noel, Vega remained at the other end of the bar, talking with Miguel. Done serving his customer, Chaffee joined them.

Noel decided he'd made a good first impression and hadn't overreacted to Chaffee's overtures. He might as well take a look around before the place got crowded.

The second room was separated by a doorway, open on the barside. Smaller, darker, and quieter than the main room, it was dominated by a large pool table, with just enough side room for a player to stand back and take aim. A mirror a foot wide ran shoulder height along one wall of the room, opposite the bar. Below it, a wooden shelf was just deep enough and high enough to provide a precarious perch. There were no tables or chairs. Only a half-dozen barstools.

Next to the second entrance was a huge oil Wurlitzer jukebox. And now Noel could make out several large multifaced speakers hung close to the ceiling, providing the sound. Sawdust was strewn on the wooden plank floors, the whole place spotlighted and pinspotted from a track system above the bar. The walls were painted a deep brown. It looked modest but expensive, he thought. With Redfern speakers like that, the system itself might cost five thousand dollars. Yet it all looked casual, offhand, nothing special. Were other gay bars this way? In this style? Or were Mr. X's own tastes revealed here? A hint, a clue?

People were slowly coming into the bar, filtering into the second room, coming up to the jukebox. Noel remained near the pool table, trying to be both observant and inconspicuous.

He'd have to learn the argot and behavior patterns fast. Vega had been right. He'd have to keep his mouth shut, speak offhand, obliquely for a while to disarm suspicion. Until he could convince the men he was one of them, he'd have to be quiet. And careful.

If Chaffee and Vega were any indication, Noel would also have to be a great deal looser in his speech and manners. They talked to the point, bluntly, coloring their conversation with terms he was often unsure of. But their attitude—that was what was most surprising. He'd always associated homosexuality with feminine gestures and speech. But in here it was just the opposite: an extreme manliness, unruffled, almost frontiersman calm, as though all those Gary Cooper movies had come to life. Sure! That was it! The rough clothing, the swaggering walk, the drawling speech. They were acting out cowboy fantasies. How easy for him to copy! After all he was supposed to be from the West, wasn't he?

"Something funny?"

Chaffee had come into the smaller room, was now leaning over the bar.

"Just remembering something," Noel said, annoyed to be caught off his guard. He'd have to be more careful, damn it!

"Care to share it with me?"

It wasn't a threat, or demand. Chaffee liked him, that much was already clear. He wasn't the enemy. Or was he?

"It's personal."

"How's your beer?"

"Fine. It get crowded in here?"

"Wall to wall." Chaffee hesitated, then leaned a little closer over the bar. "Buddy said you knew your way around, but I get a different impression."

Now Noel *was* on his guard. "Oh?"

"I think you're pretty green. I'm not judging, mind you. I don't give a fuck. But let Mother give you a little advice. You're going to get guys coming in here who'll tell you they'll make you a model, a movie star, a pop star, anything. Listen to them nicely, refill their glasses a lot, even take presents from them. But don't pay them any mind. Because once you do, you'll be ground up into little bits by this scene, and some of the garbage around here. I've seen it happen to good-looking hayseeds often enough."

"What about you?" Noel asked, trying to keep embarrassment from covering his face. "Haven't you played with garbage?"

"A lot. But I've learned to keep my hands clean." He nodded, then moved aside, speaking loudly to a man in the corner, "Hey, dude, you drinking or holding up the wall?"

A minute later, as he passed by, Noel said, "Thanks for the tip."

Chaffee acted as though he hadn't heard him.

Noel watched him serve the drink, then, as he watched Chaffee go into the other room, his eye was caught by something in the mirror hung high over the back of the bar. Two men he'd seen in the other room were now standing behind Noel, five or six feet apart, leaning against the wooden shelf. They seemed oblivious to each other, yet linked somehow, too. Staring at their reflections, Noel thought the one in the loose-fitting army fatigues must still be a boy, fifteen or sixteen years old. Sure enough, he held a can of Seven-Up.

The two looked at each other briefly, then away. All very subtle, with no sign at all that they were aware of each other, until one changed his pose by a fraction—head back, cigarette lighted. The other shifted his own pose in equally minute reaction, sipping from the can in his hand, moving a leg; all very nonchalant.

It only took Noel a few minutes to realize that each movement was designed to signal an intention, a fear, a question; to attract or repel; an elaborate, silent mating dance.

Finally, the younger one turned to put his drink on the shelf. The other, a dark blond, turned his head to stare at the boy, shifting his own pose several times, signaling, Noel guessed, that he didn't want the boy to go without him. The boy took a step toward him. They met, said something Noel couldn't hear, then settled back against the shelf side by side. They talked quietly. The boy smiled. Their hands met in the brotherhood handclasp. Noel thought he heard names exchanged. Must remember to shake hands like that in the future, he reminded himself: Chaffee had done it, too.

Now the two were involved in a series of quick, intense questions and answers. Noel wished to hell he could overhear them, but the bar was too empty for him to move nearer. Suddenly, the boy shifted away from the wall, and the two of them left the room so fast Noel barely had a chance to see them slip out past Max at the door.

Noel gulped down the rest of his beer, unable to hide his excitement. He'd been here less than a half hour, and he'd actually witnessed a key social ritual of this society—a sexual pickup—from inception to consummation. First time out, and he'd struck pay dirt! If only he'd been able to hear what they'd said to each other! Loomis was right. He felt as though he'd parachuted into New Guinea and witnessed a once-a-century ceremony never before seen by a white man.

"I thought you were working tomorrow?" It was Vega, behind the bar.

"I am."

"You must have something better to do than hang around here."

"You're kidding! It's fascinating. Do you know what I just saw?"

"No and I don't care. Get out of here. Come back tomorrow. Go!"

Vega turned away to wipe the bar top.

Noel fought down the urge to punch him in the face. Instead, he reached into his wallet, slapped a dollar onto the bar, and loudly said, "Another beer. And keep the change."

Buddy glowered threateningly, but he got the beer. When he bent to reach it, Noel walked over to the Wurlitzer. The play button was taped over. He punched a half-dozen selections at random.

The first song to come on had a long instrumental introduction with trumpet punctuations before a mellow black tenor sang, "I'm a free man. Yes. I am. A free man, baby. Yes. I am."

Noel's beer was open, waiting for him on the bar top. Vega and the dollar were gone.

6

Noel didn't stay to finish the beer. Within minutes, the Grip filled up as though a crowded bus had stopped and unloaded all its passengers. Noel checked his watch. He and Buddy had come in at eight fifteen. It was now nine o'clock.

He'd made his point with Vega. If he stayed on it might constitute a challenge he wasn't sure he could back up. Besides, with the bar so suddenly crowded, he felt less protected, more open to being forced into contact with possible enemies, spies, friends of Mr. X. Nor did it take long for him to see that the ordinary saloon mentality—lone men drinking silently or engaged in drunken conversation—didn't hold true in the Grip. Instead, the place was filled with motion, many people talking, moving about from spot to spot, no doubt a lot of sexual hunting, too. The currents around him, though not always definable, were powerful.

Outside the bar, the night air was surprisingly warm, and he decided to walk to the subway. Turning the corner of West Street onto Christopher was like finding himself on a busy midtown thoroughfare in the middle of a business day. It seemed that hundreds of people were out, walking singly, in pairs, or groups of three or more, coming and going slowly on both sides of the street, leaning against parked cars, chatting, standing together at corners, talking and glancing at passersby. Traffic was heavy, with cars creeping along the curbs, slowing for the drivers to lean out and make conversation with pedestrians.

The street was garish, neon-lit from bars, pizza parlors, a transient hotel. And with the lights went the omnipresent beat of rock music, seeping onto the street from businesses, apartments with open windows, car stereos; from radios set on the high steps of a Catholic church where a dozen men sat, from tape decks that swung by as he passed their owners.

Noel walked the few blocks to Hudson Street feeling strange, disoriented. Men were everywhere, and hardly any women at all. Here, joints of grass were smoked as openly as cigarettes, passed hand to hand, even in front of policemen. Single men slinking against the walls as they approached him would chant out a monotonous litany: "Loose joints, coke, hash, LSD, speed." Men cruising for sex everywhere, whether walking or sitting or standing still. Twice a man followed close behind Noel for a block or more, peripherally visible, trying to catch his attention, or saying something quiet and obscene, before turning away suddenly into a side street, or stopping and retreating in the direction he'd come from. A stocky, Spanish-looking man slightly younger than Noel hissed as he approached, then made animal cluckings behind Noel's back. Two others in close-fitting jeans and denim jackets and body-slick T-shirts barely separated to let Noel through. "Did you get a look at that number!" he heard one say as they fell away. All the men seemed of a type—between twenty and forty years old, all similarly dressed in T-shirts, open-necked work shirts or flannel plaids, with bomber jackets. Some were in full leather costumes, complete with plaited chains hanging from the shoulders or wrapped around their visored hats; some even carried motorcycle helmets, though there were no bikes in sight.

A night town. A foreign, exotic land, not ten minutes on foot from the school where he taught. Noel felt like a zoologist who has just set eyes on the prairie where the animals he will be studying are heedlessly roaming. Consumed by his observations, he forgot his discomfort. He was surprised to be brought up short a minute later.

He'd crossed Hudson Street and gone a block or so. Men were more thickly congregated here, covering the sidewalk in front of a brightly lit bar and leaning against cars. Noel was threading through this languorous gauntlet when he turned to look into the jammed bar. His eye was caught by what seemed to be a very familiar face. He stopped, moving aside, angling for a better view amid all the motion inside. Then he saw the face again, saw it glance out the window at him, and almost dive back into the mob of bobbing heads. Wasn't that . . . ? Yes! But what was his name? Paul something or other: a bright student in Noel's social deviance and criminal behavior class. But where had Paul gone so fast?

"You moving?" Noel heard a voice close behind him, and simultaneously felt two hands lightly grasp his buttocks. "Or are you waiting to get into something hot here on the sidewalk?"

Noel jumped away from the man's hands, and stumbled forward, tripping over someone's shoes.

"Don't get so excited. Some people wouldn't mind," the man said.

Dazed, Noel caught himself and turned to let the tall, crew-cut blond go by with a lecherous wink. His face was older than his clothes or his voice suggested. Then Noel saw Paul again, this time coming out of the bar. It was him!

"Paul!" Noel shouted over the chatter around him. "Paul!" The boy turned, saw Noel, bit his upper lip, and then the face was gone again. A second later, Noel caught sight of him hurriedly threading through the cars jammed in the middle of the street, looking back to see if he was being followed, then darting into a doorway.

Noel was confused. It was Paul, wasn't it? Yes. The boy had only been a foot or so away when he'd turned. He was sure it was the student. Why had he run away?

Noel pushed his way through the crowd. By the time he'd maneuvered out of the thickest gathering and was free to stop without being touched or fondled or pushed from behind, he had a thought that swept over him from head to feet like icy water. Paul *had* seen him! Seen him and run away from him. Why was clear, too. The boy was gay and didn't want Noel to find out. He was ashamed of it.

A second thought followed: Paul must have concluded the same about Noel.

"Oh, Christ!" Noel said aloud, suddenly confronting the possible consequences. How would Paul face him tomorrow? Would he even return to class? Or would he go to the dean and drop the course for some stupid reason?

Worse, what if Paul got over his own shame and confronted Noel? Suddenly it was too much to think of here on this crowded, gay-infested street. He had to get out!

Back home Noel took off his clothes, dropped them on the rocker, then took a long, hot, massaging shower. By the time he was done he felt much better. The hell with Paul, he said to himself. The hell with Vega, too. With all of them. They're not chasing me away. Boyle was right. There was something to be done with this study, and he was going to do it. He could get by if he stayed calm and played along—he would make Mirella Trent's book look like a fourth-grade composition on what she did over her summer vacation. Bitch! Giving herself airs, acting like a movie star. He'd show her!

He went through his closets looking for clothing he could wear to the Grip. A flannel plaid shirt Monica's parents had given him looked like it might do. Also an old pair of chinos from his college days.

It was almost midnight. Ordinarily he'd be reading in bed by now, or even asleep. But tonight he felt too hyped up to sleep.

Instead, he opened a fresh, college-ruled notebook to its first page and began playing with titles for the thesis. After filling two pages with writing, he decided they were all lousy. Too academic. Too sociological. Too *expected*. What he needed was something sensational: something the Current Ideas series could really push.

A distant police siren curved toward him, then away again, interrupting his thoughts. When it had gone, the title flashed into his mind and he wrote it down in large capital letters, I PASSED FOR GAY. He'd just reread it aloud, savoring it, when his phone rang, eerie sounding in the now total silence of the night.

"I understand you're to begin work tomorrow."

It was Loomis, his voice different somehow over the phone.

"News travels fast," Noel said.

"You'll get used to it. You and I will be talking every night you work. All my operatives report in. You have a pencil?"

"Yes."

"Good. Copy down these phone numbers."

All four numbers began with the same exchange—one Noel had never used before. "Do I ask for you, or what?"

"Not so fast. Let me explain. These are open numbers. What I mean is that they are currently unassigned to anyone by the telephone company. Ma Bell calls them 'loops.' So do we. The numbers will change, sometimes faster, sometimes more slowly, as they are assigned, or as new numbers come up. Whoever calls one of these numbers gets to talk to whoever is on the line. You can have a conference call for nothing with half the city."

"You mean there's no special number where I can reach you?"

"At these numbers. Not many people know of the loops. You call at a certain time and you get me. Whisper has one of them open at all times for emergencies."

Noel wasn't sure he understood how it worked.

Loomis explained. The unassigned numbers were lent out by the telephone company to Whisper. Only their police contact knew which numbers Whisper was using. Each time someone dialed the number it rang—a short metallic buzz that served as a warning to anyone already on the line. For the caller, after two rings, the line would seem to be answered: only it was possible that no one would be at the other end. In that case Noel was to ask if anyone were there, or give a code name. He was to call each night, as soon as he was off work at the Grip. He could also report in during his break. In an emergency, he was to use a special code.

"What's that?"

"For ordinary calls just use your name. You're called the Lure. Got that?"

"What's the emergency code?"

"No fishing tonight."

Noel wrote that next to the loop numbers.

"If the numbers change, you'll be notified as soon as it happens. They change often, but never all at once. So don't worry. Just memorize them and destroy what you've written."

"What's Vega's code?"

"You and Buddy are having some initial difficulties, aren't you?"

"A little," Noel answered curtly, trying to play it down. He was afraid Vega's dislike of him might jeopardize the job at the Grip and he didn't want that, not now that he wanted the job, wanted to do the study. "Nothing we can't iron out," Noel added hopefully.

"Good."

"He doesn't care for what he calls nonprofessionals," Noel said.

"He'll adjust. He told me you need clothes. Copy down this address." Noel was to go to a certain store the following afternoon after class, where he would be provided with whatever was needed to fit in at the Grip. "Whatever else you need," Loomis added, "go where Buddy tells you and bill us. Remember, nothing too fancy, huh? We have a budget."

"Don't worry. Torn dungarees can't be too expensive."

"You'd be surprised. Okay, Lure, after work tomorrow you call one of these numbers and identify yourself. Any questions?"

"Nothing I can think of." Then: "Will I meet any other agents? Operatives?"

"At the bar? Maybe. It's not necessary. You don't need to know who they are, nor they who you are. That's why I'm using you, right? You aren't just another p.c."

Plainclothesman, Noel guessed.

"One more thing," he asked, less sure of himself. "You really expect this Mr. X will meet me?"

"That's why I'm going to all this trouble, no?"

"But how will I know him?"

"Don't worry about that. Get some sleep. You're going to be out late tomorrow."

But he did worry . . . and he didn't fall asleep. He doubted the mystery man would find him, even with his close resemblance to Mr. X's favorite physical type: so many men he had seen tonight fit the description. Then he believed Mr. X *would* find him. And that was an even more disturbing possibility.

7

Mr. X was inescapably on his mind again, the following evening when Noel used the loops for the first time.

He dialed one of the four phone numbers he'd been given, heard it ring twice, as Loomis said it would, then heard what seemed to be someone picking it up. He almost expected a voice to say, "Hello."

None did. The line seemed dead. Was anyone there? What was he supposed to do now?

"Contact," he said unsteadily. Was that right?

Still silence.

"The Lure here," he said, a little louder.

The silence was immediately broken. "What's the problem, Lure?"

It was a vaguely familiar man's voice. He couldn't be certain, but it sounded to Noel like one of the voices he'd heard in the freezing jail cell.

"No problem. I'm supposed to talk to Vega."

Noel couldn't recall if the Fisherman had given him Vega's code name.

"The Star calls in precisely twenty-five minutes," the man said.

The Star? Oh, you mean because Vega's also a star in the heavens?"

"Twenty minutes," the man said gruffly and was gone.

"I want to talk to him," a middle-aged woman suddenly said. "Are you still there, Lure?" She had a motherly tone, a heavy Bronx accent. "We have all your data on file, but we'll be sending you some papers. Releases and things. Just sign them and send them back to the address on the envelope. An organization for teachers in your field. You'll receive pension benefits. And health insurance, including a comprehensive hospitalization and surgical policy. No life insurance, I'm afraid."

"Naturally," Noel replied, chilled as he was by her words, and the quick thoroughness of the organization.

"That's all for now, dear," she said. Someone's aunt, someone's mother, Noel thought. Probably at a desk in an office somewhere. "Just sign wherever there's an X," she added. "Bye now."

X again, Noel thought. "Wait. Can I get the Star on any line?"

"Yes. Any of them."

But before the twenty minutes had passed, Vega called him.

"What's up?" Vega asked.

"Nothing. I just . . . Didn't you want to show me around?"

"Yeah? So?"

"How's tonight? I begin work at eight. You, too?"

"I'm not working the Grip tonight."

"Maybe another time?"

"No." Firmly. Then: "You're right. We'll do it tonight. I'll pick you up. We'll eat out. Then you go to work."

Despite the quickness with which he invited Noel, Buddy was subdued, thoughtful, even morose when he arrived.

He grumpily finished the last beer in Noel's refrigerator, only half paying attention as Noel brought out clothing for Vega's approval. The only item from the previous night was Monica's jeans. With them, he wore a red-and-white close-fitting baseball shirt with bright red half sleeves, a green-gray nylon bomber jacket, and work shoes with rubber soles, all of which he'd bought earlier that day in the small, merchandise-laden Army-Navy store Loomis had sent him to.

"Still to clean-cut for me," Buddy said. "But you are supposed to be from the Coast. It'll do."

They ate dinner at a closely packed storefront restaurant off Christopher Street, sitting at a table in the big bow windows. The place was decorated with dozens of posters from Off-Broadway shows Noel had never heard of, and huge, floppy Boston ferns hanging from the ceiling, filling every available space over seven feet high. Almost everyone in the restaurant looked gay.

Noel had a dozen questions about words he'd heard last night. Vega answered succinctly.

"What's a number?"

"You are. Or at least you're supposed to be one. A hot number."

"What's that mean exactly?"

"It means a lot of people want to ball with you."

"A hot number is someone sexually desirable?"

"Right. What else?"

"What do I talk about?"

"To who?"

"Chaffee. The others."

"Nothing. Keep your mouth shut."

That annoyed Noel again. But he went on: "What's at Sixth Avenue and Twenty-eighth Street? I saw a lot of gays there yesterday."

"The tubs. The baths," Vega explained. "Sooner or later you're going to have to make an appearance there. All the hot numbers do. You won't believe the place."

"Do you go there?"

"Is that one of your questions?" Vega demanded.

"No, I just wondered."

"Next question, then."

The evening wasn't turning out as Noel had wanted

it. Vega was hard to get to know. He was deliberately closing Noel off.

The next question was interrupted when three men came into the restaurant and spotted Buddy. Looking happy for the distraction, Vega gestured them to join him and Noel. His spirits picked up immediately. Noel was pushed off to one side of the table as the four men exchanged greetings. The names came too fast for Noel to remember. All three newcomers stared at him in the way he'd come to recognize as a basic, once-over, evaluation cruise. He let it pass. Vega began telling them an anecdote about someone named Tim they all knew. Two of the men leaned in, hanging on every word.

The third man, muscular and brawny, with close-cropped hair, small dark eyes, and a bushy mustache, inspected the menu.

"You born on Christmas?" he suddenly asked.

Noel realized the question was aimed at him. "No. Why?"

"All the guys I know named Noel was born on Christmas." He looked over the menu, decided on something, then looked at Noel again.

"You wit' Buddy?" Then, pointing to Noel's half-eaten cheeseburger, "That any good?"

"Overcooked."

A waiter appeared and there was a flurry of ordering. Meanwhile, Mr. Muscles said:

"I seen you before. What gym you go to?"

"I don't."

He was skeptical. "You look worked out to me. Gymanstics?"

"Of a sort," Noel said, intrigued by the pronunciation.

"I thought so. I can always tell. I seen you before. You live near here?"

"Noel's from the Coast," Vega said. "San Francisco."

Noel hadn't been aware Buddy was listening. Was there a reason?

"Oh. I probably seen you out dere."

"Tony was out there for a shooting recently," Vega said.

"Yeah," Tony said, smiling and revealing several recently capped, perfect white teeth. "I'm kinda a star."

"In porn flicks," Vega said. "Tony Coe."

Noel nodded as though he knew the name.

"Watch out," one of the other men said. "He'll ask you to join him in a flick."

You see, Mr. Cummings, you won't really have to look for Mr. X. He's going to find you, Loomis had said.

. And Chaffee: *They'll tell you they'll make you a movie star . . .*

"What's wrong with that?" Tony was asking, hurt, with an attitude that suggested seething violence beneath his dumb surface.

"Noel's too classy for skin flicks," Vega said sharply.

"You're just my type," Tony said, looking at Noel. "Just my fucking type. We'd look real good together. Hey, bud? Real good. I'd fix it so you wouldn't even know when the camera started."

Tony reached into his shirt pocket and pulled out a business card which he handed to Noel. It read: Reality Productions, Inc.

"Keep it," Tony said. "Call me."

Noel pocketed the card, watching Vega watch him closely. Why had he interrupted? What was going on?

A minute or so later the answer to his question flashed on Noel so hard he almost gagged on the last piece of cheeseburger. Could Tony Coe be Mr. X? And did Buddy know that? Was that what Coe had meant by saying he had seen Noel before, when he couldn't have?

While Vega had coffee and dessert, Noel tried to confirm this impression. But Coe was ignoring him, having gotten bullheadedly into an argument with one of his friends about two drugs Noel had never heard of. He was arrogant, all right. But was that enough for suspicion? He had said that Noel was exactly his type. So what? He might say that to anyone he found attractive.

"We have to go," Vega announced. "Noel's working tonight."

As they were stepping out of the restaurant, Tony Coe stood up and came over to them. In a low voice he said to Buddy, "It's a real shame about Kansas, huh?"

"Yeah. Fucked up," Vega said, quickly adding, "I never knew the guy real well. He used to come rap a lot at the Grip."

"Me, either," Tony said. "You know, intimately but not well." Changing his tone he said good-bye. "See you, too, babe," he added to Noel.

Noel waited until they had gone a block before asking, "Is he another operative?"

"Tony? I don't know. Why? I told you before, he's a porn star."

That answer meant nothing. Noel fingered the card Tony had given him. Pornography, Loomis had told him. Mr. X was into pornography.

The Grip was packed when they arrived. Chaffee hailed Noel over and put him on the side bar. It was busy, and another hour and a half passed before Noel found time to stand still and look around. A minute later he noticed Vega slip downstairs with someone.

During this first night at the Grip, Noel was openly propositioned once, flirted with dozens of times, received a ten-dollar tip from a middle-aged gentleman in full leather, was offered four drugs, several of which sounded lethal, and smoked the third and fourth cigarettes of his life.

He got home late, exhausted, and dialed the loops. For a while no one answered, then he heard the motherly voice of a woman.

"Is it urgent, dear?" she asked. "I'll ring the Fisherman at home, if you want."

"No. Don't bother."

Brushing his teeth, Noel wondered exactly what the odds were that Tony Coe was Mr. X. That white-toothed smile. The overmuscled arms and shoulders. Hands like ham hocks, like vises, hands that could twist a man's head right off his body.

He went to sleep with dawn prying under the window shades.

8

"Last call" Noel shouted.

Only a few people sauntered over to the bar for a final drink.

It had been slow since midnight. Rick said there were several big parties tonight. Noel had heard about the one at the Window Wall—a downtown private discotheque—from at least a dozen customers. It was early Sunday morning, but with the feeling of a Saturday night, and in this subculture, as in any other, all the men wanted to get laid. Most of the regulars would be at the Window Wall by now, the rest at the Baths, or lurking through the shadowy corridors of Le Pissoir, an after-hours club which featured public sex shows in a series of huge, sleazy rooms, where you or your partner-of-the-minute might be the stars at any time: employees sometimes shone spotlights on the patrons; if you didn't move out of their glare, people would gather to watch.

Noel hadn't been to Le Pissoir, of course. Nor to the Baths, nor even to the Window Wall, where women were allowed—outnumbered thirty to one. But, after keeping quiet and listening hard for three weeks, he'd heard enough to know what else was being offered to his clientele.

He told himself he didn't have to go to those places yet, that he had more than enough data from a dozen nights at the Grip to make a book. He'd built up casual relationships with the other employees, and even a few customers. He knew he was accepted as one of them. That was an important step.

Wilbur Boyle thought so, too. When Noel had finally approached his department chairman with his idea, Boyle had been cautious but obviously pleased his hint had been taken. Impressed also by Noel's initiative in taking a job right at the center of the gay world. "An enormous, but essential chore," Boyle had called it, shaking Noel's hand warmly in front of a bewildered Alison. Thank God, Noel thought.

"You ready to close out?" Rick Chaffee asked now.

"In a minute."

Noel grabbed his cash drawer, his tip box, and his pad.

"My breakage is underneath," Noel said, pointing to the liquor bottles he'd emptied during the course of his shift. The manager would tally them against the cash to see how much was sold. No problem for Noel. His customers bought, never asked for comps, and tipped well. As Chaffee had predicted, Noel was good for business.

"You going to the Window Wall tonight?" Rick asked. "Jimmy DiNadio just called from there. He said the place is hot as hell."

"You going?" Noel asked.

"When I'm done."

Noel knew *he* wasn't: he was going home and going to sleep. "Maybe. I don't know."

He took his gear downstairs to the office. The office door was shut, and Noel had to put everything under one arm, balance it there, to pull open the heavy door.

Hell! The light was off.

He reached over, feeling along the chipped plaster wall to find the switch, grabbed it, and blinked in the sudden light.

Two heads turned toward him in surprise: Buddy Vega, his T-shirt halfway up his chest, his jeans at his feet, bent forward over a naked man Noel didn't recognize right off, who was lying on the office desk as though it were the most comfortable mattress.

"Do you mind!" Vega snapped.

Noel almost dropped what he was carrying.

"The light, sweetheart. The light!" Vega commanded, nodding toward the wall switch and not missing a stroke of his hips.

"Leave it on," the other man said in a thick Hispanic accent. Now Noel did recognize him—Miguel.

"Shut the door, will you?" Buddy said. "Give me five more minutes."

Noel felt rooted to the spot at what he was seeing being done so nonchalantly—and by Buddy Vega of all people. But he finally closed the door and turned to go upstairs. Ascending, he bumped into Bob Seltzer, another bartender, who was headed downstairs.

"It's occupied," Noel said, blocking his way. He was still unnerved, aware he was perspiring suddenly.

"How occupied?" Seltzer asked, going around Noel and down a step.

"Vega's in there."

"So what?"

"He's with someone," Noel tried to explain without having to say it outright.

"Balling?" Seltzer asked, amused at Noel's obvious discomfort. When Noel nodded yes, Seltzer asked, "You got a case for Buddy?"

It took Noel half a minute to figure out what he meant.

"Me? You've got to be kidding?"

"You sure act like you do," Seltzer said, edging

downstairs. "I'm going to take a good look. I've always been a voyeur."

As upset by Bob's suggestion as he was by the incident, Noel fled upstairs.

Below him, he heard Seltzer open the office door and after a long minute say, "Oh, excuse me!" in exaggerated apology, followed by Vega's insults.

Only a few customers were left upstairs. One, dozing off at the Wurlitzer, was being tapped hard on the shoulder by Killer Max. Max, Noel knew, was dying to eighty-six someone tonight and had probably found his victim. Chaffee was on the wall phone, doubtless talking to Jimmy DiNadio again; he cupped his hand over the receiver when he saw Noel.

"I thought you were closing out?"

"I was. Vega's screwing someone down there."

"Again? Well, close out here," he said, making a space on the counter. He returned to his intense, whispered conversation with Jimmy. Noel knew they were lovers and on the rocks these days. Rick was doing what sounded like a lot of explaining and apologizing.

"We're closed, gentlemen," Max shouted, holding the door open and shoving Sleeping Beauty onto the sidewalk. He turned around to see if any stragglers were left, then seeing none, locked the door. "Christ, what a pile of losers tonight," he said, coming up to the bar where Bob had joined Noel closing out his register. "They look like rejects from a geriatrics ward at Bellevue."

Bob was counting out loud now, pointedly ignoring Max.

"How about a date tonight?" Max asked Bob. "I got some new chains."

"Forget it, Quasimodo," Bob said. "You're about twice as old and ten times as ugly as anyone I'll go on a date with. Go bother Noel."

Bob Seltzer had a live-in lover of five years and usually two or three smaller love affairs going on all at once, Noel knew. And a second job, in a bank. Where did he get the time for it? Noel wondered. Max also knew about Bob's complicated love-life. It never stopped him from coming on.

"Dream about me tonight," Max finally said, hitching up his leather pants, and waving to Chaffee who was still on the phone.

"Give me a break," Bob said, when Max was out the side door and Noel had locked it after him. Without explaining he asked Noel, "You want some reds or Tuinals? Cheap tonight. Close-out sale."

He flashed a handful of electrically colored capsules in a triangle of white paper. Noel knew that these combination barbiturates, far from being used as sleeping pills, were considered superrelaxants and valued by many gay partygoers.

"I'll take some," Rick called. "How many do you have?"

They did their deal while Rick tried to finish his conversation with Jimmy. Finally he gave up and came back to the bar.

"I'm going to kill that little bastard when I get my hands on him."

"With Tuinals?" Noel asked.

"Are you kidding? He eats them like Sen-Sens." Still muttering, Rick joined the two of them closing out his register, every once in a while breaking out into conversation: "Don't ever marry a Sicilian, Noel. They're worse than shit. Jealous as hell."

"Noel isn't the marrying kind," Bob said. "He's a loner."

"I used to be married," Noel let slip out, feeling a new camaraderie. "To a woman."

"Buddy's married, too. You see how seriously he takes it."

"Screwing guys is a Puerto Rican's idea of birth control," Bob said. "Hey, I'm short seventy-five cents. Sue me."

"I'm even," was Noel's reply. He'd waited for some reaction to his confession. When none came he felt relieved.

Vega came upstairs and let Miguel out the back door. Bob had gone over to the phone. Rick took all the register boxes one on top of the other downstairs to the office, stopping long enough to say to Vega, "I understand you were doing something fancy downstairs. I hope you cleaned up?"

When Noel and Vega were alone, Buddy said, "You should have stuck around, you might have learned something."

Their eyes met and held each other's across the bar. Vega couldn't miss the disgust Noel felt.

"If I want to learn I'll look it up," Noel said sharply.

Vega glared back disdainfully, then punched open a beer for himself, gulped it half down, and left the bar.

Noel called down to Rick that he, too, was leaving.

"Aren't you going to the Window Wall?" Rick asked, coming up.

"I'm beat tonight."

"Hey! Noel?"

"Yeah?"

"Whatever's going on between you and Buddy, you better get over it. It's no good for the business, you know what I mean?"

"There's nothing between me and Buddy."

"I told you I didn't want your personal life in the bar," Chaffee warned. Then, more kindly: "Forget him, man. He's got kids and all. C'mon out partying. Meet some other guys. They're like flies on the Wall tonight. Believe me."

At the same time that Noel realized how wrong Rick was, he also realized how conveniently wrong he was: misunderstanding his and Vega's hostility as a sex problem suited Noel just fine, a reason Noel was not going out or being seen out.

"Thanks, Rick. You're right, I know. But not tonight."

"Next Thursday, then. There's big party there. You come, hear?"

"Yes, Mother," Noel teased back. "Good night. Say hello to Jimmy."

"If I see hin."

Outside, the streets seemed especially empty. A few cruising autos crept along; only two guys stood talking in the doorway of an open-all-night greasy spoon that seemed to attract all the castoffs and low-life the area had to offer: teased-hair, peroxided young blacks with silver eye-shadow and hormone-instigated, budding breasts only half hidden beneath loud-patterned blouses; alcoholic bums of all ages who'd only recently gone over the edge, who would nod out in a booth until thrown out; poor teenaged straight couples talking animatedly, probably about their problems, more than likely buzzing on a speed high all night.

Noel didn't go inside. Neither would most of his customers at the Grip—most of whom were middle-class professionals by day, and who preferred the more stylish Art Deco decorated diners farther up the West Side.

"Hey, man! What's your hurry?"

Noel turned to the voice. Just stepping out of the diner doorway holding a white Styrofoam cup of steaming liquid was the boy Noel had first witnessed being picked up in the Grip, the day he'd gone to get a job. His name was Larry Vitale, Noel knew. He came into the Grip pretty regularly, and never went home alone. Little Larry, Bob Seltzer and Rick called him. Not only because he was still a minor, but also because of his small, tight body. He and Noel had exchanged maybe fifty words so far, but several times Noel had looked up from some work at the bar to see Little Larry smiling mischievously, as though they shared a secret.

"Want a sip?" Larry offered the cup. "It's coffee."

"No, thanks."

"It's usually awful," Larry said, sipping. The face he made confirmed the coffee's reputation. "I had a rush for it."

Larry leaned against the brick wall of the diner, one boot propped behind him on the wall for balance.

"What's your hurry?" he asked again. The mischievous smile surfaced.

"I'm going home. Tired."

"That's too bad," Larry drawled, almost slurring the words. "I'm sort of high right now. I thought we could get Luded up and go play."

As the boy talked, Noel was thirteen years old again. The other boy was his cousin Chas. Chas was speaking in that same tone of voice, urging Noel to join him in a thick brace of bushes at a distance from Chas's parents' house, where no prying eyes could see them, while they smoked a cigarette Chas had stolen from his dad and inspected the contents of each other's short pants.

Noel shrugged. "Sorry. I'm beat. I woudn't be any fun tonight. Believe me."

Childlike disappointment creased Little Larry's face. He looked even younger than his sixteen years, like a little cupid, cute and sexy. A little male Lolita. Then he grinned again. "Another time."

"Another time," Noel said, putting a hand on Larry's shoulder and applying enough pressure for it to be construed as something—a promise, a contract. He knew that at least was required.

"Later, babe," Little Larry said, apparently satisfied.

He spun away from the wall, out of Noel's grasp, scraping the bricks with his boot heel, and slowly took off toward the straggly park that fronted the Hudson River at the end of the street. He stopped for a second to finish the drink, then tossed the cup into an overflowing wastepaper basket.

Noel remained where he was, watching Larry walk away, his young body swaying slightly on the worn-

away heels of his cowboy boots, the slight bow of the
slim legs, the snug, exact fit of the faded denims on
his buttocks, how the belt tilted to the right slightly
where the boy's heavy ring of keys pulled it down.
Between the loose jacket flapping open and the belt,
a few inches of shirt stuck out and a tiny triangle of
skin was exposed.

Who the hell was Little Larry anyway? Just another
runaway who'd settled into the scene and adjusted
fast?

"For all I know, the little squirt could be Mr. X,"
Noel told himself.

A half hour later, Noel said the same thing to
Loomis on the loop.

"I thought you said he's a kid?" was the response.

"He is. But you asked for the one who was different, didn't you?" Noel protested. "Admit it, Loomis.
It's not working out as you thought it would. It can't
be, if Little Larry is the best I can come up with."

"There was the actor," Loomis said. "What was his
name?"

"Tony Coe. I thought you said he and his film company checked out?"

"They did," Loomis confirmed. "But look on the
bright side. There hasn't been one murder, one takeover since you're there."

"I'm a lucky talisman now?"

"What's your complaint, anyway? Everyone should
be in your position. You're getting material for your
book. You're well-liked. Well-paid. What's your beef?"

"No beef. I suppose I'm just tired." And unable to
deal with the tension of not knowing whom he was
looking for, Noel wanted to add, *I just thought I was
wasting your time*. But Loomis was onto another
topic.

"How are you and Vega getting along?"

"The same."

"Is that better or worse?"

"A little worse tonight."

"You want to talk about it? I have time."

Noel did want to talk about it. He had no connection with Vega at the bar. He hardly ever saw him. Vega never explained things to him, never gave him hints, ideas, not even warnings. He supposed he didn't need any more information. Nowadays people asked *him*, for Chrissakes. He knew more than many others. He felt comfortable with everyone but Vega. Chaffee was like an older brother, giving sound advice, even if his perceptions were way off. Bob Seltzer like a younger brother who was a skirt-chaser: except that Bob chased men. Even Max was easy to get along with, the way a large, slightly intelligent, potentially lethal pet dog can be. They accepted Noel, and he, them. And because of that, so did everyone who came in. Everyone except Buddy Vega.

"I don't mean to judge him," Noel said, allowing his long list of grievances to pour forth, "but I can't help it. He doesn't have to . . . you know, do it with so many guys."

"It's confusing to you?" Loomis asked. "Because he's married?"

Sometimes Noel felt as though he were talking to a psychiatrist. "It's upsetting. But I'm not sure why."

"Don't worry about it. Keep out of his way. You don't need him anymore. You're all set up there. Now just sit tight."

"All set up," Noel repeated.

"Call tomorrow," Loomis said. "You know what, go around a little. You aren't working. Go into one of the other bars. Have a drink. Get friendly."

Noel saw the point. "All right."

All set up, Noel thought, placing the telephone into the receiver. With comprehensive hospital insurance, but no life insurance. And no hint of who Mr. X was.

Hell! It could be Buddy Vega.

9

Business on Wednesday evening was relatively slow, and Noel was beginning to feel like a character in a Eugene O'Neill play listening to human woes and offering half-cocked advice over the bar, when Buddy Vega came in with Miguel.

"You still mad at me?" Buddy asked, when Miguel stepped over to the pool table in the other room. "Miguel's roommate had some people over. We had nowhere else to go."

Noel said he didn't much care.

"Good!" Vega said. "It's none of your business, anyway."

He let that sink in before saying, "You going to the Window Wall tomorrow night? There's a big party there, you know."

"I don't think so."

"You better go. I have it on good word that your man X will be at that party."

"So will everyone else in the city, from all the talk I'm hearing," Noel shot back. "What's the chance of meeting him in a crowd that large?"

"I also have it on good word that X has heard about *you.*"

That stopped Noel for a second. Despite the shiver it sent up his back, he answered, "Through who? You?"

"Just go, will you? Use the loop. He'll tell you the same thing."

"I will use the loop," Noel said, making it clear he wasn't taking orders from Vega, no matter how relevant they might be.

Buddy saw he meant it. He scowled and went to join Miguel at the pool table. They remained there for another half hour, then left the Grip, arms around each other's shoulders. Still angry, Noel watched them go.

On his break he slipped out and walked two blocks to a public phone where he called the loop. After a short while he got Loomis. The Fisherman said he thought it was a good idea for Noel to go to the discotheque, even though the odds were against him making contact with Mr. X. Somehow that annoyed Noel even more.

He had barely returned to the bar when two Latin men got into an argument. Before Max could get to them, the smaller one was shoved by his boyfriend out onto the street and socked in the nose. In a second the two of them were slugging it out.

Everyone left the bar or went to the windows. The two Latinos were bruised and bleeding before Max and two other men were able to separate them. Even with their arms pinned, they swore at each other and kicked out, both trying to score a final blow.

"*Maricón!*" the smaller one shouted suddenly, spitting the word out with a mouthful of phlegm.

The other one broke out of the hold he was in and attacked his friend, diving headfirst into his stomach. It was another few minutes before they were dragged apart by friends, one to a car, the other inside the bar to wash up.

"*Maricón!*" the smaller one shouted outside the Grip as he rode by in someone's Ford, sticking his finger up in the air in a fuck-you gesture.

The lover was in the bar at the time. He leaned against the wall and began to sob quietly, his shoulders heaving, his head hidden. Suddenly he turned around, his face livid and contorted with hatred. "I'm going to eat that fucker's heart!" he shouted, staring around the bar with wild eyes, then ran out.

Everyone in the Grip was animated by the incident for the next half hour. Noel was especially agitated. The men's fight had brought out all the hostility he'd been hiding against Buddy Vega. He realized with horror exactly how much harm they could do each other.

All he would have to do was call Vega a *maricón*. . . .

10

It was about ten o'clock the following night and Noel was revising the glossary of new words he'd picked up working at the Grip, so engrossed in it that when his phone rang twice he was halfway to picking it up before he stopped himself in midgesture. Sure enough, there was no third ring. He waited. It rang twice more, then stopped suddenly. Wasn't that the Fisherman's signal? He waited again, but the phone was silent, so he went back to work.

He had more than seven pages, almost a hundred entries of words, their pronunciations, definitions, and usages. All dependent on the fact that they might be changed at any time—the argot being a living language. But all hundred words were real. Most of them totally unknown to anyone but the denizens of the gay world who used them. Even if he did nothing more on this project, Noel believed this glossary would be an important achievement. How you called something signified how you perceived it, how you related to it.

Calling someone you slept with a "trick" or a "number" or a "lover" or a "friend"—all common, though different gradations, meant something. The same held for whether you called a close acquaintance a "brother" or a "sister"—generally a closer term. It fascinated Noel.

The phone again. Signal complete. "Lure in," Noel said. He hated the code name business and the spy-work bullshit it came from.

"That you?" It was Loomis.

"You called, didn't you?" Noel asked. His blood was pulsing like mad in the thumb holding the receiver. "Or was that a test?"

"No test. You going to that party tonight?"

"You said I should."

"Right. But be a little careful, Lure."

Now his blood was really racing. "Careful? How?"

"Just try not to behave in too unusual a manner. Fit in a little more."

"What's up?"

"Nothing much. Maybe nothing at all. Just a few things I've heard. You've aroused some suspicions."

Shit! Noel thought. That's all I need. "Like what?"

"Nothing much. But just in case, I'm going to have someone cover you."

The Fisherman had never done *that* before. Now he was really jumpy. "Will I know who it is?" he asked, trying to keep calm.

"No. Naturally not."

"Who's suspicious?"

"I'm not sure. But it's someone connected with the Grip. Not one of the other employees. Maybe the silent partner. Our friend owns the place, even though his name isn't on any of the papers."

"X you mean."

"Mister X," Loomis corrected. "Yeah. I don't know who it is. You notice anyone coming in to talk to Chaffee a little off-color?"

"I'm not sure."

"Well, just be careful tonight, that's all. It's probably nothing."

Vega did it, Noel thought, as soon as he hung up the phone. Goddamn you, Buddy, are you working for Whisper or for X? Who else could it be, if not Vega?

It certainly wasn't Rick Chaffee, Noel concluded at midnight when he saw the manager of the bar. Noel had been invited for a pre-Window Wall get-together at Rick's downtown loft, only a short walk from the disco club. The manager of the bar greeted him like a long-lost brother, and it was hard to believe that Rick wasn't as sincerely pleased to have Noel join them as he professed.

A half-dozen other guests were sitting, talking, and smoking grass on the two low divans and the huge pillows that had been pulled up to a vast, rectangular, glass-topped coffee table that looked handcrafted. Among them were two couples Noel had seen in the bar, as well as Jimmy DiNadio in a rare shared evening with his lover, and a slender, heavily made up, and relatively attractive woman about twenty-five years old whom Noel immediately tagged a fag hag.

"Glossary Number 67: Fag Hag," he had written earlier that evening, "A female hanger-on of the gay scene. A heterosexual woman of any age, social status, and profession, who parties with, often lives with, sometimes (rarely) sleeps with, and usually becomes den mother and confidante to a loose group or family of gay men. She is usually unattractive, or pretty but overweight, generally afraid of men and sex, always lonely and usually riotously funny, believing her purpose in life is to make gay men happy."

This one's name was Wendy, and she had a real Southern accent and eyes that were large, blue, and very hard. Noel took a place on the other side of the table from her, next to Jimmy DiNadio.

"It's a good thing I know Chaffee doesn't fuck with the help," Jimmy said, one hand on Noel's shoulder as they faced each other. "Otherwise . . . mmm." He uttered a warning sound and made a very Brooklyn Italian gesture with his open hand.

"He didn't even try," Noel said.

"Give me a break. He tried. I know him, huh? You getting off on this stuff?"

Noel was in fact getting higher than he could recall ever being on the few tokes of marijuana he'd been smoking as though it were a cigarette. He offered the joint to Jimmy, who refused it.

"Get loaded, man. Double your trouble, double your fun. Everyone at the Wall will be in a state. It's why the energy is so high."

Introductions were made in the usual offhand manner, and Noel took a glass of white wine, listening to the beat of the dance music that thudded out of different corners of the room from tall speakers. Even the lighting was flickering, low. Soon everyone was talking a bit louder, gesturing more exaggeratedly.

"Everyone off now?" Rick asked. "Jimmy? Wendy? How about you, Noel?"

"I'm ripped," Noel said.

He wondered why Vega wasn't here, and was about to ask why when Chaffee said, "Time for some nose candy!" lifting aloft a small translucent vial of white powder to a chorus of oohs and aahs. "Uncut," Rick said, like a barker in a sideshow selling a patent medicine. "From the shady hillsides of ancient Peru! Grade A. From my favorite dealer, who is deeply in love with me."

Noel hesitated as the ritual of snorting cocaine began. But he couldn't demur. Not when he recalled Loomis's warning to do nothing to make himself different or unusual tonight. More grass was produced, and Wendy and two others began passing around assorted pills.

"Let's go!" Jimmy suddenly said. "I'm not going to wait on line all night in this condition."

Everyone agreed, but it was another twenty minutes before they got out of the loft and the huge stor-

age elevator delivered them downstairs. Noel had to
lean against the walls for support as the car suddenly
stalled, then dropped a foot. Everyone but Jimmy and
Rick gasped. Wendy struck Chaffee on the shoulder in
annoyance. Noel lost his breath, and his vision swam
before him.

"Get over it," Rick said, not unkindly. "It's just a
little trip. There's going to be a great many more this
witching night!"

They fanned out, covering the entire empty tarred
street.

"We're on comps!" Rick shouted. "My name gets you
in if we're separated." He threw an arm over Noel's
shoulders and they walked a few feet behind the others. "Glad you came. No kidding."

"So am I," Noel said.

"How do you like Jimmy?"

"He's cute."

"That's just the trouble. Too cute. If he didn't have
that 'kiss me, please' face, I'd've dropped him long
ago. No shit!" He hugged Noel closer. "Tonight we're
going to find someone for you."

Noel managed what he was certain was a lopsided
smile as a response.

"If I had your looks, I'd be particular, too," Rick
went on. "No matter what other people said. But the
Wall's going to be carpeted with the absolute hottest
of men tonight. You'll have your pick."

The conversation was beginning to worry Noel. He
hoped Rick would forget him and not do a matchmak-
ing number he'd have to squirm out of later. Then he
saw his opportunity.

"What *are* other people saying?"

"That you're stuck up. That you think you're too
good for anyone. That you think you shit strawberry
ice cream."

"Maybe I do," Noel said lightly. But he felt awful.
That was the second warning tonight.

They had turned a corner. Suddenly there was

traffic—taxicabs double-parked, dozens of sleek long
limousines with drivers, crowds of noisy partygoers
who filled the street in colorful, shifting groupings.
This was the scene of the party. But Noel would have
known it anyway.

If it weren't for the bottom story, the building
would have looked like any of a score they had passed
already: cast concrete, dull brick, unlighted windows,
five stories high, nothing special. What was special,
however, and what gave away the place's name immediately was the bottom floor—composed of thousands
of foot-square frosted glass blocks a foot deep, and
illuminated from within somehow so that they glowed
out onto the street and sidewalks. A wall of glass that
curved around corners into deep-set entrances where
people were already entering, jiggling tambourines,
clacking sticks, shaking maracas. Overhead somewhere, scarcely audible, was music.

Before Noel could think what it all reminded him
of, he was swept up from behind by Rick, Jimmy, and
the others and slid into the glass-walled corridors of
the Window Wall. The floor graded up to a circular
portal with glass doors etched with Art Deco silver-
ing. The beat was stronger, the music closer.

Rick gathered his guests at a silver ticket booth, like
those in an old-fashioned cinema, greeted the employees by name, called out, "Eight with me." Through
that set of doors, the corridor curved left.

"Coats everyone!" Jimmy commanded.

They milled around in the corridor while he disappeared with their outerwear. Noel felt oddly relaxed
but slightly dazed.

"Nostrils!" Rick said, brandishing a tiny spoon of
cocaine. "Now the other one. Fine."

On top of the grass—a mellow high like strong wine
to Noel—the cocaine added a sudden alertness, a
slight distancing effect. Not at all unpleasant, he decided, though rather subtle for such an expensive
drug.

He was being instructed to put the coat check in his wallet or some equally safe place.

Grabbed by Jimmy on one side, Rick on the other, Noel felt himself propelled around another bend of glass-walled corridor into a huge, arched, mirrored entranceway. The music and lights struck him like an electric force.

"Ooooh eeee! Let's party!" someone shouted.

Noel was half lifted off the floor, floated across carpeting past mirrors, hanging globes, mobiles, paintings hung on wires, statues on pedestals, all bathed in a constantly changing wash of lighting, and thrust into the middle of the swirling, chaotic dance.

11

In the twenties and thirties, the Window Wall had been one of Lower Broadway's largest and most popular department stores. You entered through a half-dozen incurving foyers into one of several small, circular lobbies, that sloped to a mezzanine surrounding the huge, four-story main floor. Escalators curved gently down into the central space from another, partially open level, two stories above.

When it was renovated, the inside of the building was totally gutted except for the dozen circular pillars that tapered gracefully to the distant ceiling, now wrapped in Mylar for maximum reflection and refraction. Also retained from the original construction were all the curved-block-glass walls that had once surrounded offices, cosmetics counters, and rest rooms. Some of these were only waist-high, others a story tall, forming semicircular bars, or enclosing more than a score of living-room-sized lounge areas on the mezzanine level. The largest and most striking block-glass wall dominated the ground-floor dance area, jutting out ten feet above it like a medieval balcony, set with sliding windows usually kept open by the disc jockey and lighting engineer who worked their electronic magic from this booth.

Up the long escalators was Mirror City, featuring French cuisine and staffed by a dozen chefs who had once worked in uptown restaurants with names found in society columns and the fancier guidebooks. Part of the restaurant was enclosed by the serpentine walls of glass blocks, part of it open, overhanging the dance floor, screened by opaque floor-to-ceiling baffles to subdue the music and partying below. Across the open area, opposite Mirror City, were more lounges, most of them dimly lighted for slide shows and feature movies. In one lounge, cabaret acts performed; another held a piano bar.

The floor above was closed, except to employees, and consisted of offices and storage space, as did part of the floor beneath the dance area. Here were the huge bathroom lounges, decorated like the rest of Window Wall in Art Deco style, and equipped with showers, saunas, steam baths, and changing cubicles. Surrounding these were a half-dozen smaller rooms, almost caves, where pornographic movies flickered on a wall and figures engaged in slow, almost silent sex on the sofas and pillows strewn across carpeted floors.

This deep-pile carpeting was repeated in slightly varying shades everywhere in Window Wall, except the huge central dance area—a slightly raised hardwood floor. The carpeting was complemented by furniture in rich, soft fabrics: chairs, sofas, steel-and-glass coffee tables that might have come from a Park Avenue duplex. Hundreds of palm trees in ceramic tubs dotted the lounge areas, sometimes half circling small gardens with marble fountains and stands of exotic

flowers. More flowers—huge, sensual, perfumy calla
lilies—were set in tall vases, scattered randomly about
the place. As were various contemporary sculptures,
prints, graphics, watercolors. Two huge curved murals
in the restaurant were signed by artists so prominent
even Noel had heard of them. Mirrors were everywhere, in all sizes, reflecting the subtle, ever-changing
colored lighting. The omnipresent glass-block walls
were like disconnected sections of a labyrinth.

The discotheque must have cost hundreds of thousands of dollars to renovate and furnish, thousands
per week just to keep in plants and fresh flowers.

But even more astounding was the crowd Window
Wall offered. Hundreds of men with sweat-glistening,
shirtless torsos held each other tightly on the dance
floor, grinding into each other's bodies, whirling,
stomping, shouting with animal pleasure. Gorgeous,
long-legged women in scanty disco outfits—halter tops
and sheer slacks—their arms around each other's
shoulders, or waists, stood together in doorways smoking marijuana, kissing deeply as their limbs slowly in-
tertwined. White, black, and Latino straight couples,
as at home as anyone else, grasped each other in a
sensual connection by placing a finger in each other's
mouths, or hooked in a belt loop.

The lights changed constantly, more slowly in the
lounges, but intense, jabbing, frenetic around the
dance area. Shadows. Half-glimpsed profiles. Silhouettes. Hands reaching out to stroke your cheek. Bodies
sliding past so close you felt not only their touch but
their heat. A caress at the crotch. A bump from behind which turned into a slow grind, then was gone. A
swift, airy brush of lips on the nape from someone
who faded into the crowd when you turned to look. A
reptilian tongue flicking out of the mouth of a heavily
cosmeticized woman close to your ear. The sudden
grasp of your shoulder, and the instant apology as the
muscular giant who'd done it realized you weren't the
person. His cornstalk hair matted with sweat, perspir-

ation glittering on his pectorals, now pink, now crimson, now lavender as the lights shifted.

And the beat, the constant, steady, relentless dance beat you could just lay back into and trip out with, slowly, slowly, effortlessly, until you weren't even there anymore but off, off, tripping. . . .

"It's the lights," her voice said softly.

Noel realized he'd been smelling roses.

"The lights hypnotize. And the music, of course."

Her voice came from somewhere close by. He heard her hair swoosh and slowly opened his eyes.

The shock of rose attar. A tumble of hair so black and glossy and thick you wanted to touch it to test its density. The caress of her voice once more.

"The music, yes. And you, too, my darling, tonight." The voice stopped, rising to a breathtaking caress, her accent soft as the Seine threading through the Rive Gauche.

When he opened his eyes again, she was gone.

Noel staggered to his feet, took a minute to get his balance, felt immediately better, looked around the lounge area to see who she was and where she'd gone. Unable to find her, he went over to the nearest bar.

"Honnn-nneee! You look wasted!"

It was that girl from Rick and Jimmy's, whatever her name was, standing right near him, shaking and shimmying as though she had a tiny motor hidden away in her pelvis and couldn't find the switch to turn it off. Behind her were Rick and Jimmy.

"Glad you came?" Rick asked.

"I'm not sure," Noel said. He shook his head, trying to clear it. But he really felt a great deal better than he was letting on. He'd gotten over the peak of his drugs this evening and was slowly descending again, able to handle it.

"Well, *I'm* sure," Jimmy said. "You were on that dance floor for almost an hour without a break. We had to pull you off before you killed us from exhaustion."

"Release a lot of tension?" Rick asked.

"I suppose so."

"How do you like the club?"

"I've never been in anything like it."

"There *isn't* anything like it."

"Not true," Jimmy corrected. "There's Clouds. That's uptown."

"Yeah, but we couldn't fuck on the dance floor up at Clouds," Rick said.

"We don't fuck on the dance floor here."

"But we could if we wanted to," Rick insisted.

Jimmy made a grimace, then turned to Noel. "You see the dipshit I have to put up with? Men I like. It's the male ego I can't stand."

"You have exactly the same ego," Rick challenged.

"That's the problem!"

"And the fun," Rick came back, hugging Jimmy, eager to please him. They hesitated, then began to kiss. Noel watched them a minute, then turned around to the long bar, embarrassed. Somehow he never really believed Rick did this, though he had always assumed it. It was weird, seeing it. Weird.

He turned fully around, facing out toward the dance floor, past a mirrored portal like the one they'd come through into the Window Wall. Silhouettes of couples were pressed against the portal's mirrored walls, holding each other close, kissing. Most of the couples were men: a few mixed. Unlike the Grip, this was the heart of Loomis's metaphorical jungle. Mr. X's turf. Enemy territory.

The attar of roses again.

Noel turned to see where it was coming from. There were no flowers nearby, only flowing Boston ferns hung everywhere over the bar.

"Hey, are you guys going to boggie?" Wendy asked.

"Not now," Jimmy said, his words half smothered by necking.

The smell of roses, still. And now the hair, too, unmistakably the same hair passing by Noel. Her voice, too, although it took him a second or two to be certain, and he couldn't hear what she was saying to the young man she was walking with.

Noel kept his place, but shifted his position until he could follow them around the curve of the bar, where they stopped, surrounded by dangling fronds of fern. The man merely leaned over the top of the bar, and a bartender was there, taking his order.

Meanwhile, the woman turned and gazed at Noel, and as she did one hand went up to brush the dark hair away from her face. Her dark eyes said, *Go on, admire me, I know I'm beautiful*, before she half turned away, toward her companion, showing Noel the high slim shoulders bared to a low V, emerging out of her high, small buttocks.

She was talking to the man, very close to him, but he looked at Noel instead, until their drinks were set in front of them. Noel stared back at the lucky man with the sultry, slim European beauty at his side. Just right, he thought to himself; visually, exactly the right companion for her, this sturdy, young strawberry blond with the tiny, well-cropped mustache, the clean-cut features, the deep-set, almost Slavically angled eyes. The two of them might be models for an expensive brandy advertisement in some glossy, overpriced magazine.

Drawn to her, Noel couldn't take his eyes off the pair, even though the man was now intensely glaring—as if to warn him off.

"You like that type?" someone asked behind Noel.

"What type?" he asked, turning enough to see the voice belonged to Miguel, Vega's friend and sex partner from the Grip.

"The Decadent WASP Type. The sharecropper's kid making good."

"Is that what she is?" As he said it, Noel realized

what a stupid slip it was. Miguel arched one eyebrow and pointedly said:

"That's what *he* is. Or what he'd like to think he is."

"You know him?" Noel asked, hoping to undo the damage.

"He's on the scene," Miguel said enigmatically, leaning against Noel in a way that made him take half a step back.

"Are they always together?"

"Sometimes. Sometimes he's alone." Miguel still didn't seem convinced. He went on to say, "She's Alana De Vijt. A big model. Several hundred bucks an hour. He's Eric the Red. You've heard of Eric the Red, haven't you?" A challenge.

"Can't say I have. I'm from out of town, remember?"

"A lot of guys from Frisco know Eric. He's one of the city's hottest dominants. Probably the best-known sado in the country."

"He looks like an insurance salesman," Noel said.

"Very clean-cut," Miguel agreed. "But hot. H.O.T."

Several people came between Noel and the couple. He was sure Miguel was lying about them. The man had clearly not liked Noel looking at his woman. Where were Jimmy and Chaffee? Gone. Dancing probably.

"You really never heard of Eric the Red?" Miguel insisted.

Noel didn't like Miguel, nor the nasty way the question was asked.

"Sure. His son, Leif, discovered New Foundland in the eleventh century."

"I thought you was on the scene in Frisco?" Miguel went on.

"A little."

"I thought you were. Buddy said you were. He said you worked in a hot, hot place out there. The Slot. On Sixteenth Street. Didn't you work there? Huh? Huh?"

That sounded like a trap. Noel began to think fast.

"So what?" Noel challenged back, fighting down panic.

"Or maybe you had a lover out there?"

"Of sorts."

"Oh, yeah! Who? What was his name?"

"You wouldn't know him. He was very straight. At the university."

"That's in Berkeley. Across the bridge. Remember?" Real insistent now, real obnoxious.

"And the Slot isn't on Sixteenth Street, either," Noel hazarded.

"Oh, yeah! Where is it? Who the fuck do you think you're jiving, man? Not me!"

Miguel glared at him. The questioning, the threat, scared Noel. He knew it was from Vega, all his doing. But it wasn't any the better for that. If Miguel weren't the one Loomis had heard the "rumors" from, that person was probably nearby. Noel knew that if he left now, moved away, it would be interpreted as giving in, admitting he was a decoy.

"Well?" Miguel said, his face contorted now, only inches from Noel's. "Well? What do you have to say about that, man?"

Noel slowly leaned back against the bar: "I say the Slot is not on Sixteenth Street. And I say you're full of shit!"

Miguel stared at him as though unable to believe it.

"Full of downs, I'd say," someone drawled nearby.

It was Little Larry Vitale, coming up between the two of them to the bar. He put one hand up on Noel's shoulder, and winked at him.

Why did he do that? Unless . . . Jesus! Could Little Larry be the cover Loomis said would be watching Noel?

"You got any reds?" Miguel asked in a totally different tone of voice.

"Ate 'em all," Larry said.

Miguel turned around and began asking other people for downs.

"You having a good time tonight?" Larry asked, still half holding on to Noel, talking in his exaggerated drawl.

"A ball."

"Watch out for that spic. He's crazy as shit," Larry whispered. "Hey Miguel! Come here and tell Noel why they call you Maria the Loca?"

If Larry was the cover what was he doing now?

"Hey, Little Larry. You know this guy?" Miguel asked.

"Sure I do."

"Yeah. Well I don't like him. He's not straight."

"Neither are you. Neither am I."

"You know what I mean. Don't go twist it up. Somethin's not right about him."

"How many Seconals you on?" Larry asked.

"Three. But I always take three to go dancing. You sure he's all right? You two gettin' it on?"

"Yeah. Why? You jealous?"

Noel felt the boy's arm circle his waist, taking the belt in a loose grip. He had to be the cover Loomis had sent.

"No," Miguel said, backing down, "I guess not."

"Good. Why don't you just fuck off now," Larry said, "and leave us be?"

Miguel didn't like that. But he moved away, talking along the bar to some other people, asking for downs.

"That guy gives me the creeps," Noel said.

"Me, too. We'd better get out of here, now." So he *was* Loomis's cover!

Noel took that as an order. A few minutes later they were trying to push through the crowd at the coat check counter.

"Hey! You leaving already?" Jimmy DiNadio asked.

He spotted Larry, gave a significant look at Noel, then got Rick's attention, and nodded toward Noel and Larry.

This might be the best thing that happened tonight, Noel thought, his leaving with Loomis's cover. They were certain to think he and Larry were going home to fuck. Let them.

Although it was three in the morning, there seemed to be people coming in all the time, all of them trying to check their clothes.

"We'll be here an hour," Noel groaned, as they looked over the mob in front of the counter.

"Give me your coat check," Larry said. "I know one of the girls. I'll get our things fast."

Noel did as he was told, and leaned against one of the mirrored entranceways, watching the crowd of newcomers, among whom were several Grip patrons who recognized him with a nod or short greeting. Loomis had been right: coming here tonight had probably been the best all-around way of establishing his credentials with this group. But where was Larry with the jackets?

Noel wandered to the edge of the crowd again, failing to find his little companion. When he turned back to the entranceway where he'd been waiting, he was surprised to see Miguel going out and down the ramp fast, followed by someone larger and somewhat familiar. But they were gone in a flash, and the lighting was so dim and the changing colors so distorting, Noel wasn't certain.

"Here we go," Larry said, thrusting the bomber jacket at Noel. They swung on their outerwear and walked down the ramp.

"I thought I saw Miguel leave," Noel said. "With another guy."

"Yeah?" Larry asked, clearly displeased. "Who?"

"I couldn't see."

It was raining hard outside, the unexpected storm further blackening the darkness just beyond the bright glare of the club's strong lights. No one else was waiting in the circular foyer. Noel and Larry turned up their collars and walked out.

Larry walked fast, silent, through the downpour. They crossed a side street and turned down a barely lit deserted street fronted by blank-walled warehouses on each side. Noel began to get nervous.

After another block and a turn onto an even darker street, he turned around and thought he saw two figures suddenly dart from the sidewalk into a doorway.

"Come on," Larrry urged, waiting for him to catch up.

"How much farther?"

"A little more."

The downpour worsened, and they hurried, leaning in close to the partially protecting building walls. But Noel couldn't help but look around again. Again he saw the two figures, and this time he was certain who they were—Miguel and Buddy Vega.

He grabbed Larry by the shoulder and shouted in his ear. They both turned to look, water streaming over their heads and faces.

"I don't see anyone," Larry said, and looked at Noel strangely.

"I'm soaked. Let's run for it," Noel said, trying to hold back his fear.

They sprinted another block or so, then around a corner and into a deep entryway with a steel door. As Larry was opening the elevator door, Noel looked back at the street. It was empty. Not even a parked car. But he was certain they'd been followed.

At least with Larry he'd be safe.

12

He felt even safer when they arrived at the large, split-level loft and Little Larry carefully locked the elevator's steel door behind them.

"You live alone?" Noel asked, trying to regain his poise.

"Me and some other guys."

On either side of the dimly lighted living and dining areas, staircases led to other rooms. Larry dropped his jacket, got a towel for himself and Noel, and began to dry himself off, leading Noel up one stairway that rose above a very contemporary kitchen and breakfast nook.

"Come on," Larry said, motioning Noel to follow.

"This is my space," he said, closing the door.

It was a large room with no windows but a sizable skylight, decorated as Noel was beginning to think half the city was: sparse furniture, deep carpeting, pillows everywhere, a small table, a bedspring and mattresses dominating the room, with a tumbled rug throw covering it. A large closet with sliding wood doors held an elaborate stereo system—tuner, amplifier, turntable, and the ubiquitous reel-to-reel tape deck which Larry flicked on, moving to slide open another door to reveal a small bar.

"I've got vodka and wine," Larry said. "Get comfortable. Sit down. Take off your shoes."

Noel did, removing his work shoes and propping himself against the bed.

"How are you feeling now?" Larry asked, sitting down close to him.

"All right. Thanks for getting me out of there."

"A pleasure," Larry drawled. At the same time Noel felt the boy's hand slide over his thigh and come to rest high up. What the hell?

"What's wrong?" Larry's hand had stopped with Noel's involuntary flinch.

"Then Larry wasn't Loomis's cover! Who was he? Not Mr. X? He couldn't be!

"You all right?" The boy's tone was even. "You can talk, can't you? You aren't dusted, are you? That new crystal going around is freaking a lot of people." His hand didn't move, radiating warmth from Noel's inseam like a heated metal glove.

"No," Noel managed. "I guess I got a little too high tonight."

He began to get up, succeeding in getting the boy's hand off him, but not in getting enough balance to stand. He slid back into the pillows.

Larry laughed the way a child would: with open delight.

"Where are you going, man?" He leaned forward and put both hands on Noel's thighs. Before Noel could understand what was happening, the boy moved in and brushed his lips.

Larry pulled back and cocked his head to one side.

"Don't tell me: you don't like to kiss?"

He wasn't Mr. X. He wasn't. What a joke!

"Not really," Noel admitted.

"Miguel was right. You *are* strange."

Not Loomis's cover, either. But almost as bad as either Mr. X or Miguel. The way Noel handled himself here, now, with Larry would determine his reputation at the Grip. That in turn would determine whether or not Noel would be discovered. And if he were discovered, no need for an abandoned warehouse. They could kill him in his own bed. Consequences. Lots of consequences out of this. Go easy.

"I'm a little weirded out," Noel explained, fixing a look on the boy's dark young eyes. "You know, with Miguel and all . . ."

"He's got the hots for you. A lot of guys do. You know what they call you? The San Francisco Virgin. Funny, huh?"

"Because I don't go to bed with someone every night?" Noel asked, pointing the remark as an accusation.

"No, man. Because you don't go to bed with anyone! Not in a month. It's unnatural. Probably unhygienic, too." He began stroking Noel's upper thigh. "Look at you! You don't even like being touched, do you? What are you into? Kink? Fists? Scat? Tell me, man! If I haven't done it, I'll try it. I want to please you. What is it? S and M? Bondage? Come on. Tell me. It's cool."

He would, Noel knew, he would.

"No, really. It's just that I'm not up to it. I've had a hard week at the bar, and . . ."

"Why don't you just relax?" the boy said softly. "That's it, just lay back and relax a little, man. You don't have to do a thing. All right? That what you want? It's cool."

Noel allowed himself to sink into the pillows around him. Quick young hands began carressing him as he thought, Yeah, let him do it. Lots of guys did. Truck drivers at rest stops, armed forces men off base, hitchhikers in front seats of cars, anyone, everyone. It meant nothing. The boy's hands were warm, experienced, eager, loosening Noel's belt, pulling down the denims, lifting his shirt, warm against his navel and abdomen and thighs. Everyone got blow jobs. Why not he? He was horny. He'd think of Monica. She used to do it sometimes. Never any good at it. Not like Larry now, his tongue circling Noel's navel, traveling up to his nipples, then down his rib cage into the space where his hipbone began, then over the thigh and . . . Blow jobs. Head fucking. Cocksucking.

Words from gymnasium locker rooms. From sudden adolescent revelations, followed by an embarrassed silence. It had always excited him to think of, always excited any boy or man he'd ever known. And this kid was good at it, Jesus! What was that he was handing up? A popper. Glossary Number 156: Amyl Nitrite. Drug used for victims of angina pectoris. Discovered to be one of the grooviest of sudden highs. In one nostril, into the other. Here we go. Jesus! It really did get you high! And this kid is incredible! Jesus! Who would have thought? . . .

He climaxed so hard his body went rigid and he involuntarily sat up, trying to push the delirious boy's head away, fell back again, and finally got Larry off him and rolled over.

When he looked up, Larry was breathing hard, smiling that shared, forbidden-fun, mischievous smile. "You like that a little? Huh?"

Noel felt the fur underneath him like a thousand caressing hands.

"I guess you did. Why don't we take a rest? Have a little wine, some grass, and do it again?" He smiled. "Maybe a little something else, too?"

The boy stood and slowly stripped down, then lay down next to Noel: lithe, androgynous, waiting, smiling.

Noel awakened suddenly, sitting up in bed.

His first thought was that he was not in his own apartment. His second was that he had failed to do something.

Then he saw Larry stretched out next to him, an arm thrown over Noel's pillow, the fingers seeming to twitch as the boy slept. Their movement had probably awakened Noel.

He pulled the sheets over the warm young body, feeling more like a parent or elder brother than like someone who had sexually used the boy in a flurry of unexpected, drug-induced passion only a few hours before.

He hadn't been disgusted by it then. More than anything, he had felt the same experimental, scientific detachment that he felt observing pickups and overhearing conversations at the Grip. Now, he thought, only a month and I'm already going native. The degenerating jungle rot has begun. Better slow down.

Loomis! He hadn't called Loomis last night to report in. That's what was still undone.

There was a telephone next to the bed. Too close to Larry. Better do it downstairs.

The living room was empty, the door to the opposite balcony room closed. The others had gotten in after 5:00 A.M., just before he and Larry had finally fallen asleep.

Noel closed the bedroom door and crept downstairs. The kitchen phone seemed the safest: it was underneath Larry's bedroom, far from the other rooms. Cupping one hand over the voice box, he began to dial the loops.

And stopped. He couldn't remember any of the numbers beyond the three of the exchange.

The silence of the undialed call reproached him. He clicked the receiver and began again. First the exchange, then—what was it? A six? A nine? All four numbers Loomis had given him had the same first digit. Which one? He dialed the exchange again, almost expecting the numbers to follow of themselves. Once more he stopped at the fourth. Six? Or nine? Hell! The drugs he'd used last night must have blown a few circuits. A little grass? Some cocaine? That's ridiculous. Nine or six? Loomis was expecting him. But what if he thought Noel had been hurt or . . . what if operatives were out looking for him? At school? At his apartment? Nine or six, damn it! Which one. Six, he decided, and dialed.

"Nine, eight, nine, zero."

He spun around. Larry was standing naked at the kitchen doorway. Noel froze, the receiver in his hand.

"Or nine, eight, four, seven," Larry said, coming into the room. "Go on. Dial."

Noel put the receiver in its cradle.

"Why did you do that? The Fisherman is waiting."

"The Fisherman?" It sounded numbly out of Noel.

"Loomis. Go on. Dial."

Noel was inert—churning with questions, fears, panic.

Larry came over to him. Involuntarily, Noel flinched away. The boy didn't notice; instead he picked up the receiver and dialed. Noel watched, fascinated, as though he were seeing his own execution.

"Shut the door,," Larry said. Then, into the phone, "Peter Pan reporting in. I have the Lure with me."

Noel had just closed the door. He looked around in disbelief.

"Then you *were* the cover!"

Little Larry smiled his mischevious smile.

TWO

CASTING THE LINE

1

May, 1976

"Yes, yes," Wilbur Boyle said, glancing at a page or two of the manuscript Noel had handed in a few days before. "Excellent. An excellent beginning. The glossary is an especially good idea. I'm more than satisfied."

Good, Noel thought. If Boyle were satisfied with a mere fifty pages—most of which were index, glossary, and charts—he'd be knocked out by the rest.

"These semantic progression charts are fine. Very clear. Likewise these artificial kinship tables you prepared. Very professional."

Noel had not seen Boyle this oily, this enthusiastic, since the day he'd joined the teaching staff, over three years ago.

"Now let's talk about next term," Boyle went on.

"If you want, I'll take the same classes as this year."

"You won't be taking any classes."

"I won't?"

"No. Do this project right, Noel. Work all summer and take a sabbatical next term. You're due for one, anyway. You're already funded, I know. Clever of you to go through that upstate group. I would never have thought of them. If you need more money—we'll do something about it from the press. But you are employed at this bar, aren't you?"

"Not take *any* classes next term?" Noel repeated, astonished.

"None at all. Work on this." Boyle held up the manuscript and shook it, as if for emphasis. "Students can do without for a term. But *this* . . . this has got to be completed now. It will do more for your career in the department than you can imagine. Believe me, Noel, big things! Bigger than you imagined when you took on the assignment."

His rhetoric ended, the department chairman stood up and handed the papers to Noel.

"Keep it. That's your copy," Noel said.

"Yes. Of course. I assume your grading is completed?"

Noel felt brushed off by Boyle's vague promises, and uncomfortable about not having the security of classes the following term. "I handed the last grades in today, before coming in to see you. It was a lot of work, with the bar job and all. . . ."

"That's why I want you to devote all next term to only this."

The buzzer on his desk rang.

"I'll have all summer," Noel protested. "Three months."

"That won't be enough. You'll see that I'm right."

Boyle took the call. In the midst of it he seemed to realize that Noel was still in his office.

"Good luck. Keep in touch," he said in dismissal.

Outside the department chairman's office, Mirella Trent was sitting on Alison's vacated desk, one long leg crossed over the other, her skirt pulled up high, filing her fingernails.

"He's all yours," Noel said to her.

She looked up in surprise, then looked at him again in a more critical manner. God, but she was heavily made up these days, Noel thought as their eyes met, so much kohl around her eyes she could have stepped out of an Egyptian mural.

"Exactly what are you up to?" She nodded toward Boyle's office.

"Wouldn't you love to know?"

"You're in cahoots," she said.

"You bet we are. See you later."

"Noel," she called after him, "close the door."

He did, but not behind him. He went back to where she perched on the desk. She hadn't moved.

"I thought you were going," she said in what he recognized as her seductive voice.

"I am." Instead he ran his index finger over her crossed leg, from her kneecap slowly up to the hem of her skirt.

"You never used to stop there," she said. "Don't you like me anymore, Noel?"

It was an understated question given their relationship. After Monica had died and Noel had come to work at the university, he'd been immediately attracted to Mirella. Even then she'd been the brightest young thing in the department. She was intelligent, witty, worldly, knowing about everything and seeming to know everybody. Most important, she'd been wonderful to go to bed with. Irresistible, in fact.

But it wasn't long before her less attractive qualities were revealed. Mirella was unabashedly ambitious, unscrupulous, self-centered, inconsiderate of him or his feelings—and invulnerable. He found sexual gratification with her, but never affection, and certainly no consolation. He'd get fed up with her demands and arrogance, they'd argue, tell each other nasty things about each other, and break up. Only to argue, to reveal their basic dislike of each other, and to break off again. It was like the worst relationships Noel had ever heard about from friends—and so far from what he'd had with Monica or what he wanted—that he vowed to keep away from Mirella for good. Their last breakup had been this past November. They'd barely spoken to each other since. And now she was starting up again.

"Well? Don't you like me!"

"I like to fuck you, Mirella. But beyond that, I don't think so."

He'd meant to be ruthless with her. But she didn't seem the least bit affronted. She simply laughed low,

held his hand on her thigh, until her warmth began
seeping up to his fingers, and he pulled away.

"That's honest enough," she said flatly. "But you've
always been honest, haven't you, Noel? Even when it
was against your best interests. And I *am* seeing someone. But I'll be in town all summer. You know where
to reach me."

He began to tell her not to hold her breath waiting
for him to come to her, but merely said, "Have a good
summer."

As he walked out of the office, he heard her hum-
ming behind him.

The senior class placement chart had been posted
on the bulletin board outside the department office.
Noel edged past the dozen or more students gathered
around the list, nodding to several from his classes,
congratulating Gretchen Strauss on her honors, saying
good-bye to them, and exulting in the last day of the
school term, as though he were a student himself. For
a moment he forgot there would be no next term for
him. Only the bar, the shadow world, the dangerous
games with Mr. X.

At the bicycle rack outside the building he saw
Paul Warshaw just unchaining his Peugeot. For the
past two months, Paul had seen Noel behind the bar
at the Grip, but had never approached him—always
going to Buddy or Chaffee or another bartender—
never saying a word to him there or in class.

"That was a fine paper you handed in," Noel said,
unchaining his Atala. "Have you thought about expanding it for possible publication?"

Paul seemed tongue-tied. He muttered his thanks;
no, he didn't think it was a good enough point to be
amplified.

"What classes are you taking next term?" Noel
asked. Now that he had him, he wasn't going to let
Paul off so easily, especially in this academic context
where he had a natural advantage.

Paul gave a succinct account of his schedule.

"I didn't see your name next to any classes next term," the boy suddenly said.

"Sabbatical."

"Oh?"

Noel found himself appraising Paul. The lad was good-looking, with a fresh young complexion, a light, brand-new mustache just coming in—young, but older than Larry Vitale. Not streetwise like Larry, of course, but then who was, at any age? Cute, though. Large dark eyes. Long straight hair that fell across his forehead and had to be brushed back by hand. He must do well at the Grip.

"I thought . . . I thought maybe you were thinking of giving up all this," Paul said.

Noel supposed he owed Paul some sort of explanation. But he couldn't be too careful what he said, and to whom.

"School isn't everything, you know."

Paul also realized it wasn't an answer. "I really admire you," he said. It sounded sincere.

"What for?"

"For not giving a fuck what other people think of you."

"What *do* they think?"

"You mean you don't know?" And, as Noel didn't, Paul asked, "Have you been in the library john, stall number three?"

"Can't say I have," Noel admitted.

"There's some graffiti there about you," Paul said, and began to blush. "I . . . it's not there anymore. I wrote over it."

"What did it say?"

The boy looked pained. Then the words came in a torrent. "It said 'Professor Cummings is a class-A cockteaser.' I didn't write it."

"I didn't think you would."

"Don't you care?"

At the moment, Noel didn't care. Paul's anguish, his anger about the graffiti seemed to be enough. Last year, three months ago perhaps, Noel knew he would have fallen apart. Perhaps he would again, sometime in the future. Not today. Not with larger issues at stake.

"You *don't* care," Paul said triumphantly. "That's why I admire you. You don't care who knows. You flaunt it. Others on campus admire you, too. I know they do."

"Don't take it so hard, Paul. Okay?" Noel said, playing out the big brother role the boy had established for him in the last few minutes. "Relax a little."

"You're making it easier for the rest of us guys on campus, you know. Thanks."

"Don't mention it," Noel said, and swung onto the Atala. Paul mounted his bike, too. They rode up University Place together and separated with a wave at Fourteenth Street.

Christ, Noel thought, life got stranger every day. Not only had he just lost all job security here at the school, but he was also becoming a positive homosexual role model for young college men. Everything seemed to be getting more topsy-turvy every day.

2

"Yes I'll wine and dine you
Take you anywhere you wanna go
And when the night is over
I don't wanna see you no more.

All I want is a one night affair,
I've got to have a one night affair,
Oh I'll hit and run son-of-a-gun
I'll hit and run."

Jerry Butler sang out the words, the organ trashing the rhythm line in the background, the violins taking off again. Noel listened and sang along to the infectious melody, the honest words, tapping on the edge of the bar. He'd come to know most of the songs on a new four-hour mixed tape in the weeks he'd worked at the Grip, even better in the last week and a half since he'd been made assistant manager of the bar. Butler's song was one of his favorites: a favorite of other patrons, too, even if it was several years old, probably for its sentiments, Noel thought.

"Well you see I've been a lonely man
And I want you to understand

Oh, I'll never let you
under my skin
'cause I don't want to
see you again."

"Can I help you?" Noel said. The guy was obviously new to the place, looking around and keeping his distance from the bar itself. He looked scared to hell. In a timid voice he ordered a Bud and, holding on to the can for dear life, went to hide in a corner. He needn't have bothered, Noel thought. No one else really noticed him; the Grip was having one of its rare, absolutely hot-looking crowds tonight. The newcomer was outclassed by miles.

"New kid in town," a patron named Cody who'd watched it all said to Noel.

"I'm always kind to the handicapped," Noel replied, enjoying the sense of shared superiority. He must have looked that frightened the first time, too.

Not anymore. It was almost his place, he was so comfortable. From behind the bar, slightly elevated by the platform, he gazed over the crowd securely. Especially after two months, with the semester over. Especially with Chaffee away from the Grip so much, readying a new club in Chelsea. One more business to add to the Grip, Billy's, Le Pissoir, Window Wall, Clouds, and—from what Noel had heard rumored—a dozen other bars and discos outside Manhattan. Mr. X's conglomerate.

Noel sang out the words, performing for Cody and whoever else was nearby.

"Don't give me that shit," Cody muttered. "You're the heartbreaker."

"Get over it," Noel told him.

"Call for you, Noel. It's Chaffee."

"Cover me for a minute," Noel told Bob Seltzer, and went to the phone.

He and Rick had a short conversation about the following week's schedule, an almost unnecessary talk, since both knew it might go haywire any minute, their staff was so out to lunch. Noel sometimes wondered if he hadn't been promoted because of his steadiness, compared to the irresponsible behavior of so many other bartenders.

"I'll have Bob and Jimmy DiNadio cover you tomorrow night," Rick concluded. "Buddy will keep an eye on things."

"I'm working tomorrow."

"Not there. We have a company dinner to attend."

"A company dinner?"

"Dorrance wants to meet you. A few other guys will be there. Cal Goldberg from Window Wall, Geoff Malchuck, Nerone, I don't know who else. Come down to my loft and we'll go up together."

"Where?"

"Uptown. The East Side. Some fancy town house off Park Avenue in the Sixties."

"Dorrance is the head of . . . of all the places?" Noel had to ask, barely able to get the words out for the brainstorm he was having. No one had ever mentioned Dorrance except as the man who got the receipts.

"To all intents and purposes," Rick said. "I don't know. I've only met him a few times myself."

"X," Noel breathed out.

"What?"

He caught himself. "Nothing, Rick. I was just talking to someone here."

Chaffee was busy apparently; he bought the lie, and repeated they were to meet the following evening at eight o'clock, his place.

Finally! He was finally going to meet Mr. X. Loomis would utterly freak when he heard. Noel would let the Fisherman bullshit him as usual when they spoke that night on the loops, then when he was done, very casually, of course, say, "By the way, I'll be calling in late tomorrow night. I'm having dinner with X." The old cop would bust a gut when he heard.

"Well, man, you look happy," Cody said, when Noel returned to his spot at the bar, snapping his fingers. "Just get laid?"

"Better than that," Noel said. "I just got paid."

"On a Wednesday?"

3

Loomis wasn't all that surprised.

"Dorrance?" he asked again, as though he knew the name well.

"William Ernest Dorrance," Noel said. "You know him?"

"He's not listed as owning any of the places."

"He's the silent partner," Noel reasoned.

Loomis didn't answer directly. Instead he asked, "You're having dinner with him tomorrow night?"

"Not just him. All the company managers will be there. From Le Pissoir and Window Wall and Clouds, too. All of them." Noel was a little hurt by Loomis's lack of enthusiasm. "Dorrance especially asked to see me. I'm only an assistant manager, remember? He didn't have to."

"So this powwow may all be just a ploy for him to get a look at you?" Loomis offered. "All right. As long as others will be there. Where is it?"

"Some town house in the upper Sixties, Rick said. I don't have the address. Aren't you even a little pleased that I'm finally making contact with him? That's what you wanted, wasn't it?"

"*You* sound pleased."

"I am. I'm excited," Noel admitted.

"Well, don't get so excited that you drop your guard. You know what a vicious pervert you're dealing with, don't you?"

"I'll be careful."

"Remember, he only wants to take a look at you."

"I know, I know."

"Dress carefully. Wear something nice. Make a good impression."

"You sound like my late wife did whenever I went for a job interview," Noel said, laughing.

That seemed to sting Loomis. In a completely different tone of voice he said, "Remember, you won't get any help from me where you're going. I won't be able to cover for you as I did the last time."

Noel was still angry about being taken in by Little Larry. "That was some cover!"

"It got you out of trouble, didn't it?"

"I wasn't *in* any trouble. Just a downed-out queen on my back."

"Well, it could have been worse."

Noel was tiring of the lecture. "Don't worry, Fish. It'll work out all right."

"Just be careful. Observe carefully. I don't mean things like address and phone number; look at everything. I'm going to grill you about every detail of this dinner party," he said. Then the phone went dead.

4

A *middle-aged manservant* let Noel and Rick into the foyer of the town house and ushered them over to two chromium-plated elevators. They were expected on the second floor, he said in a thick Scandinavian accent, then dissappeared into one of several doorways that dotted the long corridor until it opened out into a large space with floor-to-ceiling windows overlooking a backyard garden lighted from the house.

Noel had the jitters—even with the five-milligram Valium he'd taken at Chaffee's loft. His stomach felt as though insects were waging a territorial battle. Rick seemed quiet all the way uptown in the cab. Was he nervous, too? Or merely pondering his continued problems with Jimmy DiNadio? Hard to tell. Rick could just clam up suddenly and mope.

Told to observe, Noel observed that the elevator led to five floors plus a basement. When it opened on the second floor, people were already gathered. Tim Matthews, manager of Billy's, brother bar to the Grip, was talking to someone Noel hadn't met, gesturing wildly to make a point. He spotted them instantly.

"Look what Rick dragged in. Better get out of that elevator, kids, it's programmed to shoot to the roof. You all know each other, don't you?"

"Geoff Malchuck," the tall, rangy, dark-haired man said, extending a hand to be shaken in the familiar peace salute.

"This," Mathews said, "is the famous, the legendary, Noel Cummings." A big, rawboned, round-faced, buck-toothed redhead, Tim Matthews was so unredeemably social as to merit the drag name "Marge" someone had laid on him years before.

"For once, word of mouth is right," Malchuck said, holding on to Noel's hand a little too long. Noel was used to this, and got out of it easily. "You ought to come by Clouds sometime. I'll put your name on the comp list." The offer was accompanied by the most obvious cruise. Ordinarily, Noel would say or do something to clear the air. But this was the enemy camp. He didn't think he ought to go out of his way to make anyone dislike him too much, if it could at all be avoided.

"Everyone's here now," Tim said, leading Noel into the center of the huge room. It was two stories high, surrounded by balconies. Two were merely passageways, the others opened to rooms. Amid story-and-a-half-high trees in large planters were a dozen sections of brick leather seats and a long, curved, bronze coffee table. It reeked of money—crystal vases, Stellas and Ellworth Kellys on the walls. Long-stemmed birds of paradise everywhere. The same aesthetic as Window Wall, but brighter, finer, probably more expensive; naturally scaled down. Every detail said to Noel, "Mr. X lives here."

Rick asked to use a telephone in the library: another skirmish was brewing with Jimmy, Noel guessed.

"Chaffee's a bundle of laughs tonight," Tim chuckled.

"Lover trouble," Noel reported.

The living room was so large they had half crossed it before Noel was able to make out who was on the sofas.

"What do you think of it?" Geoff asked, as though he were the owner.

"A real dump," Noel said. "Maintenance must be hell."

He had come with the others to the coffee table and was accepting a glass of wine Tim offered when he saw the two people hidden from him until then. The glass almost slipped from his hands in surprise. One of them was a slightly balding, tall, thin man with a prominent nose and large calf eyes, introduced as Hal something or other. Noel didn't catch it, he was too interested in the other person: the same beautiful European woman with her soft, luxurious accent and thick dark hair from that drugged night at Window Wall when he had left with Little Larry.

"Noel Cummings," Tim said. "For those who don't already know."

Neither of them stood or indeed made any movement to greet him, but Noel felt himself suddenly the focal point of their eyes. He settled himself in one of the leather sofas, next to Malchuck, across from the woman. . . . He didn't smell her attar of roses tonight, but an almost imperceptible perfume of lilacs drifted across the coffee table from her.

Noel had returned to the disco club twice since that first time, to be seen and to see, he had told Loomis; in reality, both times he'd gone he'd hoped to see her again. Everywhere else he'd gone on the gay scene he'd expected to suddenly hear her voice thread through conversation and the omnipresent overlay of disco music, to see her lovely profile and dark eyes. It had never happened. Yet here she was, tonight of all times, and here, in Mr. X's living room. It was the perfect distraction from his fears and insecurities. Better as a calmative than the Valium he'd taken. He couldn't really believe anywhere she would be could be dangerous to him.

"What kind of name is Alana?" he asked her.

She shrugged and smiled a quick, tiny smile. "I don't know."

"Her parents wanted a boy. They already had the name chosen—Alain," Tim said. "And when she came along, they had to make do."

"You are always so mean to me," she said, but sounded delighted with the explanation.

"I think it's a lovely name," Noel said. "Exotic."

"Perfect," she said. "I am exotic, too, no? I was born in the Orient. Hanoi. My father was with the consulate there."

"Is that true?" Noel asked.

"Does it make a difference if it isn't?" she said, and laughed again.

"You're a model, aren't you?" he tried another tack.

"A model," Tim put in. "Honey, Alana is *the* hot model in the world."

"They hang expensive clothing on me as though I were a coat hanger, then turn me this way and that for the camera," she said. "I am like a mannequin in a store window. That's all."

Noel sensed she wasn't being self-deprecating as much as trying to bring the reality of her job into focus. Before he could say anything, she asked:

"And what do you do, Noel?" She pronounced his name with two clear, long syllables, as no one else had ever pronounced it before. He liked the way it sounded.

"I'm a bartender."

"Oh, how *déclassé*," and she laughed again, this time putting one hand to her mouth.

Noel found himself completely charmed.

Another couple came over to the sectionals: two men in their mid-thirties, dark-haired, dark-eyed, mustached, bearded, identical but for details of dress and features, obviously together.

"I'm bored playing Perle Mesta," Tim said. "You all introduce yourselves. I'm going to find a husband. Anyone's husband!"

"Cal Goldberg," one of the men said. "Burt Johansen," the other said, and both sat down opposite Noel, helping themselves to wine. Noel had heard both names before. Cal managed the Window Wall. Burt was his lover, a textile designer with a large international market.

They took precedence over him with Alana, tossing names and gossip back and forth for a while before they settled back on the sofa, arms around each other, and began looking around the room.

Noel took the opportunity to ask Alana what she had against bartenders.

"There he is!" Cal said loudly, looking at someone behind Noel. "Burt was just asking where you might be."

Alana also glanced behind Noel, with a look he was hard pressed to define. Doggedly, he went on talking to her. "We make good money. We're out late at night, true, but . . ."

She wasn't listening. She stood up and went behind the sofas, out of his sight, and then came around to the other side. With her now was the intense-eyed blond man she had been with at the Window Wall.

Cal and Burt moved over, and the couple sat facing Noel.

It was obvious she'd been waiting for the man, that they were together again. Both were expensively dressed in one-of-a-kind slacks and blouses in pale-colored soft fabrics—in contrast to the denims and cowboy shirts of the others. Noel tensed again immediately. He resented the intrusion, resented Alana sitting there, so evidently pleased to be there with him.

"I'm Eric," the newcomer said to Noel, without a hint of friendliness in his voice. His eyes weren't black as Noel had first thought, but a deep blue, almost purple, in this lighting. Strange eyes.

Noel said his name and both men sat back and
sized each other up.

"I hear you're doing real well at the Grip," Cal
Goldberg suddenly said. It took Noel a second to realize the question was directed at him. It was casually
said. Too casual? Noel didn't know whether he or the
business was meant by the comment. Whether it was a
pleasantry or a challenge.

"It's a steady crowd," he admitted.

"I heard it's really gotten hot lately."

"A little. Of course it's nothing like the Wall."

What were Eric and Alana doing at what Rick had
called a company dinner? Everyone else here was obviously allied with the company. Were they? Where
was Rick? Still on the phone? And Dorrance. "Marge"
had said everyone was here. Did that mean Dorrance
wasn't going to show up?

"They pack 'em in all right," Geoff was saying of
the Window Wall. "What was your crowd last week?
Two thousand?"

"Fifteen hundred," Cal said. "We limit."

Was Clouds not doing as well as the downtown
club? Noel wondered. Or was this the usual interne-
cine banter?

Every time he looked across the table, he saw Eric
staring back. Once when Noel met his eyes, the other
held his gaze for a long time before saying something
to Alana too low for Noel to catch. It made him even
more unsettled, but he had to control his annoyance,
he had to. Not that he expected to be assassinated before dinner. Mr. X was too slick to do anything as stupid as that even with good cause. But because everyone in the room was a potential informer.

Rick suddenly appeared, in surprisingly good spirits. He'd probably had an argument with Jimmy. Rick
was always in a better mood after a good fight.

Chaffee became the focal point of the room as he
and then Cal and Burt, then Tim and Geoff and Hal,
too, talked about the complexities of opening a club.

They shared experiences in hiring help, setting up schedules, dealing with construction crews, commiserating over plumbers and electricians, the inadequacies of DJs and lighting engineers.

Still no sign of Dorrance. If he didn't show up, Noel's nerves tonight would have been for nothing. Loomis would be philosophical. But the contact would still not be made. Noel knew how important it was that it be made—by him.

Eric seemed impatient, as though he, too, were waiting for Dorrance. Alana listened, refilled hers and Eric's wineglasses, lighted joints of grass to pass around, and generally acted as hostess.

When she spoke, the low-toned, accented, rippling voice sent shivers through Noel. "Tell me, Rick. You are going to make this new club raunchy, like Le Pissoir?"

"Worse," he said.

"Far worse," a few of the others put in enthusiastically.

"If that is so, it will be very exciting," she replied, her lovely dark eyes lighting up with mischief. "It will become very popular with the beau monde. If you want I will make certain they come. Claude. Dee Dee. Azia. Women will be allowed, yes?"

"You're always welcome, Alana," Rick said. "But except for special events, it will be only guys."

"Why don't you send a few of those numbers you're always posing with?" Tim asked. "You know who I mean."

"Oh, they will never come," she declared. "They are all so uptight."

"Some of them might," Eric said. "Sometimes the prettier they are, the more they like to have their faces pushed in shit, no?"

There was no doubt the question was directed at Noel, a personal insult. He knew why, too, as a putdown in front of Alana. Nothing more. What had Miguel called Eric? One of the hottest sadists in the city?

That might be so, but not at Noel's expense. And not in front of Alana, either. Besides, all this might just be one of Mr. X's tests for Noel. More than likely Eric was just a hanger-on of the group—tolerated for whatever reason. If Noel were to have any respect from the others in the future, he'd have to do something.

No one else said anything for a short, embarrassed time. Noel took up the challenge. "I understand you're really into that scene?"

"You?"

"I don't believe in one bag. Too limiting. Keeps the lid on personal growth and consciousness, no?"

He saw Alana's hand go to Eric's thigh, as if to restrain him. But Eric smiled as he answered. "I forgot you Californians are really into all that high consciousness crap."

"It's a lot easier to clean up than the other kind."

"Not always. Your problem is you haven't found anyone good enough to show the other side of sex, little buddy. If I thought you had half a mind, I might be persuaded to give you a lesson."

The tension in the room was thick as smog.

Alana frowned, the others didn't move, didn't say a word. Eric was plainly enjoying the exchange. And Noel—though he was beginning to feel he might have underestimated Eric's status in the group—wasn't complaining either. It was a relief from all that laid-back business he'd walked into, filled with possible snipping and digs he might not be aware of. A release, too, from the jitters. Besides, sadist or not, Eric was just another faggot. Noel wasn't afraid of him. He couldn't afford to be now.

"Somehow," Noel said, deliberately slowly, "I seriously doubt that you could show me anything worth my time."

"If a lady weren't present, I'd give you a taste."

"I wouldn't think a small inconvenience like that would bother you," Noel shot back.

"Eric," Alana said in a small voice, "please. Stop."

"Why? He loves it," Eric said, eyeing Noel. "It's probably the only way he can get off. Or can you get off anymore?"

"Not on you, I can't." Noel reached for his glass of wine.

Eric's hand lashed out, grabbed Noel's before he reached the glass, jerked it toward his mouth. Noel followed, pulled out of his seat and half across the table before he realized what was happening. The wine spilled, the glass rolled onto the carpet.

Without a word, Eric pulled Noel's hand closer. Noel was balanced now and pulled back, a test of strength so wrenching that Noel lost. Eric put the thumb inside his mouth.

"Hey! Come on, you guys!" Tim said. Everyone sat up. Alana was crouching away from them.

Eric's grip was like steel. He took the thumb out of his mouth long enough to say, "Sit down, 'Marge'!" then hunkered down on the other end of the coffee table and inserted Noel's thumb again, this time lightly biting its edges.

For an instant Noel was certain from the crazy glitter in Eric's eyes that he would bite it off. Instead, Eric took the thumb out again, looked at it, and with exaggerated relish began to suck on it as though it were a piece of candy. His eyes narrowed to slits, staring level across the table at Noel. Then Eric closed his eyes and released his grip. Noel slowly withdrew his thumb.

"Jesus!" Rick said next to him, but somehow miles away. "That was hot!"

Eric sat back on the sofa and laughed.

It was a few seconds more before Noel realized his hand was free. His heart thumped like a bongo drum. He stood up and fell back onto the sofa.

"Oooh eee," "Marge" said, slapping his thigh. "That was *sexy!*"

All of them were suddenly laughing and chatting.

Alana gave Noel a napkin. He must have looked as baffled as he felt, because she began to wrap it around his thumb.

"I'm not hurt."

That made Eric laugh again.

"Wipe it," she commanded.

Noel did, still trying to figure out what had happened, why he felt so drained.

"I told you I'd give you a taste," Eric said, standing up. "You'll be back for more."

He pulled Alana up to him.

"You can see how much I enjoyed it," Eric said, holding the obvious erection through his pants. "How about you, little buddy?"

When Noel didn't answer, Eric took Alana's hand and held it there.

"I'm bored," he said, wrapping his arms around her, forcing her closer. "Let's go fuck."

She didn't protest. Noel knew it was all show, for him.

There was a tinkling from above.

"Dinner is served."

Noel looked up. The servant was on the balcony, a sliding panel opened behind him to the dining room.

"Where's Dorrance?" Geoff asked.

"He'll be here in a minute," Eric said. He and Alana were dancing a slow arching tango. Her head was thrown back, her liquid laughter entwining them.

"You coming up?" Rick asked Noel.

Something indefinable had happened; Noel wanted to puzzle it out longer. But he followed the others.

At the top of the stairs, he heard Alana's voice saying softly from the living room, "Thank you, darling."

"What for?" Eric asked.

"For not being cruel."

"Don't be stupid," Eric said tonelessly, without rancor. "Let's go eat."

5

Dorrance wasn't in the dining room.

They seated themselves haphazardly around the large, circular, white-topped table, leaving two seats empty, one next to Eric and one next to Alana. She was playing hostess, easy, almost childlike, in her element. Eric was quiet, brooding again. Noel wondered what Alana's relationship to Dorrance was. What it was to Eric. His mistress? His nursemaid? His plaything? What was Eric to Dorrance? Could he have been in that warehouse, keeping the cigarette lighter flame high? Or had he slashed at Kansas? If the past five minutes were any indication, that role would fit Eric's taste. Noel's right thumb still felt odd, as though some subtle venom was in Eric's saliva.

"I chose the wines tonight," Alana declared. "This one, for the appetizer, is from California. If I didn't tell, you would never guess."

Conversation centered on the decor of this room. Only Cal and his lover had been there before.

It was the most unusual dining room Noel had ever been in, a half circle, cantilevered over the terrace and glass enclosed. A circular skylight five feet in diameter had been cut into the ceiling.

On a clear night like tonight, one could look up and see the constellations. Pale, diaphanous curtains uncovered enough glass to show trees swaying slightly close by. Serving bars had been built in. The table was built in, too, its center a two-foot hollow containing chromium hot plates and food warmers. There were deep, firm-cushioned armchairs, fine bone china, and more silver utensils than Noel could imagine would be needed for one meal, all bathed in pale amber from recessed lights on the ceiling and under the edge of the table.

Dorrance's taste? Or Alana's? Everyone seemed to be giving her the credit.

"You're French, Alana," Tim began a question, "how do you find the Parisian discotheques?"

"She's Belgian," Eric corrected: his first words since they had sat down.

"They are not like here, Tim," she said, pronouncing his name "Teem." "They are all so chic. Everyone is afraid to move too fast, afraid they will blur when a photograph is taken. They are not funky at all."

Dorrance had just stepped onto the balcony.

"There you are," Alana said. "We were waiting."

"You needn't have," he said in a thin, reedy voice. Behind him was a large, very handsome young man wearing the usual macho gay getup: vest, plaid shirt, faded denims. Neither he nor Dorrance seemed in a good mood. The young man was introduced to Noel as Randy Nerone, manager of Le Pissoir. He looked especially white-faced, tense, as though they had just completed, to neither's satisfaction, an intense altercation.

Dorrance sat between Alana and Tim. The only other empty seat was between Eric and Geoff. Hesitating, Randy took that one.

Dorrance was in his fifties, slender with a fine-boned New England face. His silver hair was cropped close to his head, his temples indented, as though crushed by a pair of giant pincers. His eyes were large, a watercolor blue, his lips thin. He was evidently concerned about his appearance. Dressed in an openneck fine sports shirt, seersucker jacket, and dark trousers, he gave the immediate impression of a Catholic priest out of uniform: a cool, even-tempered demeanor, slightly world-weary, possibly cynical and witty.

The pale blue eyes surveyed the table and came to rest on Noel.

"You're the new one. Neal, is it?"

"Noel. Noel Cummings. I'm helping Rick."

"That's right. Doing rather well, too. Keep it up. Geoff. Tim. Burt, Cal. I see every nook and cranny are represented tonight. Nice to see you all under one roof and not in any apparent mischief." He took Alana's hand. "Thank you. This was a good idea, all of us together."

And that was all. Not five words more of conversation throughout the remaining five courses of dinner, and those only to ask for the salt or how someone was enjoying some dish.

Business was casually done—Rick's problems at the new club, minor annoynaces at Clouds or Window Wall. Not a word more to Noel.

Despite his disappointment, Noel observed Dorrance, trying to understand him without benefit of intimacy. Not a hint, not a clue to his personality or methods of operation.

Except one, a tenuous one. Malchuck offered in passing that a new gay women's discotheque was opening.

"Did you hear that?" Dorrance asked Eric.

"It's been checked out," Eric reported. "I don't think it's anything important. Alana and I are going to the opening night. I'm going to fix her up with a nice hot dyke."

"I've tried it," she said, "it isn't really me."

"Once you've had a really hot lesbian you'll never go near a man again. Tongues of steel with rotary motors," Eric said.

"You always make conversation about sex," she said without a hint of annoyance. "Always."

"He's just horny," Cal said. Then, to Dorrance, "You should have seen the thumb job he gave Noel before."

"Eric's always horny," Dorrance said.

"Just like my father," Eric was quick to reply. "Go on, say it."

The challenge wasn't picked up. Evidently a long and complex relationship existed between these two. Dorrance's attitude was almost paternal toward Eric, the younger man's spoiled and rebellious. Noel couldn't figure out whether Eric was Dorrance's right-hand man or heir apparent.

Even more confusing was how Eric seemed to go out of his way to be pleasant to Randy, who arrived at the table in a foul mood but was slowly charmed by Eric's whispered conversation to him. Something had upset him before. What kind of threat had Dorrance made?

A minute later Randy's and Noel's eyes locked across the table, and Noel felt as though he were looking into a slightly distorted mirror. Nerone's hair was curlier, his features more Latinate. But everything else was the same: coloring, eyes, even the symmetrical good looks. No wonder Dorrance hadn't even glanced at Noel; he was already busy with Randy.

Who in turn was no longer paying attention to Eric, but instead managing to keep a steady, interested eye on Noel, playing a dangerous game, flirting right in front of Mr. X.

Dorrance didn't seem to notice. Or if he did, didn't seem to care. Studied indifference? Or was he through with Randy? That could be fatal. But Randy seemed oblivious to Dorrance's reaction. He was interested in Noel. That was plain.

For a minute Noel wondered what it would be like with Randy. Different than with small, lithe Larry. Randy was large, muscled. The same face. Like masturbating while looking in a mirror, classic narcissism. Why am I thinking this? he wondered. The conversation? Alana? Eric's mouth around his thumb?

The manservant appeared to clear the table, insert-

ing the used dishes into a built-in dumbwaiter which
Noel guessed must go downstairs to a ktichen.

At that moment, Dorrance stood up.

"I'll pass on dessert."

"You have to go?" Alana sounded disappointed. She,
too, stood up. "But I have that movie you were asking
about. *Viva Maria.* We are going to show it tonight."

"Tomorrow night," he said.

"Is that the one with Brigitte Bardot and Jeanne
Moreau?" Tim asked.

Alana took Dorrance's arm.

Noel kept expecting the older man to make some
sort of sign as he left the room. But nothing passed
between them. Then Dorrance was gone, and Alana
was back at the table where the talk had gone from
movies to the real versus the publicized love lives of
film stars.

At least he's made contact, Noel said to himself.
Dorrance would be cool. It would be a while before
he would show any interest in Noel. At least until
Randy was out of the house.

And Loomis would be satisfied.

6

After dessert, Alana stood up and led the others
downstairs where one wall, covered before with a
large folding Japanese screen, opened now to reveal a
private movie theater: deep-pile swivel chairs for
twenty people, a sixteen-millimeter screen, a projec-
tionist's booth.

Behind the elevators another sliding wall was ajar,

revealing the library where Chaffee had called his lover.

Noel's first impulse was to look at the books. What Dorrance read would tell a great deal about the man—his interests, how he thought. The others were occupied, so he slipped in. Three walls of shelving, but only one—admittedly the longest—contained books. The others were filled with reel-to-reel tapes and film cans. Noel was trying to find the organizing factor for the arrangement of the books when he became aware of someone else in the room with him.

"Some collection, huh?" It was Randy Nerone, who walked directly to the film shelf. "Look at this. *Ben-Hur, Bringing Up Baby, Broken Blossoms,* and that's only part of the Bs."

"Nice what money can do," Noel said.

"There's a swimming pool upstairs. I'm going up. Care to join me?"

It was said casually enough, but Noel got the feeling the invitation was for more than a swim.

"I thought I'd watch the movie."

"I've seen it," Randy said, obviously disappointed, but shrugging it off. "You can always see a movie."

"Marge" looked in. "Get your popcorn and chewing gum. Main feature's about to begin."

"I'm going upstairs," Randy said. "Top floor. If you change your mind."

Everyone but Randy and Eric was in the screening room; even the manservant—his work done for the moment, Noel supposed—had taken a seat in the last row.

Alana was in the front, swiveling around to talk to Cal Goldberg and his lover. The seat next to her was empty: probably saved for Eric, Noel thought.

She half turned when Noel took the seat, but finished what she was saying to Cal and Burt before turning forward again.

"I hope I'm not taking anyone's seat," he said.

"There are plenty of seats left."

He couldn't resist looking at her. This close, he verified that the lilac perfume was hers. Her tanned, almost uncosmeticized skin glowed in the half lighting so that her high, model's cheekbones, something he'd never liked in a woman before, seemed to take on extra highlights. Her eyelashes were long; they looked real. Her eyes dark and soft. Her hair like a thick curtain of night sky.

"You have seen me before?" she asked. "That is why you ogle me?"

He loved her use of the word "ogle."

"At the Window Wall," he said.

She looked puzzled now.

"You are either a very stupid or a very courageous boy."

"I'm neither. I'm not a boy."

"Man, then. But you are ignorant of what it is to provoke Eric." She pronounced his name with a soft—almost Viennese—"ch." "Yet you've done it twice already."

"Is he your lover?" Noel asked, deliberately ignoring what she was saying.

"Why do you need a definition for what we are? We simply *are*. Isn't that enough?"

"Does he cheat on you only with men? Or with other women, too?"

"You are very curious," she said, but she didn't seem angry or annoyed. "Listen," she leaned very close to him so he could feel several strands of her hair sweeping lightly over his cheek, "this I know for certain. Eric wants you. Don't even think of me. Go with him."

"What if I don't want to go with him?"

"Then you are stupid. Eric always gets what he wants. Always!"

"Is that how he got you?"

"Ssssh," someone said behind them.

The lights dimmed and the screen in front of them displayed the opening credits.

Noel settled back and became absorbed in the film. He felt placated for everything that had happened

with Eric this evening by the exchange of those few
private words with Alana. Even though their content
was disturbing enough. Eric was someone he'd have
to deal with, someone dangerous, unpredictable, someone close to Dorrance.

He scarcely noticed when Alana left her seat. Then
he began to wait for her to return, his attention divided. Twice he turned around to see if she'd come
back and sat in the rear. No. After a while, he, too,
left the room.

The manservant followed him out to the living
room. "There," he said, pointing to a door next to the
elevators.

How did he know whom Noel was looking for? The
man had turned around and gone back into the
screening room.

Noel went to the door and looked in: a lavatory.

She hadn't returned when he peeped into the view-
ing room and wasn't in the living room, or the library,
or up in the dining room. Already upstairs, Noel decided to see if she were on this floor. There was a
balconied living room, with sectionals and plants similar to the ones downstairs, then a short corridor, the
two elevators, and a door on either side of the hallway. He tried the right one. Locked. The left one was
open, though. He looked in, then stepped inside.

It was a sitting room and a bedroom half hidden by
a folding screen, the platform bed strewn with gowns
and blouses. Beyond the bed was a half-open door to
a dressing room: racks of clothing. A soft, variegated
clash of colognes surrounded him. It must be her
room.

He was exiting when the corridor door was suddenly pulled open. Noel stepped back: Eric.

"Looking for something?"

"No."

"Or maybe you were trying on one of those?" he
said, nodding toward the dresses on the bed. "I didn't
really picture you as the drag type."

"I'm not."

"See. I thought not. What are you doing here, then?"

"Looking for the bathroom."

"There's one downstairs."

"I got lost."

Eric moved aside to allow Noel past him, then stepped out into the corridor, leaning against the wall in an exaggeratedly casual manner as Noel pushed for the elevator. He unexpectedly joined Noel inside. When Noel punched the button for five, he said, "The film is one flight down."

"I thought I'd see the pool. Randy said it's on the top."

"What exactly do you do at the Grip?"

"Tend bar." Noel didn't like Eric's attitude, or being in this enclosed space with him. "I'm assistant manager at the moment."

"You like the job?"

"It's all right."

The elevator opened on a glass enclosure with sliding walls opening onto a planked sun deck set with trees, bushes, benches, and lawn chaises. Noel turned left, stopping at a brick wall inset with a metal door: a head-sized oval window showed the pool inside.

"You seem to know where you're going now," Eric said.

The pool was roofed in by a polyhedron solarized glass, tinted pale gray. Two diving boards, a few more chaise lounges—on one farthest from the door was Randy Nerone, lying as if asleep, naked, on his stomach. There was no sign of Alana.

"There he is," Eric said behind Noel, "the boy with the golden buns. Go on."

"Aren't you coming?" Noel asked.

Eric hung outside the doorway. "There, before you, lies a hundred and seventy-five pounds of New York's hottest stud, just waiting. Don't think I didn't notice you two at dinner. Or were you expecting someone else to be here? You seem disappointed."

"Like who?" Every danger sign flashed on in Noel's mind.

Eric half smiled; his eyes seemed to flicker from pale to deep purple with reflections off the pool water.

"I just left her. She's downstairs. Watching the movie," Eric said.

Careful, Noel told himself. He's seen you looking at Alana. He knows you're interested. He's no fool. He'd expose you in a minute. Get you into real hot water with X.

"Alana?" Noel asked. " 'Fraid not, man. I'm not into fag hags. No matter how nice. She's all yours."

Randy heard them. He looked up and shouted, "Hey? Are you coming? Or what?"

"Alana's not my style," Noel said.

"Is he your style?"

"Isn't it obvious?"

"He's waiting," was all Eric said.

Noel shut the door behind him. Eric remained outside but the threat of him was still with Noel. Damn! Eric didn't believe him. Noel was getting so close to Dorrance, and this creep was going to screw everything up!

"Who were you talking to?" Randy asked, looking up, not moving from his prone position on the lounge.

"No one." Noel knew that Eric was still there, watching them through the little window in the door. "How's the water?"

"Warm."

Noel peeled off his shirt and sat down at the edge of the chaise lounge to remove his shoes. As he was untying the laces, he felt a hand at his waist: Randy unbuckling his belt, opening his zipper, trying to pull down his pants. Christ, Noel thought, out of the frying pan into the fire!

"What's the hurry?" he asked. He strained to see if Eric was still at the window.

Randy dropped his head back down onto his outstretched right arm, making a loud moan. "Oh, shit!" he suddenly said.

Noel had gotten up, taken off his pants and undershorts, ready to dive into the pool. He was certain now Eric was watching them. "What's wrong?"

"Nothing. Tension." Randy looked back at Noel. "How about giving me a rubdown? My back and shoulders feel really knotted up."

"I've never done it before."

"Begin at my neck and work down," Randy said. "Do you mind? I'm real tight. I had this big argument with Dorrance."

This might be a way to get information and give Eric something to look at, Noel thought, so he leaned over Randy's back and began to massage the thick, tanned neck, imitating a masseur.

"Better straddle me," Randy said. "It'll be easier."

Noel got up and knelt on either side of the massive body. Randy put his head down into his folded arms again and arched his back, flexing the spine right down to his thighs. He was enormous, Noel thought, like some huge, sensuous statue come to life—a Rodin, a Michelangelo.

"What are you waiting for?" Randy asked.

"I'm not waiting," Noel said, and leaned forward to begin the massage. As he worked over the man's upper back, he felt the heat rise from Randy's skin to his own. Every movement of his hands on Randy's body brought a soft mutter, a groan, a twist of a limb, a flex of another muscle. Noel felt as though he were mounted bareback on some large animal. He began to perspire.

"That feels terrific. You really know how to do it, don't you?" He inched up a little on the lounge. "Go a little lower down, man. It's *really* tense there."

Moving down, Noel found his legs suddenly wrapped up in Randy's. "Hey, we're caught," he said.

"I know." It was said with amusement.

"Well, let go."

"Why? Does it bother you?" His legs tightened around Noel.

Noel tried to pick Randy's hard-muscled legs off the backs of his thighs. "He's watching."

"Who's watching?"

"Eric is."

"So what?"

As he said it, Randy twisted almost to a sitting position. Noel lost his balance. His left arm was pulled in front, his right arm crossed over against Randy's chest. Noel was now pinned arms and legs on top of Randy.

"I give up," he said. "You've had your fun."

"Not yet I haven't," Randy said.

Noel began to feel the warm flesh under him slowly begin to gyrate, and then to move forward and back under him. He was sweating now, burning up with the proximity. He felt his face flush with shame, tried to reason with Randy. "Hey! Don't do that," he said in Nerone's ear, only an inch from his mouth. Noel was cursing himself for being duped.

"Why not?" Randy answered in a low, faraway voice. Then, "Why not, huh? Afraid of something? Afraid of a little fun?"

Noel struggled to free himself, but Nerone only held on tighter, still gyrating, still taunting him. When he finally couldn't fight anymore, he collapsed against the big, hot, smooth-skinned body. The flesh that met his groin seemed to reach up and envelope him. In seconds he felt pulled into undulating softness.

"Jesus!" he gasped.

"It gets better, man," Nerone said. "Believe me. I can either get you off this way, or I can let your arms and legs loose, and really let you take me. Which will it be, huh, man?"

Noel's body began to answer for him. His kindling point had been hit, and he knew suddenly without willing it or wanting it, that there was no going back now. Randy would get what he wanted.

Noel closed his eyes, trying to fantasize he was with

a woman. That worked for a while, then was unnecessary—all he could think of now was how to reach orgasm as fast as possible. His entire body seemed to be embedded in that point of him that was more tightly clasped than he could ever recall it being.

"Yeah!" Randy hissed, letting Noel's arms loose. "Put it to me your way, man. Yeah!" He seemed to be vibrating from inside out.

Inside him, it was as if a dozen hands were opening and closing around Noel all at once.

"I hope that son of a bitch is still watching," Noel mumbled as the mindlessness of climax swept over him.

7

"Who else was there?" Loomis said.

"Myself, Chaffee, Malchuck, Tim Matthews, Goldberg and his lover, Dorrance, Eric, and Alana. Oh, and a manservant. Okko, or Okku, Randy called him."

"You didn't mention Randy."

"Sure I did. Earlier. He came upstairs with Dorrance. They'd had an argument, I said. Remember?"

"Now I remember," Loomis admitted.

"Maybe it's because I told you that over an hour ago."

They had been on the loop at least that long, going over detail after detail. Noel felt finally that he was earning the money that had arrived in a long, pale blue envelope two days before: his salary from Whisper. Of course it was in the form of a stipend payment from a fictitious Social Work Research Agency in Albany, supposed to be helping to finance his thesis. Noel hadn't minded depositing the check in his account. But this repetition was getting tedious.

"Let me get this straight," Loomis asked. "Randy's the one you said was the Mr. X type. Right? What happened to him?"

"Nothing. He's leaving Le Pissoir. Going back to school, he said. Dorrance told him it was bad timing. He wanted Randy to stay on for another month."

"He told you that?"

"Randy did. We talked."

"At the pool? Where were the others?"

"I told you. On the second floor. Watching a movie."

"Except for Dorrance. Who'd already left the house?"

"I assume. But I don't know where he went. No one said. And, except for Eric. He was watching us outside the pool."

"What did Nerone say about Dorrance?"

"Only that they'd argued, then reached some sort of agreement. I still don't know why he invited us to his house for dinner."

"It's not his house," Loomis said.

"It's not? Whose is it?"

"It belongs to a corporation called Raynita, an affiliate of the Hull-Redfern Electronics Corporation, Rye, New York. The tenant listed with the city tax register is Eric Hull Redfern."

That was odd, Noel thought. Why hadn't the Fisherman told him that before he went? Not that it made any real difference. Or did it? Wasn't Noel supposed to be trying to find Mr. X based on his life-style? What was the sense of trying to psych Dorrance out through someone else's home? Noel decided to let it slide for the moment. Instead, he said, "Well, that might explain Eric's attitude toward me."

"Hostile. Suspicious. That is . . . he was sort of interested in me. He played around as though he was. But it wasn't clear, either."

"You rejected him and he got hostile? Did he talk to Randy, too?"

"During dinner, yes. You know, Fish, I couldn't really figure this Eric out. He came on to me sexually, yet he lives with this beautiful woman."

"This is the same guy who's called 'Eric the Red'? The well-known sadist?"

"That's right."

"Then he's gay," Loomis reasoned.

"But they're lovers. I know it. You would know it."

"How?"

"Because he didn't like me looking at her."

Loomis was silent a long time.

"What's wrong? Are you still there?" Noel asked.

"Noel," Loomis said quietly. "Noel. Noel. Noel. Listen to me for a minute, will you? If you're supposed to be homosexual, which you are supposed to be, you're not supposed to look at another man's woman, except if you're crazy about her dress or something. And with someone that close to Dorrance, too! Don't you care to live to be middle-aged?"

"It's all right," Noel said quickly. "I fixed it up."

"How?" Loomis didn't seem persuaded.

Noel was silent. Then he said, "While Eric was watching outside the pool, I sort of let someone . . . you know?"

"With whom, if you don't mind telling me?"

"Randy Nerone."

"Jesus! You *are* crazy. I thought he was Mr. X's boyfriend?"

"I was trapped into it. I had no choice. I didn't want to do it, believe me."

Silence. Then: "When do you see Dorrance again?"

"Who knows?"

"You *have* to see him again. You've already made contact and you've survived. So, it's working, as I thought it would. You're further than any of the pre-vicious p.c.'s. Didn't I tell you that Mr. X could smell a cop? He hasn't even really *noticed* you. We have a good thing going, let's not have it slip away from us. I want you to see Dorrance again. In that town house, if possible. The offices are probably there."

"I don't know. Eric didn't like me at all. And Dorrance hasn't even nibbled yet."

"He nibbled on Randy, didn't he? Stick to *him* until Dorrance invites you back."

"But Randy's leaving in a few weeks."

"Get back into that town house," Loomis said. "I don't care what you have to do to get in there.

Noel had never heard that tone of voice from Loomis before; he didn't care for it at all. "Or whom I have to screw to do it?" he asked harshly.

"I didn't say that, Lure."

"But you meant it."

"It couldn't have been all that bad. What did you do? Tell me. You didn't . . . ?"

"I told you enough already," Noel said as curtly as possible, hoping to discourage any further discussion on the subject. He'd been bothered by it, had badly felt the need to confide in someone about it, if only to confirm for himself that he really had been forced into it. Loomis was the only person he could confide in. But now that he had, Noel wished he hadn't said a word.

"Guys do it all the time," Loomis said airily.

"Evidently." Couldn't Loomis see that wasn't the point?

"I mean you don't have to be homosexual to do it. A lot of guys do it when there are no women. In prison. In the Navy."

"I don't care," Noel said. The Fisherman hadn't been there, with Eric looking in the little window, with Randy's body wrapped around him like a python, what the hell could he know?

"I'm not kidding, Lure, I had a buddy who was in Japan after the war. Big blond guy. Swede or something. He goes into this geisha house where the people have never seen anything like him, right? So the girls are scared shitless, thinking he's some sort of devil. And they send out one of their teenaged brothers, all got up to look like one of them. The Swede's drunk on rice wine. So it wasn't until he was done with the kid . . ."

"I don't care," Noel repeated, not hiding his annoyance now. "I'll chalk it up to experience. You know, for the book. Empirical research. Going native. Big anthropological breakthrough, as Boyle would say. Can I hang up now?"

"Sure. Sure," Loomis said, evidently perplexed by the tone of Noel's voice. "But stay near Dorrance, hear?"

"I'll try."

"And be careful, will you? If you want a piece of ass, do it quietly."

"I just had a piece of ass," Noel said.

"You know what I mean. Good night, Lure."

8

"*I'll take all that stuff uptown*, if you don't have the time," Noel offered.

He was with Chaffee in the downstairs office of the Grip. Rick was surrounded by paperwork connected with the opening of the new club: construction contracts, bills, estimates, letters of agreement.

"It would save time," Rick said. Then: "You like going up there, don't you?"

"Don't you?"

"Not really. Too fancy for me."

"The last time I was there, I saw *Beauty and the Beast,* and listened to two Charlie Parker tapes that were never commercially released. Not to mention other amenities—Primo Acapulco Gold grass and the best coke in town, just begging to be snorted."

He knew Chaffee was well aware of the good drugs and other fun available at Redfern's place, but Noel still wanted to make sure Rick took it as the only reason for his going there.

"Bullshit, Cummings! I know why you're really going there."

Oh, oh, Noel thought. Here it comes. Vega's told him I'm an agent for Whisper. This is it. Because if he knows *so does Mr. X.*

"Well, don't keep it from me." His voice was light, joking, but he had to move closer to the desk to keep the sudden spasmodic jerking of his left knee out of Rick's sight. The office seemed cramped as a grave. He broke out into a sweat. Rick kept smiling.

"Hey, I know." Rick was offhanded about it.

"What do you know?" Noel asked, trying to be equally casual.

"I've got eyes. You're looking for a rich husband. You and Eric are getting it on, aren't you?"

Instant relief. "You're kidding. You were there when we first met. He can't stand me. It's like fire and water."

"Or oil and fire. One feeding the other."

"Well, it's not. I go up there because I like the amenities. Can you blame me?"

"I still think you're bullshitting me. Here, go on. Get." Chaffee handed him the envelope.

"These don't have to go right away, do they?" Noel asked. "I'd like to stop at home. You know, clean up a little."

"In case water and fire do start to mix?"

* * *

On his way to the apartment, Noel stopped at the newsstand three blocks from where he lived. As he entered, a woman was at the counter talking to the proprietor. Another customer—a man—was looking over the extensive shelf of paperback books. Noel glanced at them, then went up to the counter, set down the manila envelope he'd taken from Rick, nonchalantly covered it with his jacket, and went over to the book section.

The woman left a minute later, and the proprietor disappeared into the back room. As planned, the envelope was gone, taken by him into the rear of the store where Noel knew a Whisper operative would immediately photocopy it in preparation for putting it on microfilm later on. The whole process seldom took more than five minutes, but Loomis had insisted it be done extracautiously.

Noel glanced over the paperbacks, then selected some magazines and thumbed through them.

"Try this one," the other customer said. He was holding out a body magazine. He must have been in his mid-thirties, with a ruddy, pleasant face, small blond mustache, long, curling reddish hair, dressed in an expensively cut French or Italian suit with one of those drop-dead forty-dollar silk ties seen only in shops on Madison Avenue.

"Thanks, I've already seen it."

"You live around here?"

A Whisper operative—despite the expensive clothing—also waiting to have something photocopied? Or, one of X's men who'd somehow discovered what was going on here? He hadn't turned around when Noel had come in, nor when the manila envelope had been taken. But Noel decided to keep him occupied anyway, at least until the papers had been slipped back under his jacket.

"A few blocks away, why?"

"Haven't I seen you before?"

"Probably. I come in here often."

"No. I meant somewhere else. Downtown. In the Village."

"I tend bar. The Grip."

The man's eyes narrowed as though he were picturing Noel behind the bar.

"And you read *Psychology Today, Human Nature,* and *Scientific American.*"

"I'm not illiterate. I went to school."

"Fallen on hard times?"

"Sort of. It doesn't bother me."

"What did you study?"

"Psychology." Noel held out the magazines. "The usual. I thought I'd become a clinical psychologist."

"I have a friend at the Upstate Medical Center." He named someone Noel had never heard of. "Maybe he could help you. You have your degree, don't you?"

"Everyone has a degree," Noel said, playing out the role he had just adopted.

"My friend could set you up with something. And if that didn't work maybe you could try something else. I know a lot of important people."

"No kidding?" Noel said, all innocence, trying not to behave as though it were the oldest line in the history of mankind.

"Why don't you come around the corner? We'll have a smoke, a drink, talk this out."

"I can't right now. Someone's expecting me in half an hour."

He heard the storeowner return, the barely audible rustle of his jacket being lifted, the envelope placed under it again.

"Maybe another time," the man said, handing Noel a business card.

Bill Clay Flanders III, it read. An address nearby: no apartment number. He must own a town house. So he wasn't a fake.

Noel had a sudden floating feeling. Here was an attractive, well-heeled, totally inoffensive person offering to help him out after only a few minutes. Of course in return Noel would be expected to put out: but lots of guys did that for nothing. Noel knew without having to ask that Flanders would keep him if he wanted.

It was common enough among most of the gays Noel had met. Rick had suggested it was the reason Noel was going up to Redfern's town house, not knowing that he was following orders, trying to see as much as he could of Dorrance, if only to placate an increasingly edgy and annoying Loomis.

But this business of being kept was an accepted part of gay life. Almost Socratic, the older, more established man helping his younger, less established lover. Noel had heard in the Grip of guys who'd been sent through medical school by older men, set up with trust funds by lovers needing tax rebates, made titular salaried heads of corporations, kept in style, often with nothing more than companionship required, then lavishly settled when the inevitably breakup occurred. Not wives. Not mistresses. And while often adopted, not quite sons either. Opportunities like this had never been open to Noel before; now they seemed to happen once a week.

Noel pocketed the business card.

"I will." Noel flashed what he hoped was a significant look, though he was certain he never would call Flanders or see him again. For the briefest moment he had the terrible certainty that Flanders—and not Dorrance at all—was the man Loomis was looking for. Sheer paranoia, he told himself.

Flanders had put the magazines back on the rack and was at the door.

"I'll take these," Noel said to the proprietor, who never looked up at Noel as he made change for the magazines.

"See you later," Flanders said cheerfully.

Noel half turned to acknowledge the good-bye. But Flanders had already stepped out.

By the time Noel reached the sidewalk, Flanders

was already on the next corner. Noel thought to catch up with him, if only to convince himself that Flanders really had nothing to do with Whisper or Mr. X. He had broken into a trot when there was a shout behind him.

He spun around, saw the storeowner waving what Noel immediately recognized as his jacket. Noel saw that Flanders had also stopped at the sound of the shout, perhaps waiting for Noel to catch up with him. Noel went back for the jacket.

He had just reached for it, and was thanking the storeowner, when he heard what sounded like a car careening out of control in front of them. Both men looked around, saw the big sedan suddenly appear from around the corner of Twenty-ninth Street, swerving wildly.

Before they could call out, they saw Flanders—in the middle of the street—also turn to the source of the loud noise. The sedan seemed to aim away from him. Its brakes screeched. Flanders threw up his hands to protect himself, then was spun around like a top as the fender brushed against him, and the car sped past and raced up the avenue. Flanders seemed to totter for a long second before he fell straight forward as though a giant hand had slapped him down.

Noel's heart and breath stopped.

"He's hit!" the storekeeper yelled, and pulled Noel along with him toward the corner.

Flanders was facedown in the gutter, his hands spread out on either side of him, not as if he had been breaking his fall, but as though he'd been knocked unconscious.

The storeowner bent down to him, muttering. Noel remained on the curb, petrified, staring at the blood as it poured out of Flanders' ears and nose in spurts, and from his forehead, which must have taken the second impact and concussed. In seconds a thin yellowish liquid began seeping out of Flanders' head, encircling the fast-growing puddle of deep crimson blood.

A crowd gathered quickly, and Noel was soon pushed back among them. Sirens were screaming toward them. Then someone was nudging Noel away from the corner.

"You'd better get out of here," the man said, as if in command, and in such an odd tone of voice that Noel stared at him. It was as if he knew something Noel did not.

Had Flanders just been assassinated before his very eyes?

"Go," the man said. Noel dumbly moved away.

9

Dorrance was in the big first-floor office of the Redfern town house. He greeted Noel more warmly than before, but with Dorrance that was like gradations in the temperature of a refrigerator.

"You're very conscientious," Dorrance said, taking the manila envelope and inspecting its contents.

"I didn't have anything else to do, and Rick was real swamped." It was two hours after the street-corner hit-and-run death, and though calm again, Noel couldn't get Flanders's image out of his mind.

Dorrance went through the papers thoroughly, but quickly, as though he had a photographic memory.

Noel used this time to study him again. Something about Dorrance repelled him, even if he weren't the mastermind of so much evil and mayhem. He was cold, efficient, extracautious, always polite and tactful, precise, well-spoken: nothing out of the ordinary, nothing that suggested more than a career diplomat or a successful bureaucrat. What was frightening was how unextraordinary he was, how dull, with his expected good grooming, his a la mode haircut and clothing. Unimaginative. That was it. Nothing unique about him; at least nothing apparent. He reminded Noel of a washed-out version of Wilbur Boyle, his department chairman. He and Boyle would get along very well, Noel thought, have a long, insincere conversation: they were of a type.

"It all seems to be in order," Dorrance said, getting up from his seat. He closed the envelope and locked it in a desk drawer. "Now, would you care for a drink?"

That was a first. "Sure," Noel said. Perhaps Loomis was right, the more Noel hung around the more he'd be noticed.

Dorrance ordered over the intercom, and they took the elevator up to the large living room on the main floor where Okku, the manservant, was just setting the drinks onto the coffee table.

"Help yourself to some music," Dorrance said. "I don't know what's what back there. Eric and Alana usually select it."

The stereo system Redfern had installed in the house was magnificent. It consisted of a preamplifier, radio tuner, two phonograph decks, two reel-to-reel tape decks, and a cassette deck attached to dozens of speakers for each floor, all hooked up to a central series of powerful amplifiers somewhere on the basement level, thousands of watts strong. All the equipment was touch-operated: shiny black surfaces and subtle, scarcely marked keys were all that you saw. All the electronics were Redfern manufacture—the latest, the most expensive, Noel guessed.

He chose an hour-long cassette copy of a tape just delivered to the Grip. He adjusted the volume and returned to where Dorrance was seated in a leather rocking chair, looking out at the back garden.

"Eric and Alana seem to be out today?" Noel asked, trying to make conversation.

"They're in Bermuda for a few days."

Noel sat down. "So that's why it seemed so quiet."

"They and their friends can get awfully noisy at times," Dorrance said, almost wistfully, Noel thought. "Tell me something about yourself, Noel."

Noel almost gagged on his vodka and tonic. Here it was.

"There's not much to tell."

"You're not a stupid young man. Educated. To what? College level?" Noel nodded yes. Dorrance went on. "Yet you're working in a bar, why?"

"You're the second person to ask me that today. You might call it disillusionment with the groves of academe, I suppose."

"Understandable," Dorrance said. But he didn't sound convinced. "Go on."

"Well, when I came out a few years ago, on the Coast," Noel lied, the words flowing out of him they were so well rehearsed, so often said recently, "I decided I was tired of the hypocrisy. I wanted to live my own way, and that didn't fit in too well. The last holdout was my lover, in Berkeley. When I walked out on him it broke the last tie to my old life. That's why I came to New York."

Dorrance was rapt. Bought it hook, line, and sinker, Noel thought.

"And you like being at the bar?"

"It's all right."

"You like one-to-one contact with the public?"

What was he getting at? "It isn't ideal of course," Noel said, "but until I figure out what is, it'll do."

"The reason I ask is . . . well, perhaps *you* can tell me why I'm asking all these questions?"

Noel wasn't certain whether he'd been led into a trap unaware, into some revelation he hadn't meant to make. For what seemed an eternity, he sat, holding his glass, looking at Dorrance, feeling like a block of ice that had been left to melt on the expensive carpets. What did Dorrance know? What the hell was he up to? Slow down, Noel told himself. Calm down. Answer him.

"I'm not sure I know what you mean. Unless it's that you're expanding and all."

"Exactly. We are expanding. Rick's club. Maybe another one on the Coast. You seem to me to be the kind of person we need. Conscientious, smart, popular, responsible."

"To do what?"

"Nothing right now, except what you're already doing. You're comfortable at the Grip. Others are comfortable with you there. We'll see how you work out and what best fits your particular talents. Then, when we're ready, you'll be ready, too. For the time being, stay at the bar. Rick will be away a lot. It'll need a steady hand."

"Right," Noel said.

"Good," Dorrance said.

That was it. No offer. And certainly nothing personal. Dorrance was like a corporation officer informing the junior executive he was being watched, put in line for promotion. Definitely all business. Nothing sexual. Not a hint of a come-on. Was Dorrance shy? Asexual? Or was he up to his ears in debt to Eric—the real money? Loomis would be disappointed. He'd expected so much from Noel. So far all he had was—what? A few photocopied papers? And this offer.

There was a call for Dorrance, and he took it on the library extension. Noel refilled his drink and nursed it, trying to find a way to present this new information to Loomis in a manner that would not totally devastate him.

"That was Eric and Alana," Dorrance said, several minutes later. "They both said hello."

"Both? I'm surprised to hear that," Noel said. "I didn't think Eric cared for me too much."

"Sometimes he shows how much he cares in odd ways," Dorrance said. "If you're done with your drink, I'll drive you downtown to the bar."

Not another word passed between them until Noel got out of the plush, dead-silent, powder-gray Bentley sedan in front of the Grip on West Street.

10

The following night Noel wasn't working at the bar. Until three o'clock the following afternoon, when he began an eight-hour shift at the Grip, he was free.

This sudden freedom, after three hectic months, made him extremely restless. He ought to work on his thesis, or go out and investigate more gay life for it. He still hadn't been to the Baths or any back-room clubs, and his experience of bars was limited to a few in the Village. But that wasn't what he wanted to-night.

Paul's words that last day of school kept coming back to him. He suddenly found that he did care, he cared very much. But at least he didn't have to worry what students would write about him on bathroom walls for the next three months; for the next eight months, unless Boyle changed his mind.

Boyle might be right. Look at Mirella Trent: one class this term, and that one a seminar for advanced students, most of whom were doing fieldwork, lectures at various other universities. Mirella Trent was on easy street.

He showered and then moped for the next hour, telling himself he was being foolish to waste a good night off, the first in months that he wouldn't be at the Grip, at Eric's, or working on his thesis.

"What's wrong with me tonight, anyway?" he asked

his image in the mirror. "I'm disturbed. Emotionally charged up. Over nothing. Nothing."

The minute he said it to himself, he knew it wasn't true. What he was, was horny. Just plain horny. If nothing else, the weeks of working in a gay bar had conferred that much physical honesty on him. Once Noel accepted it, he felt immediately better.

He resolved to go have a light dinner uptown at a well-known singles bar on the East Side. The place served mediocre food but was known to attract young professionals of both sexes, who, like himself tonight, admitted they were looking for lovemaking with no entanglements.

> *All I want is a one night affair.*
> *Hit and run son-of-a-gun.*
>
> *Don't want to love you*
> *Don't want to make you my wife;*
> *Don't want to see you*
> *everyday for the rest of my life.*

The words of Butler's song came back to him with renewed force as he shaved, they were so applicable to his situation. He sang the song, making up new words, skipping or slurring over those he couldn't recall, as he dressed.

He felt a little odd in pressed slacks, sports jacket, and an open-necked shirt as he hailed a cab up Madison Avenue. It seemed too dressy, too formal, compared to the jeans and T-shirts and body shirts he'd been wearing lately, with their easy, formfitting grip.

The place was packed when he arrived, and Noel had to wait at the bar for a half hour before a sneering waiter deigned to show him to a minuscule table in a corner. By then he'd already begun his second vodka martini and taken a look around.

There were women all right, but in twos and threes or coupled with men. Several noticed he was looking at them: work at the Grip had taught him what constituted a heavy cruise—it worked on either sex. But the petite blonde with her movie-star face and trim body seemed more interested in her spinach and bacon salad and her dowdy female companion than in Noel. Ditto for the sultry, long-limbed brunette facing him, whose every gesture said, "You can look but you can't touch."

Twice during his meal, Noel took the longest possible route to the men's room, where he stood reading pseudointellectual graffiti until he figured it was time to come out again. Each time he saw another woman who might be picked up, if something about her were more inviting, more alluring. Each time he returned to his corner table alone.

Then it was eleven o'clock. Surely some of these women knew the place's reputation; one of them must be on the make, too! But the one time a fairly attractive curly-haired, reddish-blonde sauntered past him and then back again, all he could do was mutter a halfhearted hello and look out the window.

It was then that Noel realized he was comparing them to another woman. One's eyes were too light. One's hips too stout. One too made up. The blonde was inane looking. The brunette too self-conscious. But who was he using as an ideal? Monica? Maybe Mirella? No.

Noel was asking for another coffee when a group passed in front of the restaurant and lingered a few feet away from where he sat. When a woman with dark, lustrous hair became suddenly visible, Noel almost stood up. But then she turned toward the window, and of course it wasn't—who? Alana! How could it be? She was in Bermuda. Dorrance had said so just yesterday.

The group moved off, and left Noel with a depressing thought: he'd been comparing all these women to one of the world's highest-paid fashion models, a woman who smelled of roses and lilacs, who lived with another man. And who didn't care for him. Noel called for his check.

By the time he reached his apartment, the depression really hit. But he still felt restless, frustrated.

He could cab across town, pick up one of the numerous prostitutes who walked the Minnesota Strip off Forty-second street—so called because so many of them were from the Midwest. Or he could try to settle down to work. Or take an ice-cold shower and forget about it.

He opted for the shower. He had just turned on the water full force and was stepping in, when the phone rang.

"Hi," a man's voice said, "what are you up to?"

Noel couldn't place the caller.

"I was about to take a shower."

"Yeah? Wish I were there."

Now he did place the voice. "Randy?"

"Took you long enough to figure it out."

"We've never spoken over the phone before."

"I thought maybe you forgot who I was."

"No, I didn't forget." How could I forget? Noel wanted to say.

"I was at the Grip a few minutes ago. Buddy told me it was your night off. I figured you'd be out on the town."

Buddy, huh? Noel had been trying to avoid him ever since that night he and Miguel had followed them to Little Larry's place. So far, Vega had stayed out of Noel's way, doing nothing in the least bit suspicious. How did Buddy know about him and Randy?

"I'm just here at home," Noel said. "You know Buddy?"

"We all sort of work together, right?" Randy said. "We know each other. I wouldn't say we were real friendly, if that's what you're asking."

"Just curious," Noel said. "He say anything about me?"

"Only that you were off tonight."

A long pause, then Randy said, "Well, I just called to say hello and to see what you were up to."

It was evident from his tone of voice he had something else on his mind. Noel waited.

"You're not mad at me, are you?" Nerone suddenly asked. "You know, about what happened? I know I got a little carried away. I'm not usually so aggressive like that."

"That's all right."

"You're not busy or anything, are you?"

"No."

"I just scored some dynamite grass, and I'm right in your neighborhood. Why don't you invite me up?"

"Really good grass?"

"The grass is fine. What I'd really like is a replay of that pool scene the other night, what do you say?"

Noel thought fast. Was he supposed to believe Randy just wanted to make love with him again, or was there something more? Maybe Vega had put Randy up to it. Making sure that this time Randy would blow Noel's cover if he didn't say yes. For whatever reasons Vega had. Buddy must know how close to Dorrance Nerone was, or maybe still was. Word would get back to Mr. X fast enough, unless Noel came up with a really good excuse, and it seemed a little late in this conversation for that. It was a test, another goddamn test! And whoever was responsible for the test—Vega, Mr. X, whoever—knew that Noel was going to fail it unless he played by the rules: and the rules said Randy Nerone got laid by Noel tonight whether Noel liked it or not.

"Are you still there?" Randy prompted him.

"Yeah, still here," Noel said. "Sorry, thought I heard someone knocking on the door." It was a lame excuse, but better than none.

"Should I come by?" Nerone asked. "Or what?"

The bitch of it, Noel thought, was that Randy seemed to be innocent of how he was being used by Vega, by Mr. X. Simple, guileless, oversexed Randy

would feel a little hurt if Noel rejected him tonight.
Whereas Noel would be putting his noose in a neck if
he did.

"Sure, Randy," he said, "come on by. I'd really like
to see you."

He could hear Nerone's relief and pleasure in his
sign-off. He gave his address, then shut off the
shower, changed into a pair of worn jeans and a T-
shirt, threaded a tape on his reel-to-reel, dimmed the
lights, and waited for the downstairs buzzer to ring.

For a moment he thought to call Loomis and find
out how he could get out of this. But after their last
misunderstanding over Randy, he already knew what
Loomis's position would be. "Lots of guys do it,
Lure."

When the doorman buzzed up to announce his
guest, Noel stood in front of his mirror. He was supposed to be the Lure, the Bait. Look at me now. I'm
the one who's caught on the hook: anywhere I turn
I'm caught on it.

He hoped Randy Nerone's grass was strong tonight.
He was going to need it.

11

═══════════════════

"Is Randy Nerone working for Whisper?" . .

"Whatever gave you that idea?" Loomis asked.

"Is he? Or isn't he?" Noel insisted.

"You know, Lure, you're getting to be neurotically
suspicious."

"And you're getting to be psychotically demanding."

There was a long pause. When Loomis spoke again, it was in a tone of voice that Noel had come to recognize: annoyed-and-determined-not-to-show-it.

"Why don't we start from the beginning again?"

"Fine with me. Is Randy Nerone working for Whisper?"

"If I tell you he isn't, will you believe me?"

"Probably not," Noel admitted.

"Then why should I bother?"

It was Noel's turn to be silent. *Because I'm sleeping with him,* he wanted to say, but couldn't bring himself to do it. Because Randy is the only one I'm sleeping with. He's my only cover, my only credential that I'm just a normal, man-loving homosexual. I'm doing it despite myself, overcoming long-ingrained habits and ideas about sex and about my own sexuality. I'm as disturbed by it when it's easy with Randy as when it's difficult. It scares me as much as Mr. X and his henchmen do. It's my only security. So it damn well had better be security. *That's* why I have to know if Randy Nerone is working for Whisper.

"Are you still there, Lure?"

"I'm here."

"Let's not argue," Loomis said. "You're tense. I'm tense."

"I'm not tense. I'm just not happy with all your demands."

"What demands? That you go to a party that some people would kill to get to? What's so difficult about that?"

"*I said* I was going to the party at Bar Sinister." That was the name of the new Dorrance club Chafee was opening.

"Fine. What's the problem? Stick close to Dorrance and be ready to report tomorrow night in full detail."

"If I'm sticking so close to Dorrance, who's going to be watching Redfern? I'm sure he's the hatchet man or something like that."

"He scare you?"

Noel didn't like that question.

"Because if he does," Loomis said, "don't worry about him. He's just a big-mouth, rich-kid fag. All talk."

"I'm not so sure of that."

"Because of that model he's hanging around with?"

"I'm sure he's putting it to her," Noel said. "And . . . other things."

"So he's bisexual. It's very chic to be bisexual this year. I read all about it in *Time* magazine. Good night, Lure. And, Lure?"

"Yes?"

"Don't ask so many fucking questions you don't want answered."

12

The party Loomis talked about was to be held at Redfern's town house before Bar Sinister officially opened its doors to its select membership.

In addition to Noel and the other members of Mr. X's growing conglomerate—Matthews, Malchuck, Goldberg, et al.—another hundred or so guests had been invited, friends, co-workers, and hangers-on of Redfern, Alana, and their friends.

When Noel and Randy Nerone arrived it was after midnight and the party was in full swing. The two main floors of the town house, the outside terrace, and the pool floor were spread with men and women in bizarre and garish costumes working up toward the time when Bar Sinister—an after-hours club—would open its doors for late-night perversions and promised

grotesqueries which would not end until long after
dawn.

Since Noel had entered this scene, he lived more
and more at night, usually not getting home until after
4:00 A.M. He slept during the day, waking only at one
of two in the afternoon. Just a few months before, half
his day would have been over by then. Now, he lived
in a night world.

"Should we go straight up to the pool for old times'
sake?" Randy asked as he and Noel got into the elevator.

"You go, if you want." He had to find Dorrance.

The party was audible long before the elevator
doors opened up onto the second floor. In the library a
hastily constructed DJ's booth with double turntables
had been set up. Every speaker in the house was emit-
ting the incessant beat of funky rock music.

"There they are," Matthews greeted Noel and Randy's entrance to the main floor, "the two beauties!
Never since Castor and Pollux has there been . . . or
was it Damon and Pythias? Oh, who gives a flying
fuck? Who's got that Dust?"

They managed to elude Matthews, who was swaying wildly toward them, and Noel headed Randy up
the side stairs to the lounge overlooking the crowded
living room.

Downstairs, the sectional had been redivided, set
more or less in a shallow rectangle on one side of the
big room. The rest was given over to dancing and
general milling about.

"I'm not entirely sure I'm ready for tonight," Noel
said, looking over the many heads downstairs for
Dorrance's close-cropped gray one.

"Here, have a hit of this," Randy said, offering Noel
a slim, tightly rolled joint. As usual he was in a good
mood, his body vibrating against the railing as he
looked over the assemblage with a sort of proud pro-
prietorship. Noel wished he could feel as comfortable.

Often as he came here, he always felt under surveillance, his every action monitored.

Having missed Dorrance downstairs, Noel looked around the balcony floor. Could he not have come to this shindig? Unlikely.

Alana appeared from her sitting room, arm in arm with a tall, willowy black woman who inclined her stunning head low to whisper in Alana's lovely ear. The woman wore a space-fantasy costume, silver lamé halter top slashed in front to her navel, girdled with a thickly wrapped belt that looked like a leather bull-whip, and turning into skintight lamé slacks right down to her ebony patent-leather boots. Her hair had been pulled back from her face and gathered by some kind of silver pin. In comparison, Alana looked like a little girl, her skintight black leather slacks disappearing into similar boots, her loose-fitting, sheer blouson softly feminine next to the hard glitter of her companion. As they appproached the balcony, Noel could see Alana's blouse was cut almost as low as the black woman's—the skin between her breasts looked as soft and white as satin.

Alana seemed genuinely delighted to see Noel and Randy.

"Now you must meet someone very special to me," she said to her friend as they came up to the men. Noel wondered if Alana were gay too, or bisexual.

"This is my great *amie*, Veena. And this is Noel and Randy." She pronounced the second name Rondee. "Veena Scarborough is the wonderful disco chanteuse," she explained to Noel.

Veena detached herself from Alana, put her hands on her hips, pursed her mouth, arched one curving eyebrow, and stared intensely through her silver-sheen makeup, in the pose she had made famous on the cover of her first platinum album.

"Oooh! I just love white meat," she purred.

Randy laughed. Noel felt like a fly that had just inadvertently landed on a Venus's-flytrap.

"And you two mean to tell me you're together, too!" Veena added, sidling up to them and instantly encircling them with what appeared to be several arms and legs. "Why, honeys, I would pay, and I do mean cold fucking cash, to see you two get each other off. I swear I would."

Unlike Noel, who was paralyzed by the attentions of the Amazon, Randy returned her caresses in joking kind.

"Catch us later at Bar Sinister," he said, and casually popped one large mahogany breast out of its silver lamé casing.

"Let go!" she protested, slapping his hand away. "You don't want none of that. And anyway that ain't no ordinary tit, you know."

She pulled away, but left her breast bared.

"Let's blow some coke, honeys," Veena said, and commenced to search through a silver lamé reticule that hung from her thong belt. Finally she found a little turquoise pillbox, and opened it to reveal a tiny mountain of glittering powder.

Noel looked at Alana, who was smiling like a fond mother over the antics of a favorite child.

The cocaine was passed from Randy to Noel, who in turn offered it to Alana. While she sniffed at it delicately from a tiny Art Nouveau spoonlet, Noel stared at her a long time, until she looked up at him. But a second later, her eyes took on a sudden high glaze from the drug, and she laughed.

"They won't let me in no back room clubs no more, honeys," Veena was complaining to Randy. "And I can't blame them. Why I got me a throat like a boa. It just destroys those poor boys," and she laughed. Waving the pillbox in the air, she pulled Randy over and began a slow grind to the music.

"Nice party," Noel said, through the fine, misty haze of the cocaine.

"You don't care for my friend?" Alana asked.

He shrugged.

"Well?" she insisted.

"If you really want to know, I think she's weird."

Alana smiled. "Eric is right. You are a prude. I love Veena. She's wonderfully funny. Like a cartoon. She takes nothing seriously. Nothing at all."

"She doesn't have to. She's had a half-dozen hit albums. She's filthy with money."

"And you don't care for that?"

"Not really."

"Then you must abhor me. I'm filthy with money, too. How much do you think I earn standing around looking like a mannequin?"

"I never thought about it."

"Sometimes, I earn four, five hundred dollars in an hour. You should model, too, you know. If you want to be rich so badly."

"I never said I wanted to be."

"Oh, you didn't say it. But you would like it. You are jealous of us, because we do so well." She stepped back, looking at him, and teasingly put up one finger as though she were an artist looking at a newly painted picture. "I think you are the perfect size. A perfect size forty. Yes?"

"So?"

"You would do well. They make clothing to perfect sizes. Usually that size."

"And be looked at by everyone?"

"You are looked at by everyone already, no?"

"It's not the same thing."

"You are very glum. You are in a bad mood. You hate my party, don't you?" she suddenly said. Before he could answer, she had turned from him. "You depress me. Good-bye."

"Wait!" Noel followed her, but she had floated down the stairs and was just another dark head in the mass of people. "Damn it!" he said. It seemed that nothing he ever did around her was right.

He turned around again, saw Randy and Veena sitting in a corner: she was telling his future by looking at his palms, he was laughing at almost everything she said. They were enjoying themselves.

Looking out over the railing again, Noel spotted Dorrance at last, his silver hair shining like a beacon from his spot in a corner near the doors leading to the screening room. With him were two younger men, both dressed in heavy black leather outfits, engineer's boots, leather pants, body-fitting leather vests over bare chests. One was dark-haired with a full beard. The other, slightly heavier, was fairer, with a big brush mustache, and a long thin scar running like a crescent from his left eyebrow to his lips. Unlike some of the other guests whom Noel had seen before, these two looked like rough characters. X's henchmen?

"You like that?"

The voice alone made Noel stiffen: Eric.

"You know what I like," Noel said, and nodded past Eric's face to where Randy and Veena were sitting.

"The nigger?"

"Fuck yourself," Noel said nonchalantly and turned to check out Dorrance and his pals again.

"The dark one is Bill Solomon. The other is Estes Dewhurst," Eric said, leaning close to Noel and following his glance. "They specialize in threeways. Their pet is something called number eighty-seven. Both of them screw you at the same time."

"They look like SS torturers," Noel said.

"Stockbrokers."

"What?"

"Solomon, Dewhurst, Chatto and Dine. One of the biggest new houses on Wall Street. Only five years old, but with one of the snazziest portfolios you ever laid eyes on. Jimmy Chatto's here somewhere, and so is Janet Dine."

"Thanks for the tip. I don't have anything to invest."

Noel felt that Eric was looking at him very closely. Probably deciding whether Noel believed him or not. Stockbrokers. They could, of course, be stockbrokers. One rule he'd learned early was that, on the scene,

people weren't exactly—or sometimes even anything at
all—like what they appeared to be.

"You must know a lot of important people," Noel
said. "Rock stars. Movie stars. Politicians."

"I do. Bankers. Multinational executives."

"I'm impressed."

"You'll find them all here tonight, and later on at
the new club."

Noel wanted to get away from Eric, to get together
with Dorrance. He stood up and tried to get Randy's
attention. "And what am I supposed to do? Feel gay
pride or something?"

Redfern stood up, too, and blocked Noel's view.
"You know, I really don't get you. I just don't."

"There's nothing to get," Noel said. "Don't worry
about it." He started to move around Eric, but Eric
grabbed his arm hard.

"Is that today's lesson, Professor Cummings?"

Noel felt for a second as though the balcony had
given way beneath him. He fought to regain footing.
Despite the look of obvious triumph on Eric's face, he
managed to say, "Excuse me, will you? I see my friend
is calling me."

Eric let go of his arm, and Noel walked over to
where Randy had indeed seen his signal and stood up,
feeling, as he crossed the ten feet to Randy, as though
a pistol were pointed at his back.

Randy was still talking to someone who'd joined
him and Veena. His right arm came out and reached
casually around Noel's waist, pulling him in close to
his own body. And, for perhaps the first time in his
life, Noel felt he had never needed another person's
contact, another person's caress so much, no matter
how automatic it may have been on Randy's part. For
a second he'd been falling. Now he felt grounded,
safe. So safe he was able to look around. Eric had disappeared.

"You been smoking Dust over there?" Randy asked
after a few minutes.

"No. Why? Do I look bad?"

"A little. Did he give you a hard time about me?"

"Eric? Why should he?"

Randy hesitated. "You didn't know?"

Noel searched the man's large dark eyes for an answer.

"Before you and I met, Eric and I were . . . well, it never really worked out and I thought he might trash me to you."

The information startled Noel. It seemed all wrong, but he couldn't say why. Yet he didn't disbelieve Randy.

"He didn't say a word about you. You mean you and Dorrance . . . ?" Noel had to straighten this out. "You had argued and all that evening."

Randy laughed and his arm hugged Noel closer. "Come on. Don't play head games with me. Dorrance is an old man. You didn't really believe that?"

"I guess not," Noel said, knowing for certain now.

"It was Eric. But I couldn't get off on him. Too rough for me."

Noel stared at Randy: inside him levers began to click click click click like one of those slot machines in a Las Vegas casino. But they all stopped short, and no answer came up.

"You have that look in your eyes again," Randy said.

"What look?"

"I don't know what it means. Sometimes it means you're about a hundred miles away. Sometimes I think it means you don't really like me."

"You know I like you. You're my friend, aren't you?"

"I don't know. Sometimes I really don't, Noel."

"You did a few hours ago," Noel said, reminding Randy of their lovemaking before the party. He needed this man at this moment, not only for the safety he felt with him, but because Randy was going to tell Noel something very important. Noel was sure of it.

"Yeah! That was crazy!" Randy said. "Let's go downstairs and boogie."

"Didn't I see Dorrance here a minute ago?" Noel asked. "I wanted to say hello to him."

"I think he went upstairs with some other people. The roof is open tonight," Randy said. "Don't you want to dance?"

"Later. Do you mind?"

"Do you want me to stay down here?"

"What do you think, that I don't want to be seen with you?" Noel asked. "Come on."

Noel was glad of Randy's company a few minutes later when the elevator doors opened on the top floor. There were about a dozen people on the roof garden: a man and two women off to one side, and the others opposite, grouped around Dorrance who was talking with unusual intensity, Noel thought.

Not knowing the others, Noel and Randy advanced toward Dorrance.

"It's got to be done soon," he heard one man urge. It was one of the two leather-clad stockbroker/lovers Eric had pointed out to him earlier.

Others agreed with him. None of them noticed Noel or Randy, they were so intent on what they were saying.

"It will be done soon," Dorrance assured them. "But Eric absolutely believes that we have to wait until the time is right."

"It's right now," one man said.

"We've waited long enough," the other leather number said, disgusted.

"You'll just have to wait a little longer," Dorrance said. He was facing away from the others, and was the first to spot Noel and Randy, who had stopped a few feet away from the group.

"It's long overdue already," one more voice put in.

Dorrance gave him a stern glance, then said in another tone of voice, "Some friends are joining us. Noel. Randy. You all know each other?"

The others turned as though on cue.

"Hey, hot guy," the blond, leather-dressed man said to Randy.

"We'll talk later," Dorrance said, low, to one of the other men.

In seconds, the group dispersed and reformed around Noel and Randy. Introductions were made, hands shaken all around. Noel watched helplessly as Dorrance excused himself and went over to the others on the roof, talked to them briefly, then disappeared down a stairway next to the pool door.

13

A half hour later Noel was no closer to Dorrance. Loomis would have a fit it he found out. He had to get to him, if only for a moment. If the party *were* seeded with Whisper operatives, they'd report that he and Mr. X were seen together.

Noel excused himself from the small group Randy had gathered and began searching for Dorrance. Here and there he came across familiar faces—people he'd seen at the Grip, some whose photos he'd seen in magazines and newspapers. That man with the shock of platinum hair had to be Jerry Kovacs, the avant-garde playwright, and Noel was certain the pretty, chubby girl in the corner, with a slim black boy on either side of her, was María Antonia Díaz-Juárez, the tin heiress.

He'd combed the main floor and was climbing up to the dining room when he spotted Dorrance by the elevators, just pushing the button and checking his watch.

By the time Noel got there, Dorrance had descended. Noel took the second elevator down.

Two couples, one straight, one gay, were coming in the front door when Noel got out on the first floor. They were snorting cocaine and groping each other. He went to the office and knocked. No answer. The door was locked. He knocked again, louder. Still no answer.

Maybe Dorrance had gone up to the pool again.

He got into the elevator and pressed five. It must have been prepushed by someone else; it went down to the basement.

"Hell!" Noel said when the door opened to the strange, dark lower floor. But a door was ajar. He let the elevator close behind him, and pushed the door fully open.

He was just in time to see the front of Dorrance's Bentley slide up the steep driveway, stop for a second at the street, then take off, before the automatic garage doors began to close again.

Where was he going? Not to the Bar Sinister. With all the people here going over, too, he surely would have taken a few of them with him.

Noel closed the hallway door, found the wall switch for the lights, and stood for a minute thinking. He ought to follow Dorrance, find out where he was going. If he were leaving the party, where he went would be important.

But how to follow him? Getting a cab at this hour, outside the door, would be near impossible. He might wait fifteen minutes before an empty one arrived.

He looked at the low-slung Mercedes SL coupe, then bent down and peered inside. The keys were in the ignition. It was a signal. He shouldn't ask questions.

Without another thought, Noel got into the car and turned on the ignition. In front of him, the garage doors automatically opened. It was a minute before he had located all the necessary switches and buttons to operate the car. Then he drove up the ramp and out, noticing, with satisfaction, the doors close behind him, and hoping no one had seen him leave.

Two blocks east, he spotted the big Bentley. Noel decided to hang on at a distance, in case Dorrance recognized the pale, metallic blue coupé. It was low enough that he could easily hide behind most sedans and keep the Bentley in view with only one car between them.

Dorrance swung downtown. Noel followed.

At Sixty-third Street, the Bentley took the short, curving ramp onto the Fifty-ninth Street Bridge. Noel opted for the same lane, keeping two cars between them. The Mercedes took the hundred-and-twenty-degree curve as though it were a straightaway. It handled like a dream.

At the end of the bridge, Dorrance went through the various turnways onto the road leading to the Long Island Expressway. Noel stayed about an eighth of a mile behind in the same lane for the next ten minutes or so. The highway was empty, fast moving.

Examining the side pockets of the seat, Noel found a stick of grass and several cassettes. Keith Jarrett's *Köln Concert* was handmarked: probably taped from records. Noel popped it into the deck opening at his knee height and was serenaded in quadrasonics by the funky, pristine piano.

A minute later Dorrance turned onto the Grand Central Parkway. Noel swung the SL from the third lane onto the service road with utter ease. Jarrett's piano was building a fantasia out of isolated chords like silver.

He almost missed the turnoff Dorrance took, and had to cut fast in front of another car to take the exit ramp leading up. The coupé lunged forward like a great cat let off its leash.

At the end of the ramp, Noel slowed down to a stop. He was atop a road overlooking the parkway, with an unimpeded view of Flushing Meadow Park slung out below, the lake glittering blackly in the necklace of tiny lights from the surrounding street lamps.

This was a residential area: medium-sized houses, some single, some attached. Not too many cars on this road.

The Bentley was ahead, turning off the service road at a major thoroughfare. Noel followed. The road narrowed, rose and fell like a ribbon in the wind for the next mile and a half.

The next turnoff was sudden: up a hilly road left. Noel shot past as Dorrance made a sharp right into a driveway. The Mercedes glided to a stop. Noel looked in the rearview mirror.

Dorrance got out of the Bentley, locked it, and walked up the stone stairs of a large, white, two-story frame house with dark gables and roof.

Noel waited, double-parked on the silent street, expecting Dorrance to come out any minute and drive off again. But when the front door opened again, it was a young girl who came out, unlocked the car, and drove it into the garage alongside the house.

Noel waited another five minutes, feeling increasingly nervous as a face peered out of the lighted window of the house he was parked alongside. He hoped the observer wouldn't call the police.

As no one came out of the white frame house, Noel slowly backed up until he was parallel to it. There was a brass address plate: 57–38.

Lights blazed from both floors.

Noel inched forward to where the winding street crossed another road. There he swung a U turn, and again glided past the house. The downstairs lights were off now, only one on upstairs. It was two o'clock. The SL coasted down to the main road, where he spotted the street sign hidden high in the foliage of tall trees—Edgeware Road.

"I know where Mr. X lives," he said out loud, as he swerved back onto the Grand Central Parkway:

"57–38 Edgeware Road, in Queens. I know. I know," he repeated, then flipped the cassette to listen to Jarrett's moody playing until he was back in Manhattan.

There must have been a sensing device between the Mercedes and the garage door: it swung open as soon as he sidled over the edge of the down ramp.

He drove in, got out, watched the door close, and turned to leave.

Then the garage lights went out.

Noel remained still for a second. Did he hear someone else there? Or was that his own breathing magnified in the closed, echoing hollow space?

He took three steps to the door into the hallway, groped for the handle, turned it.

Another hand covered his on the doorknob, gripped it hard.

The lights went on again. Noel blinked, pulled his hand away, and fought down a dozen sudden fears. Before he could regain his vision, he'd been pushed up against the metal door.

"You think you're funny, don't you, Professor Cummings?" Eric said, his face inches away from Noel's.

Noel had seen that look before: in the eyes of wolves about to attack defenseless prey. He went rigid.

"I wanted a drive."

"Sure."

"So I took it."

"That's my car, you know."

"I brought it back, didn't I?"

"This time."

Noel's initial fear was beginning to dissipate in his anger at Eric. "You'd never miss it," he said. "A twenty-five-thousand-dollar car to you is like a Three Musketeers bar to anyone else."

"Where did you go?"

Noel heard the edge in his voice, but brazened it out. "For a drive."

"Where?"

Odometers didn't lie. Redfern would check the one on the Benz.

Staten Island. Jersey. Back over the bridge. Around."

"You're lying."

Eric's hand was pressing a fist-sized lump through his ribs. But Noel couldn't see any weapon. If it came to it, they were evenly matched.

"You're lying," Redfern repeated. "I know you are."

Redfern was dangerous, maybe even a lunatic. But—close as he was to Dorrance—he had to be dealt with now, or he'd never let up on Noel. He'd bully him any chance he had. And that wouldn't help Noel to get close to Dorrance. No way.

Slowly, calmly, Noel said, "Why don't you go fuck yourself, man?"

Eric moved away. The pressure was suddenly lifted off Noel's chest. Then, pivoting quickly, Eric slapped him backhand across the face.

Noel recovered from the blow and dove headfirst into Eric's middle, slamming him against the side of the Mercedes. Eric grabbed him, they wrestled, fell onto the garage floor, rolling, grabbing recklessly at each other, until Noel suddenly let go and managed to get to his feet. Eric sprang up. They faced each other, arms and hands out, circling slowly, eyeing each other's throats, faces, heads, eyes, mouths—anything that would be soft and hurt.

Eric put down his hands and straightened up.

Certain this was a ruse, Noel kept on guard.

"I don't believe it. I just don't fucking believe it," Eric said in a strangely broken voice. He turned away from Noel and walked over to the garage door, where he continued to repeat the words, punching one hand over and over into the open palm of the other. When he was done, he turned around again.

"Why do you do these things to me?" Eric said. "Why? Only one other person in my entire goddamned life can irritate me to the point where I want to smash him, really smash him. You know who? My father. That's right. Go on laugh, big sociology professor. Laugh."

Noel straightened up, hoping it wasn't a mistake.

"I'm not laughing."

"You don't deny it, then? Being a college teacher?"

"Why should I? Everyone knows it."

"Then why work at a bar?"

"That's my business."

"There you go again, goddamn you! Can't you be human for one fucking minute?"

They glared at each other, and suddenly all the levers that had been going click click before with Randy, all clicked into place. Jackpot. Eric was Mr. X. Not Dorrance. It was Eric. And here he was, facing Noel and asking for something, trust, or honesty—something. And if he didn't get it—what then? A razor blade across the eyes?

"I'm doing a book on gay life. That's why. The university press at my school is going to publish it. It's long overdue. If I don't do it, I probably won't get tenure. I'm even on sabbatical next term to finish it. It's a view of gay life seen from the inside. I've gotten a grant to help me with it. If I don't do it my career is washed up. It's going to be a breakthrough study."

He could see Eric was wavering.

"You chose it because you're gay?"

"My department chairman chose it."

"But you are gay?"

"More or less."

"Which? More? Or less?"

"Ask Randy Nerone. What do you think we do together? Read Margaret Mead to each other?"

"No. I guess not."

"I suppose I'm bisexual," Noel said. Eric seemed to believe him; he wasn't going to fuck it up now. "Like you. Like everyone probably."

"Is that what your book is going to be about?"

"No. It's going to be about social structures of the

gay scene and its imitations and adaptations of general cultural mores."

Eric stared at him. Something was going on inside his mind; Noel wished he knew what.

"All right." He shrugged, seemed defeated for the minute. "All right. Let's go upstairs and clean up."

Noel tried not to emit the sigh of relief he felt. He put out his hand: "Shake?"

"No," Eric said, "that would imply trust. I don't trust you."

"I'm sorry about that," Noel replied. It was the truth. If Eric really was Mr. X, he needed Eric's trust.

Out of the dimly lit garage they saw how soiled and torn their clothing was from the scuffle. As he pressed for the elevator, Eric said, "The last person like you that I trusted nearly got me killed."

Noel tensed again.

"Your father?"

"Get in," Eric said, as the elevator door opened. "No. I was never infatuated with my father." His eyes searched Noel's for something. Noel couldn't be sure what—sympathy, mockery?

"What happened to him, the guy you trusted?"

The elevator opened onto the second floor. The party burst in on them. Eric quickly pressed the button to close it. It was quieter on the third floor, although noise from below still reached them. Eric led Noel to the door opposite Alana's room. This suite also had a sitting room, bedroom, dressing room, and bath.

"You'd better change that shirt," he said, fingering a long tear in Noel's shirt. "Here. This one." He held up an antique Viyella Black Watch plaid that picked up Noel's coloring. "It looks good. Keep it."

Eric washed his hands and face at the little sink, and he, too, changed clothing. As they were stepping out of the room he turned to Noel. "I think Randy is over by the DJ's booth."

"You didn't answer my question."

"What question?"

"What happened to the last guy you trusted?"

"What do you think?" Eric said with a half smile.
"He was murdered."

14

"*You already knew where Dorrance lives?*"

"We've known for a month," Loomis said flatly.

"Why didn't you tell me? You let me go after him
and almost get myself killed trying to return the goddamn car."

"Who told you to go after him?"

"You said to stick close to him."

"At the party. I didn't say to go home with him."

"Not exactly in those terms, but you said I was exactly his type which was why I was chosen in the first
place."

"Mr. X's type. It looks like Dorrance isn't Mr. X
after all. Redfern is. You said so yourself."

"I didn't say he was. I said it seemed more likely."

Loomis refused to budge. "One of them probably is
Mr. X. Right?"

"Agreed."

"Dorrance doesn't look at you, couldn't care less
about you, even though you are precisely Mr. X's
type. Right? We watch Dorrance every night for a
month. He goes home to his white frame house in
Queens and doesn't come out again until morning
when he returns to Redfern's. He has a wife, a teenage
daughter, an older son in school somewhere in Indi-
ana. Right?"

"If you say so."

"I do. Whereas we can't even begin to trace Redfern's comings and goings. Where is he today?"

"Eric? In France. Cannes. That's what Randy said. Eric and Alana were going to the Riviera for a week or two."

"That's what I mean. Now, Redfern is a noted sadist, right? He's rich. Whereas Dorrance seems to be nothing more than an employee—an administrator. So, Redfern must be the silent partner, no?"

"Could be."

"Let's go slower. He's just opened Bar Sinister. You went to the opening night party. Do you know who the owner of Bar Sinister is?"

"Chaffee?"

"No, Chaffee's just another employee, as you are. It's owned by Altamira Enterprises, located in West Hollywood, California."

"The company opened the new club, I don't know for certain that Eric did," Noel corrected.

"He's suspicious of you, has been from the beginning," Loomis went on. "Yet he admits he's infatuated with you. Right? Also Randy Nerone, who is your exact type, was his boyfriend. And you told me he murdered someone. What else do you need?"

"He said the guy was murdered. He didn't say he murdered him."

"What's the difference?"

"There's a difference. Why all of a sudden is Eric X and Dorrance not?"

"Because one and one never made three, but one and one and one again *do* make three," Loomis said. "That's why. Now what is this offer he made you?"

"I'm to leave the Grip and work for Eric. I'll be going with him and Alana on trips, chauffering them, helping to entertain, going out with them to parties, working out with him down in the gym. Sort of a glorified steward and companion."

"And you'll live in the house?"

"On the fourth floor, in a guest suite: bedroom, sitting room, dressing room, bath. Except on my day off, once a week, when I can either remain in the house or not."

"It's perfect, Lure, perfect. Exactly where you should be: in his house, on the spot, to tell me anything that's going on, as it's going on. How much is he paying you?"

"Five hundred dollars a week."

"You were doing what, about three hundred clear at the bar?"

"Three-fifty. Look! I don't give a shit about the money. I don't like this setup."

"You're scared, Lure. You go and do a stupid, fake, courageous asshole stunt like stealing his goddamn car to follow Dorrance but you won't live with him, which is necessary, even for a good salary? I say you're scared. Scared shitless."

"Maybe I am. . . . I won't have any privacy."

"You'll have privacy. You just told me you have a suite on the guest floor. Who else is there?"

"No one right now."

"Try it, Lure. Tell Redfern you'll try it a few weeks. Then stick to him like a second skin."

"I won't go to bed with him."

"Who asked you to?"

"He did. Sort of. . . ."

"Better that you don't. String him along. Keep him dancing thinking about it. Think of it, Lure—fancy cars, movie stars, parties, vacations in the sun. Little snot probably has houses all over the place. When are they coming back?"

"Next week sometime."

"Tell him you'll try it out, all right, Lure?"

"I'll think about it," Noel said.

15

"*You already know the garage,*" Eric said, tapping the metal door. "You'll be given a key. It's generally kept locked from the inside."

"To prevent your guests from stealing cars?" Noel asked.

Eric ignored the remark. "These doors lead to the laundry, spare servants' rooms, a storage space, room for air conditioning and heating equipment," he said, tapping doors on either side of the corridor until they arrived at a double door straight ahead. "This is the gym."

When he flipped on the light they were on a balcony overlooking a room the width of the house and about one third its length. When the foundations had been put in, this floor had been dug one story lower. Rows of high windows opposite where they stood provided good light and some ventilation.

The gym was completely equipped. One section had barbells, rods, weights, and several pulley systems for back, shoulder, and leg exercises built into the wall and floor. Here were four press benches, a series of wall-height mirrors, and caramel-colored carpeting underfoot. Elsewhere the floor was wood parquet for resilience. Perhaps a half-dozen ropes hung from the ceiling, bound in twos and threes. Another pair had rings and coils on sliding loops for aerial gymnastics. There were also padded horses, parallel bars, and a pile of heavy mats for tumbling. An open door at ground level led behind them to the pale blue tile of a large bathroom.

"I've never seen such a well-equipped gym, not a private one, anyway," Noel said, surprised.

"Everything but a track, if you'll accept the pool for lap swimming," Eric replied. "We all use these facili-ties. Okku, Alana. I work out every day," he said, leading Noel to the ground level. "I'm here at least an hour. Usually before noon. I'll want you here then to spot me with the weights. You're free to use the gym whenever you care to."

Noel peeked into the bathroom. It was huge with urinal, sinks, toilet, bidet, a large stall shower, a steam room, and smaller sauna. Two doors—closets? Noel opened one—shelves full of towels. The second was locked.

"What's in there?"

"That's not important," Eric said.

Noel kept looking at the door. "Evidently it *is* im-portant."

"Strip down," Eric said; he'd already discarded his clothing. "Let's work out now."

"I didn't bring any shorts."

"There are several pairs in the closets. One ought to fit you."

Noel sorted through them until he found a worn blue pair that seemed likely to fit.

"I'm going to warm up," Eric said and went out to the gym.

Noel undressed, dropping his clothing on the bench as Eric had done. He had just turned the blue shorts around, preparatory to pulling them on, when he saw a faded name tag sewn in. He held the shorts and read, R. Landau. The dead disco-owner! Could Lan-dau have been the murdered man Eric had spoken about?

"Jesus!" he said, dropping the shorts as though they were on fire.

* * *

"I thought you were wearing the blue ones?" Eric said when Noel emerged from the dressing area.

"Changed my mind."

"Those look better anyway. Spot me on this bench press."

Noel stood behind the bench. Eric lay down, his head directly in front of Noel. Built into the bench were two abdomen-high metal bars with semicircular grips for resting both ends of the barbell rod. Noel lifted the weight—a considerable two hundred and fifty pounds—onto the rests and stood watching Eric's hands reach up to lift the weight, hold it parallel to his chest, then drop it slowly so that the bar brushed his nipples, then up again, a dozen times.

As Eric worked out, the muscles of his abdomen bulged until they looked as though they'd burst the skin. His breath came briefer, harder with every press, filled with little grunts that got louder toward the end of his set.

Noel's job was to be there to take the weights off Eric in case he became suddenly exhausted and couldn't reach the barbell rest with the great weight, or in case his arms locked with the barbells in midair, always a frightening possibility.

There was a real trust implied in spotting for Eric, Noel thought, watching him begin his second set of presses. A fallen barbell with this weight could smash a skull like a boulder cracking a robin's egg.

"Your turn," Eric said, sitting up and exhaling forcefully.

"I'm not into weights," Noel said. "I'll use some other equipment when we're done here."

"Suit yourself. But you'll never get the sheer strength you get from weights, you know."

Eric only required Noel's aid three times more during the next half hour. Most of the excercises didn't require spotting.

Noel couldn't help but notice how diligent, orderly, Eric was. Evidently he'd set up a system. From the

looks of his tightly knit body, he'd been using the
weights for several years. Had Robby Landau once
spotted for Eric? That seemed likely given the gym
shorts in the closet. Had he been the only other man
whom Eric had trusted? It gave Noel the creeps.

Noel was turning and swooping on the rope rings,
thinking about Landau, and it made him dizzy. He
executed a twirl and jumped down. Feeling better, he
hoisted himself onto the parallel bars and tried to recall the routine he'd used years before. Most of the
figures came back, and he did them not gracefully,
but at least without knocking the poles down.

Why was Eric so obsessed with the weights? He
had a good enough body not to need a daily workout,
a good enough physique to attract even the most
physically oriented gay sex partners. Was it for
strength, as he had said? He *was* incredibly strong for
his size and weight. But that too must be compensa-
tion. For what? For being grotesquely undeveloped as
an adolescent? Had Eric been a skinny mama's boy:
or a fat one? Or did it have to do with his father. That
had come up twice so far—once with Dorrance, and
again when he and Eric had fought in the garage.

Eric had stopped watching Noel and gone into the
bathroom. Noel waited until the shower stopped before
entering. Eric was dripping wet, a small, damp towel
wrapped around his middle.

"You aren't taking any chances, are you?" he asked.

"What do you mean?" Noel asked, all feigned innocence.

"Afraid I'll jump you in the shower? Go on, take off
your shorts. For what I'm paying I figure I'm at least
entitled to take a look at what I can't touch."

He watched Noel undress, and continued watching
until Noel had showered and was drying off.

"I'll need another towel," Noel said; "this one's too
wet." As though unaware of what he was doing, he
reached for the handle of the locked door. "Oooops!
Forgot. Wrong door."

Eric was dressed, leaning against the tile wall, arms across his chest, his eyes narrowing in a way that Noel now knew meant anger, irritation, displeasure.

"You don't stop, do you?"

"Because I tried to get in here? What's behind this door anyway, the family crypt or something?"

"You don't want to know."

"Of course I want to know. You've opened every goddamn door on this floor and purposely kept this one locked. What is this, a replay of Bluebeard's castle?"

"You're not ready."

"I know what it is anyway," Noel said. "I've heard all about it at the Grip. It's Eric the Red's Red Room. Right?"

"Right."

"So? What's the big secret, since I already know what it is? Open up."

"I only open it when I'm going to use it."

Noel was dressed now, too, except for his shoes.

"Well," Eric prompted, "are you ready?"

"Forget it," Noel said, tying his Adidas. "I'll never be ready if that's the case."

They went upstairs. In the elevator Eric said, "Someday I'll tell you all about pain and pleasure."

"What's wrong with right now?"

"You're not really interested."

It was true. Noel was repelled by even the possibility of what he might find behind the locked door in the big, blue-tiled bathroom: masks, tools, thongs, racks, instruments of torture: who knew what?

"I didn't say I wasn't interested. I said I wasn't into it."

"Everyone thinks it's just being jaded. Isn't that what you think? That I've done everything else—everything!—and I'm just bored with sex, that I play with all this, because it's different, kinky? Isn't that what you think?"

"Something like that."

"It's not true. There's an entire aesthetic to inflicting pain, to domination, if you will, and on the other hand to being submissive, that you can't begin to understand until you've experienced it. Of course there are a lot of jerks around, of all sexes and genders, who are just out to hurt. Barbarians! Done right, it's an art. An art with great refinement—a stretching of sensory abilities we seldom even notice. When someone steps into that room, and few do, he knows in advance he is going to come out knowing a great deal more about himself—his attitudes, his fears, his desires, his thresholds—than when he went in. He comes out of that room altered forever. Not on the outside—that would heal anyway. But inside. Where only he can see it."

"And what about you?" Noel asked. "Do you come out altered, too?" As he said the words, he knew he had made a mistake.

Eric stopped, looked at him, and his upper lip curled slightly. The moment of confidence, coming that much closer to trust, had been burst, stupidly, unthinkingly. No way to mend it.

"You always have to put me down, don't you?"

Without waiting for an answer or apology, Eric stalked onto the terrace. Abashed by his mistake, Noel followed.

Alana was in a lounge chair, clad only in the bottom of a scanty bikini with a print scarf around her head. She was surrounded by glossy foreign magazines and sun lotions.

"Come look here, my darling," she greeted Eric. "There's a wonderful new place we must visit. In the Andes!"

16

Noel was in his bedroom reading a Castaneda book Eric had insisted he try, when the phone console buzzed and lit up green: the call was for him. In the two weeks he'd lived in the town house, Noel still hadn't gotten used to the system. Outside calls were automatically answered, whatever name was requested was color-coded, relayed to each floor, where the console would buzz and flash, until someone answered.

This call was from Alana.

"I thought you were at a shooting?" Noel said.

"I am. But there is something we need here in the studio. A manila envelope with some male head shots I forgot. Would you be an angel and bring it to me?"

"I guess. Let me check with Eric. He's been with someone from the Coast all day. I doubt if he'll need me."

Noel knew a messenger could as easily be used to deliver the envelope to her. But perhaps she was feeling neglectful of Noel. They hadn't had much contact since he'd moved in. A few times he even thought she was avoiding him to lessen any tension between him and Eric. This might be her way of making it up to Noel.

"Okku will give you the address. The envelope ought to be on the lamp table of my sitting room. Can you bring it soon?"

"As soon as I tell Eric."

He transferred her call to Okku, who answered

from the kitchen. Then Noel buzzed the intercom red, for Eric. No response. He buzzed again. No answer. Maybe he and his visitor had gone out.

Noel easily found the envelope Alana had wanted. It held a dozen or so data sheets on male models: photos and specifications.

Dressed for outdoors, he was on his way out when he saw Okku.

"If Eric comes back, will you tell him where I've gone?"

"Mr. Redfern is not out," the manservant said and pointed down with one finger, before turning on his heels and going toward the back of the house.

Noel's first impulse was just to leave and assume the message would be conveyed. But who could tell what Okku wold do? He'd had no signs from the stolid Scandinavian that could be construed as anything remotely like friendliness. He'd better check out with Eric himself. Capricious as Redfern was, he might decide to lose his temper over a triviality like this.

Okku had pointed downstairs, but the gymnasium was empty. There were signs that the two men had worked out earlier—a towel draped on a press bench, some barbells off their racks, on the floor. But there was no sound of showers running. The big bathroom was lighted—also as though recently in use—but also empty.

Noel was turning to go back out when he noticed something amiss in the room—the second door, the door to Eric's Red Room, the door he had never seen open before, was ajar.

Eric said that door was only open when the room was in use. Could that have been the purpose of Henry Steele's visit from San Francisco?

Noel tried to picture the man—a long-legged, slim-hipped, cowboy type, over six feet tall. Then he tried to picture the long body clamped to a marble-topped table in the room, crisscrossed with leather straps, his

head perhaps masked, his eyes blinded, his flesh arching and twisting with pain/pleasure—like the photos
in the S and M magazine someone had brought to the
Grip, that everyone had pored over a few weeks before. Noel could imagine Eric's role easily enough. He
expected to hear a shriek of excruciating pain issue
from the room at any second.

He'd leave a note upstairs, hoping Eric would find
it. That's what he would do. But wait. If Eric had left
the Red Room door open it couldn't have been acci-
dental. Noel was supposed to look in. It was all set up
to show him what Eric would never tell him. Or was it?
Maybe it was a trap. He'd step in, and together, Eric
and Steele would jump him and . . .

He heard voices talking. Neither loud enough nor
clear enough to be understood. One was Eric's, the
other probably Steele's. It didn't sound like either sex
or torture.

Leave a note upstairs. Or call out Eric's name. Do
something!

The mirrored walls opposite the room allowed Noel
to see inside the two inches of open doorway. The
"Red Room" wasn't red—neither painted nor lighted
red. All he could make out was some metal shelving.
More like a storeroom or office.

Holding his breath, Noel backed over to the door,
all the while checking the mirror in front of him. Feeling clammy with trepidation, he slowly pushed the
door open another inch, poised to leap out of the room
in an instant. Nothing. No sign he had been noticed
from within. No change in the voices.

But he could see inside better. It *was* shelving.
Filled with envelopes and accordion folders. An office. Steele passed by, pacing, moved out of sight
again, then finally sat down on a chair. He was still
dressed in gym shorts; he was leaning forward. Noel
could now hear him more clearly.

"It's not the same out West, Redfern. The police are
different."

"The police are the same all over," Eric said.

"But you don't have any trouble here."

"Who doesn't?" he asked defiantly.

"They don't bust bars or clubs or anything," Steele said. "Do they?"

"What's the difference; let's get back to the point, Steele. Can you deliver from your district? That's all we want to know."

"Deliver what? Money? Or clout?"

Noel never heard the answer. The phone began to buzz again. This time it was cut off in midring. Eric picked it up. Silence. Then, "Thanks, Okku. He's probably looking for me. I'll take a look in the gym."

Certain he'd overheard plans he wasn't supposed to hear, Noel slipped out of the bathroom, and Indian quiet, leaped up the stairs of the gym to the entrance platform. He stopped, took a deep breath, then called out Eric's name.

The two men sauntered out of the bathroom. Steele winked a greeting at Noel then went over to the ceiling rings and leaped up on them. Eric came over to the stairs. Had he noticed the door was opened?

"Alana asked me to bring these to the studio," Noel said casually.

"Take the Benz if you want."

"Thanks." If Eric had noticed he wasn't telling. "Any time you want me to be back?"

"No."

"See you." He hadn't noticed. Good.

Noel opened the door, but Eric called him back.

"Yeah?"

"You like my visitor?" Eric asked in a manner that made Noel unsure of how he was supposed to respond.

Noel looked over to where Steele had just completed a roll in midair, and was hanging gracefully suspended from the rings. His long torso rippled like a washboard. He would definitely be accounted a very hot number at the Grip. Well-muscled legs, arms, huge

shoulders. It was hard to picture the two of them a
minute ago discussing—what? Crime? Politics? Noel
knew they would take up the conversation the minute
he left.

"He's all right. Why? You pimping for me? Or were
you thinking of something a little more elaborate?"
Noel asked, trying to keep their talk on the flirtation
level Eric seemed to prefer.

"I'm thinking of throwing a party for him," Eric
said. "Sort of a surprise. About twenty very hot guys,
and an ounce of some golden MDA I just got."

Noel knew the drug's reputation as a semihallucino-
genic superaphrodisiac.

"Sounds more like an orgy to me."

As Noel reached for the door again, Eric added:
"Give Alana a kiss for me."

17

The photography studio was on the fifth floor of an
ancient building on the northern edge of the theater
district, one of two apartments on the floor. It must
cover half a block, Noel thought, following the thin,
frizzy-haired young blonde who'd met him at the door
through corridor after corridor lined with mural-sized
blowups of Anthony Brickoff's most noted celebrity
portraits and advertisements. After passing a half-
dozen studios—some in use, some empty—and a few
rooms that seemed to be living quarters, they arrived
at the studio where Brickoff was shooting.

It was almost the size of Redfern's living room—
although by no means as high-ceilinged or elegant.

Most of it in fact was bare, the wooden floors littered
with screens, cabinets, and various artifacts the uses
of which Noel could only guess. One area seemed to
be for dressing and makeup. Large folding screens
only half hid a portable wardrobe and a tri-mirrored
vanity table.

Opposite this area—lighted by floor-to-ceiling windows on three sides—was the set. A pale gray sheet of
paper, perhaps fifteen feet long, pulled down from a
ceiling roller, was draped onto the floor. On the paper
were four aluminum tripod umbrellas reflecting the
bright lights within at different heights and angles.
Two other tripods held cameras. More cameras, light
meters, and other photographic equipment were scattered on the floor.

A half-dozen people were in the room, most of them
sitting reading magazines, unconcerned with the
shooting. Noel guessed them to be assistants, wardrobe people, assorted helpers.

Brickoff was immediately apparent, however. He
was a giant—shaggy-haired, bearded, dressed in an
enormous old sweater and equally worn trousers and
sandals. He stalked along the edge of the paper, then
turned suddenly and began shooting Alana, who was
in the center of the paper set, dressed in something
sheer and diaphanous. Done with the roll of film,
Brickoff would hand the camera to an aide, take up
another camera, stalk the edge of the paper in a small
circle, mutter under his breath, then suddenly advance upon her, talking low, and begin shooting
again, urging her to move in certain ways or to subtly
change her pose.

Noel remained off to the side, the envelope under
his arm, watching the photo session, but mostly
watching Alana. She seemed not to hear Brickoff, but
moved as though in a dream, in another, unapproach-
able dimension where Noel could only observe and
feel.

Suddenly she stopped, then walked forward.

"That's enough," she said.

"One more," Brickoff begged.

"No. No. You have too many already," she chastised gently. Brickoff kept on shooting her, even after she left her position. She held up a hand. "I said no!"

Brickoff turned away, handed the last camera he'd used to an assistant, and sat down on the paper.

"Ah, there you are!" Alana waved to Noel whom she'd just seen. "Come here," she called across the room.

Noel held out the manila envelope.

"We don't need that," she said, taking it from him and dropping it. "Come here," she said, turning him around with both hands on his shoulders, directing him next to where she stood on the paper. "Anthony!" she whispered. "Look!"

Brickoff stared up at them as though bewildered.

"What do you think, Anthony?" she asked softly. "Isn't he precisely right?"

"Maybe," the photographer said, squinting. He didn't look impressed. Noel was certain he was merely being polite.

But Alana ignored his hesitation. "Good!" she said. "Go change. Janet, he'll wear what Peter had on before."

A woman Noel had scarcely noticed stood up and went to the dressing area.

"Go on!" Alana pushed him. "Go."

"What for?"

"I need a man to pose with, of course. We are in a lovely château garden and I am with a man, wearing the wonderful gown."

"We'll bleed in the background later," Brickoff said, standing up. He seemed a bit more interested.

Noel now understood he was to be photographed. "But I've never done this before."

"You've been photographed before, no?" she asked. "I can't believe you haven't been. Everyone has."

"Yes, but . . ."

"Go, change. For me, Noel. Otherwise I have to come here tomorrow again, all day. Three other men we had and this, this *foul!*"—she shook a finger at Brickoff—"he made so much trouble all of them ran away. What am I to do, if you don't stand here with me? Come back tomorrow, and the next day, too?'"

Noel wasn't sure whether to believe her or not. He felt certain she had engineered the shooting so that he would have to pose. But he couldn't say he minded. She had asked him so prettily, made it seem such a favor to her, he couldn't say no.

When he came out of the dressing area ten minutes later, he had been shaved, his hair brushed differently than he'd ever worn it, his face dabbed with various lotions and powders, and dressed, as only once before in his life, when he'd married Monica, in formal wear. The slim, frizzy-haired blonde thrust a sheet of paper and pencil into his hand.

"It's a release," she explained. Then to Alana, "Who's his agent?"

"I am!" She laughed. "You look so wonderfully handsome. Come look in the mirror." Then to Brickoff: "You see, my foolish Anthony, I was right. He will do charmingly. Now I will look as meltingly romantic as you wish."

Noel joined her on the gray paper, wondering what he had to do. She immediately took both hands and shook them hard until she was satisfied they were loose.

"You must relax all your body like your hands. Then just follow me as I move."

He couldn't though. He felt awkward, uncomfortable, until suddenly, during one pose, she turned into his arms and her hair brushed against his cheek. For an instant he was thrown back to that evening at the Window Wall, when he had raised his head from the myriad impressions that had inundated him and smelled her perfume, heard her voice, and then seen her hair so close to him. From that moment on, the shooting was like being part of a slow, intricate ballet where he knew all the steps but needed her to give one little prod, one tiny push to set him into motion.

They were walking through the château gardens, a distant string quartet played Mozart, the delicate interweavings of the music wafted across the night air, picking up the freshness of fountains, the sparkle of candles, perfumes from unseen flowers. A warm buoyant evening in spring. He. She. Their silent, wordless conversation—all gesture and touch and the slightest movements, each filled with meaning. Somewhere in the distance a man's voice was quietly urging, inciting them, forcing their tacit bond closer, closer. He lifted her face and kissed her.

"Perfect! Yes, wonderful! Very stately. Hold it. Hold it! Fine! You can stop."

Alana had to pull away from him, away from his light grasp on her shoulders. When she did break contact, Noel suddenly came to his senses, but reached for her again anyway.

"No!" she said curtly, pulling away and stepping out of range. "That's enough, yes, Brick?"

"Wonderful, *là!* Yes, enough for now. We might need one or two later. I doubt it. Those will do. Good partnering," he said to Noel. "Best I've seen all day. You'll look good."

Noel scarcely heard him or cared. The magic night had been disrupted. Illusory as it had been, Noel felt nothing but loss.

Alana had left the room, to change, the blond girl said, suggesting Noel do so, too.

He waited outside the studio, in the tall-windowed hallway, until she emerged. She was wearing jeans, a big hat, and a tiny vest over her turtleneck sweater.

"I have the car if you want a ride," he offered. She had moved away from him so completely before, he wasn't sure how to approach her.

"Of course," she said brightly, as though the photo

session had never happened. "Let's get something to eat. I'm so hungry!"

They ate across the street in a delicatessen.

"Thanks for the opportunity," he said, trying to get to the subject that most interested him in the least direct way.

She saw it only as he said it, not as he intended it. "Once Brick likes you, everyone will want you."

"I don't know if I could do it any other time. You know. By myself."

She insisted on being matter-of-fact. "Of course you can. Just be as you were with me."

"That's what I meant. I don't know if I could."

"Don't be foolish. It was all for the camera."

"It didn't have to be."

"Of course it did." She avoided looking at him. "Where is that waiter with our food!"

He took her hand, she pulled it back sharply. "Don't make me angry with you. Don't think you can use me as a way to make certain your injured masculinity is intact. I will not be used that way."

There was no way for him to defend himself from her charge, even if he knew she were wrong, and he wasn't at all sure. So Noel remained chastened, silent until their sandwiches arrived, overflowing the plates, and Alana cheered up again, munching pickles and borrowing condiments from the next table.

She began to talk, but with nearly every sentence she referred to Eric—something Eric had said, or Eric had done, or Eric had thought to say or do. Much as he disliked hearing this, after his own rebuke, there was much new information.

"The way you go on about him, Eric must be extraordinary."

"He is."

"How? What's he done? What's he accomplished?"

"You don't know?" She was astonished. "Why when he was a boy of fourteen he developed the basis of the transistor that all the Hull-Redfern products use. It wasn't the first, but it was the smallest, the most enduring, the most inexpensive and easiest to use. And it was the reason Redfern dominated the electronics industry. The reason for the family's great wealth. As a boy, Eric developed seventy-nine patents in his father's laboratories that are used today. He still goes to the big upstate laboratories when he has some wonderful new idea. He custom-designs all the music systems in Window Wall, in Clouds, all over!"

"Is that true?" Noel asked. "He was a boy genius?"

"He was a very sad little boy genius for a long time. Until he met me. Now I do everything to make certain he is never sad."

Noel began to get a glimmer of their relationship. "And what does he do for you?"

"He doesn't have to do anything at all," she said quickly. "Just be Eric."

"Then he's a lucky man."

"He helped me. When I needed help and no one else could or would. A long time ago in Paris. Years ago. I was very unhappy. I wanted to end my life, and Eric came along and he changed all that. Now I have this wonderful work that I love, and this country, which I love, and Eric and all his wonderful friends that I love."

"But you're not in love with him?" Noel insisted.

"What do you mean by love? Obsessed? Infatuated? No. I don't love Eric that way. I am grown up now. No more of that for me."

"Once was enough?" Noel probed.

She smiled at him. "You ask so many questions, Mr. Cummings, that sometimes I think you are not a sociologist but a psychiatrist!"

Noel wondered again how Eric had discovered his real profession. Had Paul Warshaw told Chaffee? Another student? Or Vega? Noel concentrated on Alana.

"Who was he?"

"A boy."

"Do you ever think about him?"

"Oh, sometimes. He's dead. He was almost a man. But with a boy's sense of life. Ideas, foolish ideals, a boy's ideals. He died with those ideals. He was surprised by that. Surprised to die also."

"It makes you sad; don't talk about it."

"I don't mind anymore. Once, yes. But not now. It was at the *manifestations de mai* that it occurred."

Noel didn't know what she meant.

"The demonstrations of the students. At the Sorbonne. In Paris. In 1968. He ran out with them the second day, knowing what the police were doing to people with their sticks and tear gas."

Noel remembered seeing film clips of the French demonstrations on TV news programs when he was in college. It seemed so long ago.

"You were there with him?"

"No! I went to the movies. Or shopping. Stupid me. But he was clubbed, beaten, they say the *flics* got him and hit him until he couldn't move. He went into the hospital. He was released. He was arrested. He was released. Everything seemed fine. He was so proud of it, so proud he had been there."

"But you said he died."

"That is the sad part. It was maybe eight, nine weeks later. We were at a café on the Boul' Mich, he and I and his friends, and they were arguing as usual about something political. That is when Robert stopped talking. He put a hand to his head, here, what is this called, ah, yes, the temple. He put his hand there and looked very white. I remember the wine he was drinking just dribbled out of his mouth, and I wondered if he were sick. Then he looked, oh, I don't know, terrible suddenly. He stood up and he shouted in terrible pain and he fell down. And he died then. Right then, with me and all his friends around him. They said it was an aneurysm in the brain, that's what the *médecin examinaire* said. How do you say that?"

"The coroner?"

"Exactly. An aneurysm brought on by a previous blow to the head. At the *manifestation,* of course. Grimaud and his *cochons* of policemen said no one died, no one was killed. They lied. Robert died. I saw it with my own eyes."

She slumped back in her chair and lighted a cigarette. They were silent as the waiter came and gave them coffee. Noel nervously forked apart a piece of rich cheesecake.

"I apologize," she said. "It is very morbid."

"I asked. I'm glad you told me."

"At any rate, those who have ideals that must be tested in real life will always die like that. They are doomed."

"Well that eliminates everyone whom I know."

"I hope so," she said. "Not for me, though."

"You still have ideals?" he asked, but realized whom she meant. "You mean Eric does?"

"Yes, he has ideals. He is very political. He is in this gay movement. He helps with money, with important people, with the government. I don't know what else. He is very busy, very busy . . . and very stupid."

"And doomed?" Noel asked, but she didn't seem to hear him.

"I think of you sometimes," she said, "as someone who might become foolish over an idea. No?"

It struck Noel as a warning. He was quick to dispel the notion. "You're kidding? Look how easily I'm bought off. I'm just a whore."

"I hope that is so, Noel. I really do hope so."

She finished her coffee, and stared at Noel disbelievingly until, unnerved, he asked for the check.

18

"You didn't tell me Eric was an inventor. You said he was a playboy."

"He *is* a playboy."

"Alana said he was some sort of child genius. His inventions made the Redfern fortune. His father merely administered it."

"What did you think? That Mr. X would be a schlemiel? I told you he was smart, didn't I?"

A pause, as Noel didn't answer. Then Loomis again: "Tell me again about this economic conspiracy."

"It's not a conspiracy."

"Well whatever it is, then."

"It's a combine of successful gay businessmen."

"Including some illegal ones."

"Most are perfectly legal," Noel said quickly. "There's a Wall Street brokerage firm, at least one bank here in the city, and another out of town, a department store, and a bunch of other businesses a step down from that."

"And Redfern provides the protection?"

"It's more like he provides the investment capital. But several of the others do also." Then: "You know something that bothers me the more I think about it? In all the talk I've overheard, not a word, not one word has been said about pornography, about brothels, about prostitution rings, about wholesale thefts or drug smuggling."

"Why should they mention it in front of you? You're

an outsider. He still distrusts you. It's your own fault,"
Loomis said flatly. "He'd be a fool not to."

"I'm not sure. After all, I do spot for him in the
gym. He must trust me to some extent."

"That's meaningless."

"It's not meaningless at all!"

"I *said* it's meaningless. Now get back to this conspiracy."

"I didn't say it was a conspiracy. *You* did."

"What are you, on the rag today, Lure?"

"What's wrong with *you?* You keep twisting and distorting everything I tell you. Do you want to know the
truth or do you want your own version of it?"

Noel remained quietly furious for the next minute
of silence.

"Get back to the financial thing," Loomis finally
said in a quiet tone of voice.

"Just don't keep distorting what I say," Noel put in,
then went on: "It's not exactly clear. According to
Alana, he's devoted to the gay political movement,
providing large sums of money for equal rights legis-
lation in various parts of the country. His idea is to
form an economic council to guide the funding. To
my knowledge they have no direct links with any militant gay groups you read about in the papers."

"To your knowledge?" Loomis put in.

"That's what I said. None of the militant leaders has
been in the town house, or even been mentioned except in critical terms. But they might be funded in
specific campaigns. Evidently, Redfern doesn't trust
them that much."

"All right. You made your point. What's this council?"

"Redfern wants to form it, with himself and another
half-dozen prominent gay businessmen as permanent
members, and another half-dozen businessmen coming in and leaving every year."

"From New York?"

"From all over. San Francisco, Los Angeles, Atlanta,

Houston, Miami, D. C., Denver, and New Orleans. Cities with large and wealthy gay communities. It will be nationwide. They haven't a name yet. When they do, they'll announce it to the press. It sounds like a good idea."

"They're not going to be too happy when the press gets wind that it's being funded by criminal activities."

"If Redfern's as smart as you say he is, wouldn't he make certain the money is clean?"

"Maybe he can't keep it clean anymore."

"Dorrance could. He's a genius at that. He was the senior Redfern's accountant for twenty years. Because of him, the old man kept so much of the money he made."

"You seem real impressed by these guys, Lure. You ought to hear yourself. This one's a boy genius. That one's an old genius. This one's a world-famous model. That one sold a million records in a month. Even this conspiracy is a good idea: perverts running the country."

Noel allowed a long pause before answering. He was angry at Loomis's unreasonableness, but he wanted to try to get past that anger so he could discover why the Fisherman was being so purposefully deaf to the information he wanted Noel to provide, that he *was* providing. More important, what was Noel supposed to believe? What he was seeing every day—but perhaps not clearly, perhaps incompletely, perhaps distorted by his own fears and prejudices—or what the Fisherman insisted the facts were? Stymied for the minute, he said:

"You know, Loomis, I'm getting a little fed up with these phone calls. Why don't I just write you a letter?"

"Don't be funny. What's Redfern up to tonight?"

"He and Alana are going to a charity ball at the St. Regis."

"And you?"

"It's my night off."

"Did they invite you?"

"They invite me everywhere."

"Why aren't you going?"

"I said: it's my night off."

"Next time ask me before making that kind of decision."

"I had a previous engagement."

"I said, next time ask me!"

19

That conversation spoiled the rest of Noel's morning.

He decided to call Alana, persuade her to join him for lunch, an afternoon movie, perhaps even a walk in the park. He was sure she'd make him believe again that all he was doing for Whisper was worthwhile, even though she didn't, couldn't, know his part in it. She'd soften him up again, fill up the empty day.

She wasn't at home when he called. Okku said she was at the studio. Noel dialed there. After a long wait she came to the phone, sounding breathless.

"The proofs of you are marvelous, Noel! Just marvelous! It looks as though you have been posing all your life! You will have a wonderful career! You'll be earning your own money and won't have to feel hostile to Eric because you are dependent on him."

"How about lunch?"

"I ate. Don't you care about the photos?"

"A drink, then, when you're finished. I'll come meet you."

"I don't know when I'll be done here. Brickoff has gotten some insane idea in his head and has locked me and three other women in the studio all day, until he is done. Lunch was sent up. I don't know when we'll be done. He is completely crazy today." She waited long enough for Noel to realize she meant it. "I'm sorry, Noel. Really. Maybe tomorrow."

"All right, tomorrow." But he couldn't hide his disappointment. Interrupting her apologies, he hung up.

An hour later he decided to smoke some grass Randy had left at the apartment. It only took half the joint to get him pleasantly high. He put the remainder in his wallet, thinking it was too beautifully sunny a day to stay inside moping. Downstairs, he got the Atala out of the storeroom, dusted it off, took it to a nearby gas station to refill the tires, and then rode down to the Village.

Here the streets were filled with strollers, shoppers, people on errands, or just loitering about enjoying the sun. It seemed on afternoons like this that the entire Village population was either unemployed, or worked at night, or only on rainy, cloudy days. Christopher Street was as crowded as any Friday or Saturday night, and as he rode along the curb, Noel slowed down, took off his T-shirt, and began to say hello to people he knew, flirting with strangers, riding around in large, aimless circles in the middle of the road, playing catch me with trucks and buses, then zooming over to greet some guys smoking on the corner—in general acting to perfection the persona of the hot-looking number, naked-torsoed on a sunny day, riding a ten-speed bike.

After a while he rode over to the concrete-covered waterfront park, and from there, up a few steps to the Morton Street Pier. From the end of the pier he could see up and down the Hudson River, north to the Palisades and the George Washington Bridge, down to New York Harbor past the Statue of Liberty to the Verrazano Bridge. Elegant ocean liners, vast, seagoing freight carriers, tugboats, speedboats, fireboats on patrol, the flow of the river below. Above, airplanes of

all sizes, from superjets to Cessnas, police and airport
transportation helicopters, innumerable kites.

Noel put his bike down, bunched up his shirt for a
pillow, and lay down on the pier's wooden protecting
ledge, thinking that he would never have seen this
place if he hadn't become a part of gay life. He was
enjoying the cool breezes that played on his naked
chest, the hot, steady June sun striking down on him,
the subtle lap of water against the pilings of the jetty.
In minutes he felt relaxed.

"You sleeping?"

Noel looked up—his vision swimming with the Hudson's reflections brightly spotting the figure in front
of him—Vega. What did he want?

"Sit down."

Vega sat close enough so that his pants leg brushed
the tips of Noel's hair.

"You look comfortable," he said.

"Why not. It's a fabulous sunny day!"

"It's okay."

Noel looked up. It had been weeks since Noel had
last seen Vega. Since he'd left the Grip, he'd deliberately avoided him. Out of the lighting of the bar
Buddy looked thinner, his features harsh, sunken.

"Don't drag me down to where you are, man. Here,"
he handed Vega the roach of grass from his wallet,
"get high. It'll cheer you up. It did me."

"You smoking now?" Buddy asked, taking the joint
and lighting it.

Where's your slimy pal, Miguel, your henchman?
Noel wanted to ask. Instead he said, "Keep it. Finish
it."

"This Redfern's weed?"

"No. Randy gave it to me."

Buddy sucked on the roach, finishing it and throwing it up in the air, catching it in his mouth like a
trained seal with a herring. "It is good. You like it uptown?"

"It's all right. Today's my day off."

"What are you doing there? Watching Dorrance?"

Noel didn't know how much he ought to say. "Who knows what I'm doing there? Redfern offered me a half-assed, high-paying job, so he can be around if I ever decide to let him into my pants. And Loomis said to take the job."

"Oh!" It came out of Vega sounding like a low-toned bass drum, filled with inexplicable resonances.

Buddy became more talkative. He was pretty much manager of the Grip, now that Chaffee was at Bar Sinister all the time, and Noel uptown, he said. He liked working at the Grip; it paid well enough.

Noel suddenly wondered if he didn't have Buddy all wrong. Maybe Vega didn't know that Little Larry was also a Whisper agent. If not, that would justify why he and Miguel had followed them home from the Window Wall that night. Of course it didn't explain Miguel's animosity, but that could have been just a bad drug trip that one night.

"Are you sorry you joined up?" Buddy asked.

Noel's previous distrust returned. "I don't know. Why?"

"You don't sound too happy."

"I'm not happy about Loomis," Noel hazarded. "We argued again this morning. Sometimes he really pisses me off."

"On purpose."

"I don't think so. We just can't get along."

"You did before. I say he does it on purpose."

Buddy's certainty made Noel wonder. "Spill it," he said.

"I don't know if I should," Buddy began to say. Both of them sat up and looked at each other. "I used to think you were a real schmuck," Vega said. "When I said he does it on purpose, you didn't disbelieve me, why?"

Noel evaded it. "I don't know why." Then as Buddy began to stand up: "He lies to me. Tries to make me believe certain things, hides other, important things from me, that's why."

Vega sat down again. "You like Randy?"

"What's that have to do with anything? Oh, all right. Yes, I like Randy."

"I know you're balling with him. I want to know what you think of Randy."

"I'm not in love with him or anything like that. I couldn't be . . . with another guy. But I like him, I like being with him. We have fun." Noel enumerated Randy's qualities ending with, "And he's never asked me to do anything I didn't want to."

"Like blow him?"

Noel answered, looking away at the river. "I guess you know."

"He likes you, too. He's helping you, Noel."

"So he *is* working for Whisper?"

"If you don't already know, I can't tell you."

Noel didn't even try to press for an answer. He thought about Randy, whom he'd seen last night for the first time in a week: his handsome face and smooth-as-silk skin, his happy-go-lucky attitude, that found a joke in almost anything. Jesus! Loomis must have placed Randy in the town house before Noel. He must have been the in-house agent, before Noel replaced him, but he hadn't worked out to Loomis's satisfaction.

To cover up his silence, Noel asked, "Has he complained to you about that?" How much did Randy tell Vega?

"Randy? No. He never complains. He thinks you're a little uptight, that's all. He can get blown fifteen times a day, if he wants."

"I guess you're right. But before this whole business began I never had sex with another guy."

"*Bullshit!*"

"Oh, well, with my second cousin when I was thirteen years old. But that doesn't count. Most preadolescents fool around."

"You had sex with two guys when you were in college. In your senior year. You were part of an initiation ceremony. You and some other frat members got shitfaced drunk and carried away and you gang-raped two pledges."

Noel was flabbergasted. No one knew that. No one but he and the dean of schools. Not Monica. Not even his parents.

"The kids brought charges against seven of you, but it was all hushed up somehow, and everything worked out." Vega seemed to take pleasure saying it. "So don't give me that crap!"

Noel felt he was suddenly treading the very beginning of a path that had opened unexpectedly—perilously—in his life.

Vega seemed more of a danger than ever before. "How do you know that?"

"You don't deny it?"

"Don't game with me. I ask how do you know it?"

"I read it. Page fourteen. A psychosexual history of the subject with special reference to sexual identity and violence. Your dossier, if you haven't figured it out by now. Compiled by Whisper."

Noel was stunned. "My dossier?"

"We all have one. You. I. All of us. It's some fancy reading. Better than a paperback novel. Filled with hushed-up scandals, sex, violence. Real dirt. Mine came up in the Navy. Loomis got all of it right, gotta hand it to him. But I'd always fucked around with guys. When I was a kid in P.R. I used to be a real macho hustler. Fourteen years old."

"Does Randy know?"

"You don't believe me, I can tell. Come take a look for yourself. I have them up at my apartment."

"What else do you know about me?"

Vega was gloomy. "I didn't read everything. It's all in the dossier. Come take a look for yourself."

"How did you get hold of them?"

"I'm not going to answer that," Vega said. "And no,

Randy doesn't know." Their eyes met. "I wouldn't do
that to him. He's too nice a kid. And he trusts
Loomis."

That implied Buddy didn't.

Vega stood up. "Well? You coming?"

Noel felt as though the path that had veered off a
few minutes before was becoming more definable. He
knew if he stood up and went with Vega now he'd
never retrace his steps again. But he had to see the
dossiers to believe: he had to know what Vega was up
to.

Vega cabbed uptown to a largish building in the
West Eighties where he had a good-sized, sunny, rail-
road apartment with a tiny backyard. Noel followed
on his Atala.

Buddy introduced a small, thin, pretty, dark-haired
girl feeding three children in the big kitchen as his
wife, Priscilla. The smallest child was still in a high
chair; the others, four and six. All of them were
healthy, good-looking, bright.

As was the apartment. Next to Redfern's place it
looked middle class, but it was clean, well furnished,
well kept, with a stereo, color TV, children's toys
strewn about, and picture books open where they had
left them to go have lunch, even a child's record
player.

"This is Noel Cummings," Vega told his wife. "He
works for Whisper, too. I told him about what I found."

"Buddy! Why?"

"He's all right. Someone else has to know, that's
why."

She stared at Vega in disbelief then came over to
Noel, facing him squarely. "If you are a good man,
then listen to my husband. If not, then leave this
apartment right now and be content that I don't tear
your eyes out."

"Stop that, Pris," Buddy said, angrily pushing her
away.

"I mean it," she said to Noel, ignoring Vega.

"Stay with the kids." Buddy said, leading Noel into the living room. He went into another room, then returned with a series of accordion folders containing manila envelopes. He went through them, found one, and gave it to Noel.

"This is a copy?"

"A copy of a copy. Have a beer, make yourself comfortable."

Aside from many pages of information Noel already suspected Whisper had on him were bank statements, credit union reports, employment records since he was a teenager, his driver's license, and school reports dating from kindergarten.

And two other startling documents.

The first was titled "First Encounter with the Subject: Use of Plan J-23 for total instant psychological breakdown." It was dated March 2 of the current year, the day after Noel had witnessed Kansas's murder. It began:

> Although certain the subject was unallied to the perpetrator(s), we nevertheless decided to implement plan J-23, an instant total breakdown test. The subject was incarcerated over an hour in a dark freezing cell, threatened, ignored, and finally assaulted under controlled conditions by four operatives (18, 301, 75, 111) to ensure the total release of any remaining defensive devices. I then interfered, as previously planned, and setting myself up as savior for the moment, immediately gained his full trust for the preliminary interview.

Which was detailed with exact fidelity to what Noel could recall of the first meeting, interspersed with various comments by Loomis.

The second document that Vega had starred for Noel's notice was a full psychological profile of Noel, beginning with his earliest school and doctor's reports, evidently compiled and interpreted by Loomis—whom, it appeared, was Dr. Loomis, M.D., Ph.D. Diplomate in Psychiatry. This portrait gave the history Vega had talked about, including the fraternity hazing incident. As he read, Noel saw his character, his personality, over more than two decades, his psyche itself laid bare. The final paragraph was shattering:

> The above information, in conjunction with many taped conversations with the subject, displays a case of arrested infantile psychosexual development characterized by impulsive behavior alternating with overcaution, both at the most inopportune and even self-destructive times. His easy dominance by members of the opposite sex, well documented above, is still not as total as his susceptibility to control by an older, parental male—as illustrated in clauses 15, 76, 119, 234, etc. above. He is vain, conceited, easily flattered, believes without much proof that he is mentally and emotionally superior, is lazy, and must constantly be prodded into action, is occasionally rebellious, only to fall even more deeply into submission—all arising from a deep belief that he lacks ability, importance, and worth, and by the very realistic fear that he is and always was a homosexual. These factors make the subject an exceptionally high class rating: 1.

When Noel looked up from the page several minutes later, he felt as though his heart had been surgically removed from his body without him ever feeling the stroke of a scalpel.

Priscilla had joined them, sitting on the arm of Buddy's chair. "I'm sorry I yelled at you before," she said. "You ought to read the terrible things they say about Buddy."

"Well?" Vega asked.

Noel didn't know what the question was. "I feel like

when I was eight years old, and I hurt a friend, put a stick in his eye or something like that. My father spanked me for the first and last time in my life, but I'll never forget that spanking. How angry he was."

"Now you see what Loomis thinks of you."

"I didn't know he was a psychiatrist."

"Class-A operative. Number one rating he gave you. Right next to Mr. X. Aren't you?"

"Loomis thinks so."

"Then it will get a lot worse," Buddy said darkly.

Noel didn't understand that. He was still trying to accept what he'd spent the last hour reading. Given that everything written about him was true, how in hell could Loomis conclude he was homosexual? All those years with Monica! His affair with Mirella. And one little drunken incident to unbalance it, to tip it. It was unjust! Unfair! Unfair!

Vega was talking again, saying vague things in enigmatic phrases: the dossiers were not the worst of it; something else was behind it, something far worse; he wasn't sure what, but he was going to find out.

"I'm sorry," Noel said, finally stopping Vega. "I'm not following you. I need time to think about this. You won't show this to anyone?"

"Don't worry. It's locked up. But even if nothing comes of it, remember! You read it. You held it in your hands and read it! Remember that!"

"What do you expect to come of it?"

"I don't know."

"Buddy!" his wife warned. "Shut up, until you know."

20

After all that, the stupidest thing Noel could have done that night was to attempt to make love to Mirella Trent. That's what he told himself several times that evening with her.

The first time was when he picked her up in her large, spacious Upper West Side apartment. She offered him a seat and a drink. He took the first, refused the second. That was when she—still standing—asked him whether he liked the sweater she was wearing—a forest-green turtleneck that clung revealingly and gracefully. Or, she asked, should she wear this?—holding up a Chinese silk blouse. Of course it was a come-on. Noel saw that as it was happening. Why else would she draw attention to her body, especially her beautiful breasts, unless she had more ideas than merely dinner?

During dinner he thought of it a second time. Almost from the minute they sat down in the small Italian place she had taken him to, she began to make it known through hints and various subtle allusions that Noel had a reputation among women for being both attractive, mysterious, and aloof. Might it have something to do with his late wife? Mirella said she'd heard that Monica had always seemed deliciously satisfied, enviably so. A woman beautiful as Monica—so charismatic—must have been approached by scores of other men, and yet had never once been even whispered about; that was intriguing. Her absurd "first date" game turned him off, as much as her stockinged foot under the table, rubbing his inner thighs and crotch, turned him on.

After the long, leisurely dinner, they walked a half-dozen blocks through the warm June night back to her apartment for an after-dinner drink. Even before they had entered her apartment, Noel began to make love to her.

Stupid. He could have ignored her hints and allusions. Their foolish, rotten relationship was bound to begin again.

But he had to know if Loomis was right.

Stupid, because now he knew. As far as Mirella could tell, Loomis was absolutely wrong. Noel was as healthy and lively and accomplished a heterosexual partner as she or any woman could have wanted. Years of making love to Monica had perfected his techniques, taught him the weaknesses, the vulnerabilities, the various turn-on spots of a woman's body, and the timing, too. Without giving that much thought to it, he carried out a bravura performance—one that might have been filmed for sex instruction classes.

He kissed her deeply, holding her neck cupped in one hand. From there he moved all over her face with his lips, down to her throat, around to first one ear then the other, then to the nape of her neck, lifting her short, dark hair away, then, around to her throat again, to the cleft where her breastbone began, all the while deftly slipping his hand under garments and through zippers, across her shoulders, down to her lovely breasts, aureoles of mocha outlining the tanned flesh, responding with her erect nipples surrounded by tiny gooseflesh pimples that told him all was just right. Then, the sweater off, the skirt dropping slowly first in front then sliding from in back, he moved down farther, gliding along her creamy skin to her tummy so suddenly soft amid the hardness of her wide, hard-boned hips, down to the tender-as-butter thighs, then up again briefly with his tongue deep into her navel, then down again past the silken frizzy hair to kiss her lower lips, his hands all the while caressing moving stroking fondling breasts buttocks hands thighs feet . . .

And she so effortlessly finding herself twisting once more with pleasure at the touches of this man she didn't really like, thought was weak, easy to dominate, too uncertain, too mild-mannered for her really. This man who would not stop even though she asked him, then begged him, then couldn't any longer stop his compelling wet hunger until he had the very inner webbing of her gyrating with warm and cold and hot and ice, and as he demanded it she gave it, oh, gave it, resisting at first then no longer able to resist. Gave it so gratefully, his film-star face, his sweat-curled, shiny hair, his eyes that rose up to meet her afterward as he mounted her, asking for her to give it yet again, this long-muscled, hard-fleshed semideity, this mystery to her and yes, again she could no longer resist and gave it to him, and once again, too, leaving herself and all qualms to let him enter behind her this time, a new pleasure for her, one she'd only heard of and difficult, constricting at first. Then, as his hands guided by hers moved in front of her, inside her, at the same time, and she relaxed so utterly into his hunger and rhythmic ferocity, she was a queen with her favorite, a whore of Naples with a young GI, a frontier woman in the adobe hut, and he was lovelier than any woman or man or child she'd ever seen before, the exhausting, panting everyman.

As far as Mirella would ever know and tell, Loomis was wrong.

She looked at the clock.

"I can't believe it! Only midnight. I thought we were together for hours and hours," she said, then leaned over looking at him, smoking a cigarette. She was afraid to touch him, afraid she would never stop if she did; that having tasted she would have to devour all of him. "Noel?"

"Ummm."

He seemed off somewhere she couldn't be.

Then he sat up, went to the bathroom. After a minute or two she heard the toilet flush. He came out, looked at her, then began picking up his clothing.

"Where are you going?"

He didn't answer, hastily got dressed. She was disappointed but tried not to show it.

"Will you call me?"

"I don't think so," he said tonelessly.

Now she began to feel cheated. "Only one-night stands," she asked, meaning to be sarcastic. "Or only one time per customer to spread the wealth around?"

"I'm seeing someone," he said, leaning over to pull on his shoes. "A guy." He looked up for her reaction, then tied the shoes.

"That's the worst line I ever heard, Noel."

"It's true."

Perplexed, she let him go, saw him to the door, and stood there—wearing only the top of her pajamas as he waited for the elevator only a few feet away, expecting something more; she felt she deserved more.

"I really don't believe you, Noel."

He looked toward her as though to say something very important that would explain everything, then he turned to face the elevator doors that had just begun to open.

"I *don't* believe you!" she shouted once more, enough for him to hear it echoing inside the overilluminated elevator car hurtling down.

21

Noel missed his transfer point on the subway. When he looked up, Forty-second Street was long gone. The train was just pulling into Fourteenth Street. He got out of the car with the intention of trying the Canarsie Line across town, then going up again nearer to where he lived, via the Lexington Avenue Line; or, taking this train back uptown to Forty-second Street and the crosstown shuttle.

"Lost in Greenwich Village. That's what you look like."

The familiar drawl drew Noel long before he located its source—then there he was, Little Larry, arms akimbo, a smile on his face, leaning against a subway steel girder. "What's up?" Then, as Noel didn't answer, "Where you going, man?"

"Who knows."

"Oh—oh. We don't sound happy tonight, no, sir. Hey, how come you're not with your new friends tonight?"

"It's my night off."

"Me, too. Take the local. We'll go raise hell in the Village."

"I don't know. I think it would just depress me."

"Get high. Get laid. That's the way to come up again."

"I just did. That's the problem."

"Oh, yeah. Do tell. But over a drink at the Grip," Larry said, closer now, moving away from the platform edge as the local pulled into the station.

Noel stepped in with Larry and out again a minute or two later on Christopher Street, beginning to tell Larry what had just happened with Mirella.

Vitale was sympathetic and Noel was too full of it to keep it to himself, so he let Little Larry worm the whole business out of him as they walked the half-dozen blocks to the Grip.

There they ordered drinks and found a fairly quiet spot.

"It's clear to me what your problem is," Larry said, leaning cockily against the bar, and looking over the crowd. "Jesus! What a shitty crowd tonight. Trolls. Dragons. Lizards. Things that go squish in the night. Ecch! Hi ya, Tom! Casper."

"They're playing 'One Night Affair,'" Noel said, realizing the song was on again, as if in mockery. "Well? What's your great elucidation?"

"Strange as it may sound, I think you are a true bisexual. Like Buddy here. Hey, Bud, help me pick up Noel's spirits. He's in the dumps 'cause he just balled some chick to the moon, and never came himself."

"Stop using so much coke," Vega said, leaning over the bar. "It numbs up everything."

"I didn't use any coke," Noel said, half bothered by the sudden exposure of his private life.

"But you *have* been using it. Up at . . . well, you know where."

"That's not the problem!" Larry interrupted. "Are you going to listen? As I said before, here you are this exotic breed, the true bisexual. And you made a simple error tonight of getting pussy when you wanted cock. That's all."

'Whaaat?" Noel wouldn't buy it.

"Speaking of which," Vega said, "Randy was in looking for you tonight."

"Christ! That's all I need," Noel said.

"Let me put it this way," Larry went on. "Let's say you're in the mood for Chinese food tonight, right? But the only Chinese restaurant is closed. The only place

that's open serves pizza. Now pizza is fine, wonderful,
right? But when you order the pizza and eat it, it just
isn't as good as it usually is. Why? Because you
wanted Chinese food! Very simple! You have to get
laid the right way tonight. You'll rebalance your
moods and your desires and feel terrific!"

"You're so full of shit I can't stand it," Noel said.
But he felt better for having talked about it, and
amused by Larry's advice.

Little Larry seemed about to be taking his own advice. He turned to a tousle-haired, farm-boy type next
to him, and began a very heavy come-on. Noel was
surprised when Vega leaned over the bar and whispered:

"He might be right. At any rate, it's nothing to get
hysterical over."

"I'm not hysterical."

"You were when you walked in. Calm down, will
you."

Noel stared at Vega until Buddy moved away to
serve a customer. It's easy enough for you to say, Noel
wanted to shout. You've been sleeping with guys since
you were fourteen. You found out early. Like Larry,
who'd told Noel he'd found out when he was twelve.
But at twenty-eight! Twenty-eight, damn it, never
once suspecting, this of all possible futures lay ahead.

It was easy enough for Vega with his easygoing
Caribbean upbringing, playing with other boys in the
mangrove patches, then going for a dive in some clear
pool or tropical beach. That at least was natural,
meaningful. It was not like seven years of being with
Monica, after a childhood and adolescence where
everyone agreed you could be crippled, aphasiac, mentally retarded, and you were still better off than
being—queer. The stupid jokes in locker rooms, the
epithets—"faggot, girly, fag, queer, queen, cock-
sucked"—aimed to sting worse then any others. The occasional glimpses of real queers at a bowling alley or
movie theater—limp-wristed, swaying, slim, lisping, ef-

feminate-acting, garishly dressed fifties queens. And only one glimpse was necessary to see they were a breed apart, to be shunned, despised, as though they carried a terrifying disease.

Of course one or two of his high-school classmates turned out to be homosexual. But he'd been so attached to Monica and so distant from anyone but her and her friends that when those old friends were thought of at all, it was as people who'd selected an unconventional way of life that barred them from the real felicities: marrying, having babies, being with other couples, and having good times.

Then he'd begun to teach in the Village and that attitude, and the terminology, changed. "Gay" was the term—gay clubs, gay dances, gay demonstrations, gay this and gay that.

Faggot! You can't whistle you know, if you're a queer. Wear green on Thursdays; it's a symbol, it's a sign. Hanging out in showers, looking at another guy, or worse touching him even by accident, and you're queer, a fairy. Don't brag about the girls you made it with—faggot! Hey, man, let's go knock down some fags, beat the shit out of them. Yeah! Or better still, let's not! *Comment ça.* The Third Sex. The Love That Dare Not Speak Its Name. Urnings. Perverts. Queer as a three-dollar bill. I don't want my son to grow up to be a sissy! Isn't my boy a real little man? You don't mean you're one of *them!*

"Twenty-eight fucking years of programming. And today I am the victim of my own damn acquiescence in it."

"What's that, Mac?" Someone next to Noel asked.

"Nothing."

"Well?" Larry said, turning to Noel. "Are we going?"

"Where?"

"Uptown. To trash."

"I don't think that's a good idea," Vega said.

"Who asked you?" Larry shot back.

"Look at him! He's in no condition . . ."

"He'll never be in a better condition. You got a customer, Mr. Vega," Larry added, and watched satisfied as Buddy moved off.

"I thought you were working on someone," Noel said to Larry. He half resented Vega's interference.

"Later for him. I'm hungry for Chinese food, baby. Pizza won't do. Let's go."

"I don't know."

"Here, take this, it'll put you in a sleazy mood."

Noel looked at the big, flat, white tablet Larry handed him. It was scored on one side, marked on the other 704.

"You're kidding. A Quaalude will put me to sleep."

"A half won't. Take half now, the other when we get there. Go on," he commanded, "do it. It'll put you in a sleazy mood."

Larry almost did it for Noel, but finally Noel took half the pill and washed it down with a slug of beer. Larry disappeared into the increasingly crowded barroom, and Noel hung out at the bar, finishing the beer, until he could no longer clearly revolve in his mind his own despair as the Quaalude began to take effect, relaxing him, making him begin to forget his despondency. Soon the rhythms of the music from the Wurlitzer seemed all pervading.

"Let's go," Larry said, suddenly at his side. He steered Noel out the door, and they began walking uptown along West Street.

The hard yellow glare of the streetlights reflected off the metal buttressing of the closed-to-traffic West Side Highway. Little Larry talked dirty from the moment they left the Grip, wrapping one of Noel's arms over his shoulder, half dancing along on the sidewalk. Noel didn't mind. For the first time today he felt okay, the half Quaalude took off all the edges, softened everything, making walking effortless, as though he were on a moving sidewalk.

After a few blocks, Larry lighted up a joint, and

they took turns smoking it. "You're going to like this place."

The grass added a slight twist to every one of Noel's perceptions—still peaceful, but a bit off center, like going down what seemed a really high curbstone across acres of street, and up again, climbing a hill to the other curbstone.

This intersection looked familiar. Why?

He stopped and looked around. Then he saw it—the abandoned Federal House of Detention. Its grilled-over windows, the garbage thrown against its walls, broken glass on the sidewalk, the big front doors solidly locked against junkies and kids. Noel hadn't been there since that dread March morning. Now he looked away. It was just an old building, after all.

But he had to check across the street, too, under the highway. Sure enough, there it was, the warehouse where it had all begun. Even *it* had lost its foreboding and mystery. Even *it* was ridiculous. He began to laugh at how ridiculous, laughing so hard he couldn't get the words out to explain to Larry, and so he contented himself laughing as they walked past it, until Larry hushed him, whispering that they were at Le Pissoir.

Membership was required to get in, but the doorman knew Larry, and somehow knew that Noel was part of the "family" as he said, waving them inside.

In the big, red-painted elevator, Larry began to play with Noel, who didn't bother to resist, nor even much care, even though two other hot-looking dudes also in the elevator couldn't take their eyes off what Larrry was doing.

The doors opened to a burst of funky music and deep red lighting. It took Noel a minute to see a large loft room with bare walls, plank floors, to the left a simple stand-up bar, a bit brighter, with a few guys standing, drinking. Other rooms were visible beyond this one in both directions, shadowy figures stalking through them. Aside from the music, which wasn't

even as loud as in the Grip, there was no noise, except
for what once or twice sounded like a gruff command
from a room behind the bar.

Noel immediately ordered a beer and dropped the
second half of the Quaalude without being told to.
Larry began talking to the bartender and Noel leaned
against the bar and tried to get his bearings in the
darkness.

Before he had, a man came out of one of the rooms
and stood in front of him, saying something that Noel
didn't understand. Tall and fair-haired, he was naked
except for a double-wrapped chain around his waist,
and a leather bracelet on each wrist. He was well
muscled, his body oiled to gleam in the red lights. Two
little metal rods had been stuck through his nipples.
As Noel watched, the man flexed his pectoral muscles
and the little rods jumped. He began to laugh. The
man reached out and took Noel's hand and showed
him how to twist the rods sideways. Noel pulled his
hand back and turned around to the bar. Behind him,
the man whispered something; Noel turned around
and threw his beer at the guy: a thin curtain of it flew
out, covering the man from head to toe. He stood still,
then fell on his knees and began kissing Noel's shoes
until, disgusted, Noel kicked him away. He backed
off saying what sounded like, "Thank you, master,
thank you," until Noel turned back to the bar and Little Larry.

"Looks like you made a friend."

"What a creep."

"You'll find more like that in there," Larry pointed
behind the bar. "That's for the pros: S and M, water
sports, scat, fists, pain, the works. I think you'd better
check the other one. People are apt to be a bit more
affectionate."

"How can you see anyone?"

"You can. Don't worry. Have a good time."

"Where are you going?" Noel asked, aware that his
words were coming out slowly, slurred.

"Into the romper room."

Noel remained at the bar watching shadows pass and suddenly coalesce in doorways. Two guys next to him progressed from necking to heavy petting into full sex, their shirts came off, their pants dropped. Noel made room for them. Soneone else nearby ordered a beer, and began rubbing his crotch, while staring at Noel. Others gathered to watch the two men make love. Noel moved again. The bartender, an attractive bearded fellow Noel had seen before in the Grip, was having his nipples bitten by a patron leaning over the bar. Over the speaker system Noel heard words that he first thought were song lyrics. It was repeated, clearly a man's voice saying, "Back bar, got a guy here who'll take care of that bloated kidney for you."

The room was filling up, forcing Noel farther from the bar. Every face around him seemed an archetypal image of luxury, sin, eroticism, temptation, lust: eyes shining, hungry; lips wetly open; tongues lolling sensuously; bodies gliding to focus now on a shoulder, now on a well-developed chest in the shifting red light.

Despite his haziness from the drugs, Noel determined to get out. As he reached the elevator, the doors opened. A rush of people massed toward one room, carrying Noel with them.

He seemed to enter a bubble. He could still hear the music, but muted, subsumed in a sough of sliding, rubbing sound, as of many bodies in constant motion. Hands reached out touching him lightly, tentatively, and as he turned away from them, he moved into other hands, other bodies, stroking, caressing. Then he was floating along, slowly turning, bodies sliding against him, hands more forceful now, someone opening a shirt button, someone else unzipping him, someone else lifting his shirt from behind, a hand slipping down the back of his trousers. All the while he was moving, revolving through the mass of bodies, until he saw a face near him that looked familiar, kind, and hands reached out for him.

The face bent to his and he felt caressed all over, hands in front, in back, until his clothing was open or off, and he felt freer, more flexible, more comfortable with this stranger kissing him slowly all over. In tune with the music, thinking nothing, unwilling to think, letting himself be guided, shown what to do, how to do it, Noel let go.

22

"Get up! You have to leave!"

Noel turned over, feeling sawdust under him. Someone was shaking his shoulder. Groggy, he sat up. The music and bodies were gone. Silence. Emptiness. The red lights still shone dimly. Someone was hunkered in front of him, great concern on his face, shaking Noel awake, repeating that he had to get up and leave.

"Is this yours?" The man held out a twisted bunch of material that separated into a vaguely recognizable shirt. He looked down. His trousers were on, the belt undone. Christ! He must have fallen asleep right here on the floor. The Quaalude Larry had given him had finally put him out.

"C'mon," the man urged, extending a hand, rising himself. "Get up. You have to leave."

He helped Noel up, and even helped him to put his shirt on, all the while urging him to hurry, looking around as though someone else were in the room. But Noel still couldn't shake himself fully awake. He

might go to sleep in a minute, a second, but he tried
to do what he was asked, finally slurring out a question:

"What time is it?"

"I don't know. Six. Seven. In the morning. Here,
buckle that up. C'mon!"

"Where's my jacket? I was wearing a jacket," Noel
managed to recall the fact, and turned around to look
for it. Scattered sawdust, mixed in with cigarette
butts, spilled beer cans, plasticene cups half crushed,
used, snapped-in-half amyl nitrite capsules littered the
floor. What was that pile of clothing in the corner? It
must be in there.

The man jerked him back. "It's not there! It's in the
checkroom. You checked it."

He had to help Noel out of the room to the check
counter. Only two jackets were left hanging, one of
them Noel's lightweight Windbreaker. As he put it on,
he heard the wail of sirens.

"They're here," another man said, looking into the
room.

"Shit! I want him out!"

"Through the stairway," the other suggested.

"Hurry."

Noel had just opened the stairway exit door when
two policemen began coming up.

"Who's this?" one of them said, pushing Noel back
out the door and into the loft. "Who's the manager
here?"

"I'm the assistant. Reed," the guy who'd awakened
Noel said.

"Who's this?" the policeman asked of Noel again.
"Where was he going?"

"Someone who crashed here. I was letting him out."

"Hold him. Everyone else who's here, just stay still."

"There's only the three of us," Reed said.

"Oh? Well, let's see what you got to show me." He
turned to Noel. "You two stay here."

Noel sank down against the wall and watched the two cops follow Reed into the big room where he'd been awakened.

"Here, have a cigarette. It might wake you up," the other employee, Jerry, said, lighting one for each of them. He seemed scared, nervous.

"What is it? A raid?" Noel asked.

"No. We don't get raided. Worse than that."

"What?"

Reed and the two officers came out of the room, conferred apart so that Noel couldn't hear what they were saying. The bigger one asked in a louder voice where a phone was and was directed to a wall phone near the bar.

The other cop, younger, slimmer, a bit more sympathetic with his long fair hair, said to Noel, "You don't look too good."

"Someone slipped me a Mickey last night. What happened?"

"A guy was cut up in there." He pointed to the room. "Really worked over."

"Dead?" Noel asked, knowing the answer already. Through the fogginess, he suddenly realized what was under those clothes that Reed wouldn't let him go near.

The other policeman was loud on the phone. His words were clear from where they were.

"Yes, the whole business. Privates cut off. Throat slashed. Must have crawled out of the bathroom where it seems to have happened into another room where people were. Probably choked to death on his own blood. No. No weapon . . ." (to Reed) "You didn't find anything?" (back into the receiver) "No, nothing . . . who knows . . . probably the same freak who killed the others. It was dark in there. Lots of guys. It would be easy."

Noel was beginning to sober up fast. He'd slept peacefully, drugged to sleep, only a few feet from where this poor guy had choked to death on his own blood! Only a few feet away. For how long? Could it have been hours?

Reed came out of a small room with steaming cups: the smell of coffee. He offered some to Noel.

"You should have hurried," he whispered as Noel sipped.

"You find any identification?" the cop on the phone shouted.

"We know him," Reed said. The other employee nodded.

The cop talked another minute, then hung up and came over to them. "I need positive identification, witnesses. Let's go." As Noel hesitated, he said, "You, too. Come on."

In the big room the lights were off, the painted-over windows partially opened to show gray daylight, feeling damp, muggy. The clothing had been removed from the head and torso. The body was twisted on the floor with one hand stretched out, the other curled underneath. The black, rich ringlets of hair were splattered with blood, the face, too, the chest and shoulders stained with a dry crust of blood like a bib, the neck a blur of red-brown.

"Positive identification?" the big cop asked, notebook ready.

Noel looked at the body, revulsion making him sway.

"He used to manage the place," Reed said in a small voice, turning to look at Noel, biting his lower lip. "Didn't he?"

"You know him?" the policeman asked Noel who looked down at the figure again, now beginning to make out details: the eyes, the nose, the mouth.

"Name?"

"Randy Nerone," Reed said.

"That right?" the cop asked Noel. "Hey, shake him, Bob. That right?"

Noel nodded. "Yes, it's him," then turned away and began to vomit until he thought he'd never stop.

THREE

HOOKED

June, 1976

"Yeah! Lure here."

"Why didn't you call in sooner?" Loomis asked harshly.

"I couldn't. I was down at the precinct house all morning."

It was only noon, but Noel was exhausted. The horrors of the morning hadn't ended with his recognition of Randy as the mutilated body he'd slept in the same room with—drugged as he'd been, annihilated by his surrender to everything that was taking place in the back room. That had only been the beginning. He'd been dragged down with Reed and the other employee still left in Le Pissoir to the police station where all three had undergone hours of questioning followed by waiting, then requestioning by someone else—the detective assigned to the case. They'd probed him, homed in on him, humiliated him with their leering innuendos about what was already so obvious—what he'd been doing in the club in the first place. It had been the worst morning Noel could remember in a hell of a long time.

"You mean about Randy?" Loomis asked.

"I see rotten news travels fast."

"What were you doing there?"

"Thanks to your little buddy, Larry Vitale, I woke up there. Not ten feet from where Randy never did wake up."

"What do you mean? Were you doing research for your book?"

The question was so ludicrous, Noel said, "Sure. Sure. That's exactly what I was doing, research. Until I got slipped a loaded Quaalude."

"If you can't handle drugs, you shouldn't use them," was Loomis's reply, and that seemed even more ridiculous.

"I have to, Fish. Everyone else on the scene does, you know. You want me to be just like them, don't you? You said so. You said you didn't want me to stand out from them, didn't you?"

Loomis didn't understand. His words were unemotional, flat. "You're upset, Lure. Just give me a few more facts, and we'll talk about this later. When you're feeling more yourself. All right?"

"I'm feeling fine," Noel said, wanting to have it out now, not later. "And if I'm upset because a friend of mine got his own cock shoved in his mouth, well maybe your friends at the precinct house should have shown a little consideration for my feelings, eh? It was a very educational experience, Loomis. More valuable for my book than almost anything else I've seen or done. Now I *know* what it's like to be gay and under suspicion."

"Calm down. You weren't arrested, were you?" Loomis said, as though that solved everything. "What did you tell them?"

"The truth. That I was drugged and was awakened much later and told to leave when they arrived."

"That's all? Surely they didn't think you did it?"

"They sure pretended they thought so. The first one to question me said I'd probably gotten hopped up on drugs and done it to Randy and couldn't remember I'd done it. Can you believe that! Then Reed and another cop pointed out that Quaaludes are tranquilizers, not the kind of drug that makes people go out and kill. It was a pretty withering moment. Made the detective look like a real asshole. So he demanded a urine sample, to make sure it *was* Quaaludes I'd been on."

"And they still held you?"

"Yeah. Seems while I was out of the room, Reed dropped a little bomb about me and Randy knowing each other. It seems that Randy'd heard from Vega that Larry and I were going to Le Pissoir, and came that night looking for me. Naturally the minute I got back in the room, the cops hit me with that."

"Say that again," Loomis asked curtly.

Noel repeated it, then asked why.

"Who else knew you were going to be there?"

"No one. No one but Larry, who took me. Why?" But before he was done asking, Noel had another question. "You don't think what happened to Randy was aimed at me?" He almost stumbled over it, it was so off-the-wall, so frighteningly possible.

"Could someone tell you two apart in that place?"

"Randy is—was, I mean—bigger than me. Otherwise, I don't know. It's pretty dark in there, until you get used to it."

"You didn't tell anyone at Redfern's, did you?"

"No. I wasn't there all day."

"Oh, that's right," Loomis remembered. "You had a date. What happened to that?"

"I *had* it," Noel said. "Then I met Vitale on the subway and he took me to the Grip, and we had a drink, and from there we went to Le Pissoir. I was staggering stoned long before I got there."

"Little mischief maker," Loomis muttered so low Noel wondered if he had heard it right. "Go on," he said, louder, when Noel had stopped talking.

"Well, when Reed blabbed all this, I had to—you know—admit that I knew Randy and all. They tried to make me admit to having killed him in some kind of lovers' quarrel. But I told them we weren't lovers. And Reed and Jerry said that while it was known that we saw each other, that it was also well known that it was an open relationship. So that theory stank, too. But it was a real down experience, I assure you."

"What did you tell them about Whisper?"

That was the question Noel was waiting for. It made him pause now, as it had made him pause in the precinct house.

"What could I say? With Reed and the other guy there?"

"What *did* you say?" Loomis demanded.

"Well, I thought I had to tell them and I tried to do it indirectly, you know, by giving them stupid kinds of hints, like they'd ask me something, and I'd say I would whisper it to them. They never caught on."

"Not even the detective?"

"No. I'm sure he didn't catch it."

"I doubt that he knows about the operation," Loomis said, satisfied. "In the future, Lure, should anything like this happen again, don't say a word. Don't even hint. We'll come fix it up."

"Like you did this time?"

"We got the news late."

"Five hours late?"

"I was busy. By the time I found you and called, you'd been released."

"Bullshit."

"You're upset, Lure. I said I was busy."

It would be just like the Fisherman to let Noel rot in a police station all day, as he'd let him become defenseless in the abandoned Federal House of Detention months before. But Noel wasn't going to let Loomis know he knew that. He'd keep that knowledge, and the bitterness of that knowledge, to himself.

"You still there, Lure?"

"Yeah, sure."

"All right. We'll talk later. Go on back to Redfern's and get some rest."

"I'm not going."

"Look, Lure, I understand how you feel but—"

"But I'm not going back to that town house! Not for a few days at least. I don't want to see Eric. I'm afraid of what I'll do to him."

"That's perfectly understandable, Lure. But now,

more than ever before, you have to make sure you don't screw everything up. One false move after this, just the slighest hint of hostility now from you, and he'll know. . . ."

"I've been hostile to him from the day we met. He's no better toward me."

"But you can't show him that you think he's responsible for this. He'll know why—and who you are."

"That's why I don't want to see him. Not until I calm down enough to look at him without wanting to strangle him," Noel explained.

"Fine. Maybe that is the best way to do it. Get control of yourself. That's the surest way to nail this heartless bastard!"

The instant the Fisherman said it, Noel felt the hate in his voice as an almost palpable thing. More palpable somehow than Noel's own grief and anger over Randy. Perhaps because it wasn't tinged with gratitude, unconscious until now, that Randy was dead—Randy who'd initiated Noel so deeply into homosexuality. Sure, that must be the reason why his own anger couldn't be as strong as Loomis's—because Loomis had no guilt, no mixed feelings.

And, as Noel hung up on Loomis, he wondered, too, if the Fisherman didn't have a more embracing enmity, one of longer duration, with more experiences, more grief, because he had more deaths and mutilations to tally against Eric than just this one.

What if Loomis did know about the fraternity gang rape years back? What if he did think Noel was a psychosexual? What if he had tested him severely, was still testing him? It was all for an unswerving, determined, and just cause, wasn't it? Other men were more ruthless, more unscrupulous in attaining their ends—their puny goals of greed, power, influence. Loomis merely wanted to rid the world of an insane criminal.

Once he thought that, Noel realized it was the counterbalance he had needed the night before, when he'd become hysterical—as Vega had been so fast to

point out. Seeing only from his own perspective, Noel
had hated Loomis. Rising above it, above his puny
little ego and its problems, he now saw how he fit
into the larger picture. Loomis's almost sacrosanct
cause would be Noel's cause: his just anger would be
Noel's noble fury: his controlled purpose, Noel's goal.

Noel would get even with Eric for Randy's death in
his own way. And he would take his time doing it.

Despite that decision, it was another three hours
before Noel could bring himself to call the town
house.

Okku answered, which was lucky.

"Please tell Mr. Redfern I won't be able to come in
for a few days," Noel said, acting as though it were an
ordinary job, he an ordinary employee.

"Hold on! Hold on!" the manservant said.

Noel heard a buzz, then a ring, and before he could
figure out that Okku had not been interrupted on another line, but was connecting him to Eric, he heard:

"Noel?"

Too late. Noel tried to control his voice and the anger he still felt.

"I'm not coming in for a few days," he said.

"Listen. I heard from Reed and Jerry that—"

"Right!" Noel interrupted, not wanting to hear another word, not another syllable of the hypocrisy.
He'd heard from Reed and Jerry! Sure, he had! "See
you later," Noel managed to get out and quickly hung
up.

He kept the phone off the hook the rest of the day,
took a Valium, a shower, then went to sleep. He'd
been afraid of dreams, horrible dreams, but thankfully
none came.

When the downstairs buzzer rang three days later and
the doorman said that a lady had come to visit Noel,
his first thought was that it was Mirella Trent. He
didn't want to see her and was signaling back to tell
Gerdes not to let her up, when he received a loud
buzz and the slight electrical shock that meant Gerdes
was leaning on his end of the button. The old man's
cracked voice announced, "She's coming up."

Noel cursed once, then looked at himself in the mirror. He was unshaven, unwashed, unkempt, wearing
jeans that ought to have been laundered a week ago.
He hated being seen like this. Well, maybe Mirella
would be disgusted and leave. Of course, perverse as
she was, she might find it a turn-on; she'd always professed a taste for workingmen. He didn't want her,
though. He still felt too much resentment toward her
for what he'd discovered about himself the last time
he was with her.

Suddenly it was too late to do anything about his
appearance or the slovenliness of the apartment—the
doorbell was buzzing.

Defiantly, he opened the door for her. "Yeah?"

"You look awful. Have you been ill?"

It was Alana, not Mirella.

Noel fell back from the door. She looked at him
once more, then came in, shut the door, repeated her
question, and put a cool hand up to his forehead. He
brushed it away.

"I'm fine," he said.

"You certainly don't look fine." She was wearing the lightest hint of patchouli today, but she smelled as fresh as a mountain cascade. He felt even slimier next to her.

"I thought you were someone else," he said lamely. He felt completely unprepared. He looked awful, the place was a mess. She was like a rare Ming vase suddenly placed in a Chinese Laundromat five steps below street level. She didn't fit.

She sat down in the big rocking chair, let him get her an ashtray and a soft drink, and rocked back and forth gently, alternately looking at him and outside through the tall windows, smoking a St. Moritz cigarette as though she'd been here many times before, as he foolishly reiterated that he was not ill, but had merely been upset, needed time to think, to be alone.

"It's such a lovely day," she said when his words had come to a dead end. "Why don't we go out?" It was as if she hadn't heard a word he'd said, though he knew she had. "I'll wait while you clean up. Perhaps we'll go for a walk in the park. Or have lunch. We never did have that lunch," she reminded him.

All so tactful, so gratefully said, Noel couldn't refuse her.

Fifteen minutes later he was walking with her to the parked Mercedes. Alana handed him the keys and slid into the passenger seat.

It was a glorious June day: a few high, motionless clouds, like wads of cotton, but bright sunlight reflected off the streets and glass building facades as they drove up Sixth Avenue.

At Fifty-seventh Street they stopped for a light, and Noel turned to her with a sudden, insane idea. "Let's split somewhere. To Mexico. Just you and I. I have some money, some credit cards we can burn. We'll live in an adobe hut. Go swimming. Make love all day. Eat tacos."

She laughed tentatively for the first time, then broke into a laugh. "I don't like Mexican food."

Before he could suggest an alternative route, she said, "Why don't we walk into the park?"

When they had locked the car, she took his arm and let him promenade her into the park, first on a broad paved path, then past the swan pond, onto a cutoff, going north, deeper into the park, without saying a word.

She seemed to know all the byways. She steered them away from the more frequented areas, until they had skirted the carousel, past the Tavern-on-the-Green, the Delacorte Theatre where Shakespeare was given at night, into a secluded little hilly area with a green-lawned dell that Noel had never seen before. They stopped there. Alana looked around, and finally sat down on a flat sheet of basalt, set like a dark gray tablet amid the grass. Loosening the kerchief she'd been wearing around her head, she shook her hair free, long, almost blue-black in this light. Noel didn't see anyone else in the little valley.

"There!" she said with relief, and lay back on the flat rock, her hair spread out, her thin silk blouse looking as fragile as Japanese paper against her skin.

"I'd like to kiss you," Noel said, leaning over to do it.

She held up a restraining hand. "No. I promised."

"Promised who? Eric?"

"Of course. The first day we saw you. At the Window Wall. We agreed then. Either both of us, or neither of us."

Alana smiled as she said it, so Noel took it for a joke. He pushed her hand aside and leaned over her again.

She sat up, eluding him. Her smile was gone.

"I said I promised, Noel."

"You can't mean it?"

"Of course I mean it. I would never break a promise to Eric."

"You already did," he protested. "You kissed me once before. Remember? In the studio?"

"That was for the photographs. It wasn't real, Noel."

He sulked for a minute. She lay back down again.

"Why did you bring me here, then?" he asked.

"To talk to you."

"Why here?" He realized he was being suspicious, but didn't care.

"Because I like it here," she replied simply. "I hoped you would like it, too."

That made his suspicions even more foolish.

"Why don't you lie back and relax?" she suggested.

He hesitated, then joined her. The stone was warm against his back, smooth, soothing. Above them the clouds seemed to have vanished; the sky was a pale, ringing blue.

"All right," he said, deliberately harsh, "talk!"

She was silent at first, and, he thought, angry, but then she quietly said, "There's so much to say to you."

He wouldn't help her a bit.

"First, I want to be certain that you know how much we care for you, Noel, both Eric and I, because that is most important. These past few days we both missed you a great deal."

"What's the matter? Was Okku too busy cooking to spot for Eric's weight lifting?"

"Eric loves you. You don't do him justice."

"Sure."

"As I love you, Noel. No. Differently than I do. But he does."

"All right, let's assume I believe Eric loves me, what next?"

"He needs you, Noel. He is going through a bad time right now and he needs your help, your support."

"*He's* going through a bad time?"

She seemed surprised by the intensity of his reaction. Sitting up on one elbow, she looked at him bewildered. He wanted to play with her hair desperately, but figured that would constitute an advance.

"Yes. It is true. I would know, wouldn't I? Eric is very upset about, well, you know, this ghastly business about poor Rondee."

Alana believed that. Noel could tell looking into her eyes—now brown, now black, now flecked, now even bluish in the sunlight—innocent, guileless eyes. She believed Eric was upset about Randy's death.

"All right. So he's upset. What else?"

"Nothing else. Eric needs you by him now. He wants you near him. I know you have your differences of opinion, but try to . . ."

"It goes beyond differences of opinion. One reason I haven't been to the house is because I feel more than ever that my position is a false one there."

From her puzzled look, he instantly wondered if that hadn't been the worst thing to say. He tried explaining it away.

"I really can't live off him, live with him, and I can't return Eric's interest, or infatuation, or whatever it is. I can't. He doesn't attract me. He doesn't turn me on. Just the opposite."

"No. No. You are wrong. I have seen you together. You are like a snake charmer and a cobra. Sometimes one is the charmer, sometimes the other. Everyone else has remarked it. It's a strong and unusual attraction you have with Eric and you are foolish and wrong to deny it."

"Well, I don't see it."

Noel wondered if Eric had ever told her about his taking the Mercedes the night of the party and the fight they'd had in the garage. Probably.

"Then you are choosing not to see it," she declared. "The attraction exists. Now, I think that right at this moment you are merely a little confused and . . ."

"Is that what you told Eric to explain why I'm coming on to you?"

"Don't make a bad joke, Noel. It is true that you are a little confused. You don't know yourself what you are or who you want to be."

"You win, Alana. I'm confused. Several days ago I made love to a woman and although she was completely turned on, I wasn't. Later on that same night, I made love to several men."

"In Le Pissoir?"

"In the back room there. That night I really let go of myself. I did things with absolute strangers I'd never thought I'd do. Things I'd scarcely heard of. I wasn't disgusted about it. I didn't feel it was awful or wrong. But neither was it all that gratifying. And if it weren't for the drugs and atmosphere, I doubt that I even would have been interested. So you tell me, what is sex all about? A little pleasure, a lot of work, and for what?"

"If that's how you feel, you must stop."

"Stop what?"

"Sex. All of it. With men, with women. Stop for a while and don't think about it."

"But that's not dealing with it."

"*Foul!*" She tapped him lightly on the cheek. "You just told me you cannot deal with it. No? Sex is not so important. Do other things instead."

In the three days of furious thinking and rethinking since he'd awakened on the sawdust-strewn floor of the back room, *that* particular idea had never even struck him. She repeated it again, and again he was forced to admire her clearheadedness.

"Put it aside," she said; "there are more important matters now: yourself, me, Eric, being friends. That is very important, no? You always want to kiss me, to make love to me. Why not be my friend, first? And Eric's friend, too. He needs friends more than ever now. And so do you, Noel."

That last remark irritated him. He wanted to grab her and tell her she was talking bullshit, Pollyanna nonsense. But her simple solution cut through his overwhelming confusion like Alexander the Great's sword slicing through the Gordian knot.

Alana must have been aware of what was passing through his mind; she looked down at him as though her beauty and sympathy would lead him exactly right.

"No sex for a while," he said. "And I won't try to kiss you."

"You'll feel better. Believe me."

"Maybe."

"You will." She sat up and leaped off the rock. "Now! Let's go to lunch. Then we will see Eric and tell him."

"Tell him what?" Noel asked warily.

"That you'll come back to the house. That we'll all go to the Hamptons together, which he needs so badly right now. And that we'll all be friends. Come on, lazy. Get up."

Glancing at her as they strode arm in arm back through the park, Noel wondered how she would take the news when it finally came, as it must, of the kind of monster Eric was. He knew it would be shattering to her. His only consolation was that he would be there, a friend and potential lover. She would need and want him to be there, to help her get over the shock.

"You look better already," she said. "You see how easy it is?"

3

Eric joined them in the sidewalk café attached to an elegant hotel on upper Fifth Avenue. He sauntered in so casually, sat down so naturally, that it was a full minute before Noel registered it as an intrusion on the lovely afternoon he'd been enjoying with Alana.

"I asked Paul-Luc to call me if you came here," Eric explained, ordering a Zubrowka vodka on the rocks from the slightly embarrassed waiter. "I thought you might be here. This is Alana's favorite afternoon spot."

She kissed Eric lightly on the cheek. Noel stared for an instant, which Eric didn't seem to mind. Then Eric said exactly what would have infuriated Noel three days ago. Now, it only seemed unnecessary:

"I know you were fond of Randy. I'm very sorry to hear about what happened to him. I can't think of anyone who deserved it less. It was rotten. Everyone liked him."

His words were innocuous enough, expected, given the situation. Yet they held an unexpected anger that Noel couldn't quite understand. Could it have been a mistake, and Eric really was sorry it had happened? He had always liked Randy, Noel knew. Or was he a consummate actor? Or even worse, did Eric have some kind of psychosis that allowed him to sanction such an act and then to blot it out so thoroughly that he *could* be sorry later?

"I guess that's the danger of places like Le Pissoir," Noel replied, conventionally enough. "Anyone can be the target."

"But why Randy?" Eric insisted. "With all the real shits around."

"No more, please," Alana begged.

Even an Oscar-winning performer wouldn't go that far, Noel guessed. The psychosis theory, then.

"Just one thing more," Eric apologized to her. Then, to Noel, "I don't think Randy was the intended victim. I think he was mistaken in the dark for you."

First Loomis, now Eric. It freaked him. "For me? Why me?"

Eric's drink arrived, he sipped at it. Slowly turning the glass in his hands and avoiding Noel's eyes, he said, "To get at me. That's why. That's what it's going to be like staying with us—with Alana and me. You'll be in constant danger. All of us will be."

"Eric!" she pleaded. "You said you wouldn't."

"I have to tell him that." He turned to Noel. "Now you know the worst."

Noel was so twisted by the new tack Eric had taken, he almost couldn't answer. He felt disarmed by the warning, then angry, then thrown back into confusion: the psychosis theory wasn't working. Maybe it had been a mistake. A freak killing. Both Eric and Alana were looking at him for some kind of response, so he said:

"The police think I did it."

"That's what Reed said. Don't worry, we'll get you the best attorney if it comes to that. I doubt that it will. They have no case. By the way, what the hell were you doing in there anyway? That was the real shock to me."

It was too long and complicated to go into, so Noel told him it was research for his book.

"Oh, Christ! I might have known. Well, you sure did a good job of it."

"Why? Did people talk?"

"People always talk."

"What did they say?"

"That you were stoned, hot, trashy, outrageous. Don't worry. All that's good for your reputation." Suddenly his lips opened in a smile. "I'm sort of sorry I missed it. It must have been like the Virgin Mary losing her cherry at an Elks convention."

"You bastard," Noel said, but he laughed, too, and soon all of them were laughing at how Noel had in one night turned around his previous aloof, distant, cold reputation.

They were still laughing when Alana glanced at her watch. It was nearly six o'clock.

"I thought we'd get out of town for the next few weeks," Eric said, suddenly sobered, "until all this blows over."

"I'm not sure I can," Noel admitted, "the police."

"Dorrance fixed it. You can. How about it?" Eric asked, looking closely at Noel.

I think he was mistaken in the dark for you. "All right," Noel said.

They paid the bill and walked out onto the street. Eric and Okku would fly out tonight: would Noel mind driving with Alana?

Noel would be delighted, he said, as Eric stopped half a block away from the sidewalk café at a flat, waist-high silver coupé parked at the curb.

"How do you like it? I just bought it."

It looked more like a piece of contemporary sculpture than an automobile. "What is it?" Noel asked, trying to read the stylized nameplate set into the vents of the front grille.

"A Lamborghini. Like it?"

"It looks like it belongs on the lawn of a suburban museum," Noel said. "It's extraordinary."

Eric got in and the window shot down. Then he signaled for Noel to bend down for a final word.

"Drive carefully. If you have any trouble at all, there's a loaded gun in the Benz. Inside a fake ceiling in the glove compartment. Alana knows where it is."

Alana bent to kiss Eric. He waved, and with a single light touch of the steering wheel, pulled out of the spot and roared down Fifth Avenue.

4

———————————————

What I don't understand is why you need a place like Le Pissoir?" Noel said.

It was their fourth day at the villa. Noel and Eric

had just finished a leisurely jog up and down the mile-and-a-half-long driveway. Eric's house was off the double lane road that ran from Springs to Amagansett. Now, they lay on rafts in the large circular pool, talking, floating under the shade of three large trees that had been left at one end of the pool when the compound was constructed. If they stood, they'd be near the only open portion of the terrace—a balcony overlooking a several-hundred-foot drop over rough rock cliffs. Northeast, there was a magnificent view of Napeaugue Bay and Gardiners Island. On clear days, standing at the railing looking due east, you could see as far as Montauk Point, and north to the Connecticut shore.

"I'm involved with both Bar Sinister and Le Pissoir because if I didn't run them someone else would. Only I do it better," Eric said. "There have been back-room bars since the early sixties. I've upgraded the whole thing. I sell liquor at uninflated prices. I have a controlled membership so there aren't too many undesirables. I've made the atmosphere cleaner, sexier, more attractive, safer—yes, Noel, safer—fire exits, sprinkler systems. A dozen ways out of each place in an emergency. Check out some of the competition. Firetraps, pigsties, cleaned once a month, if at all, and staffed with insolent, gay-hating slobs."

"It's still exploiting a weakness," Noel said.

"Or fulfilling a need," Eric came back. "There are two sides to it. If you add Clouds and Window Wall, it all changes. You know how special their clientele is. Movie stars call up for memberships. And the Window Wall has the best party crowd in the country. You've been there. You've seen. That's exploiting, too, according to your theory. And I'm in business, I admit it, even though I feed all the income from the clubs right back into them, or into new ones. But in my places people get what they pay for—and a little more: quality. That's not the way the mobs run their places. All they're interested in is skimming the cream off the top and letting the place go to pieces in a year or two. My clubs have reputations. Each is unique. They endure."

"But why have them at all?"

"The discos? There's a need for great entertainment places where people will party. It's the same with the fuck bars."

"But why is it all so back street, so seedy, so sleazy?"

"At first it had to be that way. People didn't want to see gays congregating for any reason. They still don't. You're aware of that, aren't you, Noel, despite your ivory tower existence?"

"It's become a ghetto."

"Maybe so. But now it's a voluntary ghetto. A place where teenagers can't gang up on one drunken queen; if they do, a vigilante group forms and keeps the kids in line. The kind of place that just doesn't exist except in a few spots: Fire Island, parts of San Francisco, Manhattan's West Side."

"But it's all so underground. And the connections with crime, why that?"

Eric smiled. "Everything I do is a crime in this state. I live with a woman I'm not married to. I sleep with men and can be busted for sodomy. I take drugs, most of which are illegal. Everything I do is considered a crime, and I am a criminal. You, too. All of us. You tell me why gays have traditionally allied themselves with organized crime even when they knew they were getting ripped off. How were you treated by the police a few days ago?"

Noel didn't have to be reminded of that.

"You see," Eric said, taking Noel's silence for assent. "And you're a valued member of society: a university professor. You have to begin *there*, with the oppression, to understand why the gay subculture is the way it is, otherwise your book is going to be another crock of academic shit."

"If that's so, then change it, don't reinforce it."

"We're trying to do that. What we are reinforcing is a common identity and shared interests so that gays don't see themselves as abnormal criminals but as a justifiable minority. Through laws and politics we'll move on. We're only at these first steps, baby. The Mattachine Society is only twenty years old, you know." Eric looked up sharply as Noel was about to speak. "Hold on. Looks like we have company."

Noel followed his glance across the pool where Okku had led a burly, suntanned young stranger out onto the terrace.

Before Noel could get a good look at him, Eric shouted:

"You're one hour late, McWhitter."

"You don't look like you're going anywhere." The stranger walked alongside the rim of the pool toward them, Okku following.

As he advanced, Noel recognized him as the bouncer at a private discotheque in Southampton he and Eric and Alana had gone to the night before. Eric had talked to McWhitter at one point, buying him a drink during the bouncer's break. At first, Noel had thought it was merely a pickup. The overmuscled, baby-faced, big-bodied McWhitter definitely looked as though he liked his action rough. But Eric had come home alone.

"That's the second mistake you made so far, McWhitter," Eric said in his most menacing manner, without moving an inch from his position on the float. "Care to try for number three?"

For a second, Noel thought McWhitter was going to jump into the pool and attack Eric. His features settled into a tight, prognathic grimness; his clear green eyes darkened suddenly, as though some protective opaque membrane had come instinctively down over them. His hands tensed at his sides. He said nothing, made no move for what seemed a long while, a looming presence at the poolside, until Eric broke the silence.

"I see you're sulking. That's mistake number three, McWhitter. Get lost."

"You said you had a job for me."

"I said to come at eleven o'clock to talk to me about a job. It's past noon now. Get out."

"You said you had a job."

"Okku, throw him out," Eric said, and began to turn over onto his stomach, at the same time paddling the water on one side to face the float toward the two men.

"What about my job?" McWhitter complained.

"Try sitting on it," Eric suggested.

McWhitter looked back and forth between Eric and Okku, as though trying to make up his mind which to tear apart. Then, raising one fist high in the air, he charged right into the manservant.

The rest was very fast. Okku sidestepped him, spun around, grabbed McWhitter's arm and shoulder, and threw him forward. McWhitter fell hard, but leaped up again as Okku came crashing down on him, feet first. McWhitter siderolled, rose, and catching Okku off balance, spun him off the ground like a corkscrew, punctuating it with a probing karate chop to Okku's lower abdomen. Okku seemed to fall back in great pain, then suddenly jumped forward with two open-handed blows, one to McWhitter's head, the other to his body. The bigger man dropped to his knees and seemed to grip Okku at the hips while the blows rained down on his neck and head and back. But in a second, Okku was up in the air, lifted by McWhitter and swung by his calves over the railing.

Noel jumped off his float and swam to the edge of the pool.

"Don't move or I drop him!"

McWhitter swung Okku in a wide arc, then looked back at Eric, who hadn't moved an inch from his prostrate position, chin in his hands as though he were lying on the living room carpet watching a wrestling match on television.

"Well?" McWhitter shouted. "Do I get the job, or do I drop him?"

"Can you cook?" Eric asked.

"Cook?"

"That's what I asked. Can you cook?"

"I don't know. Hamburgers, things like that."

"The man you want to drop is one of the best cooks in the state. French, Chinese, Italian, and American regional dishes are his specialties. If you let go of him, you can still have the job. But you'll have to do all the cooking."

McWhitter looked at Okku's outstretched body. "He's a good cook?" he shouted back at Eric.

"That's what I said."

"I'm no cook. I'm a masseur. Isn't that what I told you last night?"

"You're hired," Eric said, and rolled over on his back again.

McWhitter swung Okku back onto the terrace side of the railing, setting him down gently enough. He said, "I hope you're okay, mister. Didn't mean anything personal by all this, you understand?"

Okku got up and away to a safe distance. He seemed unhurt, only slightly shaken.

"When do I start?" McWhitter asked.

"Right now," Eric said casually. "You can go now, Okku. Thanks. Come on, big boy. You can swim, can't you?"

McWhitter stripped off his clothing, revealing a spectacularly muscled body. Raising his hands as though about to pray, he arched and dove into the water, sliding under to the other side and coming up smoothly right at the head of Eric's rubber raft. Lightly touching it as he dog-paddled, McWhitter shook the water off his face and immediately kissed Eric's lips.

"Do you mind?" Noel heard him ask in a small voice, husky with some emotion. "Working out always gets me a little excited." Then he turned to face Noel, a look of assessment. Not friendly.

"How excited?" Noel heard Eric ask.

"Real excited."

"Then let's get the hell out of this pool," Eric said.

A minute later Eric was leading McWhitter in through the glass doors of his pavilion. He winked at Noel, and even shrugged as though to say, "Would you believe this?"

Then the curtains were pulled.

5

Left alone, Noel felt at loose ends, with nothing to do, yet with an itch to do something, anything.

He checked in on Alana. She was napping, blissfully curled in her pale blue silk sheets. He decided not to wake her.

The kitchen was empty. As he poured himself a drink, Noel heard the familiar sound of the washing machine downstairs in the laundry attached to the garage. Wasn't that just like the phlegmatic Okku—one minute hanging a hairbreadth away from death, the next doing the wash.

Then it flashed on him: now was the perfect time to call Loomis. It had been four days since he'd checked in.

The first loop number he dialed from the living room pavilion was picked up immediately. Noel was about to identify himself when he heard a young-sounding woman say a bright, "Hello!"

It was the first time such a thing had happened to him. The number must have been assigned. He made an awkward excuse about a wrong number, and hung up, hoping one of the other three numbers was still unassigned.

The second call was picked up on the third ring. The familiar silence that followed told him he'd struck an open loop. He waited a minute or so to be sure, then said, "Lure here."

"Hold on, Lure," a vaguely familiar voice said, and left him hanging another minute.

"Where the hell have you been?"

It was Loomis—pissed off.

Noel wasn't fazed. "I couldn't call until now."

"Where are you?"

"Redfern's place in Amagansett. Everyone is busy for the minute. It's the first I could get away."

Which wasn't exactly true. The reasons he hadn't tried to call until now were more complicated. He was still resentful that Whisper hadn't extricated him from the humiliations of the precinct house. He had found himself enjoying his new status—not as sex object, but as friend, confidant to a minor extent of Eric. He had been enjoying Alana's company—limited as that was. Enjoying the lazy, hot, sunny weather and the lazy, comfortable life at the villa.

"You're calling from inside? What are you, crazy? He'll trace it. I'll call back. Hang up."

"No! Okku would be sure to pick it up," Noel reasoned. "Besides I don't have anything to report. Just one thing. A new person just appeared. A bodyguard, I think. His name is McWhitter. He used to be the bouncer at a small disco out here called Blue Trousers. That's all I know of him."

"How much longer are you staying there?"

"Don't know. A week. Two weeks. All summer."

"Isn't there a pay phone nearby?"

"Fifteen minutes by car."

"Shit! Don't call then. We can't take chances."

"Of course if anything should happen—" Noel began but left it hanging.

"Doesn't he have to go into the city at all?" Loomis asked.

"He did yesterday. Okku drove him to the East

Hampton Airport. He flew in, and was back out at the house a few hours later."

"I don't like having you out there by yourself," Loomis said.

"I'm not by myself."

"He doesn't suspect anything?" Loomis asked.

"Why should he?"

"Remember how angry you were?"

"I remember. It's no problem now. Mainly because I don't think he did it."

"Of course *he* didn't. It was one of his . . ."

But Noel had thought it out over the past few days. "No," he said, "I'm sure he isn't responsible for it."

"Come on, now. You certainly don't believe that crap about it being some creeping homophobe?"

"I don't know what to believe. But I'm pretty sure Eric didn't do it. What was his motive?"

Loomis was silent, thinking. "To have you to himself."

"No way."

"Then revenge. For Randy leaving his employ."

"He got over it. He was financing Randy's return to school."

Loomis's voice was pinched when he answered. "Look, he must have known both of you were there that night. He might have done it just to have the police on your back."

"He promised to get me a lawyer," Noel said. "I can't find a motive. Neither can you. Admit it."

"Then who did it?" Loomis asked, piqued now.

"You're the detective. You tell me."

There was a pause, then, "All right. I'll get some people on it. By the way, watch out for Vega. He knew you were there, didn't he? That both of you would be there?"

"I thought he was on our side," Noel said.

"Maybe," Loomis said ominously. "All right, Lure. Call again when you can. But not from the house. Do you hear?"

The old cop was becoming more bizarrely suspicious every time they talked. Vega responsible for Randy's death? It was ludicrous! It would be a long while before Noel would subject himself to Loomis's idiocy again. Being out here was a perfect excuse.

He hung up the phone and was unconsciously playing with a candlestick on the mirrored phone table when he noticed unexpected colors reflected and looked for the source.

Alana—in a blue bathrobe, standing arms akimbo, at the glass doors leading from the living room to the pool terrace. She had a look on her face Noel had never seen before and couldn't decipher. How long had she been standing there? What had she heard? He'd been talking in a low voice.

"Hi! Have a good nap?" he asked brightly.

"*Pas mal.* It was very hot. Who were you talking to, Noel?"

Christ, she had heard something. But what? How much?

"A friend. In the city."

"A friend?" Her odd look hadn't changed. She kept her pose, and that menaced him with all sorts of awful possibilities.

"Some guy I know," he said, as nonchalantly as possible. "He told me he sometimes came out to the Hamptons. I thought I'd see if he was coming out this week."

Despite the glibness with which he lied, he was sure she didn't believe him. She couldn't have heard any of the conversation from the doorway. Could she? He got off the sofa and went over to her.

"Are you angry with me?" he asked. "Because I'm not following your good advice?"

"I'm not angry," she said, but avoided his touch.

"I was a little lonely. Eric had a visitor. You were asleep. Okku was busy. It's all right. He's not coming out here. I'm safe."

She looked at him as though she were about to tell

him she knew everything and why was he lying to
her? But all she said was, "I hope so, Noel. I hope you
are safe. For all our sakes."

Now he interpreted her look as one of concern, and
he felt treacherous, rotten.

But before he could give in, she had turned and
gone out onto the terrace. She pulled off the blue
robe, and naked and gleaming tan, plunged into the
pool.

6

If Alana had told Eric of the phone call, there was no
evidence of it during the following week. Life at the
villa continued its usual leisurely pace. With the addition of Bill McWhitter, of course.

Eric and Bill were together all the time now, going
for jogs lasting hours, driving out together in the
Mercedes, disappearing at what seemed prearranged
moments from the few dinners where outsiders—
friends of Eric and Alana's from nearby—were invited.

"Young love," Noel said, following one such disap-
pearance.

"Young lust, I'd say," Dorrance commented. He'd
been at the house all day, on business. He would fly
back to Manhattan in the morning.

"And I'd say you are both jealous!" Alana put in.

"Of whom?" both asked.

"Of . . . of everyone," she replied, laughing.

It was a little bit true of himself, Noel had to admit.
To have Eric's constant attention and interest and
have them suddenly withdrawn was annoying. Better,

of course, Noel said to himself. He didn't want to get
too close to Eric. That made no sense. That made him
act stupidly, dangerously. Like his stupid insistence to
Loomis that Eric hadn't killed Randy. He still believed that was so. Eric had just plain *liked* Randy too
much to be implicated in his death. And he had nothing whatsoever to gain by it. Whatever other faults
Eric had, wastefulness was not one of them. Still, Noel
had been foolish to be so insistent about it to the
Fisherman. Why raise suspicions at all? Loomis might
already be onto Vega for finding those dossiers.
Could that be why he had tried to plant suspicions
about Vega in Noel's mind? Perhaps. And who knew
what Vega's real motives were for revealing those papers to Noel. Except perhaps to sow dissension between Noel and Whisper. He had never liked Noel.

Working it out one night when the paperback he'd
been reading had begun to bore him, Noel decided he
didn't fully trust Eric or Loomis, or Vega, or—worst of
all—Alana; not now, with that phone call hanging between them. She had never referred to it, hadn't done
or said anything at all to indicate she even recalled it.

But Noel could not forget the look on her face as
he'd turned to see her standing there. It had to be settled between them. So, with the intention of finding
out exactly what she had overheard, Noel chose the
Tuesday after the loops call to request a day off.

They were at breakfast, on the pool terrace: Eric,
Alana, McWhitter, and Noel. The bodyguard had relaxed since his rather aggressive arrival, although he,
too, was working, teaching Eric jujitsu and karate
every afternoon.

"You want a vacation from *this?*" McWhitter asked
in disbelief.

"He's entitled," Eric said. "Go right ahead, Noel.
Take the day, if you want." Then, to Bill, "He hasn't
been getting laid as regularly as you have, you know."
Back to Noel: "What are your plans?"

"I don't know. I thought I'd go over to the Tiana boys' camp and rape a few six-year-olds."

"Man! That's weird!" McWhitter said.

"Don't listen to him," Eric said. "He's got a date, don't you, Noel?"

"With Alana. If she wants to come. You'll have to wear a bikini top, though, I'm warning you."

"To Tiana?" she asked. "That's so far."

"We'll find a closer beach. A public beach. I want to see some people."

She looked at Eric. "What about you two?"

"We'll just hang around here, discuss theology," Eric said.

Several hours later Noel and Alana arrived at Southampton Beach. The nearest occupied blanket was twenty-five feet away.

"Well," Alana said, "here are all your people!"

Noel ignored her remark and began to spread suntan lotion on her shoulders.

"I can do that," she said, but he held the tube away from her and went on meticulously covering her already butterscotch-colored skin with a thin veil of rapidly melting liquid. "I think I didn't need to wear a top at all," she said. "Don't do that, Noel. It tickles."

Unable to resist, he had followed his index finger inside her navel with the tip of his tongue. She gently pulled his head away and finished putting on the lotion herself.

The sun beat down stronger here than at the Redfern villa. The water in front of them was calm as the Caribbean, with a tide breaking languorously on the shore. Noel had wanted to be alone with her, away from Eric, from the villa. But the minute he realized she wouldn't allow him even to begin lovemaking, he fell back on the blanket, letting the glaring sunlight break up the ocean surface like a pointillist painting in golds and blues and whites, until his vision—even through polarized lenses—seemed to fragment, and spot red when he closed his eyes.

When he turned over and looked at her, Alana was sitting up reading a magazine.

"What is it you want, Alana? Really want?" he asked.

She looked over the top of the magazine, then around at the various objects spread on the blanket. "Nothing," she said.

"I mean what do you want out of life?" he asked.

The upper part of her face was in shadow from the brim of her sun hat. "Nothing," she said again, slowly, deliberately.

"Everyone wants something," he argued. "If not for themselves, then for someone else. Their children. Those they love."

"One grows up," she said. "One realizes certain things one longed for a great deal mean nothing."

"Like what?"

She put a hand on his shoulder. "Don't make me think about the past anymore. Please. You are restless. Let's go swim."

It was like diving into a huge blue pool, the water was warm, calm. They swam along shore, then frolicked, diving and coming up under each other, then walked side by side at the surfline.

Her hair dried in long ringlets that were so black they seemed tinted with blues and browns and reds, as though all the shades of the spectrum were signaling their presence. He felt even more frustrated.

"Do you know why I asked you here today?"

"Because you wanted to see people."

"Because I wanted to see you alone. I never see you at the villa."

"You exaggerate. I am there all the time."

Now, Noel told himself. It had to be now. "Remember last week, when I called my friend?"

She didn't answer.

"Remember, Alana, the day McWhitter came to work for Eric?"

"I am not sure," she said inattentively, heading them back to the blanket.

"I was calling that friend because I felt so lonely out here."

"Oh?" The word came out of her toneless.

"Really. Or . . . did you think it was something else."

When she didn't answer, he prodded, "Alana?"

"I don't remember, Noel."

She was facing him, her eyes suddenly growing large. "Why don't you take a nap? That's what I am going to do."

His defeat filled a sigh. She gave him the tiniest kiss on the cheek, then sat down, lay back, and closed her eyes.

Noel sat down, too, looking at her for a long time as she relaxed, then fell asleep.

He couldn't help but compare her to Monica, whom he had awakened next to for so many years, and to Mirella Trent, whom he'd also awakened next to a dozen times in the months they were sleeping together. How inaccessible they had been to him while they slept—how private, how quiet, how different from their waking selves. But not Alana. Oddly, she seemed no different sleeping, as inaccessible awake as now. Why was that? Because they had never made love together, didn't share that important physical bond? Or because he suspected that even having her body would never be enough for him, that he wanted more from her—what she could never give him: what it seemed she had already given to Eric.

Finally, Noel fell asleep, too. When she awakened him it was near sunset. They decided to have dinner in Southampton.

Alana met friends at the restaurant they had chosen. Would Noel mind if they joined their table? Another man she knew, and some friends of his, arrived, expanding the party. They were laughing, speaking French, drinking. By the time the party was breaking up, it was eleven o'clock. Noel was content that she had at least had a good time, even if he had gained nothing but the bitter knowledge of how distant she still was from him.

At the top of the ascending drive to the Redfern villa, the porte cochere was lighted up; for them, Noel guessed, until they drove closer and saw figures moving about the Silver Cloud, the trunk and two of the doors open. What was going on?

"It's them," Noel heard Eric shout in the dark, as he swept the Mercedes over to the Silver Cloud and stopped, without shutting off the headlights.

"Where in hell were you two?" Eric demanded.

"What's wrong, darling?" Alana asked.

"We're going back to the city."

"Tonight?" Noel asked. But Alana was already out of the car.

"I can't explain why, Alana," Eric was saying to her, "but we really have to leave. Go pack. Follow us in the big car."

"What is wrong?" she asked again, angry, her accent thick.

"I don't have time to explain," Eric said. "But we aren't safe here anymore. None of us."

He had been holding her by the shoulders. Alana turned and went into the house with small, determined steps.

"I'm coming with you," Eric said to Noel. "How's the gas?"

"More than half full."

"Bill? Do you have my leather bag?"

McWhitter brought it over, and Eric tossed it into the back storage compartment. Okku had brought out the coupé top and was fitting it onto the SL. Noel helped him.

"I'll have to pack, too."

"It's ready," Okku said, and moved the bag from the trunk of the limo to the back of the sports car.

Eric was embracing McWhitter. "Keep it hot for me. We'll party tonight in town. Get some rest, will you?"

"We'll be right behind you," McWhitter said.

Eric turned to Noel. "What are you waiting for? Let's go!"

7

Twenty minutes later, as they were passing the exits for Center Moriches on the Long Island Expressway, Eric began turning around in his seat.

"Someone's following us," he said, after he had done it the third time. He opened the glove compartment. "Is that gun still here?"

"I don't know. I never looked for it."

Eric found it: there was a clang of metal on metal.

After what Noel considered the first "normal" day of his existence in months—minimal worries, suspicions alleviated—the sudden announcement that they had to leave, the sudden return to a life of perils and suspected perils, of no explanations and hasty behavior, irritated him. He'd been slowly steaming since they'd driven away from the house. Now he said:

"Put it away. I don't want you hurting anyone out of sheer paranoia." He didn't care if Eric accused him of being sarcastic, nonsupportive now.

"It's not paranoia," was all that Eric replied.

"Then why did we leave the villa so suddenly?"

"We were being watched." He put the gun back, and shut the glove compartment.

"Come on, Eric, give me a break, will you?"

"We were. I saw them. McWhitter saw them, too. They followed *you.* When you and Alana went out today, McWhitter and I were up on the roof fooling around. They were waiting for someone to come from the house, exactly where the driveway reaches the road. You must have seen them. A lighting maintenance truck and a smaller pickup. Pretending to fix something. They had binoculars. We saw them. The pickup followed you."

Noel had noticed the two vehicles, but hadn't noticed that they followed. That was interesting. As was Eric's seeing them.

"What if the pickup had a reason to take off just then? I mean, there're only two directions he could go, aren't there?"

"He followed you," Eric insisted.

"Assuming that's true, why . . . ?"

"They've been snooping around all week in one way or another. We saw some guys pretending to fish at the cove directly in front of the terrace two days ago. Naturally they would have a perfect view up."

"To the edge of the terrace? What could they see there? You two making out?"

"Okku had two strangers call during the week. Both with really lame excuses. One was selling equipment for digging wells. The other was calling for someone Okku had never heard of."

"But who are they?" Noel insisted.

"I don't know."

"Then why are they spying on you?"

"You're in as much danger as any of us, Noel. Maybe more."

"Who are they?"

"My enemies." Eric turned around again. "See that big sedan in the first lane? It's beginning to pull up now."

Noel checked the rearview mirror. There were few enough cars speeding along the highway this late at night: it was easy to see the headlights of the sedan in the first lane. It was pulling up.

"Move over a lane," Eric said. "Now!"

Noel swerved to the next lane. The sedan slowed

to parallel them. A mid-sixties Continental, black, chunky, long, tinted glass.

"Keep her steady," Eric said, tense.

Noel thought it was unlikely that the car would be following them. Even if all Eric had said were true, Loomis wouldn't be foolish enough to follow them so openly. Or would he?

"Can you see who's inside?" Eric asked. Almost involuntarily, Noel speeded up. The Continental moved to the outer edge of its lane, but kept pace.

Maybe the Fisherman was trying to scare Eric. But what was Noel supposed to do? Whoever was driving must realize that Noel would be as liable to any danger that resulted from this as Eric. If the sedan made the wrong move, who knew what crazy stunt Eric might pull? Noel decided to play it down.

"Someone might be in the back seat," Eric said, looking around.

"With a machine gun?" Noel asked.

"You think I'm overreacting, don't you?"

"*Think* you are?!"

"Then why are they holding steady with us?"

"It's a free road, Eric, really."

They were cruising at seventy-five now, the two cars gliding side by side along a curve in the highway, then descending into a straight stretch, slipping past other cars in the slow lane.

"Slow down a little," Eric said.

Noel brought their speed down to sixty; the big sedan did the same.

"There! Satisfied?" Eric asked.

"Why don't you put on some music?" Noel suggested. "Is that Keith Jarrett tape still here?" He rummaged with his free hand in the little compartment under the armrests, and looked up to see the big sedan falling out of sight.

Only to come up directly behind them.

"Shit!" Eric said. "Move over. I'll take the wheel."

"At this speed? No way!"

"They're tailgating us."

The headlights shone right into the Mercedes, illuminating the dashboard.

Noel had never seen Eric so jittery before, so anxious to take over. He almost expected him to pull out the gun and start shooting. He had to do something, had to stay in control of the car. No cars ahead. So he gunned it.

The sports car leaped like a big cat let out of a sack, almost with a life of its own. Noel hoped it would steer as easily as it did at lower speeds. Eighty. Ninety. Over a hundred miles an hour. They were slashing past landscape and trees until they were a blur, past slow-lane cars as though they were stopped.

"I think we lost them," Eric said.

They seemed to be on a different part of the highway. More cars were feeding in from some large access road. Noel had to slow down.

Minutes later, the sedan was on their tail again.

Noel saw it before Eric, slipped the car into the fast lane, and jumped out again. Because of the traffic, he had to zigzag.

"They're following," Eric said. His hand was in the glove compartment now—for the gun.

"Playing with us," Noel mumbled.

"You call it playing?" Eric asked, incredulous. "Move over. Let me take the wheel."

He made a grab for it. Noel knocked his hand away.

"I'll lose them," he said, furious now, not at Eric, who had every right to be frightened, but at the driver of the Continental, and at the Fisherman, and all those bastards in Whisper who'd sit around laughing their heads off when they heard. "You watch!"

He was cutting dangerously in and out of lanes, pushing the Mercedes up to ninety again. The sedan followed.

"Keep your eyes on them, tell me everything they're doing," Noel said between his teeth. "Every move."

In front of him, cruising traffic was also switching lanes. Noel maneuvered into a spot behind two fast cars, went around them, leading them.

"Get off the highway," Eric said. "Now. The exit."

Noel remained in the fast lane until a gap appeared between the two cars in front of him, one in each lane. He could see the exit sign just ahead, then the ramp itself. No other cars in the right-hand lane.

"He's right behind us, Noel," Eric said, panicked. "Get off the road. Go! Now!"

Noel calculated the space between the two cars ahead, close to their back bumpers.

"Noel! Do as I say!"

"Shut up, Eric!" he shouted, and at the same time rammed the Mercedes through the space, leaning on the horn. The cars' fenders were only inches away on either side of them, one car honking and swerving away.

"He's coming in after us," Eric said.

They cleared the two cars, Noel gunned the Mercedes, swerving, onto the exit ramp, praying that the wheel would turn in time, that they would clear the trees on the side of the road.

"You're going to kill us!" Eric screamed.

But the tires squealed and held; the car rocked into the curve dangerously then up the ramp. Noel braked it slowly to a stop. Out the side window he could see below on the highway. Ahead, the Continental had broken through the other two cars only to find itself alone. It had worked!

"We lost the fuckers!" Noel shouted, banging both hands on the steering wheel in glee. "They don't know where we are!"

Eric was sitting still, pale, drawn, as though someone had shoved him back against the seat.

"You enjoyed that, didn't you?" he asked in a tight voice.

"We got away, didn't we?"

Only as he said it did Noel realize what an incredible risk he'd taken. One mistake and they would have been totaled. They—and at least three other cars.

"Go back down on the highway," Eric said, and when they were driving along the road again, "pull over."

"Pull over?"

"Right there," Eric said. "I'm getting out."

The car bumped over the abutment and came to a rest on grass.

"Drive on to the house. Let yourself in. We'll catch up."

Eric got out.

"You wanted me to get away from them," Noel protested. "I got you away."

"I wanted to drive myself," Eric said.

"Why are you getting out now?"

"Because I can't stay in the car with you driving. I'm not safe."

Noel was suddenly very serious. "I thought we were becoming friends, Eric. If this is the way you trust me, maybe I'd better get out. I'll hitch back." As he got out of the SL, he added, "Better not wait up."

"I can't use this car," Eric said.

"Why not? It's yours."

"No, it's not. I had the registration put in your name."

Noel could barely make out Eric's face in the dim light of the overheads. "In my name? What for?"

"I was going to surprise you with it."

They leaned against the car. Eric lighted a joint, took a drag, handed it to Noel. Behind them was the whoosh of auto tires on asphalt. In front of them the rustle of trees. Noel was exhausted after the recent escape and exhilaration. He didn't know what to say, what to do. The least he'd expected was thanks from Eric. Maybe even shared triumph. He got nothing.

Nothing but the SL. They passed the joint back and forth.

Finally, he asked, "You're really waiting for them?"

"McWhitter will ride with you," Eric said. "I don't completely trust him either."

Silence, until the joint was only a glowing spark, too short to grab hold of.

"They tapped the phones," Eric said, "until I baffled them with a device I put together. Okku picked up the phone once to dial, right after you had finished talking to someone, and heard two men talking."

The loops! Noel tried to control his panic.

"What?" he asked. "When?"

"Last week."

"What were they saying?"

"Okku was so surprised he didn't recall. They heard him and clicked off. I've had baffles on in the city for the last few years. I didn't think we'd need them here."

So, Eric didn't know about the phone call. It was all guesswork, deduction, and the ridiculous visibility of Loomis's operatives. What a stupid thing to do! Yet it answered what could have been the worst possible discovery—the loops.

"And McWhitter?" Noel asked.

"I don't know. Maybe it's all coincidence. But none of this began out here until he arrived. His references checked out. He used to be a local hit man for the mob on the West Coast. Things got a little tight for him there. I don't know."

"Do you think Okku will see us and stop?" Noel asked.

He did see them, or at least Alana did. The Silver Cloud pulled onto the embankment and McWhitter had to be aroused from his nap and led like a big child to the SL where he was put into the passenger seat, and promptly dozed off again.

Noel followed the Rolls for a while, then the expressway met a crossover that fed in a great deal of

traffic, and Noel lost them. He had another twenty
minutes to drive by himself, thinking about what
would happen when he returned to the town house.
Every day seemed to complicate matters more. Eric
was onto Whisper, without knowing he was onto it.
Yet Noel would not allow that much information to
get back to Loomis through him: let him find out
through someone else. That might be construed as annoyance, he knew, but something about the Fisherman's methods was beginning to bother Noel deeply.
He felt stained by it. Everything about his life these
days—everything but Alana—had something rotten
about it.

"Wake up, sleeping beauty." He shook McWhitter
hard when they emerged from the Midtown Tunnel
into Manhattan. As they approached the town house,
McWhitter came fully awake, growling to himself.

"All out," Noel said at the down ramp into the garage.

"You're real friendly with Eric, aren't you?"

Noel didn't know what the bodyguard was getting
at. "Sure."

"Well that's too bad. 'Cause I don't like you."

"Get over it!" Noel said in a hard voice. "I live
here."

But he was still shaking after McWhitter slammed
the door and exited, loping over the wall around the
house in a single leap.

8

After he dropped off the bodyguard, Noel drove to find an all-night gas station where he could fill the tank and have the oil checked. He found one finally, near the Queensboro Bridge. The station attendants were all busy. While he waited, Noel opened the glove compartment. He found the fake ceiling, opened it, saw the material it had nestled in, but no gun. So Eric had taken it out of the car altogether.

Closing the panel, he found a slim leather packet. Sure enough, the car's registration had been made out in his name, sold to him for a dollar. All that was needed to make it legal was Noel's signature. Weird. The last thing he expected from Eric was the Mercedes as a gift. He wondered if professional ethics would allow him to keep it. Then he wondered what Eric expected in return: what was worth twenty-five thousand dollars? Nothing about Redfern made any sense. As soon as Noel thought one thing, Eric seemed to unconsciously go out of his way to do exactly the opposite.

When he returned to the town house, the limo wasn't in the garage. Yet lights were on in three floors.

Okku met him on the main floor. Eric and McWhitter had gone out to dinner and would probably be out the rest of the night, he said. Noel was to remain in.

That seemed to be a good sign. It meant that Eric had forgiven him for his reckless behavior on the expressway. Or, having had time to think about it, probably saw how foolish his own behavior had been.

Noel went up to his rooms on the fourth floor, showered, changed, then decided to see if Alana was still awake.

He found her a half hour later on the top floor. She was sitting in a lounge chair on the roof garden.

Noel's first impulse was to take advantage of the still beauty of the warm summer night, the flowers richly, odorously in bloom, to go to her and try to reestablish the rapport they'd had that afternoon, to make it something more.

Instead, he didn't move, holding one hand on the sliding door leading onto the deck, watching her, sensing that she was not to be disturbed right now, that she was enjoying a few rare moments of privacy, or meditation.

She broke the silence for him.

"What are you waiting for?" she said, without turning to face him. "Come and sit."

"I thought I was interrupting . . ." he began to explain. A thin mist over the night sky here, compared to the clarity of the skies over the Hamptons, made it seem as though a gauze scrim had been pulled over them. The few distant, lighted higher buildings made the deck garden float in a pool of darkness.

"You are very considerate," she said stiffly, motioning him to the chaise lounge next to hers.

"Okku said I was to stay in tonight."

"He meant that you were to remain here. You may go out if you wish, of course. They went to the Window Wall. It is only two o'clock. You can still go."

"I'll stay. I've had a pretty busy day."

He wanted to ask her for reassurances. He knew it was asking for too much. So he said, "We had an argument. In the car."

"I know. Eric said you were terrible. You frightened him, I'm certain of it. Not many people can frighten Eric."

"I'm not sure that's a compliment."

"It is your utter unpredictability that he is afraid of. His father was just so. Always, he needed him, but he could never rely on him, never trust him. Eric needs you, Noel. But you are not there for him. I don't think he completely understands that even you are not sure what you will do next."

That was a pretty shrewd estimate. "Maybe you're in the wrong business," he suggested.

"I know Eric inside and out."

"Me, too?"

"No. I am still guessing about you."

"Alana," he took her hand and she let him hold it without any protest, "tell me, why am I still here in this house? Eric doesn't need me. Especially with Mr. Muscles around."

"He'll grow tired of Bill in a few weeks. That is how Eric is. But with you it is different. You and he have a different bond."

Close to target again, he thought. And thanked her for taking his part on the drive back to the city.

"I did nothing of the sort," she declared.

They were silent for some time, then he decided to ask her some questions. He was certain she would answer truthfully.

"Why is Eric so paranoiac? Is he involved in crime?"

"Crime?"

"You know. Drugs. Smuggling. Is that why he's acting so odd?"

The minute he said it, her hand pulled out of his. Her tone of voice said what he couldn't see for the darkness: she was affronted.

"What makes you say that?"

"I don't know. Things I've heard."

"What things? That he is a drug pusher? Nonsense. He buys drugs, of course. Friends of his bring him cocaine from South America. But it is never enough to resell. And you see how generous he is with it. Every time you turn around it is finished."

"I also heard he ran prostitution rings. Women. Boys."

"Who told you that?"

"I just heard it."

"It is not true."

"And that he made pornographic movies."

"Who told you all these lies!" she asked, angry now.

"People."

"They are wrong. Wrong. They are envious. Jealous of us."

"Then why is he so goddamn paranoid, carrying guns, changing from one place to another so quickly, telling me we're being followed, that the phones are tapped?"

The last question would bring something about the phone call into the open, he supposed. But she chose not to take up the challenge.

"He says he has enemies. People want to . . . throw him away."

"To get rid of him, you mean?"

"Yes. To get rid of him."

"Who? What enemies?"

"I don't know," she said with a sigh. "Eric thinks he knows. He tells me they are fanatical against him. It has something to do with the council he is forming, he once told me."

"I thought that was just businessmen? Gay businessmen?"

"It is. Don't ask me, Noel. All I know is what he tells me. He says he must protect himself. You don't think I prefer Eric like this, do you? He is so—changed. And all these deaths around him. He tells me he is unlucky, that he should keep away from people he likes, that they are always taken away from him. He can never do anything important without losing someone he likes. He wants me to go away."

"And will you?"

"It's *you* he worries about most."

"So he told me. And in the next breath said he didn't trust me. It's inconsistent."

"That is how Eric is. He grows wilder every day. Now with this karate and jujitsu. I never know what he'll do next. I am losing my influence over him. So you must be careful, Noel. More careful than you've ever been in your life."

She took his hand again briefly to say that, then stood up, insisting he remain seated, while she went downstairs.

For a moment Noel wondered whether, despite everything, he should go to her. But in the single turning glance he had of Alana's face as she stepped into the elevator, she looked so drawn, so exhausted, that he knew he must not.

9

The mailbox in his apartment building was jammed full. He had not opened it for over two weeks. The bulk was subscription magazines, giveaways and other junk mail, cards from colleagues at school with whom he seldom exchanged more than ten minutes of conversation over two terms of classes, who seemed to feel compelled to send vacation postcards from all over the country, the world, covered with tiny, scarcely decipherable script detailing amusing anecdotes of their misadventures and curious local customs they'd encountered. Nothing from Mirella. The rest seemed to be bills.

The first envelope he opened was the monthly paycheck from Whisper, sent to him through the Social

Work Research Agency in Albany. Tearing it at one end, he reminded himself that he'd have to call the Fisherman before depositing this and doing other errands today.

But here was something new. Between the check and the statement he usually received were several pieces of blank, grainy, onionskin paper. No, not all blank. On one was scrawled: "Call on the loops from OUTSIDE your apartment!"

"Lure here," he said into the pay phone across the street from his building.

"One moment, please," the motherly operator answered. When she returned to the line, she said, "You are to go fishing this afternoon, if you are able to."

Wasn't that an emergency signal? Yes, but for what?

"I'm able to," he said, hoping it meant he was free.

"Fine." She named a movie theater on Broadway. "There's a three o'clock show. Exactly three thirty in booth number two from the entry of the men's lavatory. Do you have that?"

He had copied the message. "Anything else?"

"That's all I have, darling."

"What's the movie?"

"And have a good day," she parroted before they disconnected.

10

The film playing that afternoon was a James Bond spoof—but so diverting, Noel had to keep checking his watch to be certain he wouldn't miss the meeting with Loomis. The third time he looked it was three thirty-two.

The men's lounge was on a lower level, to the left of the central staircase. Inside was an anteroom with built-in benches, a water fountain, and grooming-aid dispensing machines. Beyond was the marble-walled bathroom itself, ringing with a cold silence as he entered. No one at the line of wall urinals. Two rows of toilet booths. Oh, fine, he thought, she hadn't told him *that* over the loop. What was it she had said, exactly? Booth number two from the door. That had to be in the first row. But wouldn't the old detective go to the back row for more privacy? Sure enough, the only booth with a closed door was the second from the right in the back row.

Noel slipped into the booth next to it, and sat down. There wasn't a sound from his neighbor. He coughed. Still nothing. These old toilets were roomy, with dividing walls that dropped to within six inches of the floor. He'd have to get on his hands and knees to see who was within, if there was someone inside: the booth might merely be closed by the management, out of order. Should he knock? Surely if the Fisherman were next door he'd have heard Noel come in. Had he forgotten to tell Noel some recognition code? Fuck Loomis and all these spy games!

Suddenly there was a cough from the next booth. It didn't sound as though it came from a young man.

Noel leaned back in the seat as far as possible to where the wall dividers did not quite meet the back wall, leaving a half-inch space. Carefully, loudly, he cleared his throat.

No response.

What the hell was Loomis up to?

Noel coughed again, louder. When that didn't elicit any response, he finally said hello.

For a second or two there was silence. Then he heard a sudden barrage of noises—the rapid rolling of the toilet paper roll, the violent flushing of the toilet and what sounded like a buckle swinging to hit the wall divider. The last sound was the metallic crack of the booth door as it opened, then slammed shut. The man in the toilet was gone.

Noel had to know for certain it wasn't Loomis playing games. When he walked out there was only one other person, a heavy-set, middle-aged black man washing his hands at the sink. Noel stopped to stare at him, and the man finished washing his hands, hastily dried them on some paper towels, and looking either annoyed or frightened or both, scurried out.

Before the anteroom door slammed shut, another hand was on it, coming in. The short, ambling figure of the Fisherman replaced the black man.

"I said to wait in the booth," were Loomis's first words. "What are you doing here?"

"The guy who just left was in your booth. This wasn't such a bright idea, Loomis."

"Shh!" the Fisherman said.

"No one else is here."

"What did you say to him?"

"Nothing. He thought I was looking for a little tea-room trade."

"For a little what?"

"Action," Noel spelled it out. "Sex, here."

"Oh! Let's get into the booths before someone else

comes in." Loomis had already headed for the back row.

"Why can't we talk here? There are only about twelve people in the whole theater. It's safe, if you ask me."

"I didn't," Loomis said, opening the booth door. "Get inside."

"This isn't number two. It's number three," Noel protested, but went in anyway, as Loomis had disappeared into his toilet and shut the door.

He heard a soft metal clank, then saw a panel of the wall divider with the toilet paper dispenser shake a bit, and jerkily slide to one side.

"Goddamn!" Noel said. "It's an honest-to-God glory hole."

"Speak low," Loomis said. "Stinks in here."

"It was your idea. I thought I'd never see a real glory hole. Who found it?"

"An operative," Loomis replied, all business. Through the rectangular space Noel could see him hunched over, as though looking at the floor.

"Naturally."

"Let's not waste time, Lure. We have some important business."

"Am I going to have to meet you here every time we talk?"

"Didn't you get those pieces of paper?"

"Sure did."

"We'll communicate that way. Write your message. Roll it up into a ball, wrap it in tinfoil or plastic wrap, and drop it outside the wall of the town house. Someone will pass by three times a day to retrieve it."

Was it Noel's imagination or did the Fisherman look different somehow? "Why all the sudden precautions?"

"Trouble. Bad trouble. I think Mr. X is onto one of our operatives. You know what that means. We can't take any chances."

"Anyone I know?"

"Your friend Vega."

"How? They never see each other. Buddy is down-town in the bar."

"Vega's been snooping around. Fooling around. Evi-dently word has gotten to Mr. X. If he doesn't already know, he will soon."

"What kind of snooping around?" Noel asked. He didn't think Loomis would admit how much Vega had found out about the way in which Whisper operatives had been chosen. Still, there was no telling what the Fisherman would tell him, or why.

"Details are unnecessary. They're classified, any-way. But I do have a pretty good word that Mr. X knows something."

"Well, I haven't heard anything about it, but who am I?" Noel said. There was something about Loomis that Noel hadn't noticed before, but he still couldn't say precisely what.

"Who's this new man in the house?"

"Bill McWhitter. Bodyguard. Masseur. Sex toy at the moment. He's super in defensive arts. Very, very strong. Almost threw the cook off the parapet at the villa. Some experience as a hit man out on the Coast. Small time, but deadly. I get the impression he'd kill me for the way I brush my teeth, without a thought. Doesn't like me."

Loomis seemed to be nodding off. No, merely thinking; he suddenly asked, "He's taken your place, then?"

"Hardly. They do fuck, which I never did with Eric. On your recommendation, remember? They are to-gether a lot. Alana says it won't last."

"What else do you know about this economic council front?"

That was out of left field. Noel had to think how to answer.

"They were all out in some Midwest town a few weeks ago. Then last week Eric got a call that really pleased him. They'd gotten a few antidiscrimination laws passed. I could get you the details."

"Where in the Midwest?"

"Kansas. Minnesota. Another state, too."

Noel had specified this, to show Loomis there was nothing illegal involved in what Redfern's group was doing, and to show that it wasn't, as Loomis called it, a front, but instead a moneyed, respectable legislative lobby group.

"And nothing else?" the Fisherman asked, unimpressed.

"Nothing but the rush home last night. It seems your men were too visible. I even saw them follow me from the villa during the day." That was a lie, but it would help dig into Loomis's mind how stupid he'd been about it.

"It's a bad spot to observe," was all he replied.

"He's jammed the phone out there, too; he told me."

"We're working on countering that. So far nothing works."

"Well, you're getting him real paranoid. Lay low for a while, will you? It's getting hot in there."

"It's not just us. It's Vega you ought to blame. He's the one making trouble."

"Why? What's he doing?"

"I told you already," Loomis said indignantly. "He's fooling around. Now let's get back to business. I want a message from you every two days at least while you're in the town house. Early morning and late evening are best. My men will be least noticeable then. Report anything and everything. And continue to be careful. I don't mind if he is getting scared. The more frightened, the sooner he'll make a real slip and that's when we go in and nab him."

He had a few dozen more dos and don'ts. Noel only half listened, still trying to assess what it was that he couldn't pin down about Loomis's appearance today. The features were more prominent; perhaps he had lost weight. His lips seemed to sneer as he spoke, and

the words to explode out of him with a cold anger as
though they tasted bad in his mouth. He made his
points with a finger poking through the wall slot.
Noel was reminded of an old Alsatian dog that had
belonged to some friends of his and Monica's when
they were teenagers. It had gone from being an amia-
ble enough creature to one that would attack any living thing smaller than itself, even leaping into the air
to catch low-flying sparrows. Finally, it had turned on
its master and had to be killed. An autopsy had shown
extreme hardening in the arteries of its brain.

Someone else came into the bathroom to use the urinal. Loomis gingerly closed the panel between him
and Noel, then flushed the toilet and left the booth.
Noel waited until both men had left, then went upstairs and watched the rest of the film. But he
couldn't get that Alsatian out of his mind all day.

11

"*Fire Island?*" *Noel was astonished.* "But we just got
back from the Hamptons."

"Fire Island Pines," Alana said. They were just finishing breakfast on the backyard terrace. Eric and
McWhitter had gone inside. "Eric has a wonderful
house on the bay," she elaborated. "We're flying out
this afternoon."

"He'll feel safer there than he does here?"

"Much safer. We know almost everyone."

"I never knew he had a place there."

"The club managers have been using it. Cal. Geoff
Malchuck. Rick and Jimmy. We may have an army at

times. You must go and pack. We are on a one o'clock
plane."

"But with so many other people around, won't that
be just more opportunities for Eric to be . . . well,
you know, the way he's been lately with us?"

"One is always safer in a crowd, no?" she asked, answering herself. She seemed so unflappable Noel
wondered if the decision had been hers. "There will
be parties, dinners, old friends to see, the beach, sail-
ing. He won't have time to think about bad things.
He'll be too distracted," she said with glee. "I'll like it,
too."

Then it was her idea! Noel didn't mind. It was hot-
ter every day, the air more polluted and close in the
city. And it would provide necessary information for
his book—a more difficult and distant project to him
every day lately. Then, too, he wasn't sure about
Whisper. Something had changed.

"You're sure he'll feel safer there?" Noel asked.

"I will!" she said, laughing, rising from the table,
kissing his cheek lightly, and running inside to finish
her own packing.

Almost from that moment on, Noel felt he had lost
the control he had so carefully built up within himself
in the weeks since Randy's death in the back room of
Le Pissoir.

Not because during the two weeks on Fire Island
he lost contact with Loomis and Whisper. It was a relief at first from what he considered a dangerous
means of communication. Since meeting Loomis in the
movie theater bathroom, he'd been uneasy about the
Fisherman, about the entire operation. It was true
that he hadn't found a minute between Alana's announcement at breakfast and the time the Silver
Cloud drove off to the East River Basin where the
two seaplanes Eric had chartered for them were waiting, engines revving, to write a message. Loomis
would find out soon enough where they were going.

It was too large and public a caravan to escape even the sleepiest Whisper observer.

No, that wasn't the problem. It was Fire Island itself, or at least the two predominantly gay communities: Fire Island Pines and Cherry Grove, where Redfern and his friends lived and played. After a respite of several weeks, Noel was thrown directly into the center of the country's most openly, flagrantly gay few square miles, two days before the season's biggest holiday—the Fourth of July weekend. The Pines was a hotbed of precisely those sexual pressures and questions he'd put aside so quickly, and he wasn't allowed to forget it for a single second. Every step he took was watched—not by spies or operatives—but by gay men on the make, cruising him, touching him, coming up to him and talking as though they'd known each other for years, hissing at him as they passed on the beach and boardwalk, making low-voiced obscene invitations, talking loudly to each other about him so he could hear, asking him for the time, though he never wore a watch out there, for a light, though he wasn't smoking, for his phone number, for a variety of sexual activities, some of which he'd never even classified as sexual. Nothing he did, wore, or said helped. The baggiest clothes he could hunt up in the house were of no use. Being rude only brought more invitations to brutalize the infatuated pleaders. Being quiet and aloof became difficult when it brought responses like, "Who does *she* think she is?" and, "Get off the act, honey, we know all about you," which infuriated Noel even more. What had pleased him at the Grip and on Christopher Street only a few months ago freaked him utterly; for the first time in his life he wished he were crippled, hunchbacked, deformed, ugly.

The setting for all this was lovely enough, Noel had to admit in his decreasing moments of objectivity during his stay at the Pines. The seaplanes had set them down on the bay shore of the island, less than ten yards of ankle-high water away from the property line of the gorgeous, cedarwood two-story house Redfern had built a few years before on the far eastern edge of the community. The top-floor deck overlooked a glorious view of the Great South Bay edged with the service communities of Sayville and Patchogue where fireworks erupted all night long, the first week of his visit. Looking east or west, the island narrowed, and from this height you could see the next few towns in either direction, each separated by considerable woods and dunes. The highest platform on the roof looked over a small grove of pine trees that stepped down to rooftops of other houses between Redfern's land and the beachfront. Birds whistled to each other cacophonously every morning at dawn and played flight games during the day. Deer families, rabbits, even raccons foraged quietly on the beach plum and Russian olive bushes around the house, until they heard a sound, pricked up their ears, then slid or crashed back into the foliage. A garden of lilies to one side of the house offered irises, tiger lilies, a dozen other varieties Noel had only seen in the flower show in the Coliseum where Monica had dragged him a decade ago. And the double mirrors of the bay north, the ocean south, only a quarter of a mile apart and easily seen in a single glance from several rooftop spots. But above all, the feeling of being away from it all, being out afloat, adrift, at sea, offshore. On the edge.

If it were only true, Noel told himself, he could have dealt with the sudden immersion in the social whirlpool that surrounded him, with the bizarre hours everyone kept, with the scattered household— everyone off doing exactly what he or she pleased, until as by magic or telepathy, they all suddenly converged. He could have gone along with the constant partying, the total devotion to disco dancing and drugs and public promiscuity—but once sex was added to it, he found he couldn't cope at all.

Changes in the house were rapid, enigmatic, unexplained. Eric dropped McWhitter as a boyfriend, just

as Alana had predicted, but that didn't mean Redfern
was drawn back to Noel. Hardly. Instead Eric had
one tanned, speedo-bathing-suited, good-looking boy
or man coming and going out of the house after another: sometimes more than one a day, and often two
or more at a time.

Noel would enter any one of the three bathrooms
and find an attractive stranger stepping out of a
shower or shaving. He would go to the first-floor
kitchen for a morning cup of coffee and discover a
blond giant he'd never seen before cooking a full
breakfast for another stranger. Two dark-haired,
bearded strangers would be lying out on the bayside
deck, another one diving into the pool. A minute later,
a young black, built like an anatomy model, would
pull a wagonload of groceries into the side door, no
delivery boy but a high fashion model merely doing a
favor for someone somewhere on the premises. In the
living room, two blond Germans who could barely
speak English would be sunk deep in the cushioned,
wraparound sofas, stoned, laughing uproariously at
morning TV cartoon shows. All of them knew someone in the house by name. All of them were attractive,
did some work or other in the city, and were interested in him. They were like sea tar stuck to the soles
of Noel's feet: always present, unavoidable, impossible to get rid of.

Worse, the entire population of Fire Island seemed
to be in love, about to fall in love, or just getting over
a love affair. McWhitter found adequate compensa-
tion quickly. Everyone Noel met—Richard, Robert,
Don, Bill, Jim, in endless duplication so he could
never recall their names—paired up within an afternoon. Even Alana had a visit from an old friend that
first week—a slender Argentinian named Guillermo,
with an accent, a superb tan, and according to one of
the Bills or Jims a shitload of money. She was gone
from the house for two nights, which didn't help
Noel's head a great deal. Not with couples of all gen-

ders kissing on the dance floor at the harbor disco,
necking on the beach, making love at poolside, on the
terrace, on the roof, in the bushes, on the boardwalks,
anywhere and everywhere Noel was.

Then there were the drugs: coke in the morning, a
joint of grass over breakfast, mescaline or psilocybin
or simple, everyday LSD to go to the beach. A down
would get them laid back enough to nap after Tea
Dance. But after dinner anything went: Noel once
counted thirty-eight different pills or spansules or
capsules divided in a few minutes among eleven people.

He had tried to keep up with them the first few
days, but just maneuvering the boardwalks was a dis-
couraging prospect. Even when he cut his intake down
to a third of the usual dose, he'd be crashing all morning, sleeping off one drug or strung out on another or
sotted out on the sand, while a new party was announced to take place in six minutes.

The last straw broke two weeks after they'd arrived.
Noel had gone to sleep early, at 1:00 A.M., just as
everyone else in the house had gone out. He woke up
at dawn. Unable to go back to sleep, he went down to
the kitchen for a glass of milk and a sandwich. On the
balcony overlooking the two-storied living room, he
heard the low throb of taped rock music. It was a
common sound by now, and he didn't even think
about it. It was only when he'd gotten down the stairs
that he noticed the sofas had been pushed to the
walls, the huge pillows spread, and the entire area
from the kitchen to the deck and pool was covered
with dozens of bodies—he'd stepped into a postdawn
orgy.

He felt as though he were stranded on another
planet—everything alien and incomprehensible. Which
explained how sincerely glad Noel was later in the
day of the big orgy to hear Little Larry Vitale's drawl
behind him, as he stood in the crowded doorway of
the Tea Dance. In front of Noel, a buxom, beautiful

South American girl in a dance frenzy was having her paper dress slowly but surely ripped off her body by the gleaming teeth of her equally frenetic partner.

"Do you think he'll stop when he reaches her kazoo?" Noel asked, as the couple spun only inches away from him and Larry, and the man bent down, still dancing, and began snapping his jaws at the back of what was left of the high-hemmed skirt. "Oops! Spoke too soon."

"I saw that old club act at Clouds in January," Larry drawled, sipping a drink the same aqua as bathroom tiles in a suburban home. "Let's get out of here. Too crowded. Too many losers."

The deck was packed to the railing, so they finished their drinks and went out to the boat dock that jutted out into the bay at the harbor's mouth. The benches were already taken by couples who were practicing necking so as to look picturesque for the spectacular sunset over the water. Noel and Larry kept away from them, sitting down on the side of the jetty, their feet almost touching the high tide water.

"You out here with the rich kids?" Larry asked.

"What do you think?"

"How do you like the island?" Larry asked. Clearly he loved it. "Have you made it down to the Meat Rack yet? No," he asnwered himself, "you probably haven't had a chance what with all the local talent falling over themselves to get a whiff of you."

Noel knew what the Neat Rack was—a strip of woods between the two communities given over to alfresco sex, day and night. Sex! That's all he heard about, thought about.

"The whole place is a little too frantic for me," he admitted.

"You kidding? Get into it."

"I can't. Not yet. I'm sort of laying off sex for a while."

Larry looked at Noel's eyes. "No yellow so it ain't hepatitis; it must be VD."

"It's neither."

"Then it's mental illness," Larry declared. "You're out of your tree. That's like a diabetic locked in a chocolate factory."

"Something like that," Noel admitted.

"No wonder you're so upright."

"It shows?" Noel asked. With Larry he felt comfortable; he could be himself, whatever that seemed to be at the moment. For a fleeting minute, he wondered if he ought to ask Larry about Loomis and Whisper, about Vega and the profiles he'd shown Noel.

He was gingerly leading up to the subject when Larry hushed him. Some friends of the boy had just come onto the dock, and they soon got Noel and Larry high on Thai stick, an imported Indochinese marijuana, then they dragged them back to the Tea Dance. Noel arrived just in time to bump into Eric and Alana and McWhitter. His questions to Larry were lost in intoxication and the zaniness of the dance the others pulled him into.

12

By the time they returned to the house it was filled with people. Having had to spend the previous long holiday weekend in town, all the club managers of Redfern's enterprises and their boyfriends and lovers had come out to Fire Island for this one. All six bedrooms were in use, with McWhitter back in Eric's room and Noel asked to share his with Geoff Malchuck, the quiet, cool manager of Clouds. Naturally the house was noisier and more full of people coming

and going than usual. Noel's mood, which had been
irritable before he encountered Larry at the Tea
Dance, worsened.

Even Dorrance arrived for dinner, flying out on the
seaplane; he would be staying the night at a nearby
friend's house, he said—obviously having experienced
Eric's place on weekends. With Dorrance there, Noel
couldn't help but notice that everyone present for
dinner this evening had been present at that first
company dinner in the half-moon dining room at
Eric's town house. Ages ago, it seemed now. Everyone,
that is, but Randy. And everyone but Noel in extreme
high spirits. Even the usually dignified McWhitter
was dancing through the living room with "Marge" to
the incessant beat of the disco tapes that were beginning to drive Noel to destroy the expensive machin-
ery.

"Well, here we are," "Marge" said, when finally
everyone had gathered at the refectory-style dinner
table, "just one happy family." He surveyed the group
as though it were his own doing.

"Not quite all of us is happy," Eric said, holding up
a wineglass and pressing its wet coolness against his
cheek. "Look at sourpuss over there."

It was easy enough to follow his gaze across the
long table to Noel.

"What's the matter, Noel, aren't you feeling well?"
"Marge" asked.

"He's feeling terrible," Eric answered for Noel.
"Aren't you?"

Noel toyed with a piece of food he'd been moving
from one end of his plate to the other. Without looking
up, he said, "I've been thinking, if you didn't particularly need me here, I'll go into the city tomorrow for a
few days."

"On the weekend?" Cal Goldberg asked in astonishment.

"What's the matter?" McWhitter asked, "allergic to
salt air?"

Ignoring them, Noel went on: "It'll give you more room here." He focused on Eric as he added that.

"You aren't taking anyone's space," Alana said. "Is he, Eric?"

Eric just rubbed the wineglass against his cheek.

"Doesn't bother me," Geoff said.

"I'll bet it doesn't!" Jimmy DiNadio said.

"Well?" Noel went on. "How about it?"

"What for?" Eric asked.

"For nothing. I don't know. To work on the book. I hadn't planned on anything in particular."

"Perhaps to see Buddy Vega?"

"Perhaps. If I happen to go down to the Grip and he's there."

"Really?" Said sarcastically. "I thought you two were real close."

"You thought wrong," Noel said.

"He did introduce you to Rick, got you working, didn't he?"

"So?"

"He wouldn't bring just anyone to work in the Grip, would he, Rick?"

"Never did before or since," Chaffee said.

"How do you know Vega?" Eric asked Noel.

Everyone at the table had quieted to hear the exchange, aware that Eric was up to something. "Marge" dropped a fork; in the sudden silence, it sounded like a steel girder hitting the tabletop.

"We just met," Noel answered, alert to something he hadn't counted on.

"Balled and met? Or just met?"

"We did it," Noel lied.

"But not in California?" Eric asked. "We all know that was a cover-up story to get you into the bar in the first place. Right?"

Noel didn't understand this sudden interrogation, or why it was being made so publicly. His guard went up.

"Right. So I could get information on my book. We

thought it would be impossible for me to just walk into the Grip off the street and get a job. Especially with my background and all."

"We?" Eric questioned. "Who's we?"

"My department chairman and I. He suggested the project in the first place. You know that. What's this all about, anyway?"

"Did Vega tell you about the Grip?" Eric asked.

"He told me it was the most popular Village bar. That's all."

Cal's lover caught up with the conversation. "What book?" he asked Eric, and when Redfern didn't answer, "What book?" he asked Cal.

"Did you know Vega was married?" Eric asked.

"I found out later. Much later."

"Did you know he used to be a cop? That he was thrown off the force five years ago for taking graft?"

That was a face-saver. The news came as such a shock to Noel that he did nothing to hide it.

"No. I didn't know that. Is it true?"

"Eric, what's the point of this?" Alana interrupted.

"Let him tell you," Eric said.

"You're going to spoil our dinner," she said quietly.

"Tell everyone what's going on inside your mind right now, Noel," Eric said. "Go on."

"You think Vega is still working for the police. That the graft thing was fabricated in order for him to go undercover," Noel said.

"Very good," Eric said. "Go on."

"And I'm in league with Vega. Is that it?"

"Eric!" Alana interrupted again. "Noel's been with us all the time."

"Most of the time," Eric corrected. "Well? Deny it, Noel."

Noel looked around the table, glancing at each face, neutral, uncomprehending, except for Eric who was waiting, McWhitter who was gloating, and Alana who seemed blank-faced with emotion of some sort. Noel would get no help from any of them. And Eric was close. So close to the truth. Too close.

"Deny what? That I'm a spy for the police in your house?" Noel asked. "Why should I deny it? If it's true it would at least give some point to your childish paranoia."

"What does he mean?" McWhitter asked Eric.

"Just because I don't get off on taking drugs until I can't stand up, going out dancing thirty-six hours a day, and having sex with a different stranger every fifteen minutes, I'm supposed to be a cop? You call that an adult's life?"

"If it's my choice to live that way," Eric came back, stung.

"Well, I'm bored with it," Noel said, wiping his mouth with a cloth napkin and pushing his plate away. "And you probably are, too, which is why you've invented this whole argument tonight. Just for a little excitement in your otherwise colorless little life." Someone whistled low at the table. But Noel was off now, and didn't stop. "And that, to tell you the truth, is why I'm going back to town. To write my book. Or even to read a book. God knows, the last one I read, months ago, was the bartender's manual, which isn't exactly Leo Tolstoy."

"Wait a minute," Eric said, "I'm not done."

Noel had been about to get up. The neutrality that he had seen on the faces of their dinner companions was gone in his stupid attempt to escape. They all seemed to take the attack on their life-style personally.

"Who were you talking to at the Tea Dance?" Eric asked.

"At the Tea Dance?" Noel repeated. "Larry? Is that who you mean? Larry Vitale? You know him. He's everywhere."

"That doesn't mean we like him."

"How can you not like him?" Noel asked.

"I can and I don't. Not him and not his friends. How do you know him?"

Jesus, but Eric was sharp today. First Vega and now Larry. Had he been saving all this up just for tonight's barrage?

"He used to come into the Grip all the time. We balled a few times." He said that because he supposed it was common knowledge at the table. "If I see him once a month, it's a lot, and *always* by accident. I don't have too much in common with a seventeen-year-old-kid. Come on, Eric, aren't you pushing a little too far? If you have to have a persecution mania you might as well make some distinctions."

"Larry Vitale is all right by me," Geoff Malchuck said.

"Me, too," Rick put in. "He's never given me any trouble."

This was unexpected support. Noel decided to use it. "Look, Eric, maybe you've got a problem you ought to see someone about."

"What are you talking about?"

"Let's face it. Not everyone sees enemies in his toilet. Be realistic for a minute."

"You be realistic! People are being killed."

"People? One person. And that was evidently the work of some psycho."

"Made to look like a psycho. There've been more than one. There've been five, six that I know of. All of them related to my clubs and through them to me. Don't give me any shit about not having enemies. Don't you think there aren't people who'd like to see me out of the way?"

"Who?" Noel asked. "I keep asking, *who?* You tell me I'm an undercover policeman. That won't explain why the police are after you. Who's out to get you, Eric?"

Eric was silent, then ominously said, "I know who."

It was lame, and even Eric knew it. Noel took the opportunity to get up from his chair. "Some faceless, nameless, reasonless enemy."

"I said I know who."

"You need help, Eric. Not protection from this jack-ass!" McWhitter began to move, then turning to Eric, stopped short.

Not really certain what he was doing, Noel instinctively thought to get out of this dining room, this house.

"Where are you going?" Eric called after him, the edge of hysteria in his voice.

"Out! For a walk!" Noel answered without turning to face them. "And tomorrow, back to Manhattan."

"You haven't denied anything yet," Eric reminded him.

"I'm not going to," Noel said.

"If you leave now, don't come back. Not ever."

Noel slid open the screen doors to the deck.

"Not ever!" Eric called out again, his voice lunging at Noel. "Do you hear?!"

Noel stepped out onto the deck and took in the fresh, cool air. Holding on to the railing, he looked across the bay toward the low strands of lights, the towns of the Long Island shore. He was trembling so hard the balcony rail shook under his hand. He had to get away from here.

He followed the dimly lighted planking to the gate of the compound, unlatched it, and walked slowly, thoughtfully, to the ocean side of the island. The sea was spotlighted almost directly overhead by a nearly full moon. It must be close to midnight, he thought.

He wandered along the abandoned shoreline, finally sitting on a dune where the tires from police cars and contracting trucks had left deep, patterned tracks. There he allowed himself to shake violently all over. He felt all the muscles around his neck were knots that had to be untied, hoping the roaring, grating surf in front of him would pound away the tensions, and fears, and anger.

After a while, he felt some relief. The stillness helped, as did the balmy night air, sharp with fetid sea life strewn on the sands, and the regular thump of the waves. Occasionally, a large wave, its froth moon-lighted like glitter, would break long and straight and very hard like a crack of cannon that thundered in his ears. Then all would be silent again.

Once, looking out over the water, directly in front of him, he thought he saw the figure of a slim, naked young man step out of the surf where the water was a platinum and cobalt shimmer of reflected lunar light. Noel thought that the profile was exactly that of Paul Warshaw, the gay student in his social deviance and criminal behavior course. The boy-man seemed to notice Noel, too, and to stare at him for a minute, tentative, but as though sharing something: a moment, another perspective, an intimacy unconnected with lust, an invitation. Then the boy-man stepped out of the moonbeams and seemed to disappear back into the still emptiness of the beach, an illusion.

The tide began to turn. The breeze off the ocean became cool, sharp. Noel stood up and trudged through the clinging sand.

"*Oh-eh!*" He suddenly heard a woman's voice from behind him and turned to see her figure silhouetted on one of the raised walkways to the beach. "*Oh-eh!*" she shouted again in long-drawn-out syllables, and he realized she was calling his name.

He was about to turn to shout back to her, he had already raised his arm in greeting when the thought hit: she had betrayed him. That was how Eric had known all those questions to ask. Alana had overheard the phone call at the Hamptons villa, and had told Eric everything she had heard.

"*Oh-el!*" she shouted again. He stumbled away from her voice and its treachery, until he was running along the beach, his sneakered feet barely getting wet as he fled.

"*No-el!*" the voice followed him. But he was way past the Pines, past all habitations, and then the voice stopped and Noel sprawled in the sand, and said, "*Bitch, bitch, bitch,*" until he fell asleep.

13

"You've got to get back into that house," Loomis insisted for the third time.

"You haven't been listening. My cover is gone."

"I thought you said you denied it."

"Of course I denied it. You might not be talking to me if I didn't do something to get out of there."

Even now, talking to Loomis in a telephone booth of the pharmacy a half block from his apartment, Noel didn't feel entirely out of danger. It might merely be his imagination but hadn't two vaguely hippie-type, long-haired blonds come into the store right after him? Hadn't they begun fooling around at the luncheon counter as soon as he had gone into the phone booth?

Don't become like Eric, he told himself. After all, he had gotten the complete once-over from both of them: the same physical evaluation he'd come to expect from gay men. They were probably from out of town, the West Coast, he told himself. Nevertheless, not to feel safe even here, a few hundred yards from his apartment. . . . And here was the Fisherman giving him this total bullshit about going back to Fire Island.

"What exactly did he say?" Loomis asked, hairsplitting. It made Noel sick.

"He's onto Buddy Vega. And he asked a lot of questions about Little Larry. I don't know what else he knows."

"Goddamn that Vega! If he hadn't begun plotzing

around none of this would have happened. You say he asked about Larry?"

"He said he didn't like him, or his friends. But some of the other guys at the table stood up for him."

"Listen, Lure. You lay low for a day or so and then call him up and apologize."

"Apologize! You don't seem to understand, he as much as said he knows what I am, who I am. He doesn't need me around anymore. He's got McWhitter, who's a far better bodyguard than I am, and who even puts out. What does he need me for? He'd have to be nuts to let me within a mile of that place."

Now the two guys at the counter were conferring, looking every once in a while in Noel's direction. One of them shrugged, then got off the stool and went out. To wait outside and jump him? Or because they had somehow decided which one Noel would prefer and that one, sipping a soda, was to have the first chance to cruise him?

Loomis was asking, "What about that woman? What's her name. Wouldn't she want you back there?"

"I told you, it was she who heard me talking on the loop at the Hamptons." He tried reasoning. "How else would Eric know?

"She didn't give you away, Lure. That's why she went after you last night on the beach. To tell you that she didn't. She might have heard the phone call—or at least part of your side of it, but she's been hiding it. She's protecting you, Lure. Why?"

Noel didn't have an answer.

"I'll tell you why, because she needs you. She's fallen for you. To hell with Mr. X. You don't need him. She's your way in."

Even as Noel was protesting it to the Fisherman for a half-dozen reasons, he suspected the old cop was dead on target. It completely elated him. Then it shot him down. Because if Loomis were right, and Alana would eventually persuade Eric to let Noel back into their circle, then it would be using her feelings for another end—it would be the very betrayal that Noel had accused her of. It disgusted him even to think of it.

"I won't do it, Loomis," he said.

"You have to, Lure. We're so close now. You can't let him slip out of the net now."

"You were close months ago with Randy," Noel said. "As close as now. What happened?"

"You're wrong, Lure. We're building a case against Mr. X. We're getting all the pieces together. We're about to get him. We've got to keep him monitored. That's why you've got to be there. Every detail you give us about them may turn out to be instrumental in his capture. It's the only way to make certain the plan will work."

"What plan?"

"It's too complicated to get into right now. But it will have to be legally airtight. Once we've got him on one thing, we can throw the book at him. And you're the only one left, Cummings, the only one who will pull the strings that shut the net on him. How do you like that, eh? For Randy Nerone's sake! Huh?"

He'd heard that particular edge in Loomis's voice before. Now, it unnerved Noel.

"I'm not going back to Fire Island," he said.

"Wait until they come back to town."

"They could stay out there all summer."

"They'll be back soon. You take a rest. Read your books. Go to a movie. Keep in touch, though. I'll let you know when they've returned. It's going to work. Don't worry. So long, Lure."

The second number had left the luncheon counter by the time Noel came out of the booth. But he was waiting right outside the door, perched on the fender of a parked car, smoking a cigarette when Noel emerged.

"He had to go somewhere," the guy said in what seemed to be a rural accent. He showed a toothpastead smile, lifted himself languorously off the car fender, and began to walk alongside Noel.

"Who?" Noel asked.

"My friend. He had an appointment."

"Oh."

"My name's Zach. Mind if I walk along with you?"

Noel didn't take the offered hand; Zach didn't seem to mind. They walked along a block or so, going west, before Noel decided to be cordial to Zach, to treat him as though he were just a pickup, without doing anything out of the ordinary, until he could make up his mind about the two of them.

"You live close to here?" Zach asked: the standard opening line of a gay pickup on the street. Noel had led him away from where he lived.

"Uptown. The West Side," Noel answered.

"Oh, I thought you lived here." The ingenuous Laguna Beach smile.

"Afraid not. You?"

"No. Me either."

"Too bad."

A subway might be too deserted, especially if Zach decided he wouldn't mind going uptown, too. They passed first one underground entrance, then crossed a street, and passed another. Buses went up and down the avenues, but that might be too limiting, especially if the partner showed up. They'd approached Broadway, crossed it, still going west. Fewer and fewer people here. Nothing but warehouses, a few parked trucks. Where the hell could Noel go?

"I'm not doing anything right now," Zach said. "If you aren't, that is."

If it was an act, it was a good one. He's just trying to get laid for Chrissakes, Noel kept telling himself. Nothing really wrong with that. You're getting worse than Eric. Far worse.

"I'm from out of town. Me and my friend," Zach went on. "I'll only be here a few days."

A subtle pressure, Noel knew. They had reached a

familiar block, but Noel couldn't say why until he spotted the curved-arch facade of the Baths. But there was no one on the street he could claim acquaintance with, to drop this guy, pickup or not.

"I am a little occupied this afternoon," Noel said.

Disappointment was written across Zach's face. "Later on?" he asked.

"Maybe. I'm not sure."

"I'd really like to see you later on," Zach said, all Southern California surfer innocence. "How about it?"

"Well . . ." They had passed the Baths' entrance. No one stepped out to help break up the awkwardness.

Zach had a pencil in his hand and was holding out a matchbook cover. "Why don't you give me your phone number? I'll call in a few hours."

"That might be difficult."

"Why? You have a lover?"

"Something like that."

"I have an idea," Zach said. "I'll give you my number. At the place where I'm staying. If you can get away, just call me."

They'd stopped walking. Zach turned and went to an inset doorway of what had once been a storefront, now just black-painted glass and metal siding. He held the matchbook up to the wall and began writing.

"Here. Can you make this out?"

Noel approached, reaching for the matchbook, which Zach still held up, read the name and a telephone number. "Seems clear to me," he said.

"Call anytime," Zach drawled with a smile.

Noel pocketed the matchbook, realized Zach had put up his hand in the peace and brotherhood shake. What the hell? he thought.

"Didn't you used to work at the Grip?" Zach asked.

Before Noel could answer or pull his hand out of the sudden strong pressure of Zach's grip, the man said, "I believe we have a mutual friend. Name of Bill McWhitter."

Noel didn't have a chance to react. Zach's hand tightened to a bone-twisting grasp while his other fist darted out and punched Noel low in the abdomen. Noel was flung into the deepest part of the doorway, slammed against the metal sheet, then punched again in the same place, hard. Before he could register anything but the pain and surprise, someone else had leaped into the doorway, and now there were two pairs of hands holding him, two pairs of fists jabbing at his head, at his body, alternately shoving him against the wall. His feeble attempts at defending himself were useless. Blood ran down one eye, obscuring his vision. The punches came again and again. They began kicking at his legs until the pain was unbearable and he couldn't stop them from slapping him from wall to wall. His legs began to crumble beneath him, and he was slowly punched down and socked in the chin, in the other eye. His consciousness flashed, flickered, and finally dissolved in a series of colored spots.

Spots that greeted his coming to, he didn't know how much later, then thought only seconds later, from the hard final jabs of a shoe into his chest, and the grating cement that scraped his face, and the two voices still muttering above him. Until he went out again with more colored lights.

He came to in a warm shower that cascaded over his hair and face, washing the blood out of his eye until he could see with startling detail the grain of the cement of the sidewalk, as well as the bottom parts of three Western-style boots directly in his line of vision. He tried not to groan, tried not to move, tried to figure out whom the boots belonged to, whose voices they were, where the liquid that poured over his face came from, tried not to black out again.

"Someone's coming!" It was Zach's voice. "Let's split."

"I'm not done pissing," the other said.

"Let's go!"

Noel heard the pants zipper. Another kick in the chest bashed him against the door's edge. This time he spotted out for a long time.

14

"Give me a hand with this guy, will you?"

Noel flickered into consciousness.

"Where are you taking him?" the other voice asked.

"In there."

"Into the Tubs?"

"Look at him. He needs help."

"Call a cop."

"Are you going to help me or not?"

"Sure. Sure."

Noel felt himself lifted by the armpits. He swayed slightly, then flickered off again. No lights this time, just out.

". . . be here in a few minutes. He said not to call the police," someone new was saying.

"He's coming to," the first, helpful voice said. "How are you feeling?"

Dim red lighting. Thin wooden partitions. Three men looking over him, one perched on the edge of the bed dressed only in a towel, the others in streetwear.

"I'm a doctor," the one in the towel said. He looked like Cal Goldberg: dark, bearded, going bald. "Nothing looks broken. No, better not try to sit up yet."

Noel tried to talk: mumbled through thick lips instead.

"Better get some water," the doctor said.

"How about a beer?" one of the others suggested.

Noel tried to sit up now. He'd never had such a headache in his life. Every inch up into sitting position caused waves of nausea, dizziness, the red lights going blink blink blink.

Finally he was up high enough. Someone was helping lift him from behind. The doctor held the beer can to Noel's mouth. The cool, brackish-tasting liquid trickled down his throat and gagged him at first. But he was able to swallow more. It quenched a thirst he didn't know he had. Then he was allowed to sink back onto the pillows.

"Can I go now?" one of the men in street clothes asked. He'd been the reluctant one.

"Sure. Both of you can go," the doctor said. Then, to Noel, "These men brought you in here. You're in the Baths. You were jumped by some guys."

"Thanks," Noel managed to say.

One hurried out. The other asked, "Do you know who did it?"

Noel shook his head: his ears rang for a minute.

"I said, would you recognize them if you saw them again?" the man asked, evidently repeating what Noel had missed in the buzzing.

"Yes." He'd never forget those bastards' faces.

"I'll leave you my name and telephone number. If you ever find them and want to press charges, I'll stand witness that I chased them off."

Every contour, detail, and motion within Noel's vision was getting sharper. That was a good sign. He still felt as though he'd been thrown off a speeding semi onto a concrete embankment. The man was writing down his information, then putting it in one of Noel's front pockets.

"Thank you," Noel said. The man looked down at him.

"You used to tend bar in the Grip, didn't you?"

"What?" Noel couldn't believe he was asking the same damn question.

"I remember you from there. Pretty as you are, you're not going to look good in a mirror for a while, sorry!" He squeezed Noel's hand, then left the room.

The doctor remained, talking soothingly, and making a delicate but thorough examination of Noel's body, asking what hurt, where, how much, and if he could move his fingers, his toes.

Afterward, the doctor wrote something, and Noel closed his eyes, wishing he could do something to alleviate the throbbing ache behind his eyes, in his chest, below one rib, and especially against one shinbone. When he woke up it was because the doctor was applying ice-cold alcohol pads to his face.

"I know it smarts. You'll feel better later."

Noel already felt better. The ache in his head had lessened.

Someone was trying to get in to the room; the locked door was pulled hard from the other side.

"Busy!" the doctor said.

"Cummings in there?" a gruff voice asked.

The doctor got up from Noel's side, rearranged his towel, and opened the latch. Noel couldn't see whom he was talking to, they were off to one side. Other men, clad only in towels, passed the half-open door, curiously looking in, until they caught a glance at Noel and quickly moved on. He must look pretty bad. He still hurt all over although his eyesight was normal, and he seemed to be regaining his sense of smell: he suddenly became aware of an odor that was stronger, more pungent than rubbing alcohol. His right arm cramped as he reached up to touch his wet, caking hair. Bastards!

"Someone to see you," the doctor said, standing in the doorway. "Feel better, huh?" He waved and left.

Noel had thought for sure it was Loomis—he couldn't have been more wrong.

"It smells like a urinal in here," Eric said, closing the door and latching it shut.

Noel didn't move. Eric remained at the foot of the bed, staring down at him, expressionless.

"You come here to gloat, or to finish me off?" Noel asked.

Eric stiffened with anger, but held his tongue.

"Go away!" Noel said, and turned his head to the thin wooden partition, where at least he wouldn't have to look at Eric.

There was no sound for a while, except Noel's still heavy, irregular breathing (bastards, tried to punch in my lungs! he said to himself). Then he could make out some noises from beyond the partition: the creaking of a cot under the rhythmic weight of two bodies. It almost made him laugh. He'd made it into the Baths all right. "And I didn't even have to pay to get in," he murmured to himself.

"What?"

"I thought you'd gone."

"This isn't a hospital, Noel. You can't stay here."

"I'm staying and getting my twelve hours' worth."

"You're raving. I have the car downstairs."

"No, thanks."

"Be reasonable," Eric said in another tone of voice, softer, calmer. "Either you get up and come with me, or you'll be dragged out by the management."

"What for? So McWhitter can finish off what his pals fumbled?"

"McWhitter? What does he have to do with this?"

"That's who did it."

"He was with me all day."

Noel insisted: "They said they were from McWhitter."

"I thought they were just some street punks?"

"They followed me out of the drugstore near my apartment. One got lost. The other tried to pick me up. I couldn't shake him. Then, boom!"

Eric's annoyed condescension became intense interest. He even sat down on the cot. "Were they Spanish?"

"Spanish? No."

"One tried to pick you up. And then they both jumped you?"

"That's right."

"Yeah, that's his style, all right," Eric said, as if to himself. "Making it look like street kids, too. That's the way he always did it before."

"Did what? Who?"

"Vega. Your friend Vega. Or whoever he's working for. You see, Noel, I'm supposed to believe all this crap and take you back with open arms."

Noel couldn't make heads or tails out of what Eric was saying. He was still having difficulty grappling with any reason why Buddy Vega or his friends would attack him.

"You see," Eric was saying, "by doing this to you, I'm supposed to believe you aren't working for them. Oh, very smart. He's a mean mother, your boss. Doesn't fool around. But you know what? I don't believe it. Not for a second."

What Eric was saying was so unthinkable that Noel couldn't finish the chain of reasoning for a while. Then he did, and felt cold all over, nauseated again. He reached for the half-empty can of beer.

"They said they were from McWhitter," he repeated.

"What were they going to say? That they were from me? Would you have believed that!"

Noel thought no, yes, maybe. "Sure I would," he said.

"That's because you're so fucked up you don't know who your real friends are. I could do all this to you myself if I wanted to. I wouldn't hire punks to do it."

That seemed right to Noel. But it was confusing. His head was hurting again. He moaned.

"Let's go one step further," Eric said. "Let's say I do take you back. Not that I believe it for a minute, mind you. You following me?"

All Noel wanted was sleep. And a few dozen pain-killers. "Yes."

Only what your boss won't know is that you're
going to have to pass a little loyalty test. If you don't
pass it, then start saying prayers. Because I'll know
you're with them for sure."

"With who?"

"Shut up, Noel. Listen carefully and don't say a
word until I'm finished." Eric's voice dropped to a
clear whisper. "Listen, you and McWhitter are going
to meet Mr. Vega two days from now. We've already
been bullshitting him about opening a new club way
down below SoHo. You and McWhitter will meet him
there to discuss the place. Vega will come if he knows
you're coming, too. At a prearranged signal, you'll get
lost, leaving the two of them. You'll wait outside for
McWhitter, then the two of you will drive back. You'll
stay with me, under close scrutiny, from now until you
go with McWhitter. Got that? That's the deal."

There it was: the deal. Take it or leave it. What
Noel had most feared when he'd taken this job with
Whisper—not his own life in danger, but someone
else's. Monica in the lake. Kansas in the warehouse.
Randy in the back room. And now Vega. Another
chance. Only this time he would win. Because Eric
didn't know that even at Eric's he could communicate
with Loomis, could take countermeasures.

"Wait until Alana hears about this," Noel said.

"She isn't going to hear about it."

"You'd actually *kill* someone?" Noel asked.

"Is it a deal or not?" was Eric's reply.

"Give me a cigarette," Noel said. He wanted to
seem to think.

After he'd smoked half of it, he said, "I'll tell you
what. You can lock me up from now until after
McWhitter's done. I'll promise to make no attempt to
leave, to do anything. You can even put me in the Red
Room if you want. But I won't go with him."

"That's tempting. Real tempting. But either you go
or no deal."

"Why?"

Eric leaned over and tapped Noel's cheek. "Because you're the bait, that's why. You're going to lure that big fish into my net."

"And if I don't?"

"I'll leave you on the street. Your friends will be back for you."

The irony of the situation didn't escape Noel. But it was a fair turnaround, perhaps one Loomis could use to snare Eric. And Alana wasn't involved in it. Not at all. Which cinched it. Let Eric rush to his doom. Let Loomis get what he wanted. To hell with them, Noel didn't care anymore.

"It's a deal," he said. "A deal."

15

Once he hardened his heart to both Eric and Loomis, the rest was easy. Noel knew exactly what he had to do. He would go downtown with McWhitter to meet Buddy Vega. But he would warn the Fisherman. Let him worry about it. The matter would be out of his hands.

"I want to stop at my apartment to clean up and change," he said as he made the painful adjustments necessary to getting into the back of the Silver Cloud. Eric and a man Noel didn't know helped him out of the Baths. He was surprised to see it was early evening. The edge of the sun could be seen through the canyon of building facades down Twenty-eighth Street, slowly setting in a polution-tinted haze refracted off the Hudson River.

McWhitter took over at the door of the car, and was

surprisingly helpful and tender. Not like a man who'd ordered a mugging. More like someone who felt guilty about wanting to do it, now that he'd seen the wish fulfilled by someone else. Who were those two thugs anyway?

"I'll help you upstairs," Eric said when they reached Noel's building. Naturally: Redfern wasn't taking any chances.

Noel undressed with difficulty—the brush of denims over a thigh bruise where he'd been repeatedly kicked was intolerable. He found some codeine tablets, popped two into his mouth, then got into the shower. The water stung, then soothed. When he turned on the massage action, he felt almost human again.

Eric had sat down in the rocker and was reading a magazine when Noel came out of the bathroom. He dressed as though he were alone, and even sorted out some clean clothing from a package of still unopened laundry to pack a flight bag.

"Your phone rang while you were in the shower."

Noel hadn't heard it. He disbelieved Eric, but didn't know why he'd bother lying about it. "Who was it?"

"I let your machine answer."

"Oh," Noel said. "I didn't hear it."

"It rang three times, then stopped. I heard the machine turn on."

Noel still didn't understand. He zipped up the bag. "I'm ready."

"Don't you want to know who called?"

"I'm not in the mood for sympathy calls."

"I'm in no hurry," Eric said casually. "Play back the tape."

So that was it! He wanted to know who had called while Noel was out. There hadn't been any telephone call while Noel was showering.

"Whoever it was," Noel said, "it can wait. I still feel shitty."

"Suit yourself. Here! I'll carry that."

At the town house, Noel went directly up to his room, saying he had to rest. There, he wrote five messages on the onionskin paper, bunched them up, put them in his pocket, then took a long nap.

When he awakened and went downstairs, Okku told him Eric and Alana had gone out for the evening. It was almost two o'clock. Noel ate alone—a salmon omelet and watercress salad—in the half-moon dining room, listening to a new easy-listening tape. Then he said he was going out for a stroll in the garden.

Circling the grounds slowly, he wished to look to any observer as though he were merely thoughtful, convalescing. Nevertheless, he managed to get each of the paper balls out of the yard in ways that were almost sleight of hand, given the darkness, then turned inside the house.

He watched one of Eric's two copies of *Casablanca* he found in the film library. Just as the last reel was coming on, he thought he heard an odd whistling from somewhere outside. Looking out the window, he could make out no one to account for the whistle. Then it happened again, from higher up. Could Loomis have already gotten his message? Was this some manner of reply? He couldn't go down into the yard and raise Okku's or McWhitter's suspicions. Or risk the elevator.

He left the film running, and painfully, quietly, walked the three and a half floors up to the roof. There, he stood on the open deck for several minutes.

It hit him on the side of his head with a tiny rap. Noel located the ball of paper at his feet, and scooped it up. There seemed to be a shadowy figure on the parapet of a building half a block away, but no one else even vaguely in sight any closer. Must have been put into a pellet gun and shot over. He remained on the roof, as though admiring the night for another few minutes.

Then, by the flickering light of Bogart and Bergman he read:

> Message received. Vega will be covered. McWhitter taken care of. You will just get out. Do as told. Good work.
>
> F.M.

Outside he heard the soft thump of the Rolls hitting the rampway down to the garage. He burned the paper and sat back to watch the film.

16

"Why aren't you dressed?" Eric asked when Noel came down to breakfast late Sunday morning.

"I don't see any company," Noel responded, taking a seat and drinking off his cranberry juice in two gulps. Only McWhitter and Eric were present in the dining room, its curtains opened this morning to fully reveal the bright sunlight and greenery surrounding them. Alana had left yesterday morning for a shooting in Milan. Noel and she had met on the stairway; she had looked at his bruised face, then rushed past him to her rooms. Not a word had been exchanged.

"Get dressed right after you're done eating," Eric said, smacking the top of a soft-boiled egg so repeatedly it was a shambles of yoke and shell in his plate. He put it aside without touching it. And then, Noel knew.

"Today?" he asked.

"You're to meet at two o'clock. He ought to be waiting there," Eric said, his nervousness now smothered by his ability to spell it all out. "The two of you will go inside. Here's a set of keys. I gave him a set, too. It ought to be unlocked."

The manner in which Eric spoke of his intended victim seemed to suggest no personality, no character, as though he had already dismissed from his mind everything individual and unique about Buddy Vega in order to see him as one thing only—the enemy, that which must be eliminated.

"Here are the plans you will give him," Eric said, lifting a long cardboard tube from the unoccupied chair next to him. He took out the plans and unfurled them on the table, pointing to various parts of the diagram as he spoke. "You enter here. Make a left at the foyer, here, then go into that large room. It's two stories high. The roof is partially open. That's where the skylight will be."

"Do you own this place?" Noel had to know.

"Are you kidding? A rental agent showed it to Chaffee months ago. We had a second key made."

Eric stretched out the roll of plans again and continued: "Leave the plans with him. That's important. Make sure he opens them and begins looking at them. Even do it for him, if necessary. Then, Noel, you go here." He pointed to a small room off the corridor. "Make some excuse. You have to check the plumbing, the wiring, anything. Then you quietly go out the entry again to the street. Go directly to the car, sit down, and wait for Bill to come out again."

He made Noel repeat the instructions. When they came to the part about Vega holding the plans in his hands, Noel asked why that was so important.

"So his hands are busy when I come up behind him," McWhitter answered softly. "He won't have a chance to move. I'll get him from behind just perfect, then flick!" He snapped his closed fists apart as though garroting someone.

"Just do as you're told," Eric said. His nervousness contrasted so markedly with the bodyguard's imperturbable, almost technical calm that Noel had the sudden total conviction that Eric had never done anything like this before, as he had the equal unshakable belief that McWhitter had, often, and with no thought but how to do it with the least trouble to himself.

Noel finished repeating the instructions, looking down at his own two uncracked soft-boiled eggs, in their neat, egg-white-colored little bowl, set in turn on a similarly colored, flatter plate, set against the slightly luminescent flat white of the tabletop, and he suddenly thought, yes, this is where my life has led me, to discussing the murder of a friend among all this elegant breakfast china. The shapes and colors in front of him made him furious with their purity and unity; he wanted to smash them, all of them, to smash all the white clean pure perfect things in the world for their hollow deception, for their utter fragility.

"Would you prefer something else to eat?" Okku asked at Noel's elbow. "Oatmeal? Cereal?"

"Yes, thank you," Noel said, but by the time the cereal had come, he had reminded himself that Loomis knew and Vega would be safe, and had eaten both of the eggs.

Upstairs he wrote NOW! all over a sheet of onionskin paper, and stuffed it in his denims' pocket.

The anonymous sedan Eric had had rented for the mission was parked down the street. Noel pretended to find the paper in his pocket before he and McWhitter got into the car. He looked at it as though it were nothing of importance, tore it up, and scattered the fragments out the car window.

McWhitter drove in silence downtown, past the congestion of Sunday traffic around the bridge and tunnel, over to the West Side—almost solitary in the glaring hot weather. Below Canal Street, even scattered cars and pedestrians ceased to appear. McWhitter slowed down, turned a corner near a series of four-

story warehouses with metal awnings that jutted out
to the edge of the sidewalk. He seemed to be looking
for the address, then advanced around a second corner, identical to the first, and stopped the car.

He sat at the wheel without making a sound. Noel
saw a bright metal object transferred quickly from
McWhitter's pants to his shirt pocket. It made a bulge
and so was returned to the pants. The garrote?

The street was empty. Not a car, not a parked truck.
It was two o'clock by the car dial clock. What were
they waiting for?

"Want to have a far-out time?" the bodyguard said
so suddenly and huskily that Noel answered, "What?"

"Instead of coming back to the car, stay in the room
Eric told you to go into. When I'm finished, I'll come
in and let you screw me."

Noel was so astonished he didn't speak.

"It's the only time I can take it that way," McWhitter said huskily, stroking Noel's thigh lightly. "The
only time I can relax enough. You know."

Noel overcame his disgust by telling himself it
wouldn't happen.

"What do you say?" McWhitter asked, his big hand
moving into Noel's crotch.

"Sure."

"I promised Eric. But it will be too late by the time
I get back to the house. And," he added huskily, "if
you listen real good from the other room, it'll sound
like he's coming when I put it on him. It's real exciting."

"Let's go," Noel said.

McWhitter gave his groin one more stroke, then got
out of the car.

Even with his sunglasses on, Noel was temporarily
blinded by the glare of the white-bricked buildings
reflected off the empty asphalt road. It was beating
hot, airless, the way it must be on the prairie in mid-
summer, he thought.

At the address, a ramshackle, weather-discolored

door was shut, but the padlock was opened, hanging from the bar.

"He's here," McWhitter whispered.

Noel wanted to get it over quickly. He opened the door.

It swung on an unoiled, creaking hinge. The concrete floor of the foyer in front of them was littered with plaster dust. The entryway, dark after the bright sun, opened up into a large, windowless room, lighted from above through broken ceiling planking. Sunlight streamed in like cathedral light, sharpening each detail of fallen wood, the big slide bar, a little balcony opposite the entrance, also cluttered with debris. Noel was going into the big room when McWhitter's arm shot out and pulled him back.

"He's not here," Noel whispered.

The pressure on his forearm said to be quiet. McWhitter was listening to something. Noel only heard a slight rustle above them on the opposite balcony: probably a rat.

"He's not here," Noel repeated.

"He's here," the bodyguard said so low it was barely audible.

"Should I call him?"

"Be still!"

McWhitter let go of his arm and began sniffing the air as if he were a beagle on a whiff of scent.

Every moment was beginning to panic Noel. What if Loomis hadn't gotten his message? "What is it?" he asked.

"Go into the room," McWhitter whispered. "Unroll the plans and look around. I'm going scouting. Go on!" He gave Noel a shove that sent him into the big room.

Noel opened the plans, feeling that somehow he was now doing exactly what Vega was supposed to have been doing, that he was the intended victim, and all of this a setup, a trap to get him in here to be garroted by McWhitter. Vega had been sent somewhere else, not here, and Loomis's men would be tailing him. Noel would die here alone.

The certainty of this made him feel totally fatigued, and he determined not to fight it. He dropped the cardboard roll of plans, straightened out the diagram, and began to compare it to his surroundings. Sure enough, there was the wall with the big bar, and opposite it, the dotted lines marked balcony overhead. There, too, were the two doorways marked on the plans as lav entrances; he could even make out the ceramic fixtures in one of them. Here was the overhead opening intended to be the bar's skylight.

The sound came from behind him somewhere, so odd that he could only think of a slap on a bare behind, or the *whit* of a blowgun.

He turned to face the direction it had come from. The doorway off the foyer, where McWhitter had gone after leaving him with the plans. Then Noel heard something heavy fall with a dull thud in the little room and he knew, sickeningly, that it was Vega's body.

A long time seemed to pass. McWhitter still didn't come out. What was he doing in there? Would he come out naked, slavering with a murder-incited lust? Noel tried to make out sounds, footsteps. All he heard were the rustling of rats on the littered balcony above him.

He would leave now, Noel decided. That was what he was supposed to do, what Eric had told him to do. He would try to figure out later how Loomis had fouled up. Right now he had to get away from McWhitter and out that door.

It took a great effort to move, but when he did, he went directly for the front door.

There was more rustling behind him. Noel stopped at that noise. He was only a few feet from the front door, facing the doorway, now half closed, of the little side room McWhitter had gone into. On the ground inside, amid splintered two-by-twos, was a pair of shoes, heels up.

I'm leaving now, he told himself. But something about the shoes seemed wrong. He turned around, fascinated by those heels sticking up, and crept up to the doorway, slowly opening the door until he could see not only the heels, but the legs and the back of the body lying facedown on the floor, shoulders and head in shadows. It was McWhitter!

Relief flooded him with warmth, and he pushed the door open enough to make out Vega's tall figure standing at the head of the dead man, swaying slightly. Loomis *had* told him. Noel was about to step into the room and go up to Buddy when a new apprehension took over. Buddy seemed to be hurt, or drunk, or something, swaying there in front of Noel.

"Buddy!" he whispered. When there was no response, Noel fumbled in his pants pocket, found the lighter Eric had given him, and flicked it on.

It was Buddy Vega all right. But his head lay on one shoulder in an unnatural manner, the eyes closed, and a cord was wound around his neck twice, rising behind his head to a rafter some three feet above. His clothing was splattered with blood which thinned to dots on his shirtfront, but was staining his light-colored chinos almost to his crotch. Noel held the lighter down lower and saw the boot tips of Buddy's shoes off the ground, just brushing what would have been the back of McWhitter's head if it weren't just a pulpy, red-and-white mass on top of his shoulders.

He snapped the lighter closed, frozen to the spot, filled with the sudden certainty that he was still in the presence not only of their assassin, but of Randy's, and even before that, of Kansas's in the abandoned warehouse months before—an old and well-known enemy as sardonic and grisly as he was effective.

Noel shuddered from head to foot, then calmly turned and went out the door. As he did, he heard the odd and fatal sound again, close to his ear. *Thwut, thwut*, answered by a sharp crack of wood lathing inches away from Noel, where a charred hole and split wood said it was a dumdum bullet from a silenced gun. From the overhead balcony!

He flattened himself against the wall, knowing he would have to put himself in range of the gunman in order to get out. Silence, then another *thwut*, farther away from him, closer to the handle of the door. Another. Closer to him.

He turned sideways, crouched, then fell on the floor, rolling quickly to the other side of the entry. *Thwut*. He heard it again and felt his right ear sting as though from a wasp bite. But he was flat against the wall, close to the front door now. How to get out? *How?* To one side of him was a wooden slat. That would help. Noel lifted it out of range of the gunman, brought it to the side closest the door, inserted it gently between the door and the doorway, and sprung it The door flew open. *Thwut, thwut*. The bullets were aimed where his head would be. Good thing he'd tried it. The door slammed closed again, and when Noel inserted the slat and opened it again, he bent down to the floor and dove out the entry onto the sidewalk, then quickly moved behind the door, pulled it shut, got the latch across and the padlock shut, before he heard the sound again. A bullet went right through the wood, just missing him, and exploded against the wall of the opposite building where it made a mark the size of a fist.

What now? He spun around and ran to the car, but realized, as he skidded into the side of it, that he didn't have the keys. Whoever was inside had gotten in without a key. He could climb up out of the roof. Noel had to get out of here, fast. He edged his way to the end of one block, shot around the corner to the next street, turning around to make certain no one was after him, then across the street to the next building. From there, he just ran. Ran like hell, letting the mindless energy tear out of his chest and head, racing past block after block of deserted warehouses, hardly altering his gait to drop off a curbstone onto a street,

up another curbstone, and on and on, expecting that
deadly *thwut* to sound next to him, before he was silenced forever. Racing until he reached what seemed
to be a major thoroughfare, with a few cars on it. He
looked up to see a sign: Varick Street, then began
pounding uptown.

Someone was calling his name. He stopped and
looked around. From across the street, driving downtown, he saw someone wave at him, out of the window of a low silver coupé. Eric.

Noel looked around, then dove into the first doorway.

His first thought was that he'd been caught in a
doorway before. He'd have to get out. Then he
thought, it *was* Eric, Eric who had killed both Vega
and McWhitter and was out for him, too, though he
didn't know why. *Have to get out of this doorway.*

As he moved forward, he almost knocked Eric
down.

He was grabbed, one arm pulled up and behind
him fast.

"Where's McWhitter? Why are you running?
Where's the car?" Eric asked, pushing him back into
the doorway.

Even with his arm twisted behind him. Noel knew
it hadn't been Eric with the gun. He couldn't feel the
icy presence now, the cold delight in death he'd felt so
strongly before. No, whoever that was, it wasn't Eric.

"Let go!" he said, and when Eric did, Noel stood
up, rubbing his arm, and let the words come out of
him in a torrent. "A silencer . . . dumdum bullets
. . . after me . . . just got out . . . got both of them,
both of them! . . . no head left on McWhitter . . .
knew those weren't Buddy's shoes, he never wore anything but boots . . . wanted me to fuck him afterward . . . couldn't . . . have to get out of here . . .
after me . . . neck snapped, hung from a rafter . . .
it was the rats in the balcony, I thought . . ."

The look on Eric's face told him to stop: he wasn't

making any sense. He did stop, began trembling
again. Eric looked out the doorway behind him, up
and down the street.

"No one's there. We're going out and getting into
the car. Do you understand?"

Noel tried to say yes; it came out a stream of babble.

"No one's out there, Noel. No one will hurt you."

Noel grabbed for Eric, was shaken off. "Let's go.
Run for it."

They sprinted across the wide street, got into the
car, with Noel trying to huddle down to make himself
as inconspicuous a target as possible, as Eric gunned
the car to scream on two wheels around the nearest
corner onto a side street, then around another corner
fast, and threading through traffic, up Sixth Avenue.

When they were at Thirty-fourth Street, stopped for
a light, Noel began remembering the sound of the
bullets against the walls and Buddy's neck bent over
to one shoulder, and McWhitter's head blown off, and
the fear that he'd managed to avoid and so to survive
came on him: he began to babble and gesticulate
wildly, until he couldn't even make out Eric's face or
words or the fact that he was safe now, but only the
arctic terror in his bones, until he saw a fist come
straight at his forehead as though in a Cinerama
movie, and the screen went black.

FOUR

THE
CATCH

1

August, 1976

When Noel woke it was dark. He took the elevator down to the main floor, arriving in time to interrupt a tête-à-tête between Eric and Alana in the dining room.

"Feeling better?" Redfern called across the living room to Noel. "Hungry? We've just begun."

As soon as Noel joined them he realized that what he had taken for an intimate conversation was probably an argument. Eric seemed vaguely annoyed. Alana took one look at Noel's bruised face, frowned, bit her lip as though afraid of the words that would pour forth if she didn't keep herself in control, and served Noel without even a hello.

"Sorry about what happened earlier," Eric said quietly.

Noel didn't know whether he was referring to the shooting, the stakeout, or to Eric's knocking him out in the car. He decided on the last, least paranoid choice.

"I was a little out of control," Noel replied.

"I was afraid we were going to crash. You're feeling better now, I see."

Alana's continued silence and distance and Eric's surprising apology united the two men, however momentarily, however fragilely. After this day's events, Noel felt safe with Eric, safer with him than with almost anyone else. He felt Eric finally trusted him, too. He almost had to, now. Each only had each other to rely upon. Except for Alana, of course, so aloof now,

so busily, uncharacteristically concentrating on her
meal that Noel was sure if he hadn't arrived when he
had the two others would have been screaming at
each other.

"I almost went back," Eric confessed.

"To . . . there?"

"I had to see for myself. But I couldn't take the
chance."

Noel let out a sigh. "You wouldn't want to see it."

"I was *supposed* to go after Vega," Eric said bitterly. "And I fell right into it. Damn! Why him,
though? Of all of them?"

Noel suspected he knew why, now that Buddy's
prediction about himself had come true. Whom else
had Vega told about those dossiers? Was that enough
reason for Whisper to kill him? Or had he been onto
something more? It couldn't have been just a mix-up
this time. Whoever had shot at Noel had killed
McWhitter. And Vega had been hanged from the rafter by the time they arrived.

"That agency that's funding you," Eric began in-
tently, so suddenly and obliquely that it took Noel
some time to catch up, "who are they?"

"Agency? You mean for the book? They're only as-
sisting really. It doesn't come to that much."

"Who are they?"

"Some social research group. It was one of a dozen
my department chairman offered me. The first to respond. That's all I know about them."

"Do they know what your book is about?"

"They should; I had to provide a pretty comprehensive proposal when I applied. Why?"

"I did some research myself," Eric said. "They're
funded by some really strange folks in the West. Very
right wing. Very conservative. Very much against social change."

"That doesn't make any sense."

"Is your book pro gay?"

"It's neither pro nor con. It's a study. You know, with charts and tables of statistics."

"On gays. Which they could use against us."

"Could," Noel admitted. "But only by stretching or distorting. The book is really pretty technical, Eric. It's not designed for the layman. And it will add a great deal of data about gay life and relationships to social scientists. In that sense it's pro gay. Knowledge of that kind can't do anything but help."

He went on for a minute more, shocked by what Eric had said. He had given the stock, trained answers he'd prepared with the Fisherman. But if Redfern's imputation was correct, why use that agency to fund him and not a more liberal one?

"Besides," Noel concluded, "they have no control over the contents of the book. None. It's to be published through the University Press. If they wanted to make trouble for gays, I would think they'd go for something more sensational, wouldn't they?"

"I don't know. I don't know a lot of things lately," Eric said glumly.

They fell silent for a while. Noel tried to get Alana's attention, but she looked away or down at her plate. When she got up to leave the table, Noel reached out and took her hand.

"What's this silent treatment all about, anyway?"

She pulled out of his grasp, and stood rubbing her hand.

"Well? Answer me. If you have something to say, say it."

She looked at him now, but contemptuously. "Look at you! Aren't you ashamed of yourself?" Then to Eric: "And you, too. What's wrong with you?"

"It couldn't be helped," Eric said.

"Couldn't be helped," she mimicked him.

"Eric's right," Noel said. "He didn't know I'd be shot at."

Halfway through the sentence, Noel realized he

should stop. Eric began to gesture for him to be quiet. Alana's mouth hung open a minute.

"Shooting? So it has come to that now?"

"I wasn't hit," Noel said.

"You were nicked," Eric said. "The top of your ear. No, the other place."

Noel reached to touch his right ear, felt the small bandage. All at once the torrent of fear returned: he was pressed flat up against the wall, the wooden door swinging closed, the sickening *thwut, thwut* going past him. He fought it away, holding on to the table.

"Just like in the gangster movies on television, eh?" Noel had never seen her sarcastic before.

"It couldn't be helped," Eric repeated.

"Of course it could be helped. Just stop, stop now."

"Stop what?" Eric demanded, equally angry now.

"I don't know what. Playing games with these people. Stop doing whatever it is that is endangering us all."

"I can't. It's not what I'm doing, it's what I am that they hate."

"And what about him?" She pointed to Noel. "This man. Why is he the one getting hurt?"

"Ask him why," Eric said. And Noel felt their trust disintegrating.

She stared at Noel, as if begging him to say something. Then, "No! I don't want to hear about it. Not any of it."

"Tell her, Noel. Tell her how the people you're working for just tried to kill you. Tell her."

When Noel didn't say anything, Eric went on: "Of course it might be a mistake. A pretty big mistake, but still . . . Or maybe it was like what happened outside the Baths."

"Stop!" she screamed. To Noel she said in a calmer voice, "Go away from this house and never come back. And you, Eric, let him go."

Neither answered her, which was answer enough. "Pah! You disgust me. Both of you. Don't you understand, Noel? This is the perfect sadomasochistic fantasy for him? Don't you care even for your own life anymore?"

"Come on, Alana. That has nothing to do with it," Eric protested.

"Don't tell me. I have eyes. I see. This business makes all that back-room stuff at Le Pissoir look like Tinker Toys."

"You're wrong," Noel put in.

"And you defend him! Tell me, Eric, if it is true that these men are after you, what for? Tell me now, what for?"

"Because I won't stay down. I won't grovel."

"Ah! Politics! I thought I'd stopped hearing about politics years ago," she said scornfully.

"Someone's got to do it," Eric said. "Someone sooner or later."

"So. I see. Like Lenin and all his friends. For an idea we all will be killed."

"Or George Washington and his friends," Eric reminded her.

"Fine. Good. Do what you want. You and you, too," she said to Noel, shaking her head. "As for me, I am going away tomorrow. I'll fly back and wear black at both your funerals. Is that what you want?"

"I thought we were going to Clouds tonight?" Eric said. But she had already started across the walkway toward her bedroom. "Come on, Alana," Eric called after her, "you were never like this before!"

"And men were never such fools as you two!" she said before slamming her door.

"... *be kind enough to leave your name*, phone number, and the date you called and I'll get back to you. Beep!"

His message repeated. This call was a hang-up. The tape ran silent for a while, then Noel heard the strangled end of the telephone's ring and his message again.

It was the morning following the double death in the downtown bar, and Noel felt oddly calm. Being back in his apartment helped—small and alien as it had at first appeared to him last night. Listening to the phone message machine also helped at first. So far these past few weeks, while he was away from home, he'd been called a dozen times. By Mirella, of course, twice. But also by Monica's parents, and Paul Warshaw, although Noel still didn't know if the boy coming out of the water that night had been he. Then several hang-ups. He suspected a few were from Whisper operatives. And then the disquieting message left by Buddy Vega.

Eric couldn't have heard that call. It had been made after Noel had gone back to the town house: the very next day. It was mercifully brief, though so enigmatic Noel could recall it word for word:

"Star here!" Vega had announced himself, using his code name. "I found out more. A lot more. It involves you, me, the whole project. Those dossiers were pigeon-shit compared to this, Noel. I'm blowing the whistle. Call me."

Too late to call him, too late for Buddy Vega to blow the whistle on anyone.

He ought to contact Priscilla Vega. Surely she knew by now? Or should he check in with Whisper first? Just to make sure? If she hadn't been notified, he didn't want to be the one who dropped the megaton bomb on her.

Instead, he played out the answering machine tape to the end, sitting on a little Navajo blanket in the middle of his studio. He didn't want to talk to Loomis. Nor to Priscilla. Nor to Eric. He just wanted to remain here, comfortable, at home, safe—for the moment. Maybe he ought to leave the city, go see Monica's parents; they'd love to have him. Call Paul Warshaw and offer him a week in the sun, in the mountains, anywhere. Even if it meant making a commitment to being gay. What did *that* matter now? As Vega had said in his message, it was pigeonshit, pigeonshit!

The phone rang and he was so startled he answered it immediately. At first, there was no response to his hello, then a vaguely familiar man's voice saying, "Is this fishing information?"

"Fishing information?" Noel repeated. Simultaneously, he recalled that was a Whisper code. "Yes, this is."

"I've a Fisherman here, wants to speak to you."

A few seconds later: "Lure?"

"I thought you weren't going to use the phones, Loomis? Too risky, remember?"

"Your phone's all right now. Listen, Lure, you all right?"

"I'm talking, aren't I?"

"There was a foul-up," Loomis said. "I don't know for sure what happened. But somehow Redfern must have sent someone there before you."

Your phone's all right now. Did that mean Whisper had had a tap on him, not Redfern?

"Sure," Noel said.

"I didn't want you to see . . . anything. That's why you were chased out of there," Loomis explained. He was edgy.

"You were there?"

"Not me personally, of course."

"Whoever it was could have thrown a pebble or something. I would have gotten the message. I wasn't armed, you know."

"We didn't know."

"Sure."

"We didn't!"

"Sure."

"Stop saying that!"

"What the fuck do you want me to say, thanks for the excitement?" Who would Eric have sent? Okku? He was at home. And Eric himself couldn't have gotten there before McWhitter. There was no one else Redfern trusted enough to do it. Dorrance? In California for the past week on business. Or was he?

"I'm telling you it was a mix-up," Loomis said.

"Mrs. Vega know?"

"Yeah."

"What does she know?"

"Nothing. The standard killed-in-the-line-of-duty business."

"I'm going to call her."

"Maybe you shouldn't. What if Redfern . . . ?"

"Loomis," Noel interrupted, "I'm calling Mrs. Vega to offer my condolences! I don't care what Redfern, or you, or anyone else thinks about it. It's the fucking least thing I can do after luring her husband to his death."

"Now don't get feeling guilty about it."

"Don't worry about my feelings, huh?"

"And don't tell her anything."

"I don't even know her," he lied. "Now if you're finished with your lame excuses, I'm hanging up."

"We're getting close," Loomis said.

"Close to what?"

"To Mr. X." There was an undertone of excitement in Loomis's voice. "We've got ourselves a neat little setup for him, and he's not going to be able to swim out of it this time. Go back to the town house and hang in there. Another week or so. That's all we need."

"For what?"

"To get him. We're setting up something small and clean. We'll pull him in on that small charge. Then throw the book at him."

"Yeah, if it keeps a few of us alive, it'll be good enough for me," Noel said.

"*I told you,*" Loomis repeated, "that was a mix-up! Don't worry. No one will get hurt this time."

"I hope not. No wonder you don't offer life insurance."

Loomis was talking to someone else on his end of the line. He didn't seem to hear that last remark. He came back to the phone with a curt, "We'll let you know when it's going to happen."

"The bust on Redfern?"

"You won't be involved in it. You'll be our backup. Just in case. So sit tight. It'll be over soon. Don't call. Keep me informed with the messages." Someone else was speaking low on his end, and he finally said good-bye.

For a long while after the call, Noel began to feel relief. He had wanted this burden off and now it looked as though it would come off. As long as he wasn't the fulcrum between Loomis and Eric anymore, he didn't care what they did.

After lunch he dialed Mirella Trent. She was out. Then he tried Monica's mother. No luck there either. Paul Warshaw answered but seemed busy and said he would call back later. Finally, Noel dialed Vega's number.

Priscilla answered in a voice so tiny Noel though at first it was her little girl.

"Mrs. Vega? Noel Cummings."

There was a sharp intake of breath, then, *"Dios gracias!* I hoped you would call me. Where are you?"

"At home, why?"

"Come to see me. Right now, please. Can you?"

"Yes, but . . ."

"Right now. Don't talk," she commanded and hung up.

The phone. She knew it was tapped. That's why she didn't want to talk. Eric must have thought it was tapped, too. That would explain why he wanted to hear the messages played back, so he could hear the surveillance. Sure. But why in the hell was *Noel* being tapped?

3

_____

Next to the pictures of John F. Kennedy and Jesus Christ was one of Buddy, all of them freshly covered with flowers and each with a votive candle burning in front of it on the bureau top. That was one indication of Priscilla Vega's loss and grief. Another was that the children were gone.

"After what happened, you don't think I would keep them with me, do you? They're at my great-aunt's in San Juan by now. Except for the baby. She's at my mother's. I see her every day."

Noel, remembering her fiery temperament, had expected to see her furious, vengeful, bitter. But she was very cool. Sorrowful, yes, but purposeful, too.

"Buddy said if you got to him in time, everything would be all right," she remarked as soon as Noel had sympathized.

That meant Buddy had gone to the rendezvous knowing as much as Noel. That took courage. Noel felt even more humiliated by his role in the affair, and his fear afterward.

"I was too late," he admitted sadly, but didn't know how much to tell her.

"Buddy said if you were too late it was because Loomis had tricked him," she said, waiting for his reaction.

When Noel didn't respond, she went on: "He said I was to help you. I *will* help you," she added fervently.

"Help me do what?"

"To find my husband's murderers for one thing," she said, with a hint of the anger he'd anticipated. "And to finish his work for him."

"He found more dossiers?" Noel asked, already aware that she felt he owed her something for her husband's life, that he must do something for her. The list grew every month: Loomis. Eric. Now Buddy Vega, too, from beyond the grave. And Monica, of course. His debts.

"Yes, more dossiers. Even more terrible than before."

The big accordion folder was brought out again. Noel's depression deepened. He'd still not gotten over the last revelations. Did he really need to see more?

Priscilla gave him not the bulky manila folder, but three finely typed pages, with photostat copies of four more assorted-sized papers attached. As he began to read the top line of the first page, she read it aloud, from memory.

"AIN memo. Re: weapon. Class B, psychological. Code name: 'The Lure.'"

Noel reread that line three times.

"Buddy thought AIN stood for Associated Intelligence Network. A connection between the CIA, FBI, and state and municipal police. Buddy said it was constitutionally illegal, but that it existed anyway, and that the reason we didn't hear more about it was the bulky bureaucracy that kept it from being effective."

Noel had just fully understood the line of type. "I'm the Lure," he said tonelessly.

"Yes. We knew that." There was great pity in her voice.

"How long?"

"Three weeks. A little more."

"*I'm* the weapon. Against whom?"

"Against Mr. X."

"Eric?"

"Read on. Page two, paragraph four."

He turned the page. "August twenty-third! That's today's date."

"Yes. But this memo was written on March eighth. Read it, or should I?"

"By the above date," Noel read aloud, "the subject should be in phase five, called 'safety clip removed.' Recent events have placed him in an all-encompassing psychosexual crisis. This, concomitant with repeated attempts on his life, ought to make him chaste, utterly confused, unable to face any major life choice such as whom to trust as his friend. He will begin to turn sharply inward. Trusting no one, he will seek seclusion, possibly even try to flee the situation. At the least, he will find psychological safety only in his own home."

"That's true," Noel said. "But what's the purpose of this?"

"It *is* true?" she asked.

"Pretty close, sure," he admitted.

"You were told your mission with Whisper was to get close enough to this Mr. X so he could be trapped, right?"

Noel didn't answer. This, too, might be a trap: or a test.

"It makes no difference," she went on. "It says so right here on paragraph two, page one. This, however, is not your real work for Whisper. That is what is so terrible. Read, go on." She pointed to a spot at the end of the page, but before he could read it, she said, "You are not a lure, you are the man who within two weeks will assassinate this Mr. X. You have been found, selected, and programmed to do this particular act whether you are aware of it or not, whether you want to do it or not."

They were sitting at the kitchen table. As Noel read the page which said in different terms exactly what Priscilla had told him, he stood up, knocking the chair over behind him. *Within two weeks. That meant Labor Day.*

"It is *very* terrible," she said.

A curious thing happened to Noel then. He felt as though he were splitting into two selves. One Noel was absolutely astonished, crushed by this final disaster, the last blow of months of confusion and pain and uncertainty, the knowledge that he was being controlled by someone else; worse, turned into a robot with a deadly mission. But the other half—his professional, intellectual self—was utterly fascinated. Here he was, playing around with minority-group social attitudes and Loomis—a genius—was performing effective social-modification behavior—not on laboratory monkeys, not on children, but on *him!*

Other scientists, looking at the psychosociological model Loomis had designed, and at its solution, would call them "elegant." Mirella Trent, for example, would rave over its structural beauties.

The fragile but very real split within himself came together with one thought: how could he ever escape the Fisherman's control, when he hadn't even known until now it existed? Eric's hold on him, even Alana's, were as ribbons to steel bands.

Or was that entirely so? Reading the condition he was supposed to be in, his first thought had been, Yes, this is how it is. But his second thought had been, So what! It's not so bad. It's true. All true. But despite it all, despite even the danger, I'm alive. Not unhappy, somehow; stupidly, not unhappy. Whatever happened, it was happening to him, and would never have happened if he hadn't made a choice on that March morning at the abandoned warehouse. True, he was living on the edge. But the edge was making him more alive than ever before.

So, he didn't believe he could kill Eric. At the same time he suspected that if the circumstances were slightly different, he really just might. That was the problem.

He stopped, realizing he'd circled the table many times. He looked at Priscilla Vega, concerned, patient, holding a cup of cold coffee in her hand. Then he sat down.

"All right," he said. "Granted. I'm the bomb. How do we defuse me?"

As though weighing something, she looked him over for a long time before she spoke.

"We did not tell you this before," she began in a low, carefully modulated voice, "because you were supposed to become schizophrenic if you ever did find out. You were supposed to split apart into two people, and then destroy yourself."

"I did split apart into two people," he said. "Just now. But it didn't last."

"Which means the programming is not perfect. As Buddy and I thought. But why isn't it perfect?"

"Does it say anything in here about a woman?" Noel asked.

"Much. Two women. One would put you off, reject you. Another one you would reject after abusing her in some way. They would together make you disgusted with all women, which would intensify your problem."

Noel searched himself for the truth, then said, "But I'm not disgusted with all women. And she's the reason why not, I think."

"The one who rejected you? She's attracted to you because you are fulfilling her need for a certain type of man."

"It's true. I know it. But I don't care. Alana's too good to me. She cares for me. I don't know if anyone else does, but she does. I think that's what has thrown off the programming."

"Maybe," she said, sounding unconvinced. "But what if you are not defused now? What if you are still dangerous? Perhaps even more dangerous, because now you are an unaimed weapon?"

That was another jolt. But it made sense. It would be just like Loomis to build in every safeguard. How much of his everyday life in the past six months had been predictable, given over to someone else to determine? The man hit by the car, for instance. The night in Le Pissoir. How much more? His life had been changed not only in large areas—his work, his friends—but in details, too: the hours he kept, the stimuli around him, even the music he'd been listening to was different. His schedule was disarranged, his values shaken, his former life all but gone, and his new life constantly unsettling. Could Loomis and his computer—he had to be using one—could they predict, say, when he brushed his teeth, or if he brushed his teeth? Possible. Incredible. But possible.

"Noel!" Priscilla was shouting at him, shaking his arm.

He came back to her. "It was happening again: the splitting apart business. But it's all right. It will help me to understand exactly how to get around this."

She stared at him.

"I'm okay. Really. Now how do we defuse me?"

"Buddy had a plan. Not based on statistics or psychology or anything fancy like that. But we discussed it several times. He thinks it would work."

"Thinks!"

"Thought, I mean. Please. I know he is dead. Sometimes I can't believe it. But I know it."

Very gently, Noel asked what Buddy's plan was.

"You know why Buddy had to leave the Navy?" she asked.

"Yes, but . . ."

"Not for the reason he told you. He was a thief. He was asked to steal documents from one group by another. He was caught. It was all hushed up. He became a civilian and sometimes a man from the government would come to see him and ask for him to steal something. Then this top policeman came to ask Buddy to work for him. He knew he was a thief."

"So Buddy was supposed to steal those dossiers and show them to me?"

"Those, yes. But Buddy got suspicious about you. When he read your dossier, it reminded him of some other papers he'd come across that he later knew he was not supposed to find. Those are the reports we were not supposed to know about." She indicated the photocopied reports attached to the psychological weapons plan.

Noel began reading one, then went on to the others. Each of them detailed the activities of a former AIN control. All were successful assassins. In all four cases, the men were now retired on some sort of pension, even though one of them was younger than Noel, and all of them were happy, oblivious to what had occured. They simply did not remember what they had done.

"Look at that last one," she instructed. "Not the print, that mark there."

"It looks like some sort of institutional seal," he said, barely able to make it out.

"Buddy had it blown up and copied darker. This is it." She pulled another paper from the accordion envelope. The stamp was larger, clearer. At the top, Noel could easily read the name of the social research agency in Albany that was paying his salary for Whisper. How had Eric characterized them? "Very right wing. Very conservative. Very against social change."

Priscilla went on: "We don't know exactly who they are. But Loomis is connected with them. Buddy was certain the police do not know how deeply this group is involved. Only two copies of these memoranda were sent to the Police Department records files. Both were initialed by people that he discovered were merely secretaries. Then they were filed away in "disbursements," indexed only for special retrieval. Buddy was the first person to take them out since they were filed."

"That wasn't predicted?" Noel asked.

"Only *you* are predicted. *You* are the weapon, not Buddy. He was merely supposed to find the dossiers and show them to you. Nothing more. It was because they made it so easy for him to steal the dossiers that he got suspicious and went back to look again. This AIN and psychological weapon plan the papers kept referring to intrigued him. So he decided to see for himself. That's how he found this. It is only *you* who are planned for. He was dispensable," she added bitterly.

"But if, as you think, they killed him, then they must know he found all this, too," he said, shaking the papers she'd given him.

"No. It was his stupid telephone call to you. Your telephone is tapped. But he was so excited!" Her voice sank to a murmur.

After a minute she told him Buddy's plan.

It wasn't as complex or fail-safe as Loomis's master plan, but it sounded effective. All this material was to be brought to the attention of the police Commissioner by Noel, the Lure himself. Priscilla would go with him to corroborate everything. They'd explain how a homicide investigation had been transformed by Loomis into a psychological weapon proving ground for the upstate social research agency. They'd ask to have Loomis taken off Whisper. Noel would resign. Without the circumstances, the weapon could not be used.

Noel thought about what she said. He wasn't sure it would hold enough water with the police commissioner to disband Whisper.

"We need something more substantial," he told her. She was silent a short while, then, "What about graft?"

"Graft? Between Loomis and this agency in Albany?"

"No, between him and organized crime."

"How do you know that?"

"We monitored the loops for twelve days. Buddy had three other phones installed and connected up and we listened in on them. Anytime someone used the loops, Buddy or I would take down what was said. I used to be a stenographer."

"My calls, too?" he asked. She nodded yes. "Go on," Noel prodded. "If what you're saying is true, this is what we have to go for."

"It's true. There is a fourth emergency loop. Never used to our knowledge by anyone but Loomis. He used it twice in the time we were listening, to call a man named G or Gee. They never talked more than a minute or so, even though it was a special loop. They were always brief, businesslike, usually arranging meetings. The last meeting they had was last week. Another one is due in two days."

"So you didn't hear anything really about graft."

"Yes, we did. Both times Loomis reported progress on his 'mutual' interest with Gee. Gee in turn reported that his lawyers were working out a suitable manner of payment. They discussed the transfer of stocks and bonds over a period of a year and a half, from one dummy company to another feeding into Loomis's bank accounts. We wrote down all the information. Some payments had already been made. For previous 'bounties' which Gee's 'associates,' as he called them, were very pleased about."

"It still sounds too vague."

"As soon as Mr. X is killed, his territory will be bought up again, by some contact of Loomis's in a city agency. They'll condemn the properties, then sell them in a rigged auction to Gee's friends. Loomis assured Gee that this contact of his was already partially paid off."

"He said that?"

"You want to read what I took down?"

"No. Later. Did they mention amounts of money?"

"Absolutely. I have all the figures on paper. Loomis was to get five percent of the final price. They estimated that Redfern's gay businesses—clubs, discos, baths, bars—were worth about ten or twelve million dollars. They couldn't touch his private holdings."

"Five percent of that is a lot of money," Noel said. He now understood why Loomis was so hell-bent on eliminating Mr. X. If it were true. "Loomis told me himself that organized crime had dropped out of gay businesses because they weren't so profitable," he argued.

"Maybe so. They are profitable now. And now they want them back."

And Eric's dream would be destroyed, Noel thought. Eric's dream of an economic/political power base that would unify gays against those who'd always exploited them: the mob, the police.

"Then Loomis was lying to me all along about those men being murdered," Noel said, recalling the Fisherman's impressive first visit.

"He wasn't lying. They *were* killed. Buddy thought Whisper eliminated them in an attempt to scare this Mr. X out of all of his businesses out of the city. But he wasn't scared. And that's when Loomis tried to work out a scheme where he would pin all the deaths on Mr. X, who was closely associated with all of the victims. Evidently in the middle of that scheme he discovered these AIN control plans, and decided that would be the most efficient method of eliminating Mr. X."

"We need real proof of this deal," Noel said.

"The next meeting is in two days in a Horn and

Hardart cafeteria on Fifty-seventh Street. Loomis and Gee will meet as though by accident, have lunch, and discuss it."

"How do we get near them, how do we get proof?" Noel asked. He still had to convince himself all she had told him was true.

"Buddy bought this a few days ago," Priscilla said, going to a kitchen cabinet and taking out a portable cassette recorder the size of a small transistor radio. "To tape their next conversation. He became obsessed with what Loomis was doing, Noel. He felt sorry for you, but it was more than that. He didn't want his children to grow up in a world where it is possible to use people as you are being used."

Noel inspected the recorder, read the directions, then tried out the demo tape with the recorder under the table. It was fine inside a quiet kitchen. But there would be a great deal of background noise in a large, public restaurant. How could they get close enough to tape the two men there?

"Buddy thought I could do that," Priscilla said. "We planned to have me go to that meeting to tape them. But I don't know who Loomis is."

"I'll have to be there, too," Noel said. "Hidden."

After discussing it, Priscilla declared she would go, with her baby, not only to disarm suspicion, but to provide a hiding place for the recorder close enough to the men's voices, in the baby's lightweight, folding stroller.

She would carry parcels with her, as though shopping, speak only with a heavy Spanish accent, if possible seem to not understand English at all. Noel would check out the cafeteria beforehand to get more ideas about placement, possible problems and solutions. He and Mrs. Vega would meet the following day near the Delacorte Theatre in Central Park, as though by chance, and go over any remaining details in their plan.

"After you've taped the conversation," he said, "give

me the tapes, then take your baby and go to Puerto
Rico, to your great-aunt."

"But you will need me to tell . . ." she protested.

"If all this is true, then none of us is safe, you or
your baby."

"It is true!" she protested again. "Safe from Loomis,
you mean?"

"From Loomis, yes," he said, admiring her courage,
her resolve to avenge her husband, "but you said it
yourself, Mrs. Vega, I'm an unaimed weapon. You
may not even be safe from me now."

She looked at him, but she didn't argue the point.

4

What Priscilla told Noel numbed him. He knew that if
he began to think about its implications—as had happened before—that he would begin to split apart into
two people. As predicted. With no assurance the split
would come back together again, as it had before. But
then, wasn't he imperfectly programmed? If it were
true. Which it appeared to be. If imperfect. Whatever
that really meant. If it didn't mean everything. Which
was where the splitting began again. Stop it! he
warned himself.

He hailed a cab going down West End Avenue,
jumped in as it swerved to the curb, and immediately
began making conversation with the driver in order to
shut off the inner dialogue—what did he think of the
traffic and the best way to get to the East Thirties
from where they were, the decline of a local rock music station, varieties of drug down trips. It was bizarre

but effective therapy. Noel tipped him a dollar and went up to his apartment, calmer.

It didn't last long.

I'm a human time-bomb, he said to himself as he unlocked the door. Then he rushed to the phone to dial Mirella. He didn't know what he would say to her, but just to hear a voice from his old life would help. Or had that last time with her, the time he had screwed *that* up, been controlled, too?

She wasn't home. He didn't leave a message.

He still wanted to talk to someone. decided on Redfern. Just to hear his voice, to prove to himself it couldn't be true.

Okku answered. There were voices in the background. He must be on the main floor. After a grunt or two, Okku was gone, and Alana answered. "Eric is busy right now," she said.

"Sounds like a party."

"You are feeling better?"

"Fine. You? What's going on there? A party?"

"No. Cal and Geoff and Rick and a few other people are here. They are getting together about the re-opening party at Window Wall. Are you coming?"

"I don't know," he said, then wondered whether she was asking about the party or the town house. "If they're working, I'll just be in the way."

They hadn't talked alone, it seemed, for such a long time. He wanted to apologize: for the last time, when she'd run out of the dining room, and for his behavior to her out at Fire Island. To say, sorry, but I'm a human time-bomb and what if I'm pointed at you? He couldn't say that. Not even if it were true. And he wouldn't know that for sure until he heard Loomis say it.

"Eric said to ask you over," she said simply.

"What about you? Don't you want to see me, too?"

He could picture her talking to him. She was probably in the library, her legs thrown over the low arm of the big, tufted-leather chair, her hair hanging half in front of her, as she dandled it while talking.

"Every time I see you something bad happens. You get hurt. I get hurt. Eric becomes more convinced of his . . . whatever it is."

"Come on now, it's not all that bad," he said.

"It is!"

"When did I hurt you?"

"Yesterday. The time before. On the beach. I am tired of crying over someone, Noel. There! I've said it. That's what you wanted to hear, wasn't it?"

Part of him, yes. "I'm coming uptown right now."

"No. Exactly because of that, you ought to stay away from me. From Eric, too. Go away, Noel. Go somewhere very far for a very long time."

"Then you come here, tonight. Stay with me."

"That only ties it tighter."

What she was saying was true. Except the part about Eric. Even if Noel did nothing, went away, Eric would still be in trouble. "I'm coming. Tell Eric."

"I'll tell him," she said. She didn't sound pleased.

They were all in the big living room—Geoff Malchuck, Rick, Cal, Jimmy DiNadio, "Marge"—sitting around the coffee table, which was spread with plans, sketches, diagrams, swatches of fabrics and carpets, pads full of graduated colors. When he entered, everyone seemed to be talking at once between tokes of marijuana and sips of wine.

Chaffee spoke first. "Congratulate me. I'm a husband."

"We're living together now," Jimmy said quickly. "It's very *shared*, if you know what I mean."

"No, it's not. It's more open," Rick said.

"Open? What do you call open?"

"I call going to the Tubs together on buddy nights open."

"That's *your* definition of open."

Before the developing argument could get fully under way, Noel congratulated them, drank a toast, then sat down next to Eric, who made a space next to himself for Noel and immediately held up an artist's rendering.

It took Noel a moment or so to realize he was being asked to look at something concerning the party. More. He was being publicly asked to contribute: following his ouster from this very group not long ago, he was now reinstated, asked to evaluate something that concerned all of them. He took the drawing, held it, aware he was blushing.

"What's wrong?" Eric asked, baffled. "Don't you like it?"

"I like everything but the mirrors," Cal said.

"I don't know," Noel said. "I'm not even sure I know what it's supposed to represent." He knew this minute of acceptance, no matter how momentary, was a gift from Eric.

"It's the main part of Window Wall, decorated for the reopening party," "Marge" said. "Put on your glasses, honey. You're among sisters here; we won't tell on you."

"The mirrors are all angled twice, on hinges," Eric said, leaning over the rendering. He continued to point out the features they had already agreed upon, with comments from the others, until Noel fell by degrees out of embarrassment and into a more useful frame of mind.

The party was going to be the largest and wildest ever held at the Window Wall. During the summer the membership had been culled: laggards weeded out, newcomers who'd been frequent guests invited to join. For this party only, a celebrity list was made up; and enough talk had already gone around in society columns for it to be chic to be invited. Movie stars, top fashion designers, performing artists, various younger society figures all had been calling the club for invitations. They would all converge there on

Labor Day Weekend, because socially they couldn't afford not to come.

"But there'll be twenty members for every one of them," Eric said. "Everyone will be a star. The professionals will just melt in with the rest. They'll talk about it for months afterward," he went on, "because it will have been the most intense, interesting, the brightest moment of their careers."

It was Eric's ideal made manifest in a single party. No wonder the planning was so complex.

There were to be multiple, silent film screens, projecting five different films around the main ballroom. Hanging from above on chain pulleys would be small, hexagonal mirrored rooms, which could be opened or closed. Performers—including some of the club's more outrageously dressed members—would use those lifts. Plants were out. But Jimmy DiNadio knew where they could get a few dozen tube-metal sculptures that looked like strange trees. Cal's lover, who was to do the lighting, had already shown how he was going to light the club—noncomplementary, contrasting colors. He gave Noel a fast demonstration from a portable light unit in the living room.

"Too bad we don't have a pool in there," Cal's lover said. "On water this would be the *only* weirdness."

It was then that Noel noticed Alana wasn't present.

"She and Veena are doing a shooting together tomorrow for *Vogue*," Eric explained. "They have to be up early, so she decided to stay at Veena's tonight."

That might be so, but is wasn't the whole reason, Noel knew. She hadn't wanted to see him. Damn! Just when they could have . . . could have what? Gotten closer? Made love? Pipe dreams. Bullshit! Not included in Loomis's programming. He was supposed to be chaste, solitary. But he wasn't solitary now. Far from it; he felt a useful member of this very special, very elite group. That proved nothing. Only that the programming was imperfect. As he knew already. The split was happening again.

He realized he was being stared at by Geoff Malchuck. Not for the first time tonight. Not for the first time any day. He'd known Geoff had the hots for him since they'd first met. Geoff had never hidden it. Maybe they could get something on tonight. *That* would prove the programming was just a damn lying piece of paper.

Noel had just decided that, yes, he would leave with Geoff or get Geoff to stay over, when Malchuck stood up, looked at his watch, and said it was time for him to go to Clouds, the club he managed. They'd had some trouble a few nights before.

Without asking, Noel knew that he'd remain at the club until morning. That eliminated Geoff.

The others decided they had things to do also. There was a general getting up, a finishing of drinks and conversations.

"Anyone staying for dinner?" Eric asked. Usually someone said yes. Tonight everyone had plans. Everyone but Noel.

Noel was at the elevators, where they all seemed to be, talking to Rick and Cal about some details of traffic patterns for the coming party, when he saw Geoff take Eric's arm and gesture for him to move away from the others. They discussed something Noel couldn't hear, speaking low, rapidly. Then Geoff and the others left.

During dinner, Dorrance called from California, and Eric spent most of his mealtime talking nonstop, long distance. Noel leafed through some magazines as he ate, trying politely to ignore the conversation; it was pretty much of a rehash of what the group had discussed all evening.

The split came again while he was reading an article on sex therapy in a gay-oriented glossy. At first he wondered if sex therapy would help him. Then he read on and concluded these advanced methods were only effective for specific problems: physical problems. Not for his problem. His programming-induced problem. If that were true.

He looked up from the magazine in instant, total despair. At the same moment Eric hung up the phone and suggested they go down to the living room for coffee, the late news on TV, and some grass.

It was there that Noel came together again with a sudden inspiration. What if he made love to Eric? That would beat the shit out of any possibility of being programmed, controlled. Wouldn't it?

He looked at Eric, who seemed engrossed in the weatherman's predictions. Objectively speaking, Eric Redfern was a handsome man, a very handsome man, especially if you liked that fair-skinned, fair-haired, but tough WASPy type. He'd allowed his hair to grow a little longer during the summer. This long, it had a real wave. His mustache was less neatly trimmed than before: more casual, softer looking. He was certainly charismatic, strong, well-built, masculine . . . and most important he was infatuated with Noel. It was a brilliant idea, Noel decided.

"Are you listening to that?" Noel asked, taking hold of the remote control panel.

"Not really." Eric kicked off his shoes and leaned back into the sofa cushions. Noel switched the TV off and turned the tape deck on, then cut the volume to make background music.

"Penny for your thoughts," he said.

It took Eric by surprise. He stared at Noel for a second, then answered, "I was wondering if the party will really work. Celebrities can be such assholes if they don't think they're being treated right. On the other hand they're being told they won't get special treatment. Which they also like."

"It'll work. Don't worry about it. Now ask me."

"Ask you what?"

"You know, a penny for my thoughts."

Eric reached into his pants pocket. "I don't have any change."

"Forget it. Go ahead, ask."

"All right. A penny for your thoughts."

"I was thinking how much you remind me of one of my students. Paul's his name." That wasn't true, literally, but in a sense it was.

And Eric bit. "Is he cute?"

"Cute enough."

"Did you make it with him?"

"No. Not yet."

"Well," Eric said, "no wonder I remind you of him." He moved to pick up the phone, but Noel moved first. Before Eric could dial, he depressed the tone button.

"No," he said, "I think you're much better looking. Of course he's younger. His is only a beginner's mustache."

Eric stared at him, half-amused, half-baffled. "What's gotten into you?"

"You're much better looking," Noel declared.

"Thanks!" Eric said ironically.

"No wonder guys come from all over the country to ball with you," Noel went on. As he spoke, he lifted a finger and ran it slowly across Eric's lips. "I'd really like to thank you for this afternoon," he said, moving closer.

"Why? I didn't do anything this afternoon." Eric moved back slightly.

"Sure, you did. You made me feel at home, like one of the gang."

"Did I?"

"What nice skin you have," Noel said.

"What are you on, Noel?"

"Don't you like being touched?"

For the briefest moment, Noel asked himself what in hell he was doing. Breaking the prediction, of course, by going to bed with Eric. Yes, but with Eric? Mr. X? One of the world's foremost sadomasochists! But not always. Not with most of those Jims or Bobs or Bills out at Fire Island.

"Noel," Eric said with some alarm, "what are you doing?"

"I'm trying to kiss you." Noel had lowered them into an awkward position on the sofa; he seemed to be trying to get Eric into a half nelson.

"How come?"

"Because I want to. All of a sudden I realized how very much I want you, Eric. Now just relax, close your eyes, now."

"You are high on something, aren't you?"

Noel tried to kiss Eric again, but Eric jerked his head away and Noel only brushed the nape of his neck.

"Come on!"

"You're crazy. Come on. Stop. This is getting bonkers."

"No, it's not," Noel said, unfazed. He'd gotten both hands into play now; one was slipping under Eric's shirt up his smooth chest. The other grasped the back of the wavy blond head. Oddly, the more Eric resisted, the more excited Noel found himself.

"But why now? Why all of a sudden?"

"I don't know. Just relax, will you? You've been waiting, jerking off, waiting for this moment for months. It's here."

"But this isn't the way I thought it would happen."

"So what? Relax a little."

Eric did relax, long enough for Noel to begin to kiss him, which Eric barely allowed. His resistance excited Noel even more. By now he had forced open Eric's lips with his tongue and was kissing him, getting more excited every moment at the brush of Eric's mustache, the feel of his body underneath him, as he maneuvered them so that Eric was flatdown on the sofa, and Noel on top of him, feeling more exultant with every tiny barrier of resistance he broke down, more excited, knowing that Loomis and his prediction were wrong, all wrong, the son of a bitch!

When he felt Eric was returning his passion, he left

his face, and opening the shirt buttons, said, "Mmm. Very nice." He went directly for the jutting left nipple of the flat chest.

"Hey! You're not playing around," Eric said, as if coming to his senses.

"Who said I was?" Noel reached his hand past the flat, muscular stomach and into Eric's pants, groping there.

"Come on, Noel. Enough's enough."

"Don't tell me you aren't turned on, Eric. I can feel that you are. And I know you have conventional sex, too. You don't have chains and stuff out at the island. Or am I doing something wrong?"

"No." Eric was trying to sit up. Noel held him down firmly.

"Well, am I?" Noel demanded. "Is there something you'd like me to do?"

"Yes. Get off me."

"Why? Here we are all alone. Let's make love. What's stopping us?"

"I don't know. I'm just not . . . I don't understand."

Eric still tried to get up, and Noel continued to try to keep him down. The more Eric struggled, the more determined Noel became to possess him, and the more Eric resisted, until they were rolling all over the sofa, sweating and groaning. Eric finally managed to free himself, falling over the back of the sofa. As it began to tip over, Noel had to jump clear of it, only inches away from where Eric was slowly getting up from his fall to the floor. Suddenly they were both on their feet, facing off with each other, and Noel was so angry at Eric for spoiling it that he wanted suddenly, almost uncontrollably, to smash him, hard.

"What the hell is wrong with you?" Noel panted. "All I'm trying to do is make love to you, for Chrissakes!" He took a small step forward, and Eric backed up, on his guard, in jujitsu stance.

"I can't."

Noel's frustration was becoming unbearable. "Why not?"

"I don't know why not."

But Noel was looking at Eric's eyes just then, those multifaceted, hard-as-ice eyes, and what Eric couldn't say, Noel could read all too clearly behind the shattered gaze of those eyes: Eric was terrified of him.

Noel sobered up immediately. Somehow, whether by intuition or sixth sense, Eric knew what Noel was supposed to do to him. And it wasn't lovemaking. Once more the prediction was working. It was useless to fight it. Useless.

As Noel pulled open the door to the stairway in his hurry to get the hell out of there, he heard Eric's confused and relieved voice saying words he'd never expected to hear, now that they did no good:

"I'm sorry, Noel. I'm sorry."

5

"I brought this, too," Mrs. Vega said. "Do you want it?"

Noel looked at the paper she held. It was the psychological weapon programming for his next two weeks.

"I should burn it," he said. "Keep it with the rest of the things. We'll need it later for the commissioner."

They were sitting on either end of a large bench, no one near them but an occasional stroller along the sun-dappled path. It was a hot, windless August day.

They had met to rehearse details of the next day's surveillance of Loomis and the mysterious Gee. For half an hour they had done just that. To a passerby it wouldn't seem so: the petite Hispanic woman playing with the child in the stroller at her feet, reading her Spanish-language photonovel; the young man, face tilted back to catch the sun, apparently meditating. But both of them had been to the Horn and Hardart on Fifty-seventh Street, reconnoitering. It seemed an excellent possibility for taping.

Noel would place himself out of sight on the balcony, overlooking the three-story-high open area below where he was certain Loomis would arrange to meet Gee. From his balcony spot he could see all of them, and signal to her. He'd even taken the recorder and tested it. It seemed to be fine: it would pick up nearby conversation even over the noise.

"What if they don't show up?" she asked.

"We begin monitoring the loops again, until they do," he said. He had thought of the same question. "Here's the new cassette. It's an hour long on each side. I don't think that you'll need more than that. You know how to load it?"

"I practiced."

A tall youth with two Afghans passed them. Priscilla studied her photonovel. The young man looked like a dancer. Tall, with jutting buttocks, turned-out feet. He stared at Noel—a cruise. Noel half smiled in return. The boy went on without looking back.

Maybe he'd like a toss in the grass, Noel thought. Funny, how after last night's fiasco, all he could think about was sex. He ought to try Paul Warshaw's number again, when he got home. Or, maybe try the Tubs. Almost anyone could get laid quickly, efficiently, even superbly at the Baths, according to talk.

He realized Priscilla was speaking and had to ask her to repeat it.

"I said someone you know was at the funeral. He asked after you. He was surprised not to see you there."

She was cleaning the baby's face with a crumbled piece of pink tissue. It couldn't have been Loomis.

"He said his name was Larry. I didn't know him."

"Code name Peter Pan," Noel said.

She stood up to go, the stroller turned around. "He never used the loops while we were listening."

"You're very brave," Noel said, "to do this."

"After this I think I'll stay in P.R." she said quietly. "There the men laugh, call gays *mariposa, maricón*. But they don't kill because the gays are that way. You know? Why is that?"

An answer—long, complicated, many-faceted—sprang to Noel's lips. But he didn't even begin to say it. Instead, he whispered, "Good-bye. Stay brave. Don't worry whatever happens tomorrow."

Then he tilted his head back again, until the squeaking wheels of the stroller she was pushing could no longer be heard.

6

The vantage point Noel chose was a table at the edge of the balcony overlooking the main floor of the Automat. Only a few tables were directly beneath him. That was the serving area—food dispensed out of the two side rows of little windows and from a hot-food counter along the rear wall. Because of the noise, the heat, and cooking smells, few customers would choose to sit there, especially at this hour—after the noon rush—when there were far fewer people eating. He ought to have a clear view of Loomis and his companion.

Noel had dressed in sloppy, ill-fitting clothing and hidden his eyes with a pair of large, mirrored sunglasses. He carried a canvas bag filled with dirty laundry and held a *New York Times* open in front of him against the balcony railing, artfully arranged so he could not be seen from below. As most of the Automat's patrons were too old or tired to climb this high, only two other people were on the balcony with him: two girlfriends it seemed, having an intense discussion about a man.

He had taken a Valium at noon and had brought another with him in case the waiting got to his nerves. He was feeling quite pleasant now, taking minute bites out of his tuna salad sandwich and reading every article and advertisement in the paper. He had begun at page one. He was already past the sports page.

Mentally, he was reviewing every possibility of a screw-up. Loomis might not show. Or his friend might not. Priscilla was already here—Noel had seen her pass by the front of the Automat twice already, as though wondering whether to come in or not. She had looked up to him, and not receiving his signal, passed by again. What if she couldn't get close enough? Or what if the cassette recorder didn't work? What if . . .?

Several single men had already entered the place in the last ten minutes since two o'clock. None was Loomis. Any of them could have been his contact.

Noel finished the third section of the paper and gazed with a slight groan at the first page of the business section. Downstairs, Priscilla Vega passed the huge windows again, coming from the left. At the same time, from the right, the small, chunky, familiar figure of the Fisherman appeared.

Buddy's widow reached the door at the same time Loomis did. She ignored him, looking up at Noel. Loomis must have thought she was going in, since he pushed the door open a bit, hesitated (was he looking inside for his contact?), then pushed the door open all the way, standing back for her to enter.

The Fisherman's courtesy disarmed Noel momentarily. More overwhelming was the realization that Loomis was actually here, about to have this meeting, that he was totally responsible for the shape and context of the entire last half year of Noel's existence.

He felt the hairs on the back of his neck prickle, as though a sharp gust of icy wind had brushed him. Priscilla looked in confusion at the middle-aged man holding the door open for her, glanced down at her baby in its stroller, then up sharply.

In time to see Noel take off his sunglasses—the signal that she was to enter.

She said a word to Loomis, thanking him probably, and made a great fuss of getting the stroller inside. Loomis entered right after her, walked past where she had stopped, into the depths below the balcony. Hesitantly, Priscilla knelt to arrange the folds of her baby's little smock, and looked up at Noel again.

He'd put on his sunglasses again, but had folded down the newspaper so she could see him run his index finger across his throat: their code for Loomis.

She turned around to the door, then back up at Noel, puzzled. He signaled again, then again, hoping she would understand. She looked hopelessly confused, then her eyes shot forward toward the serving area. Slowly, even though it wasn't a signal, Noel nodded yes.

The next few minutes were agony for him. Both Priscilla and Loomis were out of sight.

Noel had put the newspaper back up again; it would only be folded down again to warn her of danger. He toyed with the idea of taking the second Valium. The scene at the doorway had been almost unbearable to him. What else would happen to jangle him?

He decided the second tranquilizer would fuzz his

perceptions too much. To calm himself, he looked over the newspaper at the various tables, checking for a single man, recently entered, who seemed to be waiting for someone else.

What if Loomis's contact were that greasy-haired, raincoated man at the only two-seat table in the place, in the far corner of the Automat? There were no tables closer to him than six feet. Priscilla would never get near enough to tape them.

As he observed, the Fisherman's foreshortened figure appeared under the balcony, carrying a full tray—hot sandwich, coffee, juice, a piece of institutional dessert that might have been coconut cream pie—and came to a stop. Looking for a table, anyone else would think. Looking for his contact, Noel thought. Or for a table where they could be alone.

The place he walked to was in the center of the room in perfect view from above, although Loomis would be facing away from the balcony, toward the window, which made it doubly safe for Noel. The table was large, designed for six to eight diners, but now had only one occupant—a man in his sixties, Noel guessed, who'd been in the Automat when Noel had come in. He'd been reading what looked to be a foreign-language newspaper, drinking one orange crush after another, alternately gripping a wrinkled, slim, dark cheroot between his teeth. The top of his head was glossily bald, as though the skin were waxed. He had a round yellow face, with deep-set dark eyes, wore a blue short-sleeved shirt, and almost identically colored rayon pants. He scarcely looked up when Loomis set his tray down opposite, then sat one seat to the left. The Fisherman didn't say a word either; at least he didn't appear to from Noel's angle of vision. Was this old man Loomis's contact? Where was Priscilla?

There she was, pushing the stroller with one hand and approaching their table. The situation—doubtless deliberately planned by the two men—was an awkward one. She stopped, looked around. Both men glanced at her.

Confusion at what to do next must have gripped her. She kept looking around her and finally appeared to be losing control. The tray in her hand closest to their table began to tip down. Noel wanted to jump up and shout to her. First the heavy ceramic cup and saucer, then the sandwich plate, then the glass of milk started to slide irrevocably, unbalancing the tray until it was certain to fall over. Noel had to close his eyes to wait for the crash.

It didn't come. When he opened his eyes again, Loomis was half standing, leaning over the table, holding the tray steady for her, then setting it down on the table edge. Priscilla made a great show of thanking him, and as he regained his seat, as though it were the most natural thing in the world, she moved the tray in farther, pushed the stroller around to the side opposite Loomis, took the chair one seat away from the old man, and once more thanked Loomis.

The Fisherman moved down one seat, until he was facing the other man directly. From where Noel sat, it seemed that the two of them began talking a little.

Meanwhile, Priscilla—clever, clever woman that she was, Noel had to admit, for pulling that off so well!— busied herself with lifting her baby out of its stroller and onto her lap, fiddling around with the packages still stuck in the stroller. One, Noel knew, held the tape recorder and was now switched on, as she glanced up sharply to signal him.

In order to block others from joining them on their exposed side, both the Fisherman and his contact moved objects to those seats—Loomis his hat and a folder (Would that change hands? What was in it?), the older man his perforated sun hat, sitting next to him on Priscilla's side of the table. Evidently they had decided she was no threat to them—she seemed preoccupied with her child, speaking to him in Spanish loud enough for Noel to catch a few words.

Not too preoccupied, Noel noticed, to take advantage of the hat's change of locale. She shifted the chair out of its place and pushed the stroller right in, flashing a smile at the old man as she did so.

As they all settled down to eat, Noel relaxed, exchanging his immediate anxieties for other ones. How long could she remain at the table, if the men decided to linger, without making it too obvious? Then he saw her take out the photonovel she had used as a screen in the park, and knew it might be a long time. But wouldn't the tape run out? Would she be able to change it there? Wouldn't it click off loud enough to be heard? It was so close to them now.

Overriding these arguments, he knew, was the real question: when he did finally hear those tapes, would they, in fact, corroborate everything Buddy and Priscilla had shown him, told him? Would they say, definitely, unambiguously, that Loomis was being paid off for engineering Redfern's assassination and that Noel was the hit man? Only if that were clear would he believe it himself. And only if he believed it would the police commissioner accept it—no matter what else happened.

Below him all was as before. Priscilla had her photonovel open on the table, was smoking a cigarette and slowly drinking her coffee, the infant in her lap catching at the paper's edge or toying with her frilled blouse. Loomis and his companion were also done eating. As they had throughout the meal, they talked not as though they had anything of interest to discuss, but in the usual, fragmented, desultory manner of retired men on park benches all over the city, with little to say and a great deal of time to say it.

"Dr. Cummings?"

Noel's head swiveled left so violently he felt a tendon pull.

"That is you, isn't it, Dr. Cummings?"

He located the source of the nasal female voice—a young woman standing at the top of the balcony stairs, holding a tray filled with food. Antonia Something-or-other. From one of his more advanced classes last term.

Having been so bold, she now seemed to regret it. "I didn't mean to disturb you," she apologized. "Antoinette Guardi. I was in your soc. crit. class last semester."

Two men were lingering on the stairs behind her. She looked behind, then smiled weakly at Noel. "Well! Nice to see you."

After his initial surprise, Noel had an idea. She would be a good cover in case he'd already been spotted here.

"Sit down, Antoinette."

"Are you sure?"

He moved his tray over, clearing a space for her. Downstairs all was as before.

"I never see any of my professors in the summer," she began, sitting down and carefully arranging the food on her tray in what Noel suspected was the order in which she planned to eat it. Then, noticing that his food was off his tray, she carefully removed every one of her many plates and cups and put her empty tray atop his. She rearranged the food again, ready to eat, all the while saying, "I never see any of my professors during the summer. Unless they teach, of course, I always assumed they went off to exotic places to do fieldwork and all."

On the first floor, the baby had fallen asleep in his mother's arms. Nothing else had changed.

"Some of us stay in town," he said. She must be twenty-one or so, he thought, very attractive in her fresh, freckled, red-haired youth. How young she seemed. He realized he must look awfully strange to her today. How the hell had she recognized him?

"I know some teachers don't do any work at all during the summer. I know your case is different."

"How do you know that? Because I'm sitting in an Automat reading a newspaper?"

She giggled. "No. Mirella Trent's my adviser. She mentioned your project to me."

"Oh."

"Well, she *was* pretty secretive about it. But I managed to worm it out of her. I think it's a fab idea."

She smiled prettily, then her even, lovely—capped? —white teeth bit daintily into her sandwich. Antoinette Guardi. Guardi? How did she end up with that name? She looked as though she'd walked off the streets of Dublin a minute ago.

"You know what I think?" she asked, and answered herself in the next breath. "I think Miss Trent's a little impressed."

"I doubt it."

"No. I think she is impressed. She told me your life-style transformation shows a deep commitment to your work. She's still kicking herself for not going to any of the orgies at the women's prison when she had the chance."

"I wouldn't believe everything Mirella says."

"You wouldn't?"

Noel wondered if she would explain why she looked so Irish with such an Italian name. He glanced aside, past his newspaper. Downstairs everything was—gone! Loomis, the contact, Priscilla, the baby, the stroller, the tapes—all of them gone!

7

Antoinette was speaking again, asking him a question.

Noel had jumped to his feet and was already halfway down the stairway.

Downstairs, he saw someone he thought was Priscilla Vega, pushing her stroller along Fifty-seventh Street.

"Hey," Antoinette called behind him, "you forgot your bag!"

He turned around and gestured for her to throw it, caught it, and bounded out the door in the direction he'd seen Priscilla go.

She was supposed to have waited until the two men were gone before she gave him the tape and left the Automat. They'd agreed on that. That had seemed the simplest part of the arrangement. Why had she left? She wouldn't be fool enough to leave with Loomis and his contact because they were still talking, would she?

Between Sixth and Seventh avenues, Fifty-seventh Street is a long block, crowded with people day or night, no different this afternoon. Only when he'd reached the Russian Tea Room, going west, did he see Priscilla Vega and her stroller ahead: at the corner of Seventh Avenue.

Sure enough, there was Loomis and his contact. And she was close enough to tape. Close enough to arouse suspicion. What in hell was she up to?

The two men were stopped, waiting for the light to change, Priscilla and the stroller hidden among others waiting behind them, Noel a good seventy-five feet away.

Without saying another word to each other, the two men turned in different directions—Loomis crossing the avenue, the older, heavier man turning north toward Central Park. Priscilla remained where she was, letting the people stream around her. Then she bent down and adjusted something in the stroller.

She turned the stroller back in the direction she had come and, spotting him, approached with a look of absolute triumph on her face. Her gambit had paid off. She had to follow the men out of the Automat to get what she felt was needed. She was pleased, exultant.

What happened next confused Noel. He'd started forward to meet her. She kept coming toward him, but suddenly her eyes darted to either side of him, startled. Noel whirled just in time to see someone move by him fast on the left, then out of his peripheral vision. Someone else was on his right, also moving quickly. The two men who'd come up behind Antoinette in the Automat? He had looked at them then, only briefly, before turning deliberately aside. Now he recognized their clothing.

As they rushed past him, Priscilla swerved her stroller through the crowd toward the entrance to Carnegie Hall. Noel's view of her was suddenly blocked. When he had pushed past the pedestrians in his way, he saw the two men approaching the corner of Seventh Avenue, looking around, gesturing. Priscilla was nowhere in sight. Then, there she was! Behind Noel, on the opposite side of the street, moving fast toward Sixth Avenue, at the curbside. She looked back over her shoulder once, then moved on again. Noel went after her. But as he neared, she glanced back. A shudder of a nod jerked her head and shoulders. Trouble. She didn't want him to join up with her. He let her pass by—keeping to the curbside, while he followed behind, wondering what was wrong.

When he looked back toward Seventh Avenue again, following the source of her evident distress, neither of the two men was visible. They might merely have been purse snatchers working as a team that she had avoided. Unless . . . ? Then Noel made out the two of them, one darting around the corner of Fifty-seventh and Seventh, the other turning and rapidly approaching Noel along the storefronts of Fifty-seventh Street.

Now he understood Priscilla's puzzling tactics. She had seen them in the Automat also, knew they had seen her and were after her. The second man was probably running around the block, hoping to catch up with her when she reached the corner. Then they would have her from in front and behind. Noel would have to reach her before that.

He kept Priscilla Vega in sight, following slightly ahead of the man, keeping against the storefronts now that this one had taken to the middle of the sidewalk, dawdling as though looking into store windows once or twice, to try for a better look at their pursuer.

The second time Noel paused, in the windowed entryway of a Zen Japanese bookshop, he got a nasty shock. The man passed right by, his eyes fixed ahead on his quarry. And the view was close enough, unobstructed enough, so that he could see the face, even with the large sunglasses that half covered it. No doubt about it, it was one of the two bastards who'd jumped him on Twenty-eighth Street. Not Zach. The other one. And they were after Priscilla. They were animals! Fucking animals!

When Noel emerged from the doorway, the man was gone. He almost walked past him without being aware of it, as the thug was now doing exactly what Noel had done—pretending to gaze into a store window while looking ahead up the street, at Priscilla.

Noel went to the curb, and saw why. She was stopped at a telephone booth, half facing away, talking into the receiver. To whom?

Noel crossed to the north side of the street to have a better view, then stood, frozen, hidden in a tobacconist's shop doorway.

Mrs. Vega was still on the phone, talking, writing down something on a piece of yellow paper, looking all around her as she talked—at the man still pretending to linger at the store window, then toward Sixth Avenue, as though expecting the other one there. Then she was done writing, and was folding something, which Noel recognized as the envelope in which he had brought the cassette to her at her West

End apartment. Noel watched her place the cassette into the envelope, seal it, and place it in her shoulder bag.

At that moment, Zach rounded the corner of Sixth Avenue. Noel saw him stop short, panting hard from his run, and look around for his partner. Damn them!

Noel charged back, across the street, threading through the line of slow-moving autos. A taxi stopped short as he raced in front of it and he nearly stumbled. His heart was racing; he didn't care. He had a score to settle.

Priscilla had begun walking with the stroller again toward the corner. Didn't she see the thug in front of her?

Another car slid in front of Noel. They were bumper to bumper. He leaped across them, one hand on a hood, the other on the trunk of the car in front of it.

When he reached the curb, Zach had spotted Priscilla. The second tough had left his place at the storefront and was running toward her.

Noel sprang to the curb, circled a small tree set in a planter, and rushed up. He shot by the man with a full-shouldered shove to the side, and saw him stumble, fall to the sidewalk right into the oncoming path of two fashionably dressed women who'd been sashaying down the street arm in arm. They shrieked, backed off, as he clutched at their skirts to regain his balance, hitting at his grasping hands. He sprawled.

Zach looked uncertain what to do—to shoot forward, or to go for Priscilla. Noel decided to make up his mind for him.

The one on the ground was getting to his feet. The two women had retreated to a doorway, brushing themselves off and talking alarmedly. Noel pivoted and, sprinting back, bypassed the women, and expertly kicked the thug in his chest just as he was getting balance from behind. He sprawled again with a loud moan. The women screamed.

Noel turned to see Zach, no longer undecided, racing at him. Behind him, Priscilla was fiddling around with the corner mailbox, trying to shove the apparently too thick parcel through. She was mailing it to him! Not taking any chances.

He turned around and this time viciously kicked down the first tough, aiming at his face, wishing he had worn heavier shoes. Then Zach was behind him, grabbing at Noel's arm. Noel was balanced for the attack. He let the arm go, revolved fast, slamming his open palm right at Zach's chin, literally picking him up off the ground, a trick he'd seen McWhitter teaching Eric at the Hamptons villa. He followed this up with a deep right into Zach's stomach, feeling the abdomen muscles contract as though with an electric shock as he hit them. Zach fell over backward. But now his friend was up again. Noel bent low and swung sideways with his shoulders, knocking him back into a display window, which shattered with a loud crash.

Satisfied with the damage, Noel jumped back, then dashed into the middle of the street, into a line of traffic, calling out obscenities, attempting to keep their attention away from Priscilla. If necessary, he'd jump back into them. Horns blared all around him.

He looked up to see Priscilla, who had gotten the envelope inside the mailbox finally, had even hailed a cab, and was now trying to maneuver the stroller inside the back seat. The baby was squalling. She looked back.

Zach went for her.

Noel went for him, jumping over the hood of a slow-moving Chevy, which braked instantly. Behind him, in the stop-and-go traffic, Noel heard a chain reaction, brakes screeching, horns honking. He missed Zach, but Zach's partner grabbed him. With a rush of elation, Noel bent, then rammed hard, head down, pushing his attacker into a wall.

Straightening, he looked toward the corner to see

the cab door slammed in Zach's face. As the cab sped off, the stroller was left behind, knocked over in the street.

Noel recrossed Fifty-seventh Street, taking cover in the doorway of Wolf's delicatessen. From the entryway windows he looked back. Zach was helping his friend up. They were arguing, distracted now. Noel knew it would only last a minute.

A cab was stopped in the westbound traffic. He had to chance it. He spun out of the entryway, staying low, and managed to crawl into the cab, keeping out of sight.

Neither of them saw him. They were still arguing. The cab was caught by the light. Noel prayed that he wouldn't be seen. He locked both doors, leaning back.

When the taxi finally did take off, he turned around and looked back. There was a crowd at the corner of Sixth Avenue on the south side of the street. The two thugs were nowhere in sight. As he strained to look, the crowd thinned out with the change of streetlights, and Noel was treated to the rare spectacle of two grown men violently stomping a tiny gray baby stroller into the heat-softened asphalt of the Avenue of the Americas.

8

By the third morning after the incident, when the envelope containing the cassette still hadn't arrived, Noel became alarmed.

He'd gone directly to his apartment, expecting Priscilla to call him. Then he remembered that she believed his phone to be tapped. So he went out—wary, nervous, expecting Zach and his murderous friend to step out of a doorway any minute—while he called her twice from a pay phone. No answer.

That night, going up to Redfern's, Noel left the answering machine on as usual, hoping she would contact him, reassure him. He assumed the package would arrive in the next day's mail—or the day after that, at the latest.

The town house was filled with the club managers, and once more the Window Wall party was the only topic of conversation. Alana still wasn't home. Okku told him she had gone to Paris. Eric said she was with Veena, who was opening a new act in France. Neither would be back until the night of the reopening party.

Eric was distant, cold. The memory of their last evening together hung between them. Noel went home.

And worried.

Had there been enough postage on the envelope? He wasn't sure the inefficient doorman wouldn't send it back. Or it might have been marked for hand delivery. He wanted to go back to the town house. He was afraid. He was a weapon—that might go off. He wished he'd taken that detailed, dated plan when Priscilla offered it. All he could recall now were vague phrases; accusations, they now seemed to him.

He decided to redecorate while he waited for the cassette. His life—his entire future—depended on that tape.

His stark white walls became different shades of gray and brown, with satiny hues of blues and pinks that only emerged at night or in different lighting. Old, much-painted-over pipes and moldings—formerly hidden behind white paint—stepped forward as design elements when he painted them in chocolate and charcoal gray. He ordered a dozen plants of various sizes from a plant store Window Wall used, and was building in planters for the larger ones, hanging the smaller ones. He tore down his loft bed and put the bedspring and mattress on the floor in the middle of the studio, heaping it with large pillows, surrounding it with small wooden cubes he'd bought, unfinished, and painted to match the walls. Most of his other furniture he dragged to the basement for storage or hauled out on the street for scavengers.

He worked feverishly, scraping walls, spackling cracks, painting undercoats, repainting overcoats, destroying, building, moving, buying, discarding, selecting colors and materials. And worrying.

What if Priscilla had been followed and caught? What if she'd gotten his address incorrect from the telephone operator? Or had copied it wrong in the excitement of the moment? What if the envelope were languishing in some cubbyhole of the main post office? What if she had been lying all the while? Or if the conversation she'd taped had nothing to do with payoffs?

He toyed with various plans—going to the police commissioner without the tape; with the materials in the large accordion folder right this minute sitting in a luggage check at Penn Station, one key in Noel's pocket, the other held by Mrs. Vega. All that might be enough to incriminate Loomis, wouldn't it? He thought about trying to track down the parcel through the postal bureaucracy—a dispiriting thought. Or trying again to find Priscilla herself, not at home the half-dozen times he called, or the two times he'd gone to her apartment.

He ended up doing none of it.

Instead, he worked on his apartment, listened to disco music, then moved over to an FM jazz station, and from there to a classical station, progressing to some of the longer pieces of music in his record cabinets he hadn't heard in months—years it seemed to him: a Bach passion, *Don Giovanni,* a recording of

King Lear, and finally a well-known actor reading selections from a translation of Ovid's *Metamorphoses.*

It was while he was listening to one of these tales for the third time—the one about Narcissus, the beautiful youth who was jealously loved by Apollo, and Aeolus, the Wind God, and who was eventually destroyed through a fatal mischance in their rivalry—that his downstairs buzzer rang.

He climbed down from the window ledge where he'd been hanging new blinds, flicked on the receiver's audio muting button, and got to the intercom panel just in time to hear Gerdes announce that a lady had come to see him.

It couldn't be Alana, she was in Paris. It must be Priscilla Vega. She had not mailed it to him at all, but to her mother or some friend. She was bringing it herself.

He said to send her up, then hammered in the last few nails of the brace, tested it, put up the blind, and finally left it half open for the late afternoon sun to filter in. When the door buzzer rang, Noel was trying to remember a few words of his high-school Spanish to tease Mrs. Vega with.

It proved unnecessary. His visitor was Mirella Trent.

He turned aside to hide his obvious surprise and disappointment. But she noticed it and stepped in gingerly.

"Well, Noel, the doorman *did* say it was a lady. I heard him."

He regained his composure fast. With a sweeping gesture, he showed her the apartment. "I thought you were delivering something."

She followed the gesture and took in the alterations. "Then it's true!" she blurted out.

"What's true?"

"What you told me. You know, about having a boyfriend and being gay and all."

"Why? Because I painted my walls? Come on, Mir-

ella. That's such a stereotyped prejudice I shouldn't
even have to tell you that all gays aren't interior deco-
rators, for Chrissakes."

She didn't seem to listen to his outburst, but instead
walked carefully all around the studio, skirting the
areas where he was still working. "Well, maybe I'm
wrong," she said. "Maybe contact is enough to develop it."

He reminded himself that she always had an uncanny
knack for being enigmatic—and irritating. "To develop
what?" he asked.

"Taste! You never had any before, Noel. Not in the
way you lived, or the way you dressed, or anywhere in
your life. Until you got involved in this project. Stereo-
typing or not."

She plumped herself down in the center of the pillows strewn on the daybed, still looking around her
with unfeigned pleasure. "Or did *he* do this?" she
asked, lighting a joint.

"Who?" Why was he always asking her questions,
like a TV reporter on the street. Who? What? Where?
Why?

"Your boyfriend." She inhaled deeply, then offered
the grass.

He declined it. "I don't have a boyfriend," he said.

"Then it isn't true?" She seemed unrelieved by this
fact.

"It was. Sort of. It isn't. It's a long and complicated
story, Mirella. And I don't want to go into it." But she
had settled back into her pillows and seemed ready to
listen to *War and Peace* cover to cover. Since he knew
she'd eventually worm it out of him with more whys,
and whens, and wheres, he decided to give it to her.
"He's dead. He was killed two months ago. That same
night, as a matter of fact," he added, probably to
make her feel guilty.

"Oh, no! I *am* sorry, Noel. I didn't mean to . . ."

She let it drop, and so did he, concentrating on
twisting a recalcitrant screw into the molding. He

wondered if she'd already heard about Randy, if she were here to give him another chance.

"I'll get right to the point," she suddenly said after a few minutes of silence, punctuated by his swearing at the screw. "I want to go to the party at Window Wall. Now don't tell me you aren't going. I've got to go, Noel."

"But it's a gay club."

"I just *have* to go, Noel. You're going, aren't you?"

"Of course. But I'm friends with the namager, Cal Goldberg."

"And with Eric Redfern, too," she added. "Don't deny it, I know you're being kept by that handsome playboy. Don't deny it."

Noel had to laugh at the way she put it. It sounded so much like an excerpt from a Liz Smith column. If Mirella only knew the half of it. And of all the crazy things, she wanted to go to the reopening party. For a moment Noel wondered if she had other motives for coming here. Then told himself no, whatever Mirella was capable of—which was a great deal—it was all ethical: her ego demanded it be ethical.

"But why?" he asked again.

"Because I told everyone I was going, that's why. And because," and here she rattled off a list of names of some of the people she'd read would be there. "That's why. By the way, is it true that Teddy Kennedy will be there?"

"I doubt it."

She went into utter despair. "I *have* to go, Noel."

"The celebrities will hang around for an hour or so, posing," he said, trying to discourage her, "then it will be just another gay club. You'll feel out of place. You'll hate it."

"I'll *love* it. I'll leave you at the door and not even nod at you during the party if we pass each other." She began to beg. "I'll never ask you for another thing as long as we both shall live." Then she turned to bargaining. "I'll stop bad-mouthing your project. I'll give you a favorable review when it's published."

"You're serious, aren't you?"

"Never more serious in my life."

"But it's only a party, Mirella," he tried once more. He looked at this attractive, intelligent, accomplished, and chic woman; a colleague, a professional rival, once a lover, a possible wife—and saw nothing but a little girl not invited to a party.

"You can't come in with me. I'm invited to the dinner that's being held before the crowd arrives."

Each word was like a tiny slap to her sizable ego. He could see that clearly.

"All right," she said, getting out of the pillows, and speaking in a low register Noel didn't recognize but instinctively knew to be her version of noble-acceptance-in-the-face-of-defeat, "you have every right in the world to do this." She was smoothing her skirt, trying to look like Irene Papas—tragic, regal—in some film version of an ancient Greek play.

Noel got down from the window ledge, walked over to the door, and began opening it. "I'll leave your name at the door," he said.

"You sweetheart!" she jumped up to kiss him on the cheek. Like a sister-in-law would kiss him, he thought. "Can you make it for two?"

"Why not?"

"Right away," she urged. "The party's the fifth, the day after tomorrow."

"The fifth?" Wasn't that within the last week listed on the plan Loomis had computed? The time the weapon was to go off? "I'll call," he said, closing the door behind her.

Where was Priscilla? And the damned tape?

9

By ten o'clock the following morning, all the plants had been delivered and hung in their appropriate spots. There were no telephone calls on his answering machine. And when Noel checked the mailbox in the lobby, the cassette had not arrived.

He called Priscilla Vega, listening to her phone ring a dozen or more times, and decided to try her at home once more. She may have decided her phone, too, was being tapped.

As ever, since four days before, he was on the lookout for the two toughs. They'd probably been sacked by now, sent back to wherever they'd come from, Noel suspected. Still . . .

No one answered Priscilla's bell. When a face appeared out the side window of the first floor of the building, Noel asked for Mrs. Vega, and was rewarded with a shrug and a quickly drawn window shade.

He decided on a stakeout at the small luncheonette at the nearest corner, within view of the front of the brownstone. A window seat was empty. He took it. Not knowing how long he would have to be here, he ordered breakfast.

He'd brought a steno pad with him and spent a long time working out details of his redone apartment. Right after Mirella's visit, he had asked his own questions about his sudden obsession with renovation. It was keeping him busy, he knew; he was doing something, something that had not even been mentioned in the goddamn report. That's why.

But there was another reason. It was the only thing he felt he still could do that he could control. The book was unthinkable. Working with Eric at Window Wall would put them too closely in contact for safety. Since the seduction fiasco, Eric had changed toward him subtly. He might still be frightened of Noel, but it was as though he had needed Noel to come on to him, to go that far, and now that it had happened, Eric was somehow satisfied, even relieved, and probably also triumphant. Besides, he was so busy these days with the party, there was no possibility he would waste precious time or energy on what he would call "negative vibes."

Noel had been staring at the brownstones—facade after facade, jutting high stoop after stoop—of the West Side street. After almost two hours of watching, only two people had emerged—an elderly couple, each with a cane, each holding a plastic shopping bag that looked empty. Noel looked down at his room plan for the twentieth time and quickly sketched in what he thought would be the perfect speaker placement. Then he looked up again, continuing his vigil.

Those six little marks he'd just made were the finger in the dike, he knew.

His next thought was an odd one—he hadn't talked to Loomis, to anyone at Whisper, since that afternoon at the Automat. Maybe he ought to call. He might not like what he heard. But when had that ever stopped him from calling?

Or was it part of his programming to call, to feel the urge to keep in contact? Of course. It must be.

There was a pay phone on the wall behind him, still within view of the apartment fronts.

He dialed one of the loops numbers last given to him, heard the familiar but now slightly sinister silence. Priscilla and Buddy Vega had listened in on this line. Who else might be listening right now?

It was the motherly middle-aged woman who finally answered. "Lure here," he reported in. "Can you connect me with the Fisherman?"

"*How are* you?" she asked, as though she knew him. "One minute, please. I'm ringing."

He wondered what to say to Loomis.

"Sorry," she announced, "I can't seem to find him anywhere."

"This is the Lure," he repeated. "I haven't been able to keep in contact. Are there any messages for me from the Fisherman or anyone else?"

"I'll look." She didn't sound hopeful.

He shouldn't have added that last phrase. What if someone *were* listening? How stupid of him!

"Hello." She was back. "Shall I read it? It is from the Fisherman. It says, 'Expecting a large, easy catch tomorrow night. Proceed as planned.'"

"Yes?" Noel wrote it down. "Go on."

"That's all there is. Should I repeat it?"

"Proceed as planned? What does that mean?"

"Don't know, dearie," she said breezily. "That's what's written here."

He thanked her and said he'd call back later.

While he'd been on the phone the little restaurant had filled with customers. Lunchtime. Probably workers from nearby. He moved his things to the back, to a two-seat table, near the phone, then ordered more food. When it arrived he shoveled it in, still thinking about Loomis's message.

It had been foolish to think that even in an emergency Priscilla Vega would use the loops to contact him. What did "proceed as planned" mean? They hadn't planned anything the last time they'd talked. Maybe Noel had missed one of the messages. He wouldn't know what to do. The control pattern would be broken. Loomis had said he was to do nothing. That meant Loomis, too, suspected that his plan had been botched somehow and that he was going ahead with the bust, not the assassination.

"My mom wants to know if you have a tapeworm."

Noel looked up. The slightly overweight teenaged boy who'd been serving him was standing by the edge of the table.

"Because if you do, she knows a doctor who'll cure it."

Behind the boy, Noel saw his mother—slim, gray-haired, plain-faced, looking back at him with concern. He paid the check. "Tell your mom I was just hungry."

"Okay." The boy disappeared.

Noel found that he was no longer looking at the brownstones, not outside at all, but at the boy as he went over to his mother, gave her the money to ring up, reported what they'd said, all of it casual, indifferent. The compact adolescent acted like a little man, but Noel envied something in him that wasn't at all adult. It seemed as though the boy really *was* indifferent to Noel, to anything but his own interests—his friends, his comic books, who knew what else? Just the way Noel had been as a child: as all children really were. Who would have guessed that the child he had been, fixing his Schwinn Roadmaster in the driveway that morning when Monica Sherman had come by, would now be doing what he was doing, acting as he was acting, being who he was? Waiting for someone. Expecting a call from someone else. Thinking about yet someone else. Fearing, resisting, denying, desiring, avoiding, all the someone else's.

He was no longer doing anything for himself, because he no longer had any self. Everything was for Loomis, or Eric, or Alana, or Vega, or an idea, or a title, or a career, or some value, a notion of cowardice that had to be overcome, or an entire set of emotions and responses about who he was and what he was supposed to be, do, and not do. He'd been programmed long before Loomis. All the Fisherman had needed to do was a little fine tuning: because long ago Noel had been set on this very path, never doing for himself, always for someone else. And if that selfishness, that self-interest he'd denied for years, was really what innocence was, he wished he could get it again.

The boy came back to his table with the change. He was holding a glass of water and a small packet of Alka-Seltzer.

"It wasn't *my* idea," the boy said.

Noel wouldn't wait for Priscilla Vega, or the call, or the cassette, or Loomis's motivations, none of it another minute more. Not today. Not tomorrow! Not ever again.

10

He awoke that day—the last of the AIN memo, he immediately reminded himself—to an unexpected, fierce morning thunderstorm, which caused him to shut off the air conditioning and throw open both windows. Now that he only slept a few feet away instead of at the far end of the long studio, this was a new luxury.

Soon enough the thunder stopped, although the rain continued steadily, putting him back to sleep. When he woke again it was eleven o'clock, a glorious sunny day with only tiny, fast-drying puddles near sewer gratings to corroborate the downpour. But the fresh breeze of early morning had come to stay for a while. He showered, then dried off by the window, enjoying the hot sun and cool air.

The morning mail did not contain the cassette—he had almost ceased to care about it—but it did include a check from the upstate social research agency for

the past month's work. An unpleasant reminder. When
he finally got around to opening it, after breakfast, he
had another unpleasant surprise: a piece of onionskin
paper was inside. On it, someone had drawn a cartoon
of a deep-sea fisher almost capsizing his small yacht
to haul in a large and quite dead giant fish. For once
Noel was happy to burn one of Loomis's messages.

His ten-speed was still in the storage room of the
building and apparently in working order. Only when
he'd ridden a block or so did he realize one of the
gears wasn't catching properly. The vehicle was as
temperamental as a thoroughbred; and like one, didn't
like being unridden over long periods of time.

He'd just gotten the gear working when he realized
he was riding past the pharmacy on Madison Avenue
where those two blond toughs had first come up to
him. Noel swerved right quickly, crossing the avenue,
and found himself in front of the newspaper store
where he'd photocopied documents for Whisper,
where that man had been run down, killed instantly.
What had been his name? Noel couldn't recall.

Too many memories. He decided to head across
town. But he'd turned onto Twenty-eighth Street, and
only a few blocks later, he was directly in front of the
Baths, passing the doorway where he'd been jumped.
Was the past inescapable?

He decided not fo fight it, just to keep riding. He
continued west, over toward the West Side Highway.
Unsurprising—given the ride so far—he had to wait for
a light at the corner where the building that housed
Le Pissoir stood. Then he rode up onto the highway
itself and really took off.

The next time he slowed down was when he recognized the configuration of the blocks below him. This
is where he'd first heard that scream. Where it had
begun. He stopped the bike, expecting some sort of
revelation to make everything clear.

On one side of the highway, the Hudson River rippled like shot silk. A white luxury liner was gliding

by, graceful as a large swan, tugboats in advance guard pulling it. On the road itself, two joggers passed him, their bouncing backs sweat-skinnned, their brightly colored shorts rippling. More bicyclists passed him. He heard an outcry from below and leaned over the railing to see where it came from. Another shout greeted him: young, excited, then disappointed voices. Twenty-five or thirty people stood in a shallow circle at the far edge of the parking area. A wide, thin wood sheet, curved-in almost to a letter C, had been placed against the wall of an abandoned warehouse. Skateboarding kids were racing toward it, up its concavity, trying to turn around at the apex, holding on until they were almost parallel to the ground, sometimes slipping so that the skateboard slid out from under them and they tumbled down the sheet of wood, sometimes making the turn successfully, and shooting down again to a cheer, until the next boy—and one girl, too—came skating at the plank.

Watching them calmed and cheered him. So he had to force himself to pass slowly by the warehouse itself, to look into the window where he had first been drawn into the spider's web that now held him entangled. It was easy to find. The green door was placed up again, its lower portion rusted with red. But behind it, amid all the litter, two men were in a clutch, kissing, caressing each other. Love in the afternoon. If they only knew!

He rode to the other railing, looked at the abandoned Federal House of Detention, then took off again, riding down the ramp at Charlton Street, then turning around and taking the West Street tour, until he'd passed the Grip, before he backtracked to Christopher Street—as ever the most strolled blocks in the city.

Skimming Sheridan Square, he saw the familiar leather vest, belted denims, shirt hanging out, worn-down boot heels, and mostly the all-too-familiar walk of Little Larry Vitale. Noel waved a greeting as he passed, surprising the kid, who tried waving Noel down. Not today: Noel wanted to keep moving. He was done here for the day.

At St. Mark's Place, he turned uptown. The long ride to the town house was fatiguing. He was more out of shape then he thought. He'd have to do more bicycling again.

Noel let himself into the side gate, dropped the bike on the lawn, and went in. No one home.

Then he spotted Okku on the back terrace, drinking coffee and talking to a freshly tanned Dorrance, in from California for the reopening, Noel supposed.

"Eric's sleeping," Dorrance relayed. Okku immediately left his seat, went in for coffee: the perfect man-servant; lucky Eric.

"It seems he got home this morning at nine, after working all night," Dorrance said. "He wants to sleep until early evening. To be in shape for the party."

"Understandably."

"And Alana—" Dorrance began.

"Is in Europe," Noel finished for him.

"No. She's here somewhere. Was last night, at least."

"She's early then," Noel said, hiding his surprise.

"She had something she wanted you to see. A package. Ah, look, Okku's bringing it."

The brown paper parcel was opened. Within were several heavy, glossy-papered, expensive European magazines. Noel went for the cream-colored envelope that sat on top and read the note she'd written:

"Look inside. You're coming tonight, yes? I must talk to you. In private. It's very important."

"Here," Dorrance offered to show him, "she's marked the pages with paper clips." He opened the magazine at the designated spot. It was a two-page spread—Noel saw the stairway descending from the open French doors of a château wing, leading through a formal garden, where, against fireworks in the night sky, a man and a woman were leaning toward each

other in a tentative embrace and a barely restrained
kiss that was almost palpable. Alana! And himself!

"The others are variations," Dorrance said, opening
the other magazines for Noel to see. Some were single
pages, others cropped to half-page size, all of them
mysterious, inviting, filled with chiaroscuro: her white
skin against his dark suit, the depths of the garden
shadows against the bright, silvered paving stones, the
fireworks display against the black night.

"It's a lovely ad campaign," Dorrance said. Then, in
a more concerned tone of voice, "Don't you think so?"

"Very nice. Alana looks terrific."

"So do you. You photograph beautifully."

"It's odd seeing myself. And yet, that's not me."

"You'll get used to it. Alana never even looks. If you
weren't in these, she'd never have brought them with
her from Paris. She thought you'd like to see how you
came out."

"But that isn't me," Noel protested. "Look at him!
He's suave, confident, romantic, untroubled. Look at
me! I'm supposed to be devastating to all sexes. Hell,
I can't even get laid."

"It's all make believe," Dorrance agreed sadly.

Noel spent another few minutes looking at the photos, just to say he'd seen them. Then he went inside.
Alana wasn't home, he discovered, checking her
rooms. Passing back through the corridor toward the
living room balcony he touched one of the other
doors. Eric's—open. That was odd!

Inside Eric's sitting room it was shadowy daylight,
drawn shades dim. Noel crossed to the bedroom door.
It, too, was open.

Eric was in bed, sleeping. Overhead a planter's fan
spun with a loud hum. Noel had seldom come into
those rooms before. Now he felt he simply had to look
in. He told himself he wanted to be certain that everything was all right. Closing the bedroom door behind
him, he quietly approached the bed.

Eric was on his back, the pale-colored oversheet was twisted around one shoulder and down to one leg as though he were dressed in a toga. Noel watched him sleeping for a minute, then backed up and sat down a few feet away in a large, comfortable chair.

Here it was, the last possible date. Here were the supposed victim and the supposed assassin together in a room, alone. Eric was totally vulnerable, Noel clearly in charge. The timing was perfect, wonderful. But nothing else was.

Watching Eric sleeping, Noel knew that even if it were incontrovertibly proven to him that Eric was responsible for Randy's death—or Kansas's, or any of the others he was supposed to have slain so heartlessly—that even then he would never be able to hurt this man. How could he? Only a few nights ago, for the first time in his life, Noel had sought a man's physical love: this man's love. And ·understood when it had been rejected. Accepted that, too. As he would accept just about anything Eric did. Because that had happened, too—he'd fallen in love with Eric as he had with Alana, expecting nothing back, not even desiring a return from either of them now, only that they continue to be themselves and allow him to be with them. The programming so shrewdly put together by psychiatric engineers and computer banks could never get beyond that fact. Never.

He suddenly became aware of a change in the room. At first he looked up at the ceiling fan to see if it had stopped. On the bed, Eric lay as before. No. Not as before. His breathing was more rapid, more irregular. He was awake: playing possum, pretending still to sleep. Noel was about to leave, then froze. Don't move, he told himself. Eric doesn't know it's you. Remember his paranoia, his fear. He thinks it might be anyone, *anyone!* And if you move, he is going to assume you are moving toward him, not away from him, to kill him, not to leave him alone. The minute you move, the programming, the super-subtle programming, is in effect. This is exactly the unexpected, unprepared for freak occurrence that Loomis was hoping for. He wakes up, jumps you. You struggle . . . don't move!

Noel was trembling. Softly, remaining as still as possible, he whispered, "Eric? Are you awake? It's me, Noel."

Eric's eyes opened, looked all around the room. He had been awake, scared, too.

"You left your hall door unlocked. The bedroom door, too," Noel explained, trying to speak in a more normal tone of voice. "Pretty bad security for someone so concerned about protection."

Eric was still checking out the room.

"There's no one else here. Only me."

"What are you doing in here?" Asked sharply. Annoying Noel.

"What do you think? I didn't like being rejected. I came to rape you."

Eric didn't take the joke. "Be serious, Noel."

"I am being serious."

"Not serious enough," Eric warned. Under the sheet, his right hand lifted, then the sheet fell away. Taped to the inside of his hand was a tiny, wicked-looking Derringer.

"Jesus!" Noel said, getting up out of the chair. "Does that thing work?"

"Of course it works."

"How long have you been wearing that?"

"Why did you come in here?" Eric asked.

"To see you. To wish you luck tonight."

"Aren't you coming?"

Noel wanted to say no, he couldn't. Something had come up. An emergency. But the disappointment was already too apparent on Eric's face.

"Sure I'm coming. I'll be here by eight. As planned."

"You really came in to wish me luck?"

"And to see you. How long have you been wearing that gun?"

"Since I'm sleeping alone."

"You mean after McWhitter . . .?" Noel began.

"Long before that," Eric said bitterly. "Since Robby Landau was killed. That's almost two years ago."

Noel flashed back on the last time he'd been in this room, the night he'd taken the Mercedes to follow Dorrance, and had fought with Eric in the garage. Redfern had said then that he'd only trusted one man and lost him. It had to have been Landau—Eric's lover. Mr. X's first victim. Noel was still staring at the tiny gun.

"What if it goes off?"

"What if I don't wake up in time? It's the chances. I'm lucky."

"A better idea would be to lock your door. Go back to sleep."

"Noel, do me a favor."

"Sure. What?"

"I'll be all over the place tonight. Stay with Alana. Be her date. Be nice to her. She needs some attention. Do you mind?"

"No. Not at all," Noel said, enjoying it.

"You tripping tonight? Everyone else will be."

"In the punch?" Noel asked.

"Through the ventilation ducts. The finest stuff. Pure. Clean. Very up. Light. Nothing heavy. Tonight everything's going to be fine. Nothing heavy at all!" Eric repeated with such emphasis that Noel wondered what he knew—and what Eric thought he could do to prevent it when it came.

11

The reopening party at Window Wall that season had been planned with infinitesimal care to make the largest possible splash. It succeeded. Long after the daily tabloids had finished writing about its immense success and the early morning sidelight tragedy that almost no one present knew about until much later on, the weeklies and monthlies took up the party. Magazines that ostensibly dealt with fashion, or high society or film or finance or music, had sent reporters and photographers, and each of them returned to his editor with scores of glossy, colored photos and nearly identical stories—that money, talent, beauty, style, the exotic, the sordid, and the wild had all come together that early September night, two thousand strong, to affirm the fact that glamour wasn't dead at all—it was alive and kicking downtown at the Window Wall.

Heiresses danced with Christopher Street dropouts who were just scraping by on welfare payments. Heavyset, aging Californian real-estate moguls and paper-thin, lion-maned British rock stars shared drinks and small talk with muscled hairdressers. A well-known Hollywood ladies' man was seen at dawn crawling out of a three-hour orgy in a lower-floor room consisting of seventeen other men and the transsexual he had unknowingly followed inside. A six-and-a-half-million-dollar transaction between a Wall Street brokerage firm and a West German bank was initiated while all six partners were sniffing cocaine in a lower lounge. A peer of France, whose family had helped crown Charlemagne, broke up with his seventeen-year-old boyfriend in Mirror City, so amicably that the young surfer/swimmer found himself settled the following day with one of his ex's houses in royal Palm Beach.

Approximately $17,000 worth of liquor and at least that much in various drugs were consumed during the party. The upstairs dinner, for a scant, select two hundred, cost only half that. More than four hundred partygoers had sex of one sort or another with at least one partner somewhere in the precincts of the club. Two DJs on double shifts from midnight to noon played 840 cuts of music, repeating only once—deliberately. Two lighting men—also doubled up—punched out 11,313 different light combinations on their five-paneled digital computers.

Naturally, attitudes changed. Two Seventh Avenue designers broke up their profitable five-year partnership and were eighty-sixed from the club after their brawl over a sixteen-year-old tart (a well-known hooker since she was eleven, seen fixing her face in the mirror during their fracas). Another designer dropped his favorite mannequin when she passed out from an overinhalation of ethyl choride, and selected a new star for his spring line from the chorus of frenetic dancers gyrating precariously atop one curved-glass brick wall. Three interior designers—agreeing for once—decided built-ins and industrial carpeting were "out," posh fabrics and a return to the Biedermeier style "in."

Fifteen guests passed out at one time or another. Fourteen were revived. The other, whom no one seemed to know or care to know, was declared a casualty. Everyone else who happened to get in through one of the five etched-glass doors eventually emerged outside again, and all seemed to spend the next three days on the telephone detailing everything that had occurred and declaring there would never be another party like it—until Window Wall reopened next year, of course.

Although the disco began only at the witching hour, the club doors opened at nine for the dinner guests Eric had invited to Mirror City. Like the party later on, this group was a very mixed affair: ribbon clerks and truck drivers and florists by day hobnobbing with cinema idols, stand-up comics, billionaires—all such distinctions obliterated by the formal wear required by the invitation, which could be checked for lighter dance togs at the appropriate time.

Expectation, excitement, and a sense of being one of the very elite ran like electrical charges through this early crowd as they arrived and were shot up to the third floor to the lounge area opposite Mirror City, overlooking the still-darkened main floor. Eric had rebuilt this lounge, tearing down the floor of offices between it and the roof and installing a dozen tinted-glass skylights to let in the night. A sixteen-piece jazz band played mellow reconstructions of the thirties and forties dance tunes, furthering the illusion of a roof-garden nightclub from that era.

It was in a round-cornered black leather sofa in this lounge—almost deserted after dinner, and once the discotheque had been opened—that Alana finally got away from her friends and admirers and sat Noel down over double Hennesseys in balloon snifters for the "very important talk" she had written to ask him for earlier.

The jazz band was in the middle of a Cole Porter medley. In the small bowls on every table, candles flickered dimly. Every frosted-glass light had been dimmed. A few couples were dancing slowly in the middle of the large room. Other, equally shadowy duos and trios sat in booths and darkened corners. The brandy fumes were heady after the three wines that had accompanied dinner, and the coke that had gone around each table between every course, and the tranquilizer Noel had unnecessarily taken at eight o'clock.

He was completely relaxed: hunger sated, thirst quenched, tension gone. Everything smelled like brandy and lilies and perfume. Everything looked muted, candlelit, butter-smooth as the sofa, without sharpness, without edge. He had taken off his tie, opened a half-dozen buttons of the frilled Sulka shirt Eric had given him to wear this evening. His legs were lifted onto an ottoman, just brushing Alana's golden tan thighs where her skirt had been raised.

They'd been more or less together all evening, ever since they'd left the town house with Eric in the Silver Cloud. But now that they were really alone, Noel wondered what she wanted to say that she hadn't been able to say before.

He glanced at her without wanting to be seen observing, once more ticking off her attractions: her soft dark eyes, her glowing skin, her slightly overripe lips, the fine planes and angles of her face, her long, thin, very European nose, her loose, heavy dark hair around her shoulders. His panic subsided into warmth.

"Well?" he finally said, so quietly he barely heard himself.

She heard it though, looked at him. "I've been practicing all day. I still don't know how to begin."

"The beginning," he suggested.

"That is most difficult. You've seen the photos."

"Dorrance showed them to me."

"Did you like them?"

"You looked wonderful."

"So do you. It is about the photos I want to talk. To begin with," she added hastily. She seemed very unsure of herself. So unexpectedly unsure that Noel wondered why. He said nothing.

"The magazines came out last week. In Paris. Berlin, Rome, Milan. They were very stunning." She immediately guessed it was the wrong word. She was nervous, wasn't she? "Very surprising, I meant to say.

Everyone in Europe wanted to know who you were."

"I'll bet they did."

"Not because of me. There have already been many offers."

"What kind of offers?"

"To pose. For art directors. For photographers. For designers. To do layouts, advertisements, fashion spreads."

"You're serious, aren't you?" he asked.

"I've been serious about this from the beginning, Noel. It is you who have always made a joke about it. Now I'm telling you it is no joke. An income of at least one hundred thousand American dollars for the first two years, that is not to laugh at, yes? If you do well, you will earn more, of course."

She looked away from him, cradling the balloon glass, and said in a lower voice, "But you must come to Europe. To live. To work. You must agree to give up what you are now doing. Your book . . . anything else you are doing. And one more thing: you must decide immediately."

Ever since Dorrance had showed him the magazines on Redfern's terrace, Noel was prepared to hear these words from her: not the details, of course. The figures she mentioned seemed astronomically high just for standing in front of a camera, the terms exacting.

"Where do you fit into this?" he asked. "As my agent?"

"As your agent, yes. But then however you want me to fit."

"What's that supposed to mean?"

"I have Air France reservations for two. The six o'clock flight. Today. I am taking that flight. With you, or alone, Noel."

"Does Eric know all this?"

"More or less."

"I thought you'd never leave him?"

"I'll see him. He'll come to visit. It is time I began to live for myself, no?" she said, so pertly that he had to laugh.

"I still don't understand how you'll fit into it," he demanded, wanting her to declare herself.

"Come away with me, tonight, Noel. Away from this stupid, this awful business. Live with me. Work with me. Be my friend, my brother, my lover, my husband, whatever you want to be."

Now that it was out, she seemed surprised. He was.

"You want me to marry you?"

"If you want to."

"Even with all that's happened to me?"

She lost her patience. "What has happened to you that is so special? Nothing! You went to bed and made love to a man. Maybe you'll do so again. So what? No one cares about that. No one will care. It is not so important. It happens. Sometimes it means something. Sometimes not. Don't listen to the voice of your father or grandfather or scoutmaster, listen to your own inner voice, Noel. I am offering you a life where it won't matter to anyone if you make love to a man or a woman or . . . a potato. Is that so difficult to understand?"

Before she finished, he reached over and cupped his hands over her own fluttery ones around the balloon glass.

"Forgive me. It isn't every day a beautiful woman proposes."

She smiled, looking fatigued, uncertain. He realized how much of her pride this little talk had cost her.

"So you will come with me?"

"Let's dance," he said.

"Say it, Noel. Say you will come with me to Paris."

"Let me think about it a minute. Come on, we'll dance."

She seemed uncertain, but followed him to the center of the dance floor, all but empty now that everyone had gone downstairs to the discotheque, allowing herself to be drawn into his arms.

The skin on her arms and through the gauzelike material she wore was hot, dry, as though she were still nervous. Her scent was scarcely noticeable: rose attar. The same as she'd worn the first time he'd seen her and heard her voice. As they swayed, her hair brushed the back of his hand. She was easy, comfortable; she fit perfectly into his arms. Perfectly.

All he had to do was say yes. He would go with her to Paris in less than a day. Possess her—Alana De Vijt, the world's most-sought-after woman, compared to whom all women he'd ever known, even Monica, were selfish, foolish, tactless, clumsy, stupid. All he had to do was say yes. He would have an international career in modeling, be famous, be seen everywhere, make more money in a year than he had in six. Go to parties, dinners, galas, resorts, spas, nightclubs. See the way the rich and the beautiful, the spoiled and the unspoilable lived. All he had to do was say yes. He knew sex would be no problem with Alana. Even now he felt a warmth in his loins he had never felt for Mirella, for other women. He also knew that he would feel easier about men. That being with her he would feel free to find out what lay behind his attraction/repulsion to them, especially to Eric. She would be discreet, out of the way, back again when he needed her. They would grow old together. Perhaps have children. Never lack. Meet movie stars. Ride in big black cars. (Who had said that to him? Loomis, wasn't it?) All he had to do was say yes. He deserved being pampered after these hellish six months. All he had to do . . . What was left to hold him back? Whisper? Hypocrisy! Tenure? Did he want it now? The book? Would he ever finish it? Nothing.

But the instant he concluded that, he knew he would never go to Paris with Alana on the six o'clock flight, on any flight. Not because it wasn't the best thing that would ever happen to him. It was. Not because there was anything to hold him here. There wasn't. But for the simple, but all-pervading reason that yesterday afternoon waiting for Priscilla Vega to show up, he'd made a resolution, the first in his life, the best in his life, to live that life, whatever it turned out to be, and not someone else's idea of it: not even Alana's.

Then he realized that the crucial day had passed: the day he was to have gone off, killed Eric.

He also remembered that this probably meant that Loomis's alternative plan would go now into action—the set up drug bust illustrated on his message from Loomis. The catch! And he knew that because Eric was so much a part of his life now, his real life that is, not the fantasy Alana had invented for him, Noel couldn't allow the catch to happen.

Trying to mask all he was feeling, he asked where Eric was.

"Upstairs," she answered dreamily, "in the office. Or in the DJ's booth. He likes to watch from there."

"Let's go find him."

She caught the urgency in his words. "Now?"

"We'll boogie a little. Don't you want to?"

"It's so pleasant here. It will be crazy downstairs."

"Let's go downstairs," he urged. "I'd like to."

"You'd have to check your jacket. Even your shirt. You know how hot it will be."

She clearly didn't want to go. Afraid he would decline her offer? Why?

"I'll leave my jacket here," he said. They had stopped pretending to dance. He took off the jacket and threw it on the sofa. "Come on. You love to dance."

"We'll never find him, Noel. There are thousands of people down there."

But Noel was beginning to break out into a sweat, even with his jacket off and his shirt open to his navel. He very gently pulled her behind him, to the solid glass doors that led to the nearest escalator, trying to hide the sudden intense fear that was rising inside him, unresolvable—until he saw Eric and knew that Eric was safe.

12

One third of the way down the long, gently sloping, slowly descending escalator, the party hit Noel so hard he had to clutch the handrail.

From this overhead view it seemed as though every inch of the place, dance floor, lounges, bars, doorways, was crowded with bodies, and every body was in twitching, jumping, swirling almost Brownian motion as though a giant electric current had been forced through the outer walls. Four hundred sweeping, twirling, blinking, shooting, stroboscoping lights utterly destroyed the shape, solidity, essence of every object he looked at. Walls, mirrors, sculptures, doors, faces, bodies were fractured into bars, circles, ellipses, cones, stripes of light. Everything moving so quickly, then shifting rapidly to another shape, another density, another brightness, that when he tried to focus on the DJ's booth—shoulder high over the dance floor— he could only make out and hold its general shape for a second before it, too, fragmented into a pointillist landscape: scallops of electric blue shoving against points of fuchsia, eradicated by slashes of red, then greens, then purples, pushed aside by dashes of orange and magenta into colors that he couldn't even begin to name or describe, never having seen or even known of their existence before.

Simultaneously, he was attacked on all sides by the sheer rush of sound. Beneath him, huge speakers ten feet tall erupted into staccatto thumping so deep he could feel its pulse in his arteries. Around him, suspended in the air, every few yards, tweeters shrieked, chattered, whined, aahed, beeped, sang, screamed. Suddenly two soprano voices in a shrill chorus were twittering at his left ear. Just under them, a dozen trumpets blared the same color red that streaked across his eyes from a reflection off a double-hinged mirror, then subsided into a punctuating throb. Beyond them, behind him, the multiple rhythms of tambourines and maracas suddenly began like chattering monkeys, like wild-eyed, screeching, tropical-colored birds of prey. Now a thin edge of stiletto-sharp silver also held the air, as the lead singer's voice began the words. Between it, beneath it, all around it was the bedrock visceral, blood-pumping, heart-strumming, ear-buzzing bass which he fought as it reached out to grip his legs like a viscous, life-sucking force. But he couldn't resist, and slid into it deeper and deeper, slid forward inexorably and was now off the rubber grip of the escalator steps and pushed far into the center of the dance floor, where he was suddenly still for a half second, like a frame from a film of a hydrogen bomb's mushroom cloud, absolutely still for the instant, as the fatal atoms did their deadly shatter. Then everything was in motion again.

Noel suddenly remembered what Eric had said to him at the town house about atomizing the air of the entire Window Wall with LSD. Everyone was tripping on it. He, too, was tripping on it.

A face sailed past him, multicolored, young, perspiring, glimmering in different colors, ecstatic. Another face caught him from another side, darker, sweat-beaded, eyes staring up, mouth opened in a complete and delighted grin. A glimpse of Alana, her head thrown back, eyes closed as though in orgasm, lips open to smile as though in on some secret, the lights metamorphosing her into sheer delight. She must be tripping, too. Everyone was. And Noel had never done it before!

But he was moving, too, because unaware that his mind was unable to come to terms with it, his body had instinctively taken off on the rhythm around him; instinctively knowing that the only way not to fall, to keep afloat, was to keep moving rhythmically in tune; the only way to avoid the dance, to progress, was to stay vibrating, to become the dance itself.

Alana's hands reached out in the colored, fractured, light-growing air between them, gliding smooth and buttery soft, evoking sudden images of dancing girls' arms in harems, of the arms of Hindu statues, of Balinese dancers' arms making strange, enigmatic symbols before his eyes. They came together behind him, around his neck and shoulders, and she glided closer to his body, and his own arms suddenly appeared in the air before him, looking odd and unnatural, but slightly familiar, and they, too, began to dance, and finally snaked around her body, changing shape and proportions with every second-long change of light or color or detail of the sound around them.

Noel couldn't take the barrage on his optic nerve anymore and closed his eyes. But that made no difference in the lights or shapes, except that now there was no point of reference anymore. The sounds continued, deeper, louder, closer to his skin it seemed, invading him. So he opened his eyes and felt terror and nausea sweep up through his body into his mouth and ears and eyes, and out of him. Then it began again, from within, only he stopped it from emerging, and it shot back inside this time, detonating every individual cell, until he could see their tiny nuclei individually shatter, and the blackness that had threatened to suck him below engorged him and he was sucked into the blackness, darker than any imaginable, until he almost thought, then he was sure, then was absolutely convinced, it wasn't blackness at all but the white, white, white of nothingness forever white. . . .

When he opened his eyes, he was whole again, Noel Cummings, as was everything else—the lights, the music, Alana, the club, the people, the dancing were there, too, a minute later. Paradox. No. Joke. First whole, then a million individual cells. There, yet not there, black becoming white, death seeming to give instant birth. Big joke. Still dancing, too. Alana turning around slowly in front of him, decomposing into billions of cells, each little cell winking on and off, moving, proving itself alive. Then all of the cells joining together to form bone, flesh, skin, muscle: Alana—with a wonderful smile. She'd known the joke all the while, of course, while he, a child, hadn't. Eric had known all the while, too. *Eric.* What Noel must do to find Eric. To include him. This trinity that they were.

But he could not move, as another wave of sights, sounds, smells, too, tastes, feelings—first inside, then outside, then inside again—began to form around him, intensifying, building to a crest within. This time he did not fight it but allowed himself to slide right into the blackness that became so spectacularly white. . . .

He came back in time to know that something had changed around his physical body while he'd been off tripping into the white. Everyone in the huge room was suddenly roaring what sounded like approval, pleasure, around him. Noel opened his eyes, saw Alana, her face shifting every second he looked at her, saw her gesturing for him to follow her gaze. Everyone else's, too. Then above them, floating only a few feet over their heads, though far off across the dance floor so that he could clearly make it out, was a giant, octagonal silver balloon, which like everything, everybody around him, kept changing its shape. No. It wasn't a balloon. Its surface was hard, reflective, all mirrors. It was an octagon, holding that shape even as it began to change, the top of it separating, until he could now see that it was one of the mirrored rooms Eric had shown him in the sketch. (Eric. Where was Eric? Why wasn't he here, sharing this, where he belonged, with Noel and Alana, their trinity?) It was actually opening up, its paneled sides dropping slowly as it revolved, like a giant flower opening in the heat of the sun to reveal some exotic secret within.

Which turned out to be a person, standing. No, not just a person, but Veena Scarborough, a hand on one silver-lamé jutting hip, another hand attached to a long, darting, silver fingernail, shaking in the air now as flakes of silver were shot off her face, her silver-embedded eyes, the stroboscope making everything vibrate to one single vibration where the senses all melted together. Now separated. An eerie, high-pitched atonal sound pierced the music blaring and thumping around her, then, as her silver-painted lips opened and she shouted, sang, shrieked, crooned, demanded, " 'Pull yourself together,' I say, 'Pull yourself together, baby!' "

The crowd roared recognition of one of their favorite songs as the silver-strobe sound shot out of her, hit Noel directly between the eyes, and he felt his ego punched to smithereens with another crest of white. . . .

And back again. And gone again into the white. Until even that became rhythmic, too, and Noel couldn't say why he'd never felt such contentment, such pure physical, mental, emotional pleasure before.

Alana had somehow gotten them over to the edge of the crowd. Still holding him, still into the beat of the music, she managed to get the two of them into a space against one wall. He let her lead him, holding onto her outstretched hand as it changed and became a snake/a tree bough/a flower/a petal/a strip of leather/a steel-curved bar/and arm again/then a hand. Alana smiled, reached up, touched Noel's fore-head. He felt her skin hot then cool then melting into him from the touch, from his side where they were up against each other. He saw Veena in her silver Queen of Outer Space costume gyrate, shimmy, wag a finger, shout to her finale, stop as though frozen, as the petals began slowly to fold around her, and the crowd rioted into shouting, stamping, giving back what she had given them.

Noel closed his eyes for a rest. The lighting was muted inside now. Easier to take.

He felt someone touching him, shaking him by the shoulder, it seemed. He opened his eyes, turned, and saw a familiar face close by. Cal. Cal Goldberg. The manager. He was motioning to Noel, pulling him and Alana behind, threading through the sidewall of people packed together all still in motion, to another wall, then up a dozen steps, and into a sudden absence of glaring lights, cell-gripping sounds. Noel turned to make certain that Alana was with him. The door was closed.

They were inside a large plush office, with sofas, chairs, coffee tables. One wall, where they had entered, was completely one-way glass looking out into the club, where the party still raged. Inside, it was almost hermetically still, calm as a pond. Noel made out other people sitting in the swivel chairs—Rick, Cal again. Someone he didn't know but guessed to be a friend of theirs.

Alana shook off his hand gently, dropped onto a sofa, motioned for Noel to follow. He settled into the pillows gingerly, having to rename, redefine, figure out everything he saw as though seeing a chair or sofa or person for the first time in his life.

"I saw you guys out there," Cal explained. "I thought maybe you wanted to rest a minute. Drink?"

"Water," Alana said. Noel nodded, unable to find his voice yet.

"You've never tripped before," Alana said to Noel. It

was not a question. Evidently it was all too apparent.

Noel searched for, found his voice. "Not like this." He wanted to tell her what he had learned, discovered, intuited, seen, felt since they'd come down the escalator. He decided it would take weeks, months perhaps.

The glass of water was suddenly handed to him. Its three-dimensionality disconcerted him for a second; it seemed alive. But he watched how she took it, and did so, too. It felt odd. The water, as he looked into it, seemed filled with living, microscopically small creatures. But she was drinking it. He did, too. It tasted like nothing. Felt strange, alive again, going down his throat.

"I hereby declare this party an A-one success," Rick Chaffee said with a much exaggerated drawl. Noel wondered why, looked at Rick. His eyes were bright: stoned. Noel's must look the same.

"If that's the case, I'm not needed anymore," Cal said quietly. "I'm going home."

"And miss the rest of it?"

"I've been to plenty of parties, honey. And I intend to go to plenty more."

They laughed, exultant, telling each other their work had not been for nothing.

There was a tap at the mirror. On the other side of the window Cal's lover, Burt, was peering in, even though he couldn't see inside, waving his hand in a circle against the glass.

Cal let him in, along with sixty seconds of music and lights and intense heat. Noel said hello. Greetings were general. Then Noel decided he had something very important to say to Alana, turned to her, saw she seemed to be resting, tripping off, her eyes closed. It could wait. He, too, slumped back into the sofa and slowly looked outside as the others talked, and he began to feel the acid in him begin to crest again. He went off into the warm Antarctica of white again.

13

He was stretched out on the sofa. The room was filled with people: Veena and Alana on the opposite sofa; Cal and his lover; Rick and Jimmy DiNadio, quietly, but intensely as ever, arguing. They noticed him first.

"You okay?" Chaffee asked.

"Fine." And he was. Everything still seemed to have its own unique, individualized presence for him—the ashtray on the table was aggressively three-dimensional. The water in the glass was almost a cartoon of water. Any movement he or anyone else made left a half-dozen afterimages, as though he were seeing through a camera lens that was speeded up to catch not only motion, but the areas in between motion.

"You catch my act, honey?" Veena asked. Before he could say yes, she went on: "It was *fabulous!* If I say so myself."

Noel sat up. Then stood up. Outside, through the office's one-way mirror, the party was roaring, unabated. He glanced past a wall clock and was astonished to see it was three o'clock. He'd been tripping for three hours already. That meant that the heaviest part of it was over.

"Really knocked me on my ass," he said to no one in particular.

"Honey, imagine what I felt like?" Veena said. "Trying to keep my balance on that thing. Let me tell you! Surfing is a cinch compared to that!"

Noel was perfectly relaxed. He was used to the drug's more obvious effects now. Still, he was both-

ered by something: a mind itch he couldn't find to
scratch.

"Well, where in this dump is the massa anyway,"
Veena said in response to something Alana had murmured too low for Noel to catch.

That was it: Eric! Eric was in trouble! He had to
find Eric. He felt a rush of the acid coming on, and
sat down. It worked on the cerebral cortex of the
brain, Noel remembered from his reading about the
drug: his excitement, fear, whatever strong emotion
he had would trigger more of a reaction in turn.

No one answered Veena's question immediately.
Then almost everyone present seemed to have a different answer. Rick had seen Eric in the DJ's booth, taking over the light panels system, he said. But that
must have been hours ago. Cal had talked to Eric via
the club's intercom, when Eric was downstairs on the
lower floor. Eric had reported a spectacular, very
mixed sex scene in the showers. But Cal's lover said
that he had been downstairs at two thirty: the orgy
had been over by then, and Eric nowhere in sight.

"I'm sure he's having a good time," Alana said, ap-
pearing very mellowed out. "He always does."

"He's up in the office on the fourth floor," someone
said almost from behind Noel. It was "Marge," flat
out on the carpet, back against the wall, feet straight
out. He looked beat. His red hair was plastered down
over his forehead with sweat, his T-shirt soaked. "I
saw him going up, just before I managed to squeeze
in here. He was with Geoff Malchuck. I saw them
going inside."

"They're probably checking out that new shipment
of coke Geoff scored," Cal said.

Noel's mind began racing. New connection. Coke.
Geoff Malchuck. Hadn't they talked at the elevator in
Redfern's town house yesterday? Could Geoff be the
setup? The trap Loomis had all ready? The catch was
supposed to be tonight, the onionskin had said.

"Who else was with him?" Noel asked.

"Some friend of Geoff's," "Marge" answered. "No one I know. Anyone have a Tuinal? I'm ready to slide into my down trip."

Geoff Malchuck a Whisper operative? He couldn't be. Or could he? Remember how closely he looked at me the day at Redfern's, just after Priscilla Vega told me about the programming?

"How do I reach the upstairs office?" Noel asked, a hand on the intercom phone.

"Push C and dial eleven," Cal instructed. No one else was paying attention. Noel had to keep it casual.

"What's wrong?" Alana asked.

He didn't respond. The phone rang and rang. No answer. He hung up and dialed again. Still no answer. Noel stood up. "See you later," he said.

Before anyone could register a reaction, he was at the door, had it open, was in the middle of the party again. After the quiet, cool calm of the office, it was like being inside a hurricane composed of lights, sounds, people, motion, insanity. He was trying to see a way around the dance floor over to the escalators when he felt a tug at his right shoulder, turned, saw Alana, her lips moving. He couldn't hear what she said, couldn't make out anything but the intense thumping bass of the music. He pointed toward the middle of the room, felt her hand slide down his back and latch onto his belt. She was going with him.

Pushing through the dizzying, dancing smash of bodies proved almost impossible. He couldn't get anywhere near the escalators. Those he did try to shove aside gave angry looks. Some even pushed him back. This was not the way to do it. He turned around to her and motioned up, jabbing with one finger, *up*.

"The elevators!" she shouted, her mouth right near his ear. "Follow me."

They had to go back the way they'd come. Precious moments lost was all he could think. And the acid was sweeping through him again periodically, although never quite coming to a crest like before. He still had to stop and try to keep it under control.

They had arrived at one of the circular lobbies outside the main dance floor. Alana reached up to tap on the curved window of the ticket taker's booth. The frizzy-haired blonde inside looked up, and smiled, recognizing Alana, waved her comprehension when Alana pointed to what seemed to be a flat bare wall, and pressed a button.

The wall slid open, revealing an elevator. Noel almost dragged Alana inside, waiting on pins and needles for the door to close.

"What's wrong, Noel?" she asked again in the sudden quiet of the elevator. She held a hand over the button panel.

"Eric's in trouble. That coke connection he's doing. It's a trap. A setup to bust him. I can't explain it all to you. You can't come with me. Go back to the party."

As an answer, she pressed the button for the fourth floor. The doors closed, the car began to rise smoothly. Noel had to lean against the wall in the sudden double rush of ascent and acid. When it stopped, he was leaning forward, poised to rush out. The doors stayed closed. Once more she was holding her hand over the button panel.

"Let me out, Alana!"

"You are certain of this?"

"Of course, I'm certain. Let me out. Go back downstairs."

"You are very high, Noel. Higher than you've ever been before. Sometimes strange thoughts occur when you are this high. Fantasies. Paranoia."

"I know I'm high. But it's not paranoia or fantasy. Believe me, I wish to hell it were." How could he explain without explaining everything, which would take time, precious time?

"But Eric is with Geoff," she protested. "Geoff Malchuck."

"I know. I know. Let me out."

She didn't move. Was he going to have to force her to?

"Look, Alana, I just know that something like this is supposed to happen tonight. I can't go into all the details right now. But I know. Geoff Malchuck or not."

Her look of concerned bafflement dropped. The mask that remained was pale with conviction, understanding, anger.

"Then Eric was right. You are a spy. An enemy."

"A spy, yes. Enemy, no. He's in trouble. Look, Alana, I'll explain later on . . ."

Her hand shot out, slapping his face hard, stopping what he was going to say next. She was shouting something at him that he couldn't make out. She slapped him again, this time knocking him to the wall of the elevator. He felt as though he were going to crest over again and slide into the white light. He couldn't afford to now.

As her hand darted out again, he managed to catch it, push it aside, and reach for the button panel. The doors slid open as he tried to keep her from hitting him again.

"Stay here. Go downstairs. This may be dangerous," he said. He pushed the panel button and leaped out just as the doors closed. He could hear her hammering on them as the elevator dropped.

He located Eric's office, tried to handle. Locked. He jiggled it, tried to force it. Then he began shouting through the door, kicking at it, trying to get in. Still nothing. Banging on it now with both fists. Then he backed up to the wall behind and charged the door, shoulders first, knocking every cell within his body to smithereens it seemed to him. Managed to collect them, backed up again, and rushed the door once more.

This time he almost knocked himself out. He heard a sick crack he thought at first was a rib, then realized was a door panel, and gave another hard shove.

The door gave. He staggered into the room, tumbling to the floor in just enough time to see the two full-length windows thrown open, and three men standing there as though in a *tableau vivant:* two he'd never seen before, Eric between them, handcuffed, being prodded from behind onto the fire escape. Eric yelled something Noel couldn't make out, as the crest he had tried so hard to control swept over him and he couldn't resist the long deep slide into it.

"He's all right," someone said. "Leave him."

He must have been out for only a second. Everything seemed as before, except that Eric was gone now. One window was closed. The second of the two men was just stepping out onto the fire escape. The catch! And he wasn't stopping it.

He got to his feet, rushing to the window in time to grab one of them by the belt, and pull him back hard, so that he stumbled, couldn't catch himself, hit the side of the desk, fell.

"We've got some trouble," the one outside shouted down to someone else. Noel crawled out onto the fire escape, felt the grating underfoot, found a handhold, swung into the man, catching him as he turned, smashing him in the stomach. He turned to get Eric and couldn't find him in the darkness. He shouted his name. There were lights now, from across the airshaft, from below—searchlights. He shouted again for Eric. Suddenly, so suddenly he couldn't keep his balance, he was being pulled backward.

"What in hell is wrong with you?" someone muttered behind him. Noel was dragged off the fire escape back into the room.

"I thought you said this one was all right?"

"He's supposed to be."

"Son of a bitch, he just bit me."

Noel felt a blow to his kidney from behind.

"Loomis said to make it clean," the other one said as Noel twisted back. He was pinned now. "Nice and clean," the man said in front of him, then hauled off and punched Noel's chin just as a new crest was coming. He felt it and the acid wave connect together. He didn't go out, although he pretended to, slumping suddenly so that he was dropped to the floor.

"Hey, wait a minute, sister! Where are you going?"

"She's the one!"

Noel tried to get up, to get from around the desk so he could see. Pain caused him to hold onto the corner to try to catch his breath, to fight off the dizziness.

"He's up again," one of them said.

Noel could make out the sound of a struggle. When the pain and dizziness subsided enough for him to stagger over to the window, he was grabbed from behind again, both arms pinned to his sides. He tried struggling, felt helpless, weak. He thought to relax completely, allowing the other to ease his grip, then Noel could jump out.

In front of him, through the thrown-open windows, the other man was trying to grab hold of someone who was fighting back hard. It took Noel a minute to realize that it was Alana. He tried to shout to her to stop. Tried to struggle free. Heard blows exchanged between them, heard her voice uttering soft, indignant, angry sounds. Saw the two bodies writhing, saw someone else appear on the fire escape, grating, saying, "Now now now now" like a rapid-fire gun. He was let go from behind and leaped up to the window frame.

Alana had gotten free. Both her assailants seemed to have let go of her. She turned to him as he reached out for her, calling her name, trying to get her inside, then saw one of the men dive forward into her, hands out in front of him.

Click. Click. Click. Everything stopped, froze, but the white of her arms flying up into the air, clutching for the railing, the grating, something, anything to hold on to in the air, before her head disappeared from sight, and her midsection and legs fled after them backward, slowly as though in a ballet, backward, like a bizarre throw in the air from some modern ballet's pas de deux.

Everything stopped, and replayed again: the hand in the air, in the water, reaching up and up, over and over. Over and over, the hand reaching for air out of the water. His groggy awakening in the rocking boat, seeing the hand clutching for air, getting up, waking with the icy plunge into the water, reaching for her, reaching for her, feeling the utter fucking helplessness of not being able to reach her in time, and the only thought he could put together was, *No, this can't be happening, not again, this can't be real, it must be the drug*.

Click. Click. Click. It went.

And ended in a short piercing scream that tore from her insides, into her mouth, and rushed at Noel, tearing the fabric of his night vision with that hand in the air before him still, now and forever, that hand clutching for air, as he heard the deep, awful sounds below halfway between a thud and the splat of a smashed melon.

He was hurling himself down the iron fire stairway, suddenly released, he didn't know how or why, racing, swerving to get down, reaching the place where the fire escape ended in a ladder. He jumped onto it, dangling on it, seeing the wet paved alley below him, people in uniforms and jackets standing around, red flashes over the opposite walls, on faces, as though a hundred flashlights were bobbing, shaking. He let go of the ladder, dropped with a thud to the ground, pushed through them all to get to her.

She was a broken doll. Her dress ripped up to her hips. One leg bent under her, the other at an angle that couldn't be right. Her head turned away from him, as though spurning him once more. Hair covering her face like a black cloth.

Someone was kneeling beside her. He looked up,

shouted to someone else. Nothing he yelled made
sense to Noel.

Eric was there, too, facing him across her body, not
looking down at her. His hands were still bound. Two
men held his shoulders from behind. He was looking
at Noel with utter contempt.

"She's still alive," someone said loudly. "Where in
hell is that ambulance! Radio the hospital to be ready
for her!"

Another siren was approaching. The crowd was
shifting now, moving to let some people through. He
saw Eric staring at him, accusing him, indicting him
for what had happened, knowing that Noel had done
it, all of it, from the beginning to now, to this. Men in
white were sliding around on either side of her.
Everyone forced back away from her. Something like
cloth slid under her. Then lifted, it must be a net. Her
body jiggled slightly, her face was still turned away,
still covered with her beautiful hair. The crowd dis-
persing now. People muttering around him. Eric just
standing there, standing there, accusing him.

The acid came on him again, making him shut his
eyes to the glare. He was still standing when he
opened them. Only now something was in his right
hand. Stupidly, dizzily, uncomprehending, Noel looked
at it—a glittering curved edge of sharp metal. Pointed.
Deadly.

"Now's your chance," someone whispered.

"He killed your girl," someone else said, then
stepped back.

The red lights picked out Eric's figure. Flashlights
wavered, only on Eric.

"I'd tear him to pieces," another voice said, receded
fast.

"He's all yours."

"He killed her."

"Get 'im, Lure."

"He's to blame."

"You let her die."

"Get him. He deserves it."

"Rip him up. He made you a queer."

"We won't stop you."

"He's all yours."

"Get him."

The knife felt like a burning ember melded to his hand.

"Get him back for all the others."

"Kill him, Lure."

"We won't stop you."

The heat of the knife was unbearable. But he couldn't drop it, couldn't shake it, couldn't let go of it.

"Kill him now."

"He made you a fairy."

"He made you kill her."

"You let her die."

"He's to blame."

Nothing to cool off the heat in his hand, racing up his arm, burning his elbow, his shoulder, his neck, his fingers. Nothing to ease the burning but to push it into something soft, wet, fleshy.

"Rip him to pieces."

"Get him, Lure."

"Kill him."

"Kill him."

"Kill! Kill! Kill!" the chorus whispered around him insidiously as he lunged around Eric, trying to stop them, to shut them up.

"KILL! KILL! KILL!" they whispered into every pore of his skin, every nerve ending of his muscles, as Noel reeled forward to sink the knife where it would stop the voices and cool the incredible burning heat in his hands. The voices urging him, urging him, insisting, insisting, before he went mad from the pain and the heat—and Noel lunged . . .

He saw Eric's face only inches away, not the mask of monstrousness, not the icy presence of death, but a

terrified brother, held-down sacrificial victim, lamb
ready to be slaughtered.

. . . Lunged and stopped, feeling his insides twist
to a bone-grinding halt, requiring every single minute
connection of bone to skeletal muscle to skin to stop
the lunge.

Heard, as though from miles away, the metallic clat-
ter of something at his feet. Saw before him Eric's
face becoming his own, then Alana's, Randy's, Monica's.

Someone was saying harshly, coldly, clearly: "Take
this one away. Book him. Come on. What are you
waiting for? Move!"

Eric disappeared, hustled away into the back seat
of a police car, pushed inside. He stared out the back
window, trying to see Noel, before he was shoved
back into the seat, and the car shot away, past the
narrow opening of the alleyway, and was gone.

Noel was motionless, floating, in release. He'd met
the test, felt its power, the programming that could
not be controlled. *And had beaten it.*

Something wet hit his left eye. He reached up; it
felt like mucus. Someone else moved in front of him
swiftly, rapidly spit at him. Then another. And one
more.

He let them, let the phlegm slide down his cheeks
and nose and chin. The shadows flitted away. The red
revolving lights thinned out, were finally gone, and he
was alone in the alleyway.

"C'mon, honey. We got to go now."

A hand reached up to touch him.

He didn't move. She brought a tiny silver handkerchief in front of him and tenderly wiped off his face.

"We got to go now, Noel. We got to go to the hospital. Come on, Noel. Rick has a car. He'll drive us."

Suddenly the release, the relief was gone. He saw
the hand groping for a hold in the air, once more
heard the scream, the sound of her landing on the

sidewalk. Everything came back clearly—with anguish.

"Come on, Noel." Veena was tugging at him. "Your woman's hurt. She's hurt bad."

14

In the hospital waiting room Rick Chaffee brought a pill and a glass of water to him. The drug was Thorazine, he said, and would bring Noel down from the trip and back to normal. Noel declined it, but Veena took one.

A young intern—a fan of Veena's, he said—came into the big room to tell them Alana was already in surgery, where she'd been taken as soon as she'd arrived. Didn't they want to go somewhere else, where it was quieter than the emergency waiting room? Noel didn't care, but Rick was in charge, and since there were a great many people staring at Veena in her silver-lamé outfit, she, too, thought it might be a good idea. Up a flight of stairs was an anteroom that looked like a small living room: two sofas, a chair, a Danish Modern affair. But it was quiet, private. And within a few minutes the Thorazine had already begun to work on Veena. She stretched out on the couch. Rick covered her with his tuxedo jacket, which looked incongruous.

Noel didn't sleep, or even close his eyes. He didn't need the Thorazine, he knew. Even though the eight hours that LSD was supposed to last were only half over, he had come down from the drug completely when he had dropped the knife meant to take Eric's life in the alleyway of the Window Wall. His vision had settled, no afterimages, no extra dimensionality to objects, none of it. But he was exhausted. The most he could do was to sit in the large chair, watching Veena sleep, watching Rick read one magazine article after another, and feeling the quiet around them.

At ten minutes after five in the morning, the same young intern who had brought them to the smaller room opened the door and quietly told them that Alana had died on the operating table. Veena woke up as he talked to Rick. All Noel could understand were disconnected words: "Massive hemorrhages." "Unexpected complications." Before the intern had gotten out of the door, the still sleepy-eyed disco star had broken out into wails of weeping, and it required all three men, another sedative, and almost a half hour before she was well enough to leave the hospital.

Noel told the intern he wanted to see Alana, and was directed to a post-op room one story above them.

Someone had brushed her hair back. There wasn't a bruise or scar on her face or neck or shoulders that he could make out. She lay as though asleep on the portable bed. He looked at her, touched her lips, felt how cold they were, then saw the paperlike consistency of her skin, always so alive and glowing before, and knew she was dead. He hadn't expected her to live. He had known in that unforgettable moment that he'd seen her hand clutching for a grip in the night air that she couldn't survive, that she was lost to him, long before he heard her scream, long before he saw her body twisted on the sidewalk, long before he was told. Seeing her now was mere confirmation.

He only stayed with her corpse for a minute before going down again. He no longer felt anything he could call an emotion.

Rick dropped Veena off and drove Noel to his apartment, attempting to get him to stay with him and Jimmy. He resisted his offer. He wanted to be alone.

It was already daylight when he entered his apartment. So he opened the window blinds, watered the plants, ran a fingertip along the wall to see if all the paint was dry, took a long hot shower, then feeling the exhaustion begin to catch up with him, lay down on the bed in the middle of the studio.

He had two fleeting regrets—that Alana had not seen the apartment redecorated, and thus understood from how much it had been transformed, how much *he* had altered; and that he had not immediately accepted her offer to go to Paris, even with what had happened, and thus given her at least a moment of happiness.

He tried to sleep, and instead remembered the entire evening in almost cinematic detail. It bothered him that she had died thinking that he had betrayed Eric. If spirits did exist after death, she would know differently: know that he had saved Eric from his worst enemy—Noel himself. Recalling the moment he had wanted so urgently to knife Eric, and how much he had resisted and why, Noel experienced again his release from Loomis's control, his relief that he had fought it. It was an outburst that racked his body from head to toe as though he were in a fever chill.

As he rose to find a handkerchief to wipe his face, his foot bumped and knocked down a parcel that had been leaned up against the wall near the door. Gerdes must have remembered how Noel had asked day after day for a parcel.

It was too big for the cassette, but when Noel opened the multiple wrappings and got past the various envelopes and stapled sheaves of photocopied pages, the envelope in which he had given the tape to Priscilla Vega fell onto the bed.

The cassette was wrapped with a handwritten note she had signed. By the time he received this, she wrote, she would be in San Juan. She had managed to tape everything they needed between Loomis and Gee. Taking the taxi, she had not gone home, but directly to the apartment of Wilson Martinez, a Hispanic congressman, to whom Buddy had already confided about Whisper and what he thought they were up to. Priscilla and her baby had stayed with the Martinez's for three days, until the cassette arrived in the mail at their East Harlem address. Noel did understand she couldn't take any chances in mailing it either to herself or to him, didn't he? Martinez had listened to the tape, read the new papers, and had called Lloyd Parnell, the police commisioner. Priscilla had given her testimony before Parnell and several lawyers. She might have to come back to do so again, if it came to trial. The tapes had been transcribed. All that was now required was for Noel to call the commissioner. Parnell would be waiting for his call—call him immediately at any hour. Even with all the evidence, Noel would have to testify to make the case against Loomis stick. Her postscript gave an address in Puerto Rico: he was to write if he wanted her.

His first thought was to drop the envelope and all of its contents into the incinerator outside his door, let it go up in ashes and smoke. Alana was dead. Eric was alive. The psychological weapon hadn't fired as it was supposed to. He wanted no more to do with it. He almost blamed Priscilla Vega for telling him what she had told him. Alana might still be alive if he hadn't known. He would still have his illusions intact, and not this—nothingness.

Then he held the cassette in his hand and knew he had to listen to it.

There were background noises: silverware, dishes, voices, a baby gibbering, a woman soothing it in Spanish, then a distinct, low-toned man's voice.

"You're certain he'll do it?"

Loomis answered. "No question about it. I told you, he doesn't have a choice anymore. It's set. He'll do it."

"What's in it for him?"

"His job. A career. Eventually money, prestige. What he wants."

"I thought he was some kind of professor?"

"He is," Loomis replied, repeating it, careful, distinct, as though talking to a child. "We fixed it up between us."

"You and his boss? The guy that found him for you?"

"That's right. His department chairman. He's the one who recommended this particular man."

"You and this boss of his are real tight?"

"Let's just say we have the same friends and connections."

That was all that Noel needed to hear. He glanced at the clock: eight fifteen. He dialed the number Priscilla had written, the commissioner's private line.

Wilbur Boyle. It was all he could think of as he waited to be put through, heard Parnell rasp that a car was on the way, they would convene the hearing immediately. *Wilbur fucking Boyle!* Which explained the agency. Which explained how Loomis knew all about him . . . which explained . . . had someone been killed just to get his attention that morning, riding along the West Side Highway? Who was Kansas anyway? An operative who'd somehow betrayed Loomis? Or was he just some hapless bum they'd found sleeping in the warehouse because he had nowhere else to go? Did it really matter? What was important was that between Boyle and Loomis they'd set up the trap for him. He'd been controlled from the first. He'd never had a chance against them.

Son of a bitch! He'd been the one who'd been lured!

15

"I think we've heard enough to consider this preliminary hearing fairly satisfactory, gentlemen," Parnell said.

Everyone else at the large oval table looked toward the far end where Loomis was sitting as though not a word said in the chambers for the past two hours had anything whatsoever to do with him. Next to him was Carl Russo, the attorney who would probably defend him if criminal charges were brought after the upcoming departmental trial. Russo was known to be a PBA agitator. He spoke for his client now.

"Naturally I will have to see all of your substantiation."

"Naturally, Mr. Russo," Parnell said wearily. "I'm certain Mr. Kirsch will be happy to present you with the rather massive amount of evidence we now possess."

Andrew Kirsch would present the evidence against Loomis at the departmental trial. He was an up-and-coming figure in the ranks, an old enemy of Russo's, the commissioner had explained to Noel.

"You understand, Loomis," Parnell said, "that in light of all this, your unit is disbanded as of now?"

The Fisherman came back from his reverie and nodded that he understood. It was one of the few times since they had entered the chamber that he seemed to have heard anything that was said. Most of the time he stared beyond Russo's head, past one of the two guards in the room, as though trying to see out of the little cross-barred window.

Silence. Even the stenographer had stopped clicking on the little lap-held machine. Everyone seemed to enjoy the quiet. Noel was startled by a plantive honk from a car horn somewhere below them.

"About bail," Russo suddenly said, leaning over the table. The stenographer began clacking away at her machine again.

"I'm afraid not," Parnell said.

"We have some pretty serious charges here," Kirsch added.

"You'll have to secure an indictment then," Russo said.

"Don't need it," his adversary replied. "These are intradepartmental matters."

"All preliminary charges are PD related," Parnell said. "Misuse of departmental funds, conspiracy to take the life of a PD officer . . ." He let his words trail away, obviously disgusted with the whole business.

They had just finished listening to the tape Priscilla Vega had made and especially the final street-corner portion in which Loomis and the man he called Gee had settled on a payment time, and amounts. Even with all the noise of a busy afternoon midtown street, their words had come through clearly. Damningly. Everyone in the room had been silent after that.

Noel took another sip of coffee from the Styrofoam cup, listened as the two police attorneys began to skirmish over procedural details. But that couldn't hold Noel's interest long. He knew he was supposed to stay until Parnell left. He knew he was the key witness. He had nothing to say except yes and no. But it was the most damning evidence so far. Now, while they traded jargon and technicalities, Noel stared at Loomis.

Not directly at him, but off to one side slightly, the

way he looked indirectly at stars in a night sky, to see the vague distant outlines more clearly.

The Fisherman certainly looked no different from the man Noel had first encountered in the abandoned Federal House of Detention, or, more memorably, sitting in Noel's apartment that late Sunday morning in March, rocking back and forth, reading the sports section of *The New York Times* just before he made his offer—which wasn't really an offer at all—to Noel. The slat-back chair was gone now, the apartment was completely changed. Noel himself was so transformed he could no longer remember what he had thought that morning. Only Loomis was the same.

When Parnell had told Noel he would have to come here and face Loomis, he had almost not come, so strong was his fear of the man after the horrors of the early morning hours. But the commissioner had been persuasive. He'd waited too long already; he wanted to nail Loomis now! Noel was too tired really to resist it, and—he reminded himself—he was clear of that control now, forever.

He hadn't felt the overwhelming hatred and disgust he'd expected when he'd come in the room and seen the Fisherman. Probably because of Loomis's own eerie aloofness. Or possibly, Noel thought, because he had gone through so many emotions, so intensely, in the last six hours that perhaps he no longer was capable of feeling anything. Even nerves got overstimulated, blocked out sensations after a while. Yet he retained a strong curiosity to know what it was that Loomis could be thinking about as the accusations were heaped against him.

The others had all decided on something, were suddenly standing, collecting documents and briefcases. Noel stood up, too.

Kirsch came over to him.

"Mr. Redfern has been released. Without bail, of course. I understand he's waiting for you in the main lobby of the Criminal Courts building."

At the end of the table, Russo and Loomis were conferring, the Fisherman, oddly enough, talking animatedly, although in a tone so low no one else could hear him, as though arguing something.

Noel headed for the door. The attorney kept up with him. Noel felt a hand on his arm.

"If you have any qualms," Kirsch said, "you ought to know what we know. After we received Mrs. Vega's material, we pulled in the half-dozen Whisper operatives who ranked closest to Loomis. Without his knowledge, of course. Between threats of demotion and intensive questioning, we discovered that there was a contingency plan in case you failed to go off. Redfern was to be placed in a common cell, seeded with a Whisper operative who, unknown to the desk sergeant, was armed. He would begin an argument and . . . We knew of that plan, however, and I made certain that Redfern was placed where he would not get hurt."

Kirsch's voice dripped sarcasm. Noel decided he would prosecute Loomis with the same ruthless will to destroy that the Fisherman had shown in all his dealings.

"Can I go now?" Noel asked. Everyone agreed he could. He had just left the chambers when Russo came out.

"My client would like to have a word with you," he said to Noel.

Before either Noel or Kirsch could reply, the defense attorney added, "Naturally both guards will be on duty."

"Cummings," Parnell asked, "it's up to you."

Kirsch didn't like the idea and said so.

But Noel's curiosity was stronger than his wish to leave. So he went into the room, approached the oval table, took a seat as far from Loomis as he'd been before. He barely heard what the Fisherman said to him.

"Go on. Ask me."

Still unnerved by how this man always seemed to

know his own mind better than Noel, he nevertheless took courage in the presence of the two burly police officers. "Have you figured it out yet?"

"Figured out what?"

"You know. Why it didn't work?"

Loomis stared at him. He was succinct. "No."

"Because of her, Alana."

"Her?" Loomis answered with such disdain his nostrils flared. "Her? She was designed to be the trigger."

It took Noel a minute to understand that Alana's death was no accident, but planned from the beginning and integral to the success of the plot. He had to clutch the edge of the table so he would not leap across and throttle the monster.

"The drug was good to me," Noel said. "The LSD. It was good."

Loomis shrugged that off.

Noel remained coldly angry. "Maybe the plan was just lousy right from the beginning."

There was no answer to that. Loomis seemed to have lapsed back into his absentmindedness. Noel couldn't stand being in the room. He got up to leave.

When he had one hand on the door handle, he heard from behind him, "It's always worked before," so matter-of-factly, that he had to shiver—and get out fast.

16

The clammy chill the Fisherman's last words induced in him didn't disappear until Noel had entered the lobby of the Criminal Courts building and spotted

Eric, still dressed in the expensive, casual-looking, white summer tuxedo he alone of all the men invited to the Window Wall dinner had been allowed to wear. He looked none the worse for his few hours in a jail cell as he paced the patterned-tile floor, staring down at the design.

Seeing Eric safe—after so many odds had been piled up against his ever seeing today's daylight—made Noel stop. He wanted to do something, to throw his arms around Eric, to hug him; to verify by touching him that Eric was unhurt, alive; to thank him and whoever else was responsible for the miracle that had kept him from being Eric's executioner. Then Noel remembered he had another task ahead—he had to tell Eric that Alana was dead.

He waited for Eric to make the first move. When the tanned face turned toward Noel, Eric appeared strained, as though he'd been trying not to think, not to cry, maybe. He ran a hand through the sun-streaked blond hair and said in a voice with no waver at all, "Nice design, isn't it?" Noel followed his gaze down to the sweeping interlocking pattern on the floor, as Eric went on: "I think I'll send someone to copy it, blow it up, make a big mural for the wall opposite the DJ's booth. She's dead, isn't she?" he said, in that same controlled tone of voice. One of his white shoes was rubbing a spot of dried chewing gum off a tile.

"She never regained consciousness."

"She never knew the truth, then?"

Noel saw no reason to hide anything anymore. "She knew who I was," Noel replied.

"And thought you were responsible?"

Noel sighed. "Yes."

"I'm sorry." A pause, then, "It won't be the same without her."

"No."

Eric had rubbed the gum completely off. The tile

was a clean pale yellow compared to the gray around it.

"She asked me to go with her to Paris," Noel said, not knowing why he was telling Eric this. Only that it was necessary. "We were supposed to leave on the six o'clock flight. She was very insistent. She had everything planned for us. She begged me to go tonight. To save you, I think."

"To save herself," Eric said. Without explaining, he went on: "Well, Professor Cummings, you almost had it made, wealth, fame, happiness. So close . . ."

"I could kick myself for not giving her that small satisfaction."

Eric was surprised. "You told her no?"

"I couldn't tell her yes."

"Because of your book?"

"The book? No. Not because of the book. I don't know why," Noel said, not wanting to have to explain it; there was too much to explain.

Eric stared, his deep-set, intense, dark blue eyes holding Noel's own eyes—not in battle, not trying to see through them to what was hidden, not competing, or demanding, or judging for once, but as though observing a major celestial phenomenon that had been in the sky all the while, but which he was noticing for the first time.

"I know why," Eric said, without a hint of superiority or triumph, as though stating a fact so obvious it didn't bear repeating, "because of me."

"Yes, because of you," Noel answered simply; it was true.

A group of people came up behind them, forcing them to move to one side, breaking the moment and the sudden embarrassment Noel had felt along with his admission. Thankfully, Eric didn't pursue it, but asked what had happened at the hearing.

"Everything's going to be all right now," Noel told him, knowing it was vague.

"For whom?"

"For us. For you," he amended quickly. "You're safe now."

"That's comforting."

"You weren't being paranoid," Noel tried to comfort him. "You *were* being hunted. It *was* a conspiracy. It's over now. Squashed."

"That bastard Malchuck. Ready to sell me out. After I gave him everything, everything! You know when I found him he was handing out towels at the Baths?"

"I never knew anything about him," Noel tried to explain. There was so much to explain to Eric, from the bike ride that morning on. "I was so wrecked on that acid I couldn't do anything until . . ."

"Forget it. Let's split. This place gives me the creeps. I called Okku. He should be waiting outside. Come uptown. We'll clean up. Get some rest. You sleep any?"

"I didn't have time. So much happened."

"I had time. But I was afraid to lie down on the cot in that hole."

He took Noel's arm and began walking out. Once they passed through the front doors, out onto the bright, hot, sunny street, Eric put his arm across Noel's shoulders. Noel didn't flinch, didn't shake it off.

"We're going to be together now, aren't we?" Eric asked.

"Yes," Noel said, amazed at how easily he answered.

"Not just because Alana would have wanted us to be?"

"That's one reason. Not the only one."

"Good. Because a lot of shit has gone down between us, Noel, around us, too. We're bound by that. We're going to have a lot of work to make it up to each other. I'm willing. Are you?"

"I have nothing else to do."

Eric hugged Noel closer, and Noel reached an arm around Eric's waist as they descended the short flight of steps onto the street. Noel felt as though after a journey of almost twenty years' duration—destination unknown—he was finally finding his way. Still uncertain as he was of that destination, he was at least certain it coincided with Eric's.

On the sidewalk Eric looked up and down for the Silver Cloud.

Noel suddenly felt a piercing coldness that even Eric's close warmth could not blanket.

The manservant was two blocks north, leaning out of the sunroof, waving at them. It was almost noon. Traffic in the area between Foley Square and Canal Street was inching toward its midday chaos. Arms still around each other, they began walking toward the limo.

Noel felt the coldness again. Not disappearing after its initial frozen thrust as before, but lingering. Perhaps he was coming down with some illness, he thought, and involuntarily detached himself from Eric, unable to concentrate on what Redfern was saying.

The sidewalk was bristling with people coming out of buildings on their way to lunch at one of the dozens of delis, and hot dog stands, souvlaki and pizza places. But Noel was immediately drawn to a figure who seemed to be deliberately keeping pace at the opposite side of the sidewalk. He was a slim, short man in dark glasses that hid most of his features, business suit, and striped tie. Noel couldn't say why he associated the continued and frightening chill with this man, but he stopped Eric, waiting for the figure to move ahead before they started up again.

He recognized the sensation, unmistakable, all pervading, as the same icy presence he'd last felt in the small high room of the abandoned saloon, surrounded by the mutilated corpse of McWhitter, the grotesque hanging body of Buddy Vega. He knew the presence emanated not from Eric who was all heart—affection, possibly lust—but from this small man.

"You're shaking like crazy," Eric was saying, as though from behind a wall of Lucite. "What's wrong with you?"

Noel couldn't answer. His entire awareness was on the man in the suit, slowing down a few feet ahead of them, as Noel began to see details: the angle of the arms, the shape of the head, and particularly the walk, that so familiar walk, that Noel could not place, though it pained him to see each step. He had to find out, had to know who it was.

He shook Eric's hand off his shoulder and hurried to catch up with the short man. As he drew abreast, he felt the cold even more numbing. Eric was joining him, saying something. Both Noel and the man stopped—as though on cue. Even with the disguising sunglasses, the completely unexpected suit and tie, Noel knew whom he faced: Loomis's last card, his final crushing trump, his law beyond the law, his vengeance outside the trappings of justice. Here was a killer as carefully programmed as Noel, but unlike him, an already proven murder machine, the slayer of Kansas and Randy and Vega and McWhitter—Loomis's ultimate, effective executioner, encased in the most treacherous of forms: seductive, childlike, Little Larry Vitale.

—Who noticed Noel, but seemed not to see him, turned past Noel, as though he were an automaton programmed to see only one face, kept swiveling around, behind them, and suddenly produced a thin, deadly, gleaming icicle which he launched into the air.

Eric saw his assailant before Noel could cry out for him to beware. With all the training McWhitter had instilled in him, Eric sidestepped the first lunge, retreated to a parked taxi, spun around with breathtaking rapidity to avoid the second jab of the glittering knife at his heart.

"Come on, bastard," Noel heard Eric breathe out between clenched teeth, "come on," taunting him, as Larry lunged again, and Eric seemed to fall over the hood of the car before his foot shot out hard, smashing the small killer in his chest, knocking his sunglasses off, forcing him to stagger slightly before he regained his balance and came on again. Eric lifted both feet off the ground and, heedless of the sweeping movements of the blade, kicked again, this time knocking the weapon to the sidewalk. Before Larry could turn around to retrieve it, he was grabbed by one shoulder, twisted around, sent flying into the fender of the car.

Noel bent down, immediately felt the warm hilt of the knife connect with something deep and ready and longing inside of him, and turned back to the car, where they still struggled.

The knife was a burning ember in his hand, melded to his arm by an urgency he couldn't explain or resist.

"It's always worked before." He heard Loomis's last words thudding through his mind, as though Loomis were inside his skull, shouting in glee. "It's always worked before."

And Noel felt the split he had fought off so successfully before, sensing this time the split was for real, that this time he would complete his mission, and wreak the final outrage, to destroy what Loomis could no longer get near.

"It's always worked before." Loomis's words danced a frenzied tarantella through his reeling, buzzing mind, as Noel turned to face the wrestling forms in front of him, feeling the urgency of the knife blade wedded to the poisoned fingers that held it, move forward, ready to strike, to plunge, to cut, slash, rip, tear, feel flesh separate from bone, tissues come asunder, nerve ends snap, synapses scream, skin split like butter, blood issue, ooze, stream, gush, cooling him—

He felt the split, saw the two men facing him, expressionless, as he froze them both to stillness— trapped against the fender of the car, both mouths open to beg, scream, cajole.

And the knife was a burning coal. It had to be

doused or the fire would consume his flesh, too, so he plunged it in, feeling the urgency take over, and the soft tissue melting under the frozen blade, finding sweet relief in the wet coolness that surrounded each thrust, cutting, ripping, tearing, upward, downward, in, across bones, muscles, cheeks, ears, eyes even, those deceiving mirrors, those lying reflectors, immersing himself in the methodical slashing and tearing, finding the split resolving itself in relief, not minding the pummeling of fists at his back, the futile attempts by mere human hands to dislodge him from this preordained encounter, but taking his time, cutting, and plunging again, feeling all time stop, feeling both the heat in his hands and the coldness that had frightened him so before evaporate now, as the head in front of him began to slide off the slimy wetness of the metal fender, the torn mirrors of its eyes hidden now, as it crumpled slowly onto the tops of his shoes, and he plunged once more into air, unable to stop himself, then stopped, and all he could feel was utter, total, complete, and life-restoring relief.

For an instant.

Before the voice repeated it's incantatory drone, "*It's always worked before*," and the relief was gone, and Noel back, one person, not two, on the Lower Manhattan sidewalk, looking down at a confusion of hair and blood and material crumpled in front of him. He looked around, dizzy with the onslaught of sensory stimuli as sounds, smells, images, sailed before him, and slowly came to a stop and became ordinary, recognizable as before.

"I've killed," he said. "I did what he wanted me to do. I've killed. He's won. He knew he would win."

Noel began to cry: a hard racking disabling weeping.

"Give me the knife," someone said. "Give it to me."

Noel did as he was told. It didn't matter now.

"I've killed," he tried to make him understand. "He's won."

He was grabbed around the shoulders, held close, as Eric's voice breathed into his ear, "*We* won, Noel. You and I."

They were surrounded by men in uniform, moving in on them. In the distance, Noel heard siren's screams, coming closer, but above their piercing wail was a calm, steady voice from within, saying over and over, "We've won." It was a victory: for Kansas and Vega, Randy and Alana, for the dead, and those who might have died. "We've won."

Dell Bestsellers

Comes the Blind Fury

John Saul

Bestselling author of
Cry for the Strangers
and *Suffer the Children*

More than a century ago, a gentle, blind child walked the paths of Paradise Point. Then other children came, teasing and taunting her until she lost her footing on the cliff and plunged into the drowning sea.

Now, 12-year-old Michelle and her family have come to live in that same house—to escape the city pressures, to have a better life.

But the sins of the past do not die. They reach out to embrace the living. Dreams will become nightmares.

Serenity will become terror. There will be no escape.

A Dell Book $2.75   (11428-4)